GW00836520

The Keeper

by Keith Jenkins

Freebird Publishing

The Keeper is a limited edition book.
Published in 2009 by Freebird Publishing
☎ 01293 405781 or 07941 637336
© Keith Jenkins 2009

A catalogue record of this book is available from the British Library.

Edited by Ian Chillcott
Proofed by Lynn Chillcott
Illustrations by Suzanne Lane
Layout and Design by Cathy Card
Image Scanning by Printwize Interact Marketing Services Ltd
Print Management by Linda Jenkins
All photography supplied by the Author unless marked.

Printed in Great Britain by
Butler Tanner & Dennis
Caxton Road, Frome, Somerset BA11 1NF

ISBN Number 978-0-9562497-2-2

Contents

Prelude – Threads   2

Part One

1   Echoes   18
2   Green is the Colour   26
3   Get Your Filthy Hands Off My Desert   36
4   A Hero's Return   44
5   Remember a Day   52

Part Two

6   Us and Them   62
7   Breathe   66
8   The Happiest Days of Our Lives   70
9   Coming Back to Life   78
10   Signs of Life   84
11   A Delicate Sound of Thunder   88

Part Three

12   Learning to Fly   100
13   A Pillow of Winds   110
14   Fearless   120
15   Let there be more Light   130
16   Childhood's End   142
17   Wearing the Inside Out   152

Part Four

18   Comfortably Numb   164
19   A Saucerful of Secrets   172
20   On the Turning Away   180
21   One of These Days   190
22   The Show must go on   194
23   Time   202

Part Five

24   Round and Round   212
25   Dark Side of the Moon   218
26   Any Colour You Like   230
27   Wish You were Here?   236
28   Astronomy Domine   244
29   High Hopes   252

Part Six

30   Piper at the Gates of Dawn   260
31   One of the Few   266
32   A Momentary Lapse of Reason   276
33   Obscured by Clouds   282
34   Shine on You Crazy Diamond   290

The Final Cut   304

Dedication

A dedication is normally just devoted to one person – not this one.

There is only one group of people that this book could be dedicated to, and that is my family- the young and the…not so young; those who have just joined us, and those that have, sadly, left for a better place.

So, this is dedicated to –

My amazing Mum, Joyce, and my mother-in-law, Beryl – once encountered, never forgotten.

My long distance sisters, Diane and Karen, and niece and nephew, Sian and Nic, who I see all too rarely these days.

Ben, the father of my two remarkable granddaughters, fellow angler, Pink Floyd and Spurs fan – how could he fail?

My wonderful children, Vincent and Christine, who continually amaze me with their wit and wisdom, and who make me so very proud to be their father.

My beautiful wife, Linda, whose strength and power of will still astounds me. She had the whole dedication to herself last time, but not now, although she so surely deserves it.

My equally beautiful granddaughter, Ayla, whose light brightens my life so much it is almost blinding.

Willow, Ayla's young sister, who arrived in this world on the day that I finished this book, and who will, no doubt, shine just as bright as her sister.

And finally, to my late father-in-law, Stan. He left us a short while ago and his passing was intensely painful, but nowhere near as intense as the sweetness of his memory – the brightest Star in the Sky.

Acknowledgements

Three people deserve special mention here, as they have greatly added to the final manuscript:-

Lynn Chillcott who, despite everything, has proofed this until her eyes almost bled, and then proofed it some more. Totally beyond the call of duty, but the whole book will be better for it.

Cathy Card, who has laid this out just as I wanted it, and then when I realised I wanted it a bit different, she's laid it all out again.

Sue (Sooz) Lane. Her illustrations and cover art are so beyond what I expected I feel slightly humbled that they should just appear in this meagre tome. She so deserves a much wider audience.

Thanks girls, I love you all.

Acknowledgements normally just include the people that have been instrumental to a books inception, characterisation, and final production. But I think there's more to it than that.

In this book I've been inspired not only by people, but also places, fish, music, sporting events, the natural world; in short - Life.

So, here's to Life, in all its guises. I've tried to do it in an Ian Drury, 'Reasons to be Cheerful' style. I hope it works –

> CHILLY: LANEY: PHIL & REG:
> ZIGGY STARDUST: CLOSE TO THE EDGE
> STEVE & JOAN: STEVE & KEV:
> PORKY: WENDY: STEVE & BEV.
> BASIL: MARY: ARNIE: JACK:
> PINK & PURPLE: CREAM & BLACK.
> ALI: HILTON: HUTCHIE: JOE:
> PAISLEY: WILKINSON: OVETT & COE.
> PAULIE: JACKO: BILBO: DAN:
> STARSHIP TROOPER: WATCH THAT MAN.
> CONNINGBROOK: HORTON: JIMBOB: SI:
> YATESY: JIMI: WATCHER IN THE SKY.
> AC/DC: CP: F: CHRISTINE: VINCENT: PENNING: SKEFF.
> RICK & ROGER: SYD & NICK
> DAVE & ERIC: THICK AS A BRICK.
> BOWIE: BOLAN: PETE & KEN:
> SONNING EYE: STANGROOM: BEN.
> WRAYSBURY: RHAPSODY: FALLOW: RED:
> ROBBIE: TONY: LINDA: FRED.
> FREEBIRD: DISCWORLD: SHIRLEY: SUE:
> TOUGHIE: ESCOTT: WINNIE THE POOH.
> SYMPATHY: STAIRWAY: MICKY D: MICKY GRAY:
> AYLA: LAYLA: WILLOW & OAK.

Life is a symphony, and these are just some of the notes that I dance to.

FOREWORD

I love life in all its various guises, and I have probably had more fun than any man deserves in three lifetimes. That fun has been enhanced, still further, by the people I have met along the way, and there is one man that stands head and shoulders above the rest.

I first met Keith on the banks of a local Army lake in the Aldershot area, it was December 1994. He had acquired a ticket to wile away the winter, until Horton warmed up sufficiently to make the fishing a more realistic prospect. I was as 'Army' as it was possible to be, and Keith…well he was just Keith, really. Dressed from head to toe in the most colourful clothing, that unfortunately didn't have a volume control, I really couldn't see that I would ever get along with the fellow. He did make me tea however, and that is simply the best way to get my attention. I didn't believe it would be possible to find two more diametrically opposed people, but very soon it was obvious we had much in common - Rugby, Cricket, Football, wildlife, music and the written word. I suspect that we talked of fishing occasionally, but we never normally found the time, and to this day we try to avoid the subject like the plague. I have met a handful of people that I could honestly say have changed my way of life with their influence. Some have passed away, unfortunately, but Jenkins, I am pleased to report, is very much alive!

Over the course of time, along with keeping the French economy buoyant with our wine consumption, we struck up a friendship that has lasted until this very day. My transition from the military to Civvy Street was made so much easier, and in many ways he steered me away from a very violent past. You see, Keith is incredibly good with words, not just written, but spoken too, and after a while I, too, learnt to speak to others instead of hitting them!

In Keith's world the pen really is mightier than the sword, and it was his writing that held my attention the most. The first thing I ever read by him was an article called 'What's the rush?' in which he described how frustrating the journey from work to the lake could be, late on a Friday evening. No carp were caught and not a rig or bait was mentioned, yet he had held me captivated in the telling. And so it was, when I started to write for the magazines, I had to look no further than him, and in a way, he set a standard to which I try desperately to aspire to. I fail miserably, of course, but I guess I will keep on trying.

Keith is the ultimate family man, and it may surprise a lot of people that he only ever does his fishing at the weekends - and even those weekends away are fairly infrequent. He lives in Crawley with his wife Linda and, although they no longer live at home, he has a son Vincent and daughter, Christine. Even Mum, Joyce, lives with him and I am proud to say that they are all my friends. Indeed, I have even become the 'stand in Grandfather' to Christine and Ben's young children, Ayla and

Willow. He is a special man, with special talents and when he set out to write his first carp fishing novel, the 'Myth', I proofed the book along the way. His understanding of people, fishing and the environment that angling is surrounded by, left me open mouthed. It was a very brave decision to write a book of fiction about carp fishing, but the end result has become something of a cult book…and rightly so!!

And so, some ten years after the release of the 'Myth' he has decided to write another, and here you have it. For those of you that have read his first book, you will be amazed at how enchanting, sad and spell binding, this second book is. For those that haven't, then be prepared to be enthralled. He is a remarkable man and a remarkable writer, but for me, the most important thing is that he is my closest friend.

Here's to you buddy.

Ian Chillcott
2009

Introduction

Yes, I know. I know!

I'd said that I wasn't going to do a sequel to 'the Myth', and yet here it is.

Despite many novel ideas that have run through my head over the past decade, the idea of a follow up to 'the Myth' wasn't amongst them, until one night in February. I sat there, mulling over the idea of adding a few chapters to the original, but I'm not a great fan of that sort of thing, so pondered the chances of a possible sequel. By two in the morning, unable to sleep because of the ideas running through my head, I realised there was, indeed, a book in there.

My life, like everyone's, has changed immeasurably in the past decade, and I wanted to reflect that in the characters within these pages so, although some are the same, naturally there are new characters as well.

I can't help but draw from real life so, once again, the main characters are a melange of personalities that I have met, either on the bank, or elsewhere, and believe me, fact is always more colourful than fiction. I've tried my best take the most 'interesting' aspects of different characters, and mould them together as best I can, hopefully with a modicum of success.

This isn't just a book about fishing, although that has always been the thread that stitches everything together. I've tried to broaden the span here, once again reflecting what we see but sometimes fail to recognise.

There's not a lot more to say, really, apart from the 120,000 words that follow, so I'll let them do the talking and hope that they say just what I want them to.

Oh, and by the way, many people have asked me 'who caught The Common, then?' Well, the clues were there before, and the answer is in here as well, you've just got to know how to look for it.

So, welcome to the world of Old Ted – The Keeper.

When it's not always Raining
There'll be days like this,
When there's no one complaining
There'll be days like this,
When everything falls into place
like the flick of a switch,
Well, my Mama told me
There'll be days like this

Threads

*P*ain and pressure.

Bright light and harsh vibrations.

Hot, dry sensations all over its scaly skin.

These were not new, the great carp had experienced them before, but now they seemed much more intense. The reason, unbeknownst to the carp, was that the last time it had been taken from its safe, watery and supportive haven, it had been almost half its present size and weight.

Then – release.

Revered but, unwittingly, abused.

As it was gently lowered back into the cooling water, its bulk now supported by that realm, the most natural instinct was 'Escape!' and so, with one huge sweep of its tail it surged out into the lake and was away, seeking the nearest refuge it could find, the best to recover from its ordeal.

The island snags were spurned, that being the most immediate source of its pain so, within very few moments, it slowed its retreat and moved edgily into the forest of snags at the north western corner of the lake; a favourite haunt in times of stress and crisis. There it would remain for the rest of the day until the events of that morning were a vague memory.

Little did it, or its captors, realise that it would not feel the sting of sharpened steel for another forty seasons, from this autumn and ten more.

'You have got to be kidding me!' said Stan, in disbelief.

'Yeah, that's what Rhodie said, pretty much,' replied Sid, wearily. He'd known that the knowledge he had to impart to his mates would elicit this sort of response, but it didn't make the telling any easier.

'But, mate… I mean… What the…!'

'Yeah, I know Quill, my feelings entirely, but I've been sussing it out all morning and it's a stone cold, bloody fact!'

Sid's morning investigations had been instigated by a phone call from one of the chaps they'd got to know on the Mere. He'd heard serious rumours that the lake was about to be closed, with no further notice, and so he'd called Sid to find out if he knew anything about it.

After a number of frustrating phone calls, Sid eventually got through to a local tackle shop owner, and then all became clear.

'This has been in the offing for years, it's just now that it's come to a head,' he told Sid. For the past year or so, none of them had given a second thought to the construction site that they passed on the way to the lake, a half-mile away. It had been going on for a few years, and they just assumed that it was a new housing estate or a small business park. What it was, in fact, was a small, exclusive housing complex with properties that began at a million and went upwards. Within six months, the first of these wonder-homes would be occupied by some very wealthy people, and the very lake complex that had been hidden from many prying eyes over the decades would be their new back garden.

Stan's mind was a mess. A thousand thoughts went through his head, and he began voicing a few of them, but Sid steadily brought him to his knees until all that was left to say was a resigned, 'So what we gonna do now?'

A mere month had passed since the capture of The Common and, in that time, despite their best efforts, no more of the larger denizens had slipped up. The 9 and the 19 had inevitably visited the bank again, but the others had just faded away – much the same as their chances of ever being caught again appeared to be doing. Since The Common's capture the mood had been, naturally, buoyant, and it mattered not that the captures were few and far between. The lake had not changed – it was still rock hard – but the fact that these huge fish were catchable, with two falling to their rods in three months, meant that there was always a chance of another incredible catch. At least one of the matriarchs was still to be caught, although the sting of its loss, the previous season, still pained Rhodie on some quiet nights.

But now, all of that hope and anticipation was dashed, and their season was, once again, left in tatters.

After delving deeper over the next few weeks, Stan discovered that the plan was more all-encompassing than just closing the lakes because the local gentry didn't want any oiks wandering around and spoiling their view of the landscape. No, it was much more complex than that.

To the west of Felcham Mere, behind the Dead Man Standing swim, was another lake of about twenty acres. This was quite a featureless, open expanse of water and home to mainly silver fish, bream and pike, plus a few small commons. The pike were of a decent size, which meant that for a few cold months the banks were trod by a hardy few, willing to hurl bits of dead fish hither and yon and, occasionally, snaring one of the glorious predators.

Then, someone decided to have a sail.

Part of the advertising blurb was that there would be a purpose-built sailing lake adjacent to the complex. The plan was to cut away most of the causeway that separated the lakes to create one lake in excess of seventy acres, room enough to tick and tack to your heart's delight. And the work was to begin in earnest in the next few weeks, so the initial reason for stopping fishermen visiting the lakes was a health and safety concern. But once the work had been completed (which included the construction of a purpose-built clubhouse) then it was millionaires only.

But God bless English Nature and rare plants and animals. English Nature's concerns were alerted a few months previously and, having sent some chaps to investigate the site, they discovered a number of rare flower species, as well as a protected species of dragonfly, and a few pretty waterfowl that were quite tasty and needed to be nurtured. So, stipulations were made that would ensure the protection of the whole eco-system. And to ensure that this was carried out efficiently and in a complimentary fashion, people would need to be employed as wardens and gamekeepers.

Suddenly, Stan could see a change of vocation on the horizon.

'You have got to be kidding me!'

'Don't speak to me like that, Quentin! I'm your bloody father and, believe me, I am not kidding. The world does not revolve around you, surprisingly, and you'll be amazed how different things will be if you just stop being so damned self-centred. When I was a lad… blah blah blah…'

Quentin had heard it all before, and had just glazed over as another lecture from his father gained momentum. Thirteen was not a good age for either party.

The memory of the news that had initiated his outburst was now fast becoming imminent fact, and Quentin was oh so not sure about the whole thing.

His father had worked in the City for many years, long before Quentin was born, and their house in the most fashionable part of Chelsea had been no sort of home for a young boy. As early as was possible, he'd been despatched to a private school and spent very few months of the year at home, which began to suit him more and more as he neared his teens.

Then the bombshell, six months ago. His father was leaving his lucrative job in the City and had decided to get the hell out of there and move to a 'lovely place in the country'. Quentin had no concept of the cost of property. He knew his family were pretty well off, and never struggled to buy good cars and big tellies and the like, but if he'd been told that the Chelsea house was worth in excess of a million pounds, it would have meant very little. The fact that the money would go a very long way to purchasing the new place in the country only served to make him wince, and consider arson. But then, he didn't understand the concept of house insurance either.

After the initial outburst, on that wet autumn day, his father had then informed him that they were going to see their new house that very weekend and so, after a seemingly endless journey in the Merc, the boredom of which was only alleviated by his PlayStation, they arrived at what looked pretty much like a building site. The reason for that was obvious – it was.

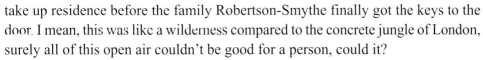

Trudging through the mud they were shown to their new house – or the skeleton of it, at least – and Quentin couldn't help thinking that, without the doors and windows in place, any number of birds and beasts could take up residence before the family Robertson-Smythe finally got the keys to the door. I mean, this was like a wilderness compared to the concrete jungle of London, surely all of this open air couldn't be good for a person, could it?

But now, the open air was beckoning and the Robertson-Smythe caravanserai was about to set sail. The Chelsea home would be missed more by the parents than the son, but as most of their friends had moved out of town over the past few years, to the Chilterns and the Cotswolds and other quaint sounding places, it was no real wrench. In fact, if they'd only admit it, that was the real reason for the move – there was nobody else left in town, just Arabs and Greeks. They'd even heard rumours of Russians coming. To Chelsea? Surely not!

As the streets became roads, and they in turn became motorways, Quentin desperately tried to find solace in his latest PlayStation game, but his mother's constant 'Are you excited?' questions were a nagging distraction, and his grunted, non-committal response only a goad for his father's anger.

In a mere two hours they were weaving along leafy country lanes, and past signposts for strange places like Nether Wallop and Over Wallop, East and West Grimstead, and a selection of Winterbournes and Winterslows. Whatever happened to Fulham and Putney and the like? And what were the inhabitants of a place called Wallop going to be like? He shrunk down into the depths of the Merc's leather chair and tried desperately to concentrate on the game, but his mother's twittering kept distracting him.

Mother's Twittering – I bet there's a place called that out here, he thought, and tittered.

Quentin's Tittering, there's another. That made him laugh out loud and he had to come up with a swift response to his mother's questioning glance.

'At least you're smiling, at last. But don't get too over excited, now.'

'Is that near Nether Excited?' he muttered, then stared intently at his PlayStation as he saw his father's scowl in the rear view mirror. His parents weren't used to his sense of humour; in fact they were barely aware of it, so this turn of events concerned them a little. That was until they saw the sign they were looking for – Felcham. After all of the exotic and bizarre names he'd seen on the way, this was positively mundane in comparison, and Quentin wondered whether he'd be able to move to a Wallop in his later years – that would be something to look forward to.

Then they were there, and the difference from his last visit was startling. There were no signs of any huge, yellow machines. The cloying mud had been miraculously replaced by lush, green grass, and dozens of young saplings were just starting to bud as the spring sunshine coaxed them into fruitfulness. The house was unrecognisable, and vast; bedrooms and bathrooms occupied the upstairs in large numbers, and the sitting room, dining room and kitchen were opulent and bright.

Their furniture had been delivered the previous week, and his father had overseen its placement in all of the rooms. Quentin's room was large and spacious, and on looking out of the window he saw where all of the machinery had gone. A few hundred yards from the house was a huge lake, and the machinery had been utilised to make it even larger. Quentin had known that there was a lake nearby, but on his previous visit, his apathy was such that he gave it barely a glance. Now, however, it was laid before him in all its glory in the spring sunshine, and the woods to the left, and across the far side of the lake, looked mysterious and strangely inviting. This might not be as bad as he'd first thought, and he strolled back downstairs for a better look, completely forgetting his PlayStation, which lay lifeless on the bed.

Another flash, followed seconds later by a distant 'CRUMP!'

The small arms fire chattered and cracked around them, spitting into the mud and swampy grass.

Ted was getting used to the slight crushing feeling in his chest after each mortar blast. That didn't stop him feeling petrified, though. The six of them had been huddled in their muddy foxhole for what seemed like hours, but in reality was no more than thirty minutes. The bombardment, however, had been relentless, and the enemy were obviously desperate to gain this piece of land. The rest of his battalion were dotted about over the surrounding acre or two of land, each hoping that the next 'CRUMP' wasn't close enough to be the last they heard.

A few minutes passed after the last explosion, the odd stray 'crack/thumps' of small ordnance ensuring they kept their heads down. Tom Shanks, always ready with a witty remark in the most dire situation, was the first to break the eerie silence.

'So, as I was saying, let's have a quick cuppa then we'll be off down the road for a dance and bit of how's yer father.'

Ted couldn't help smiling at the gallows humour that always seemed to ease the tension after these regular, near-death experiences. He rummaged around in his Bergen for the powdered tea whilst Tom and Andy fussed around with the brew kit.

There was no flash. The 'CRUMP' was so all-enveloping that it had no beginning or end, and his chest felt as if a Tiger was rumbling across it. The buzzing that accompanied his burst eardrums would stay with him for the rest of his life, as would the sight of Tom's headless corpse falling ever so slowly to the muddy ground.

Ted blinked himself back to the present and set the cup down on the kitchen table. More than half a century could not dim those images, and although he had learnt long ago to control his reaction to them, he could still feel his chest tightening until the waking nightmare faded away, lurking in the shadows of his mind until another opportunity presented itself to resurface.

Soon, the buzz was replaced by the sound of birdsong and the more welcome buzz of insect life as the woodland ushered his nightmare from memory and he was brought back to 'now'. Sutton Woods had been his home for many years now. On his eventual release from military service, almost twenty years ago, he had tried, and failed on more than one occasion, to form a meaningful relationship with any number of ladies. But, it became more and more obvious that the only company he craved was his own. This, then, led to only one conclusion – it was time to return home.

Since then, a small cabin in the woods had been his home for many years, and his affinity with all life in those woods had been enhanced through the changes of every season. His ability to survive in the jungles of Malaysia, and deserts of North Africa had held him in good stead over the past two decades, and his reliance on outside help was minimal. That's not to say that he shunned human company, far from it. A night or two down at The Green Man or The Fox was a weekly repast he craved, even if the conversation was the same every evening. At least it was good humoured and convivial, and normally quite drunken.

Then, without realising, he'd become 'Old Ted'.

Throughout the countryside, there are 'Old Ted's' in every community. Their age is always difficult to pinpoint, and can be anywhere between sixty-two and one hundred and four. Strangely, nobody recalls them in their twenties and thirties, probably because then they would just have been known as 'Ted'. A faint smell of root vegetables, wood smoke and ruminating ungulates seems to pervade him. He doesn't favour the full facial bush, just a burgeoning set of sideburns that could house a family of blue tits.

His is the wisdom of the trees; knowledge that is not so much learnt, rather gained by osmosis. How else could he know that a smiling swan indicated a possible assassination attempt on a local councillor, or that three newts 'neath a lily leaf meant a harsh frost before the next full moon? If he had been given the power of speech at birth, on seeing the four hairs sprouting from the mole on the lip of the midwife, he could have predicted that the milk in his mother's breast would be sour afore noon of the morrow.

And all 'Old Teds' have a certain mystery about them, something hidden; a secret, sometimes sinister, but invariably not. Mostly, the 'secret' is a certain talent, or an enigmatic gap in their history.

But, Old Ted had none of the above; his secret was more heroic, and unsung, and would remain as such.

Everything was going fine for Ted, then the talk in The Green Man and The Fox started to turn to what was going on at Felcham. Big houses were being built for rich City folk, and there was talk of the woods being decimated and the lakes being drained. The more the drink flowed, the more outrageous everybody became until it was eventually decided that the local councillor (who had survived the assassination attempt) should be contacted and made to do something about it. As is the way of these things, much was conjecture and bluster, but the furore was loud enough to attract the attention of the local E.A. officer, and it was soon decided that the Felcham foxglove was almost as rare as the four-spotted Felcham frogtoad! Although the stories of decimation were overblown, there were still plans to chop down a number of trees, to give better views of the lake from the houses and also to aid the sailors in their search for more wind. After much hot air, and not a little lunching, it was decided that the joining of the lakes would continue, although a small island would have to be left, as it was the habitat of a particularly rare species of orchid. Likewise, some of the trees in the northeastern corner of the Mere would come down, but the proposed plans to clear the eastern woods were shelved.

But what of all of these rare plants and animals, who would ensure that they didn't become any rarer? The only logical conclusion was to have someone with a local knowledge of the flora and fauna to look after its future wellbeing. Not a full time job, obviously, but ideal for a retired but healthy local man, maybe.

If only there was someone who fitted the bill…

Despite the sudden absence of anglers, all of the carp in the Mere were soon to face even more danger. Their natural curiosity meant that, after the initial shock of the noise created by the diggers and JCB's along the causeway, pretty soon they were frequent visitors to the area of most recent excavation because, invariably, a whole new food source would have been unearthed. If the anglers had been allowed to continue fishing on the lake, there would have been no doubt that they would have had a great chance of catching quite a few of the fish whilst their defences were down. But that wasn't to be, and the nearest to the bank any of them came was when one of the larger carp got extremely close to one of the excavation buckets, narrowly avoiding a fairground ride that could have been most fateful.

As winter turned to spring, the lake became quieter, the huge machines having done their work and departed, leaving nature to heal the wounds left behind. That

would take only a few short seasons, but the disruption to the evictees would be more permanent; in some cases catastrophic.

The carp had wasted little time in exploring the extension to their domain, and although smaller and shallower, the new lake held some inviting areas of reed bed and slowly burgeoning lily pads that would require further investigation as the days lengthened. There would surely be more larders to raid this summer.

There was still much activity, especially along the northern banks of the new lake, and this would herald a new era for the carp, where the danger came not from the bankside, but from the surface of the water instead. The construction of the new clubhouse was being completed in tandem with a concrete runway that would allow all manner of watercraft to slide effortlessly into the lake, including jet skis and motorboats that towed water skiers.

The summer would not only offer tasty new pastures for the carp to harvest, but also totally new dangers that could be ultimately fateful to some of their number.

'Come on girl; don't worry about that. The estate agent will be round in the morning. He can sort it out then.'

Stan picked up the last of the bags and hustled Jean through the front door, leaving the bundle of keys she'd been fiddling with on the table for said estate agent.

The transit van was full to brimming and their son, Stevie, was having trouble pulling down the door whilst trying to stop the contents spilling onto the road.

Dropping the bags on the pavement, Stan trotted over to hold the potential escapees whilst Stevie finally pulled the door closed.

'Okay boy, you driving this or the car?' asked Stan, knowing full well that his son would take full control of the convoy.

'Get in the car, dad. You just lead the way and leave the big stuff to me,' Stevie said with a grin, walking round to the driver's door.

Stan did as he was told and jumped in the front of his estate, removing a broom handle from the vicinity of his ear before putting on his seatbelt and starting the car.

'Well, here we go, Jeanie. First day of the rest of our lives and all that.' He knew how sad his wife felt about leaving the home that they'd brought up a family in for the past couple of decades, but he also knew that, since the kids had both left, there was no better time than now for this new start.

When he'd broached the subject, a month prior to Christmas, Jean's initial reaction was one of shock and incredulity. What would they do for work? When would they see the kids? What about all of their friends? Stan had, obviously, foreseen these arguments and had answers for all but the last.

The whole point of the move was that Stan had applied for the job of assistant warden on the Felcham Park Estate, and had been accepted. The money wasn't as good as he was getting at the moment, but the offer of a small cottage that came with the job, and an equally small rent as well, made the deal almost a no-brainer. Their house would fetch a decent sum, and with only a small amount left to pay on the mortgage, would give them a decent buffer for the first few months until Jean got settled. That part had seemed the hardest, but then she was offered a huge redundancy package just weeks before handing in her notice, and suddenly the runes seemed to have fallen perfectly.

The kids would be fine, and looked forward to the chance of a few weekends in the country, and so, as it happened, did their friends.

So now, here they were, the Peacocks On Tour. The deal had become even better when the 'small cottage' turned out to be a three-bedroom affair with a classic country garden, and was no more than five hundred yards from the Estate. Stan had spent a few weekends in the area, although he obviously knew it pretty well already, and had met his boss, John Bakewell. They'd got on well straight from the off, John being a local guy a few years Stan's senior, and they'd spent a few pleasant evenings in the local hostelries, The Green Man and The Fox, getting to know each other and the colourful locals.

'Silly sod!' said Stan, laughing, as he saw Stevie in the rear-view mirror, banging himself on the head as they went past a sign declaring 'The Wallops'.

'Just 'cos he beat you to it,' said Jean. 'Wallop! Wallop! Wallop! Ding! Ding! Ding!' she mimicked, repeating the old Mike Read joke yet again, before her husband had a chance.

'You love it', he declared, grinning like an idiot. And she had to admit that she did. Her mood had lightened as the journey progressed, and she was actually starting to feel a quiver of anticipation. This could just work.

All they had to do was find somewhere for Stan to fish because, without that, this could end up poorly indeed.

'Quentin? That's some sort of name, innit?' exclaimed Neil. The boy was a few months Quentin's senior and was seated next to him at his new school. 'Haven't you got a nickname, or something? I can't go around saying 'Quentin' all day long,' Neil continued.

'Becks, silence please!' commanded Mrs Barnes, the English teacher.

Quentin looked straight at his neighbour with a knowing look. 'So that's why they call you Posh, I thought it was sarcastic 'cos you're so common,' whispered Quentin, barely able to contain his mirth.

Posh Neil looked somewhat chagrined, but retorted swiftly with, 'Yeah, well maybe it is sarcastic, but at least I've only got one name, not two. Now that is bloody posh!'

'Becks! If you have something to say…'

'Er, we were just discussing sarcasm, Miss,' blurted Neil, realising too late that this could lead to trouble.

'Sarcasm? Well, well. That sounds a mighty interesting discussion. Can we all join in?'

Neil looked like a rabbit in the headlights, so Quentin jumped in to help.

'Well, what it was, Miss, was that I didn't realise his name was Becks, and I thought they called him 'Posh' to be sarcastic … because he's not … posh, that is.' Quentin's initial bravado soon evaporated and he looked forlornly at his neighbour, but no help was forthcoming.

'Ah,' said Mrs Flood, pensively, 'I see. But it isn't sarcasm; it's irony. However, as you both put it so eloquently, you can have the rest of the afternoon off.'

They looked at each other in amazement but, before the idea had any chance of germinating, Mrs Flood continued,

'**That** was sarcasm, boys. Now, sit down and say no more otherwise you will be staying for an extra hour after school, and that is a fact!'

Much stuttering and stammering ensued, much to the amusement of their fellow classmates, but eventually the bell came to their rescue and they left hastily.

'I just sussed it,' said Posh, as they sat in the playground awaiting the end of break.

'Sussed what?' enquired Quentin, slightly intrigued.

'Smiffy – that's what I'm gonna call you from now on,' explained Posh.

'Bloody hell, how did you work that out?' said Quentin, rhetorically. He had obviously heard of Quentin Crisp, and the Smiffy moniker had been mentioned before, although only by his strange uncle Leon and never in earshot of his parents. To be honest, he quite liked it, especially after finding out who this other Quentin was, and what he represented. What had his parents been thinking, naming him after a gay bloke? Fortunately, not many kids of his age knew of the Crisp connection, but unfortunately his newly acquired friend seemed strangely knowledgeable for one so young.

Posh just smiled, and said, 'Don't worry about that, Smiffy. What you doing after school?'

'Dunno,' said the newly dubbed Smiffy. 'What you got in mind?'

'You live over in the new places at Felcham, don't you? Have you been into the woods yet?'

'No. My mum's a bit dodgy with that sort of thing, doesn't like me playing too far from the house. You know, what with cars and pervs and that.'

Posh was a bit puzzled by that and asked, 'What do you mean, 'pervs and that'?'

Smiffy tried to explain, but his knowledge was only gleaned from his parent's threats and warnings, so the explanation was garbled and made little sense to a country boy who had been allowed to roam free for most of his formative years.

'Oh, there ain't any of that sort out here. Everybody's really friendly, although there is Old Ted.'

'Who's Old Ted?' asked Smiffy, intrigued.

'He lives in an old cabin in the woods, lives off of rooks and rabbits and that. I never seen him out there, but my dad says when he goes in The Green Man he tells some real strange stories. But mostly he keeps to himself, in the woods.'

'So, why would we want to go into the bloody woods if Old Ted's in there?' asked a perplexed Smiffy.

Posh laughed as he stood, the bell having sounded for the next lesson. 'Don't worry, they're big woods. We won't go anywhere near Old Ted's bit. I'll come round after tea and we'll see if we can find some pheasants eggs – they taste real good. Your mum'll love 'em.'

With that, they made their way to geography. Posh and Smiffy – adventures beckoning.

'Yes sir, I reckon I knows these woods better 'n most round 'ere. Could show you where the woodcock nest, and where that grand old dog fox has his lair. But there's so much more than that. You needs to listen to 'em.'

Daniel Crane looked at Ted and tried desperately to find something to pin his doubts on. There had to be something wrong with this guy. Lived alone, no dependants, been living in these woods for half of his life and knew them like the back of his hands. Rumour was that he used to be a military man, but that must have been a long time ago, and of little use to Daniel anyway. He was brought out of his reverie by that last statement.

'Need to listen to whom?' he enquired of Ted.

'Not 'whom'. What,' came the confusing reply. Daniel pressed on. 'What?'

'Yer, 'what'.'

'What?! I mean, what do you mean, 'what' rather than 'whom'?' Bloody hell, this was becoming very confusing, and he felt that the whole thing was slipping away from him.

'Ah, the woods, that's what,' Ted replied, a faint odour of wood smoke seemingly ever present whilst he was in the room.

'You need to listen to the woods?' Daniel said, realising that here was the foundation of his doubts – the old guy had lost his bloody marbles.

'Not jus' listen. Understand 'em as well. Everybody hears, don't all listen, mind. You gotta know what they're trying to say. I bin listening all my life, still don't understand all of it. Always something new to learn.' Ted sat quietly after that, his gaze steady but piercing.

Daniel felt a certain unease in his company, and was about to close the interview when Ted added, 'Got poachers, y'know? Down in Sutton Woods, near the old mill. After rabbit 'n' squirrel. Found two snares yesterday, new 'uns. Bin put there no more 'n two days ago. They'll be back so I left 'em set. Reckon tonight'll be the time to bag 'em.'

This fresh angle caught Daniel slightly off guard, and also gave him the ideal opportunity to be rid of Ted. He'd been down by the old mill himself only that morning and had seen no sign of poachers or snares.

'Okay,' he said, 'I'll meet you at dusk by the big oak, we'll get out there before they arrive and nab them in the act.' That should settle it once and for all.

How time flies, it seemed like only yesterday that he and Old Ted were sitting quietly by the old mill, watching as the two poachers retrieved their full snares. Daniel was certainly surprised at that turn of events, and even more surprised at Old Ted's turn of speed when one of the guys attempted a quick escape. He wasn't sure how it had happened, but the guy wasn't too keen in running anywhere after Ted had caught him.

Now, four months later, Daniel was awaiting his weekly meeting with Ted.

'Good mornin', sor,' said Ted, putting on 'the accent'.

He had worked out, long ago, that people expected a few things from their 'Old Teds' and one of them was the classic, country bumpkin accent. Although Ted naturally had a certain twang to his voice, his many years in the Army, often in foreign climes and surrounded by a myriad of local dialects, had softened his burr. So, in the company of strangers and locals who expected those certain somethings, he caricatured his own voice to suit. If truth be known, it was almost natural by now, but at certain times and in special company he'd drop the act and just let it flow.

'Morning, Ted,' replied Daniel, who wasn't as stupid as Ted thought, but was more than happy for Ted to be whoever he wanted to be, as long as he did what Daniel required of him. 'Anything to report?'

'Oi bin keeping an eye on the work they'm doing on the clubhouse. Seem to be going along noicely. Reckon they should be finished b' June. Then we got to beware. Once them there boats gets on the water is when the trouble starts.'

Daniel looked hard at Ted, wondering whether to mention his slide from country bumpkin to a village idiot crossed with Long John Silver! By the look on Ted's face, he'd already realised that he'd pushed it too far, so Daniel moved on as if nothing had happened.

'Right, we'll keep an eye on that. What about the East Woods, any snares?'

'No, sir, not as yet,' replied Ted, without artistic licence. 'The badger's sett in Sutton Woods seems to have been disturbed, but that might just be that big old brock from the West Woods, looking for a mate. I'll be out there tonight, seeing what's about.

'Need to do some pollarding in the West Woods as well, couple of them big old oak branches been damaged in last week's wind. Oi'll get Bert and Reg along with their chainsaw, have 'em down in a jif.'

'Something you're not telling me, Ted?' said Daniel, tentatively.

'Oh, not much, sir. Just worried about the carp. Not sure how they'll take to them jet skis and speeding boats.'

Nice touch, thought Daniel, pretend they're something totally alien to you.

'Well, you keep an eye on them and just keep me appraised of the situation. Good morning, Ted.'

Ted nodded and left, and Daniel knew that he was dealing with a very shrewd man. Honest, he was certain, but there were depths to Ted that were, as yet, unfathomed. Time would tell.

Ted strolled from the lodge to the battered Land Rover that he'd seconded a month or so ago. Within minutes, he had parked in the new clearing to the left of the clubhouse and was strolling away from there, towards the old snag tree. Only yesterday he'd spied some fish beneath it, and, with the sun unhindered by cloud, he was sure he'd see a few more today. Sitting quietly on the stump of a recently felled oak, he pulled his cap lower, to shield his eyes from the sun's glare. None of those fancy 'sun glasses' for him; his eyesight was perfectly acclimatised and he could spy the small perch beneath the tree, waiting in ambush for the shoals of small roach and rudd.

Perfectly still, he was almost a part of the land, and woodpecker and pigeon paid him no heed as they went about their business close by. Out of the corner of his eye he caught a movement in the stubbly grass to his right, then a small, pink nose appeared, followed by the whole of the shrew that it belonged to. Darting this way and that, the minute rodent was a blur of fur, which suddenly spun round and grabbed the merest tip of a worm that had emerged behind it. In a miniature whirl, the worm was extracted and decimated, then, after washing its face dramatically with its front paws, the shrew disappeared from whence it came.

Ted smiled. You don't need no TV when Mother Nature puts on a show like this, every minute of every day, he thought.

'Badoosh!'

Ted knew that sound and looked up just in time to see the water droplets returning to the lake surface; much the same as the great carp had just done.

'Here there be dragons!' murmured Ted, with a smile.

Seconds later, the 'dragon' reappeared above the surface, its scales gleaming gold and bronze, before re-entering its watery lair with a resounding crash, startling a nearby family of moorhens.

For now, all was well. But Ted wondered how long that wellbeing would last.

PART ONE

The hour is early

The whole world is quiet

A beautiful morning's
about to ignite

I'm ready for danger

I'm ready for fire

I'm ready for something
to lift me up higher.

Chapter One

Echoes

‘Oh, you ain't lost it then, Quill,' chortled Sid as he slipped the net under the beaten carp. Stan peered over his mate's shoulder to see what he'd just caught, a warm glow suffusing his every fibre.

‘Ha hah! No not at all, boy. That fought like buggery, waddya reckon?' asked Stan, massaging his aching shoulder whilst Sid lifted net and fish from the water and lowered them onto the waiting mat.

‘Definitely a twenty; twenty three, twenty four?'

Sid's estimate was bang on as the scales read twenty three and a half pounds of glistening common carp. Stan beamed for the camera and let out a small victory yell as he slipped the carp back into the lake, glad to be back by a lake again fishing with his mates – well, fishing with Sid at least.

The winter had been spent making plans, conducting interviews, arranging all of the changes that a house move entails, and no fishing whatsoever, so these couple of days in early spring were heaven sent.

Sid had called a couple of weeks earlier to enquire as to Stan's welfare - well, to take the piss mercilessly, actually – and had then suggested that they get together on one of his local lakes to have a bit of fun, catch up on things and generally enjoy themselves. If it had been down to Jean, Stan would have gone as soon as the phone hit the receiver, but it wasn't so simple. However, two weeks hence it would be. So here they were, sitting by a small lake on the Hampshire/Sussex border in the early spring sunshine, supping tea and shooting the breeze.

The previous evening, just after Stan's arrival, Sid had opened proceedings with a common of similar size to Stan's, and there had been a wordless acknowledgment between them that the last time they'd seen a common carp it had been three times that size and was now forbidden fruit.

As the evening wore on, and the second bottle of wine had been uncorked, Sid asked what Stan knew he would.

‘So, come on then, Quill, what's the chances of me and you having a little dangle over the Mere? You must be able to swing it, surely? Just one rod each, bit of sneaky stalking. You know the flavour?'

Stan laughed, but in his heart he felt oh so sad. He knew how they all felt, having had Utopia snatched from their grasp, but the fact that Stan was now a warden of the Estate made it no less difficult for him; if anything it was much worse.

'Sid, mate, you know the score. If I could, don't you think we'd be sitting somewhere else now, rather than next to this puddle?' He knew that was a bit harsh, but his bitterness was rising to the surface and he couldn't halt the flow of vitriol. 'Think about it; I see the lake every day, every bloody day, and I can't do a thing about it. Yeah, I can walk around it as much as I want, but that don't make it any easier. Imagine what it'll be like in the summer, when I'm strolling around and I see those bloody great things lying in the sun, thumbing their bloody noses at me.' Sid, always one to make light of any situation, jumped in, 'Man, I'd love to see that – carp's noses! D'you reckon…?'

'Don't!' growled Stan, and Sid could see that it was time for a change of tack.

'Well, this may be a bloody puddle, boy, but I seem to think that only one of us has caught from here so far, and that would appear to be… oh… me!'

Stan laughed, lifted his glass in salute, and reached to refill both.

'Wonder what the boys are up to at the mo'?' asked Sid.

He'd called both Buzz and Chris to see if they could all get together, but it seemed that the Mere had been the final piece of thread that had held their small band together. Now though, the tapestry was starting to unravel. Buzz had taken on a couple of government commissions and was out of the country for the next three months at least, and Chris had followed in Stan's house-moving footsteps, only his had taken him east instead of west, so they were now almost two hundred miles apart. Chris's move was also due to work, but his fishing had suffered little because, within a thirty-mile radius of his Cambridgeshire home, there were any number of large waters housing very large carp. The plan, as always, was to keep in touch and pop over to see each other every month or so but, even this early in the piece, it was evident that this just wasn't going to be viable, and the cord that had joined them for a quarter of a decade was being stretched ever so thin.

'Dunno mate, but they're missing out on a nice drop of vino, that's for sure,' replied Stan.

'So, old fella, what you gonna do for a bit of fishing from now on? Can't have you wallowing around in this puddle all season, can we? Got anything planned near to home?'

'To be fair Sid, I haven't really had the time to look; it's been bloody mental, what with getting the house sorted and learning the ropes on the new job. I've spoken to a couple of guys who've given me a couple of lakes to look at, but I just ain't had the chance,' (or the inclination, thought Stan).

'Oh well mate, you're more than welcome here for a few sessions, but I've also put my name down for that Ringwood club. They've got some bloody fish down there mate, I'm telling ya,' said Sid. They both knew of the Ringwood waters, but getting into them was a different matter as there were few places available and, if perchance you were lucky enough to get a ticket, booking up for a night's fishing was limited and on a 'first come, first served' basis – not ideal.

'Yeah, cheers mate,' Stan replied, 'but I dunno what my plans are gonna be at the moment. It's practically twenty-four/seven at the mo, what with me and John being the only two. They're interviewing for another warden as we speak. Hey, Sid, what about that? Maybe you could apply for that, boy!' The prospect suddenly excited Stan, but Sid had already thought it through over the previous couple of months and the cons seriously outweighed the pros.

Being a decade or so younger than Stan, Sid's family situation was just blossoming, and his first child was due within a few months, which meant that he had to earn as much as possible for the foreseeable future, and the warden job offered almost half as much as he could earn on a good week on the cars.

'Lovely thought mate, and what a bloody partnership that would be, but I just couldn't afford it at the mo'.

With the wine beginning to control Stan's tongue, he put forward a less than feasible case and, before long, the whole thing deteriorated into banter, jibe and counter-jibe. Soon it was time for bed.

The afternoon sun was warming enough, especially as they were set up on the north bank, sheltered from the north easterly breeze by some slowly blossoming willows behind them. A small double had fallen to Sid's rods soon after Stan's success, and the verbal jousting contest was leaning in the host's favour for the moment. As another chocolate biscuit was dunked into another cup of tea, the conversation drifted back a few months.

'So, how big do you reckon that one I caught would be now, mate?' enquired Sid around a mouthful of tea-soaked crumbs.

Stan took another gulp of tea before replying. Gazing up at a distant speck in the blue sky, he asked, 'What d'you think that is, Sid? Hawk? Buzzard? Crow?' pointing skywards.

Sid squinted and followed Stan's directions. 'Dunno, mate. There are a few buzzards around here but that'd have to be pretty high up to be that small. Oh, here we go!' he exclaimed, as the speck veered away to the left and plummeted earthwards at speed. With the wings back, the raptor noticeably picked up speed and then, claws extended, plucked a small bird from the air, just yards from a distant copse of trees. 'Bloody hell!' cried Sid. 'Did you bloody see that?'

The question was, of course, rhetorical because Stan was in a similar state of exclamation. 'Man, that is the bollocks! Bloody hell, what was it – sparrow hawk?'

'Yeah, might have been,' replied a suitably excited Sid, 'but I've been told that there's supposed to be a pair of peregrines around here as well, so you never know.'

'Who cares, mate? That was the nuts! "What, you only caught one fish in two days? Bet that was boring." Wankers!' said Stan, mimicking all of those people we all know who simply don't understand.

'Better put the kettle on again, boy. Must be your turn, innit?' said Sid whilst settling back in his chair and pulling the peak of his cap forward. Before Stan had a chance to counter, however, his right hand alarm screamed for attention, and all thoughts of tea were left spattered on the ground by the kettle. The fish put up quite a battle, but turned out to be one of those bionic mid-doubles that all lakes have, and it was soon sliding back into the lake, unaware that it had just handed the bragging rights back to its captor.

Later that evening, as they washed down Stan's fine curry with an equally fine glass of wine, Sid revisited the question that had been interrupted by raptor and capture.

'Have you seen 'em recently, Quill?'

'Seen what?' asked Stan, mischievously, knowing full well what Sid was referring to.

'Oi! Don't make me come over there, boy. You know what'll happen,' declared Sid, all gusto and false bravado.

'Yeah, yeah! You know what they say, Sid: "talk is cheap", and it don't come any cheaper than yours, fella,' replied Stan, smiling in the darkness, and pulling his coat around him a bit more, as the frosty night grew colder.

'Well, I'd like to hear them say it to me. Now come on, don't make me have to put manners on you, not at your age. You know I'm at my prime fighting weight.' With that, he got up and did some shadow boxing and a quick Ali shuffle, before swearing loudly.

'Shit, knocked me bloody wine glass over!' he declared, disbelievingly, which sent Stan into raptures and caused him to spit out a mouthful of wine before choking on it.

'Sit down, you bloody idiot!' he squawked between gasped breaths and giggles. 'You'll knock the bloody bottle over next. Sit down!'

A semblance of sanity resumed a few minutes later, with both refilled glasses placed far away from shuffling legs.

'Right, see what happens, Quill? You try to go all MI5 on me and the shit hits the fan. So, give it to me straight or we're gonna have words.' With that, Sid picked up his glass and put on his sternest face. Unfortunately, the flickering candlelight just made him look constipated and had Stan chuckling again.

Sid lifted an admonishing finger and merely said, 'Ah!' to which Stan lifted his glass and began.

'Okay, okay. I don't think my bloody ribs can take any more of this. I give in. Yeah, I've seen 'em – once.' Sid was just about to pounce but, before he could draw breath, Stan said, 'Shut! Listen! Learn!'

Sid settled back whilst sipping from his glass and Stan continued.

'The lake's changed totally. I told you they'd started digging through to the pike lake – well, that's almost finished. They've had to leave an island in the middle, which just happens to be where we saw The Big Common from in the close season.'
Sid nodded in recollection, and Stan continued: 'The snag tree's still there by the Top Banana, but all the trees behind it have been cut down. In fact almost all of the trees along the north bank have gone, right up to the Post Office.'
'Bloody hell, that must look bloody shit!' said Sid, almost to himself.
'Yeah, it ain't pretty at the mo. What they've done is cut down the oaks, but they've left a few willows and silver birches – something to do with wind flow. Anyway, they were also looking to cut down the East Woods as well, but English Nature got involved and the guy who carried out the survey is a good friend of my boss, John, so he made sure that they found some very rare species of plant and insect.'
'Nice friend to have, by the sound of it,' said Sid.
'Yeah. It was him who said they had to leave the island in the middle because of some rare orchid or something. So, the lakes are joined up now, just finishing the digging out by your pads and Dead Man Standing.'
'No!' exclaimed Sid. 'Not Dead Man Standing?'
'Yeah I know, mate. But that's gone and they're digging a little way down into the bay. By the time it's finished the lake will be about seventy-odd acres. I've had a look round the pike lake a couple of times, and there's a couple of areas where they'll definitely get, I reckon. Northwest corner and southwest corner, for sure, but I'm not sure what's in there in the way of pads and stuff. The northwest corner, just past the clubhouse, has got a few dead reeds, but they're starting to grow, so I think that might be a good area. But what else, I don't know at the moment.'
'How deep is it? Any bars and that?' enquired Sid, suddenly with his fishing head on, despite the futility of that.
'Dunno, Sid. Not had a chance to plumb it or anything, but there must be a decent depth or they wouldn't be able to have sailing boats on there. John reckons that it averages about eight or nine feet, but I'm not sure what bits. Thing is, at the mo' it don't matter. There's no fishing so I'm just gonna concentrate around the edges. I'm sure that's where they'll be, 'specially once those bloody jet skis and motor boats get out there.'
'Enough talk, Quill, cut to the chase, mate. What have you seen?' demanded Sid, draining the last of his wine and rueing his earlier Ali shuffle.
'Oh, Sid. What have I seen? Well, strangely, the day after you phoned was a very odd day. I'd been doing some work around the back of one of the houses – a bit of brickwork problem on their garden wall. Anyway, I've just finished and I'm packing my gear away when I thought I heard this splash. The house is a couple of hundred yards from the lake but the wind was southerly and I could clearly hear the coots and that. So, I put my bag down and stood for a while. Then, a minute later there it was again – badoosh! Well, I'm off! It sounded like it was coming from the snag

tree area so I set off in that direction. It was quite a nice day, pretty sunny, so the snag tree was the obvious place to try. When I got there, the wind was pushing in there but the water was pretty clear so I stood on a tree stump from one of the old oaks and got a much better view. I could see perch and stuff in amongst the roots, but you know what it's like. You stand there for ages then, just as you're gonna leave…'

'You see one of the buggers,' continued Sid, filling in the gap.

'Two,' came Stan's curt reply.

'Two! Bloody hell, which ones?'

'Well, I'm just thinking of getting down when – badoosh – this bloody great carp leaps out, but it's to my left towards what was the Back Banana. I couldn't see anything for the ripples, but I jumped down and ran to another stump. Got up. Badoosh! Bang in front of me, five yards out, bloody great mirror carp.'

'Which one?' asked Sid who was, by now, like a kid entranced by a fairy story and wondering whether the prince would get there before the trolls.

'Couldn't tell, at first. Just knew it wasn't The Common. I just stood there, peering into the water, then I saw a movement to my right and there, not three yards out is The Common!'

'What! But you said it was a bloody mirror!' cried Sid, who really wished he had never seen Ali shuffle.

'Keep up, Sid. What do you think it meant, you buffoon? There were two of 'em; The Common and one of the mirrors.' Sid nodded, realising his foolishness and unequipped with a witty retort.

'So,' continued Stan, 'The Big Common is cruising along the margins, looking huge, and then from the opposite direction comes a big mirror. They do that sliding-alongside-each-other thing, then the mirror does a one-eighty and The Common follows it. I could see the flank; it wasn't your fifty-two. I think it must have been the one that Rhodie lost because it was bloody massive! Almost the size of The Common I reckon; definitely upper fifty all day long.'

This revelation left Sid in desperate need of a drink so, as a last resort, and in the absence of any alcohol, on went the kettle.

'What happened then? Did you follow them?' he asked, whilst firing up the stove.

'Oh no, then it got weirder. I was just about to jump down from the tree stump when this voice says, 'Bigger'n when you last saw her, eh?' I turned round and there's this old geezer standing ten feet away. I didn't hear him turn up, hadn't seen him when I was walking over there, but there he was. I said, "What d'you mean?" 'cos I didn't know if anyone else knew. He just smiled and said, "You take good care of 'em; they're gonna need it," in that bizarre bloody accent some of 'em have, then he just turned and strolled off towards the woods.'

Sid was as perplexed as Stan sounded so asked the obvious dumb question: 'Who was he then?'

Stan avoided the obvious riposte and just shook his head. 'Dunno, mate. I think I've seen him in one of the pubs before. And maybe even around the woods and that. There's a couple of gamekeepers been employed so I think he might be one of them, but he was a bit strange.'

'Da dah ling ding, ding ding, ding ding ding!' sang Sid, with the usual rendition of 'Duelling Banjos' that accompany these strange tales of country folk, finishing it off with, 'Squeal like a pig!' for effect.

'Yeah, you're probably not wrong there, mate. "Big as a girt pig!" replied Stan, quoting a line from Buzz's encounter the previous year.

'Whatever though, Quill, two bloody massive carp and we can't fish for the bastards!'

Stan nodded ruefully. If truth be known, one of the driving forces behind him going for the warden's job was the hope that it might give him the opportunity to fish the lake, but that hope had faded almost immediately when one of the workmen had ventured out with a small spinning rod, just after Christmas, and had been sacked on the spot.

'Yeah, I know, mate. Don't think that hasn't crossed my mind once or twice! But there's nought I can do at the mo. I think we'll just have to play the waiting game and see how it pans out over the next year or so. Those fish ain't going anywhere and, if anything, there's every chance they'll get even bigger,'

Stan took the proffered cup of tea from Sid, and sat back to enjoy it before bed. Then it was knocked all over him as Sid leapt up to strike a screaming take on his right hand rod. Cursing, Stan jumped up to assist, wiping his cooling hands against his trousers whilst Sid grunted and muttered in the dark.

'God, I miss this,' thought Stan, as he bent to pick up the net.

Gradually, the lake's waters warmed as the spring sunshine strengthened. The great fish could do little but follow their natural instincts and one of them was 'curiosity'. The new lake was, indeed, full of natural food, and as the weather warmed, so the food multiplied. The carp took little time finding new larders and despite much bankside commotion, they could be seen cruising the far margins by the West Woods on most days. But their 'home' was still the Mere and that was where they returned on most evenings, snuffling out the grubs and larvae that were ever present in the margins of the islands and the recently denuded north bank.

As the first days of summer brought forth greater warmth and life, their existence was idyllic, and as safe as it could possibly be. But that would soon change. Work on the slipway and clubhouse was moving on apace, and rigging and sails, motors and skis were all being prepared for the opening regatta, at the end of July.

As that regatta loomed, less than a month distant, the carp were to be found in the top bay, behind the big island, recovering from the previous days' annual ritual. Scratches, scars and the odd missing scale were evidence of the frenzy of spawning

that had taken place, but there had been no lasting damage, and the warming sun and copious food would soon heal any superficial wounds. Down in weight once again, the large carp cruised lazily around the bay, rubbing against each other once in a while as if to affirm their bonds.

Life was good, but it was about to change dramatically.

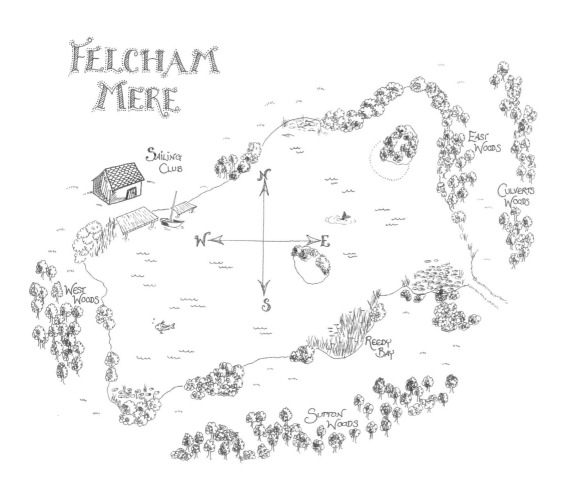

Chapter Two
Green is the Colour

Smells and sounds. Smiffy's senses were being overloaded like never before. It was like being on PlayStation, but a hundred times more intense.

The wood was alive with sounds; squeaks and whistles, creaking trees and rustling undergrowth and it was like a whole new world of wonder for Smiffy.

Oh, sure, he'd been to Hampstead Heath, and Kew Gardens with the school, and out to the country where his uncle and aunt lived, but he'd never been anywhere like this.

Posh held up a hand, commando style, and Smiffy stopped in his tracks.

'What is it?' he whispered. Posh ushered him forward with a beckoning finger, then put a hand on his shoulder to stop him. They were by a large tree, oak Smiffy presumed, and about twenty yards away was a small clearing in the undergrowth that was dappled by the sun coming through the trees.

Posh pointed to the right, to the edge of the clearing, and at first Smiffy saw nothing, bar a small, green bush. Then something moved behind it and he could see a leg and bottom of something. Posh held his finger to his lips, and they remained motionless. For no reason he could discern, Smiffy's heart was beating faster than when he'd run the hundred metres at school. He peered intently through the few branches in front of him, then, as if arriving through an invisible door, a deer appeared in the clearing, sunlight sprinkling yellow flakes across its back. Its nose twitched and sniffed before it lowered its head and took a mouthful of moss in its teeth, chewing in a strange, rotary fashion. Smiffy was transfixed, then whispered, 'What is it?' to Posh.

Before his friend had had a chance to say 'roe', the deer's head came up fast and it bounded off into the woods, leaving just a swaying branch in its wake.

'Smiffy, you gotta be quiet. I told you,' Posh admonished.

'But I only whispered,' said Smiffy, in futile defence, but he was unworried. What a sight. He'd never been that close to a wild animal in his life, except at the zoo, but that was different; there were bars and reinforced glass in zoos. They might as well have been on the telly. This was so bloody real.

'Yeah, well,' said Posh, 'they got really good hearing, and sense of smell. We were upwind so that was alright. She was a roe deer, a doe,' he confirmed.

'What? A roe, a doe; what is this, bloody Sound of Music?'

Posh laughed at his mate. 'No, you plonker! It's a roe deer and it's a female, and a female is called a 'doe'. There's also fallow deer and red deer, although you only get the reds in the forest, normally.'

'Right,' said Smiffy, chagrined, 'but how do you tell 'em apart then?'

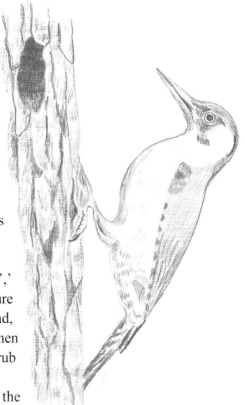

'Well, with the does it's mainly colour. The fallow have loads of white spots on the back but the roe deer are just plain brown. The male fallows have got big antlers, but the roes' are like short, spiky things.'

Smiffy stared, open-mouthed at Posh before exclaiming, 'Bloody hell, is your dad David Attenborough or something?'

Posh just laughed and said, 'Nah, Smiffy, it's something you just know in the country. Can you hear that bird?'

Smiffy heard a strident call echoing through the woods and nodded, 'Yeah, what is it?'

'Green woodpecker,' answered his friend, nonchalantly, Smiffy shook his head, 'I thought they went 'tap-tap-tap',' he said, disbelieving. Posh just smiled and pointed and, sure enough, through the trees flew a green bird with a red head, dipping and swooping before landing on a distant tree. Then came the distant 'tap-tap-tap' as it searched out a tasty grub for tea.

Smiffy just shook his head and walked away through the trees, his smiling friend ambling along behind.

Smells and sounds. A month had passed since that first, wonderful introduction to the natural world for Smiffy, and he sat with his back to the tree, awaiting the arrival of the green woodpecker that its call had heralded. And there it was, just through the trees, over towards the old mill. He'd decided that it was his very favourite bird, and since that first encounter had gleaned as much information about it as he could. He'd even taken out a copy of 'Birds of Britain' from the school library, and had identified more than a dozen in the short time he'd had it.

For now, he was alone in the afternoon woodland, Posh having had to visit the dentist with his mum, but he'd be over pretty soon, no doubt. A small movement caught his attention, to his right, near that fallen tree. Without moving his head, he looked down and, not twenty feet away, a small, dark head appeared from beneath the rotting bark.

'Rat!' thought Smiffy, immediately, but he'd seen rats on the telly and this didn't quite fit the bill. The head moved forward and brought a long, rusty brown body with it. What was it? What was it? Smiffy knew he had the answer and then, as the rodent stood on its back legs and sniffed the air, he had it – a weasel.

A bloody weasel! Right there, near enough almost to touch. Like most of the weasel's prey, Smiffy was transfixed, unable to move even if he'd wanted to. The long, sinewy body gave it an almost serpentine appearance, and that was enhanced when it bounded off through the undergrowth, spooked by the cracking of a twig in the distance. Snapped from his reverie, Smiffy looked round to see his friend walking through the wood towards him, and he couldn't contain the news within him.

Running though mulch and fallen branches he met Posh with a breathless, 'A weasel, I've just seen a weasel!'

As intrigued as he was, it is the way of kids, and adults, the world over to pour cold water on any startling revelation that they themselves have not been party to.

'A weasel? Are you sure? It wasn't a stoat, was it?' asked Posh.

Smiffy was slightly stunned by this reaction, but regained his equilibrium enough to sputter, 'Weasel, stoat, does it bloody matter? I've seen one of them and it was bloody fantastic!'

Posh just nodded, then bent to pick up a willow switch, flicking it along the ground whilst walking to the site of the recent close encounter. 'Well, it's just that it's easy to get them mixed up,' he started, quickly adding, 'but it's great. Don't get me wrong. You don't tend to see many; they're really shy.'

Smiffy sensed some doubt in his friend's voice so quickly took up that gauntlet. 'I did see it, Posh, I'm telling you. Give us a pencil, I'll draw it for you,' he demanded, indignantly.

'No, no. I believe you, but what colour was its tail?' he asked, casually.

'It was quite long, sort of rusty brown and had a black tip. Why?'

Posh nodded, 'Yeah, thought so. It was a stoat. Stoats have a black tip to the tail, weasels don't. But, bloody hell, well done, Smiffy, a bloody stoat. Well done.'

He was genuinely pleased, although slightly jealous because, after all his years in the country, he had only seen a weasel on a couple of occasions, and never a stoat.

Still, they knew where it lived now, and he was sure they'd get another sighting in the future,

'Where we going then?' asked Smiffy eagerly. Posh had told him at school that he had a bit of a surprise, and Smiffy couldn't wait to find out what it was.

'Ah, you'll just have to follow me and see,' replied Posh with a grin, and turned and retraced his steps through the wood, heading towards the old mill.

When they got there, Smiffy looked a bit bemused. They'd been to the old mill on a couple of occasions and, as wonderful and mysterious as it was, he couldn't imagine there being anything that would surprise him there.

'Come on, down here,' said Posh, climbing down a grassy slope next to one of the crumbling walls of the mill house. At the bottom, he turned right, along the face of the mill wall and along to the pool in front of it. The pool was fed by a stream that meandered through the woods and eventually came out at the south end of the Mere, about a quarter of a mile away.

'Right,' he said, 'how d'you fancy catching your first fish?' He'd found out fairly recently that Smiffy had never been fishing, never even held a fishing rod, so he'd decided that this was an art his friend really needed to learn.

Smiffy looked a little startled and then, as the idea gained pace in his head, his first words were, 'But I haven't got a rod.'

Perfect.

'Well, you have now,' said Posh, grinning even more as he leant round behind the mill wall and retrieved a fully tackled up rod, complete with reel and float.

'There you go, Smiffy. Let's go fishing.' With that he handed the open-mouthed Smiffy an eight-foot cane rod and reel, grabbing similar for himself from his hiding place. Leaving his mate gawping at the unprecedented gift, Posh walked a few yards to the edge of the pool and sat down, dangling his legs over the edge of the wall. He'd dug up some worms on the way and had them in a small pot, and so picked out a small one and carefully impaled it on the hook. As it wriggled enticingly, he flicked the bale arm over on the old reel and carefully flicked the float into the middle of the pool; the red tip gradually righting itself as the lead shot slowly sank. The bale arm was flicked back over, and with a deft twitch of the handle, the slack line was taken up and the coils straightened. All of the time, Smiffy had watched this precise operation and was amazed how simple it looked; surely he'd be able to do that first time.

The worm selection was fairly straightforward, his choice being governed by the barely discernible shakes and nods of Posh's head. The impaling was a little more difficult but, once on, the worm wriggled just as enticingly as Posh's had, so that was okay. Now, bale arm. He flicked it off and the float dropped to the floor in a pile of shot and line. That wasn't supposed to happen, and he had no idea how to right that wrong.

'Come on, Posh, sort me out,' he pleaded. But just as his plea was about to be answered, the red tip of Posh's float disappeared and he lifted the rod quickly, feeling the thrum of something on the other end.

'Bloody hell, have you got one?' squealed Smiffy, and watched in amazement as his mate lifted a wriggling, glistening silver fish from the water and swung it into his hand. 'What is it?'

'Dace,' replied Posh nonchalantly. 'Loads of them in here, but I wanna catch a chub if I can.'

Dace. Chub. They meant nothing to Smiffy, but he had the sudden urge to catch one himself. To that end, before Posh had a chance to try for his desired quarry, Smiffy was demanding assistance and instruction from him. After five minutes he had mastered the bale arm and finger on the spool to hold the line. A further ten minutes (and just two retrievals from surrounding foliage) saw him flicking his float out into the still, deep, mysterious pool. And five minutes later saw a smile the width of the Grand Canyon split his face as he held his very own, and very first fish – a spiky backed, stripy, beautiful perch. His joy was infectious, and, by the end of that first afternoon, he and Posh were both smiling gleefully at their individual successes. Posh had, indeed, caught a fine two-pound chub, and Smiffy cared not that his further five fish did not weigh that amount in total. For now, one thing was evident – a fisherman was born.

The rod and reel was not a gift; Posh had merely 'borrowed' them from his dad's shed, but when Smiffy returned home late, muddy but remarkably happy, his mother's admonishment fell entirely on deaf ears.

Yes, he knew his tea was cold.

Yes, he knew she'd told him to tell her where he was.

Yes, he knew that he wasn't supposed to go into the woods.

Yes, that was dirt under his fingernails, and, yes, he was going to wash his hands before he had his dinner.

'Dad,' he said, after having wolfed down his tepid sausage and potatoes, 'can I get a fishing rod and reel?'

His father looked up from the table where he was working and asked, 'Fishing rod? What do you want that for?'

Oh, how he wished he could say, 'Well, I just wanted to paint the roof, actually!' But that sort of retort was reserved for the playground at the moment, and would have earned him a severe bollocking if he'd tried it at home.

'I went fishing with Neil this afternoon and caught some perch and dace, and it was great. But Neil's only got one rod so we had to share. But I want to be able to go again, so can I get a rod and reel, please?'

'Not if you're going to come in late and dirty, my lad,' came his mother's response from the kitchen. Smiffy's dad raised an eyebrow and motioned with his head in the direction of the kitchen – that knowing look between father and son. 'Well, let's see, shall we. Where would you get one from anyway?'

That was all that Smiffy needed, that chink of an opening. With his foot in the door, there was no way back for them now, and by the end of the week the new tackle would be his.

Truth be told, his parents had been very concerned about how their son would take to their new home. He'd always been fairly insular, or so they thought, but then they hadn't seen him for six months of the year so what would they really know? Now, however, he seemed to be thriving and the dreaded PlayStation was left inert in the corner of his room. Everyone was banging on about kids getting fresh air and exercise, and now here he was, demanding it – what more could they want?

'That'll be too big, won't it Posh?' asked Smiffy, as he held up the eleven-foot rod in the Salisbury tackle shop his dad had taken them to. He'd brought Posh along to help with selection, as he and his dad had no idea what was required.

'No, that's fine. We won't be fishing in the pool much, there's a couple of little ponds around that we can fish, no need for short rods there,' replied Posh, so that was that. A rod, reel, floats, hooks, tackle box, a net, and this, and that, oh and that over there. Peter Robertson-Smythe barely blinked at the final total, merely handing over the card and ushering the boys into the car, hoping to get back in time for the rugby.

Posh had suggested maybe too many floats and hooks, but it was good to share, so they wouldn't be wasted! Now, it was just a case of christening everything.

'Give me a call when you want collecting, Quentin,' said Peter, knowing that the rugby was safe, the boys talking about eight in the evening. 'Have fun! Catch a whopper!' he said, and made his way back down the farm track to the main road, pleased that he'd bought the Range Rover as well as the Merc.

After a bit of juggling, all of the gear was shared out and the lads made their way to the gate, beyond which was the small farm pond that Posh had decided to fish. It was less than an acre in size, open on every bank, and had a small, reedy island in the middle of it. Nestled around it were six other anglers, their green brollies resembling out of date mushrooms. On first glance, Smiffy was less than impressed; this was nothing like the mill pool in the woods, but, hey, Posh said there were some good fish in there, so what was there to lose?

Amongst all the other purchases, two pints of maggots had been on the 'essential' list, and it was these that Posh was firing out in front of them with Smiffy's newly acquired catapult. They'd spent an hour in Smiffy's garden loading line onto the reel and getting everything into the tackle box in its right place; now it was time to put it all to the test. After an hour, Smiffy's rod remained un-christened, and all Posh had to show for his travails were a couple of perch, smaller and less pristine than those in the mill pool. Their original excitement had now waned, and gradually Smiffy realised that this may not be for him. Posh had noticed that a guy along the bank from them had caught a couple of better fish, so strolled up to see what he was doing different to them. Fortunately, the guy knew his dad so was happy to give him a bit of advice, and also some grains of wisdom – sweetcorn.

'That guy's caught a couple of tench and he's using this,' said Posh, showing Smiffy the small pot of yellow grains.

'Sweetcorn? Blimey that's a bit weird, innit?' remarked Smiffy, unsure if this was a wind-up or not.

'Yeah, well, he's had a few so I'm gonna give it a go. D'you want some?'

Smiffy was still unsure so declined, but ten minutes later he was much more certain as he and Posh were gazing into the net at a dark green tench of almost two pounds.

'How d'you put them on, then?' asked Smiffy, after his third aborted attempt had left two more grains in the grass. Posh walked over and showed him again, being very careful not to split the grains, then he pulled Smiffy's float up a further foot. 'That'll lay flat on the surface, which means the bait will be on the bottom. That's where the tench feed. Just put your rod tip under the water, then reel back slowly until the float sits up with just the tip showing. You may get a lift bite, so watch out.'

A lift bite – what was that? thought Smiffy, but did as he was bid. The float eventually sat as Posh had directed, but was a good five yards closer to the bank than he'd originally cast it. Unsure what to do, he picked up the catapult and fired out some corn, most of which landed a yard behind the float. No, he didn't think this was gonna work, this fishing thing. Yeah, it had been great in the mill pool, but if this was the sort of place where the bigger fish lived then he didn't fancy it much.

'Smiffy!' shouted Posh. 'Lift bite! Lift bite!' He was pointing at Smiffy's float, which was rising up from the surface of the water like a slowly ascending rocket, tumbling to lie on its side.

'Strike! Strike!' his friend commanded, so he did, but the rise of the rod tip was halted after a moment, and then bent down alarmingly. Suddenly, line was coming off of the reel of its own volition and wind as much as he could, he was unable to stop it.

'Tighten the clutch,' instructed Posh, but he may as well have said, 'Reconfigure the Tranthium drive and de-fibrillate the Cloomb valve!' It would have made just as much sense!

'Clutch, mate. Clutch!'

'Well, clutch away, I don't know what you're talking about,' bellowed an increasingly agitated Smiffy. The line was still being taken from the reel and he seemed powerless to stop it. Posh put his hand over the spool and, for all Smiffy knew, may have said 'Abracadabra' because, suddenly, the line wasn't being pulled from the spool but the rod tip was being pulled down again.

'Right, don't wind so madly, let it tire itself out a bit,' instructed Posh calmly. A pithy retort would have been handy, but all Smiffy had was an increasingly drying mouth, so just listened and learned. A couple of times the rod tip was pulled down violently, and the spool gave up a bit more line, but soon the lunges had stopped and, slowly but surely, Smiffy gained line and guided the fish towards the waiting net.

'Steady now,' said the netsman, then, 'Yes!'

The weight was gone from the rod, his arm ached like hell, but when he peered into the net all Smiffy could do was repeat his friends last 'Yes!' but slightly more vociferously.

'Blimey, that's a good'un, lad,' came a voice from behind. The guy who'd given them the corn had come along to see what all the commotion was, and was peering admiringly into the net. 'What's your peebee?'

Smiffy knew that it was a question but he had no idea to what it referred. Was the answer 'green' or 'seventy-one'?

'Errm, I dunno. What is it, Posh?' he replied, seeking desperate assistance from his mate.

'Well, this is mate, without a doubt,' came his friend's certain reply.

Of all the shiny, new items of tackle they'd bought, amongst them wasn't a set of scales, so the sweetcorn man fetched his along and they weighed the fine tench at just over five pounds. There were no more for Smiffy after that, but he wasn't too worried, and when Posh caught a tench just a pound smaller than his as they were packing away, and declared that it was his 'peebee', Smiffy just nodded and said, 'Nice'.

For ages after, he assumed peebee was some strange angling term for your favourite fish or something. It wasn't until a few months later, when Posh landed a pike of seven pounds and declared it to be his new peebee, that Smiffy queried it.

'No, you muppet – P.B. – personal best. Biggest fish, get it?' explained Posh, derisively. Slowly, the mist cleared, but by then it mattered not. He was well and truly hooked and, coupled with the wonders of nature that were all around, every day was a new adventure.

'How'd you get on, dear?' called Jean, as she heard Stan in the kitchen.

'Oh, had a few tench, but it was a shitty little puddle. Don't know why I stayed, really. I'll have a few words with that twat down the pub, telling me it was a bloody lake stacked with whackers.'

Stan left his boots by the back door and put the kettle on, taking off his sweatshirt whilst he waited for the kettle to boil. Jean strolled in and gave him a kiss, picking up the shirt and dropping it in the washing basket without breaking stride.

'Did anyone else have anything?' she asked.

'Yeah, Dan Becks' boy, Neil, was there with a mate. They had a couple of nice tench. I think his mate lives on the Mere estate. Got all the new gear but didn't have a clue how to use it. If it weren't for young Neil he would have lost a lovely tench.'

Jean tutted, then put the teabags in the cups.

'What?' said Stan, indignantly. 'What you tutting at?'

'Well, don't talk like that about the lad, maybe it's all new because he's just started fishing. And maybe they were there so that Neil could show him how to fish properly,' said Jean, milk in hand.

He was going to tell her how he'd helped the lads out with the corn and the float and all that, but in the end he knew it would be pointless and sound more like an excuse, so he just picked up his tea and went into the front room. Suppose they have to learn somehow, he thought, then picked up that week's copy of Carp-Talk and smiled at the face of his old mate, Mickey Charles, looking back at him from behind a forty-pound common carp. Good lad, Mick, still doing it, fella.

Learning how to fish, eh? Now that would be something to teach, wouldn't it, he thought as he flicked the pages. Where on earth would you start?

Chapter Three

Get your filthy hands Off My Desert

Ah, there she is, thought Ted. The sow made her way slowly but confidently out of the sett and into the gloaming of late evening, and Ted smiled. He loved the contradiction of an animal that was so notoriously elusive but, when seen, appeared so confident and almost aloof. The big, female badger ambled forward with that strange, rolling gait, and was followed by the five young cubs. No more than a few months old, they were remarkable miniature versions of their mother, but still not old enough to leave her side. The rest of the clan followed, with the older cubs snarling and play-fighting, and bowling over a couple of their smaller cousins.

Ted loved to watch the badgers at play, and would spend many a summer's evening sitting behind the scattered remains of an old shed near the mill, imbued with a feeling that he could only put down to one thing – family. The badgers were fully aware of his presence, no more than a few feet away, but he had been there since the sow was the size of her cubs, and had been accepted as just another part of the woodland community. He never abused that position, never interacted or helped, and on more than one occasion over the previous couple of decades had returned home almost in tears, having had to watch helplessly as one or another of the group had succumbed to sickness or injury. But survival of the fittest was high on his list of mottos, if he actually had such a list. His life, however, needed no such thing. He lived it the way he had always done; honestly, tirelessly, with compassion and bravery.

As the badgers continued to rummage for food, and snarled and growled in mock battle, the dusk slowly faded to night and Ted's mind wandered.

Why couldn't all battles be so simple? The natural world knew the need for strength and guile. Survival of the fittest was not just a Darwinian concept; it was a necessity. The strongest males of any species – elephant, lion, rat or badger – would be the ones best suited to protect the family unit. Simple fact. Very rarely, in all the encounters in the animal kingdom that required a test of strength, did the losers die.

Yes, many would be hurt, but they would go away and lick their wounds and recover and return the next year to try again. And again. And again. Until, eventually, they were either strong enough or were mortally found wanting.

Why do we have to kill those weaker than us? Ted had let that question suffuse his being for many, many years, and he was still no closer to the answer. He'd seen his fair share of corpses; friend and foe. He didn't care to remember how many of those had been his doing – far too many, that was for sure. 'Just following orders.' Much too easy a get-out clause. He still woke up, in the deep darkness just before dawn, and saw the faces, some more vivid than others.

A Burmese jungle. Hot, humid, alive with sound. Rivulets of sweat running down his back, his shirt clinging to him like a second, oversized skin.

Eyes stinging, limbs aching. The rifle in his hands growing heavier by the second. One step, move ferns aside. Another step, move ferns, check Taf is still behind you.

Movement ahead. Stop dead, fist in the air, no talking.

Ahead, to the right, thirty yards. He motions with his hand, slowly forward, be aware.

'Tak! Tak! Tak!'

Gunfire from ahead, bark splinters flying as bullets hit wood.

Down on the ground, all sensory activity concentrated on one thing – survival.

He edges forward, using his elbows to propel himself, his hands holding the gun so tightly they could crush it. Then, just for a second, a glimpse of brown skin behind that tree. Aim, carefully, there is nothing else at that moment, just the cross-hairs and that square inch of target.

Then more.

Crack!

Crack! Crack! Crack!

His shoulder hurts, his eyes sting but in the crosshairs he sees red droplets hanging in midair.

Noise, shouting, gunfire, the acrid smell of cordite. It seems to last forever, but is no more than a few minutes.

Take care, there may be more. He reaches the tree and quickly looks around it. No more standing. At his feet a body. He toes it over. A young boy. Fifteen? Sixteen? A weapon still held in his lifeless fingers, the top of his head missing, flying insects already inspecting the offerings. No vomit this time, just sorrow and disgust. No time for that; men to command and lead and save.

He stares straight ahead. Black and white, black and white. One of the badgers rolls too close and brushes Ted's foot, nonchalantly regaining its composure before waddling back to the fray. No deaths in this woodland glade.

Ted rubs his eyes with thumb and forefinger, then slowly rises. Doesn't look like the old brock from the West Woods is coming tonight. All the young 'uns are accounted for, so no outside influences are involved either. Happy with that thought, Ted turns and quietly makes his way back through the woods, his badger 'family' oblivious or un-alarmed by his departure.

'Twit-twoo!'

The tawny owl grccts him, hidden from view but obviously quite close. Ted smiles, the only one of that family to make the classic owl noise but so rarely seen. Most country folk, and a few folk visiting the country, will have seen the luminous beauty of the barn owl, but there were so many more, and, if you knew where to look, much more to learn about these night hunters. Ted follows the small stream for a few hundred yards, before veering away to the east where he knows a family of little owls will be foraging, good to see on a fine night like this.

'What is it? one of them asked.

'Dace,' replied the other lad; the captor.

From the other side of the old mill-house, Ted smiled as he watched the two lads fishing. Good to see, he thought. Not enough of that these days.

He recognised the young lad with the fish as Dan Becks' boy. Neil, was it? Though the other lad, who he didn't know, seemed to be calling him 'Posh'.

Just a nickname, same as 'Taf' and 'Scally', 'Bongo' and 'Lily'. Good names, good friends, long gone.

The other lad was having all sorts of problems with his fishing gear and Ted had half a mind to go and help out but, as with the badgers, he decided not to. They'd learn soon enough. Or give up.

He moved away a few minutes later, having seen young Becks showing the other lad what to do. They'd be fine. Then a few minutes later he heard excited shouting, just to prove that he was right.

Time to get back to work. That young Simon, his boss, had asked him to check out the East Woods because he'd had a call from one of the estate wardens that there'd been car lights behind there last night. The East Woods were about a mile from Ted's cottage, and coupled with the rather windy night, that meant he'd seen or heard nothing himself. He was a tad chagrined at that. He tried to make a point of knowing everything that was going on in 'his' woods, but he'd planned to walk the East Woods today, anyway, so if there were something to see, he'd see it.

He strolled around the southeast corner of the lake, seeing the first pads clambering for the lake surface in the bay to his left. The reeds rustled in the breeze, much as they'd done many months earlier, prior to Buzz's capture of a forty-eight pound carp.

The trees were beginning to blossom; the undergrowth beginning to rustle and bloom. Spring was working its magic once again.

Ted loved this time of year, when everything had the chance to start again. How he'd love to have the chance to start again. But would he? Would it have been different if he had the chance? He mused over that thought as he slowly made his way through the trees, his subconscious mind constantly on the lookout for something. What? Oh, he'd know when he saw it.

A faint 'crack' of a twig alerted him to someone else's presence, and his subconscious mind handed back the controls to Ted. Just ahead, through the trees some twenty yards, a man was walking up to the lake's edge, where he stopped and gazed out on the water. Ted stopped by the bole of a large willow, and watched the man crouch down by the water's edge and look around. A minute or so later he rose, stretching his legs and arching his back, as if just having awoken. He seemed oblivious to Ted's presence, and that's just the way Ted liked it. Then he heard him talking and was, at first, confused. But the man's hand by his ear gave away the fact that he was talking into a phone. If Old Ted had been in company, he would have referred to it as 'one of they mobility phones,' but he knew exactly what they were; he just had no desire to own one.

'Yeah, just in the woods to the left as you come to the lake,' the man was saying. 'Where Nick came last night. Can't see anything at the moment – nobody around.' Ted leaned against the tree and listened intently, but was unable to pick up the next few sentences as a flock of geese made their usual, vocal entrance, landing with a series of 'whooshes' in front of the man.

'Yeah, load of Canadians, noisy bastards,' continued the one-sided conversation. 'Nah, I think we need a bit more cover, wait 'til the leaves come fully. Maybe in a month.'

'Mutter, mutter.'

'Yeah, well worth it, I reckon. Every two or three nights, about five kilos per night. Some down to the left of here, where the pads are.'

'Mutter, mutter.'

'Oh, yeah! But we'll just have to make sure we can get the van down here. Might have to camo it or something. What about Dave's jeep? That might do it.'

'Mutter, mutter.'

'Yeah, right. Okay, laters.'

With that, the phone was returned to the man's jacket pocket. He then turned and quietly walked north, totally unaware of his hidden audience.

Ted waited a minute or so, then walked to where the man had been standing. He looked left and right and knew that he could only be seen from the opposite bank, which was now almost a half-mile distant, and had an island bang in front of it. He was almost invisible, and if he had a mind to, say, do some stealthy fishing, this would be an ideal place to do it. Especially in a month or so when everything was in full bloom.

With that, he traced the other's steps northwards and out of the woods, just as the man was disappearing into Culvert's Woods, whose boundary formed the northeast corner of the estate.

Hmm. If he was able to get from there to the road, he must have a fair knowledge of the area, or know someone who did. This was going to be interesting. Continuing his stroll around the lake he came to the old snag tree. He'd seen a couple of the big carp there the previous day, and hoped for a better view in the spring sunshine. He'd also seen the new warden, and not for the first time. When John Bakewell had brought him into The Fox, a few weeks earlier, Ted had peered intently at him across the bar, sure that he recognised him from somewhere. Then it had come to him, later that night as he walked past the lake towards home. A barn owl had called a few times, so Ted stopped by the lake to see if he could see it. It tended to hunt along the southern end of the lake at this time of year and, sure enough, there it was, classically backlit by the full moon. Ah, what a sight. Then… Badoosh!

Off to his right, over the lily bed, one of the great carp leapt from the water and shattered the silence with its re-entry.

Ah, hah! That was it! That was where he'd seen him before. In fact, to be precise, **this** was where he'd seen him before. By the lake, fishing, with three of his mates, last year. They were the ones who'd caught The Big Common, or so some would have him believe. And, although he'd not seen it with his own eyes, he'd seen The Common sulking in the snag tree for a couple of days. And he'd seen the demeanour of the anglers change over the next few weeks. Yes, he was sure they'd caught it but, fair play to them; they'd kept it as quiet as possible.

But tongues wag in the country, and secrets are merely stories waiting to be told. The need for a huge set of scales, even with the story of a netful of bream attached, couldn't remain untold, and although many rumours and theories as to what they were needed for circulated, there were a few who knew. And Ted was sure that he was one of them.

'Stan,' John Bakewell had told him. 'Stan Peacock – good lad; he'll do fine.'

John's assessment was fine by Ted; he'd known John, and his family, for many years and had every confidence in him. But he didn't know Stan yet, and he was just waiting for the right moment to address that.

And yesterday had been perfect. Enigmatic; that was a word he loved, and he liked

to think of himself as a bit of an enigma. So, a West Country burr, a mysterious message and we'll see where that leads us.

'How'd you know I'd seen them before?' came the question, even before Ted knew there was an inquisitor.

With that, Stan rose from behind the tree stump he'd been resting against; the very same one he'd seen the carp from yesterday. He'd come down for another look and had seen someone disappear into the woods at the far end of the bank, then he'd seen Ted come into view, so had ducked down behind the tree stump, to exact retribution.

Although slightly flustered, Ted quickly regained his equilibrium and moved on as if nothing untoward had taken place.

'Your oiys. I sin it in your oiys,' he replied, enigmatically.

Stan furrowed his brow and nodded his head ever so slightly.

'You have very good eyesight then, that's all I can say, Ted.'

Ted was, for the second time in as many minutes, slightly flustered at the use of his name, but his riposte was just as quick, and just as deadly.

'Oh. Oi can spot a peacock quill from a hundred paces, young 'un. I got twenny – twenny vision, don't you worry 'bout that.'

Stan's mouth dropped open at that, and his fluster was definitely not slight. 'How the bloody hell?'

Ted smiled, enigmatically he hoped, and then just beckoned to Stan, whilst walking back the way he'd come.

'Don't you want to see the carp today?' he asked, grasping at some verbal straws.

'They int there today, young Stan. They'm up past that there clubhouse, new hatch of mayflies for 'em to feast on. You have a look later, you'll see 'em. Now, we got business, me and you. Loik oi told you yesterday, you gotta look after 'em.'

With that, he rounded the northeast corner and made his way towards the East Woods, Stan following but without a clue as to why. John had told him to see about some disturbance that one of the house owners had heard the previous night, but he knew no more than that. He could only assume that Ted had more information on the subject.

A month had passed since that first, enigmatic, meeting and Stan was still a little unsure how to take Ted. He was an intelligent man, that was for sure, but the word 'quirky' seemed to fit him quite well, and Stan wasn't sure whether that was contrived or natural. The revelation that there may be a group of guys intent on catching one or more of the great carp, probably with the intention of relocating them, definitely grabbed Stan's attention by the throat. The fact that someone was thinking of doing that was no real surprise to him, but the fact that they knew about the fish was. But then Ted had gone through a small series of events that had slapped Stan's naiveté in the face. From the capture of The Common, to its release an hour or so later, Ted knew almost every move they had made and, as he said, if he knew, you could be damn sure plenty of other folk knew. And that sort of news doesn't stay hidden in a drawer for long.

After a bit of a chat here and there, it became evident that the would-be poachers had visited the area quite a few times since the turn of the year. A pint here, and a little chat. A cup of tea and bun there, and a little chat. Piecing together little bits of information, building up the puzzle until, a month or so ago, they'd found the piece with the lake on. From what Ted could ascertain they'd approached old Tom Stokes, who owned Culvert's Woods and the land adjacent to it, to see if it would be possible to do a bit of ferreting for a few rabbits. Money up front, whether they were successful or not, and Tom was more than happy for a little bit of extra cash, especially as they seemed stupid enough to offer more than double what he would have asked. So that was it. They had a base to work from, not overdoing it, just once maybe twice a week, and every now and then Tom would see them with a couple of rabbits and a thumbs-up. Happy days.

Of course, the rabbits were purchased from a selection of butchers, and the ferrets never left the cage, but who was to know?

So, since their first enigmatic encounter, Stan and Ted had been keeping a subtle watch on the area, usually alone, but once or twice they had met up on the south bank, near Quill's Tree, and had watched faint lights in the East Woods. On inspection, nothing much had changed, but it was obvious to Stan that the guys were popping along every two or three days to pre-bait a few areas. He wasn't sure how successful that would be, but thinking back to last close season, when they had seen those stunning sights on the opposite bank, he was sure that the carp's natural curiosity would get the better of them at one point over the next few months.

As the end of May loomed, and the weather warmed, the pre-baiting seemed to be happening more frequently, and Stan thought it would be a simple thing to catch the guys, as they seemed to be more brazen by the day. But Ted decreed patience. They had to catch them in the act, then it was cut and dried, and it sent out a message to any who would dare to follow.

'It'll be tomorrow night,' said Ted with certainty. 'No moon, gonna be a bit of a storm a-coming from the west so no chance of being heard above the wind and rain. Wind pushing in along that bank, so chances are they fish will be along there too.'

Stan looked at Ted in a new light. If he didn't know better he'd have thought he was a carp angler.

'Right. What do you reckon, then? How do we apprehend them? We gonna get a few bodies to help?'

'No need for that, young Stan. Me 'n' you's enough. And a bit of that,' said Ted, tapping his temple with his forefinger. 'Meet me back here tomorrow morning, we'll see if we can arrange a little surprise, shall we?'

With that, he walked off towards Sutton Woods, leaving a slightly perplexed Stan

gazing after him. Turning and shaking his head, Stan strolled off in the opposite direction, with a stop at the snag tree en route. It was a little late in the day, and the sun was at the wrong angle, but it mattered little to Stan. It was just somewhere to gather his thoughts and think things through. Since his outing with Sid, which had produced three fish for each of them, he'd not wet a line in anger, and the itch was getting more and more in need of scratching. He'd enquired about a couple of local clubs, and had looked around a couple of small lakes, but they really didn't do anything for him, and he could feel a tension building in him. The matter wasn't helped by the odd sighting in Felcham Mere either, which only served to fuel the need inside him. He'd taken Ted's advice, a month earlier, and had gone to the reedy corner, past the boathouse, and, sure enough, there was the mayfly hatch and there were the carp. And the roach, and bream and tench. Bloody hell, it was a float fisher's paradise, and although he couldn't get a good view of the fish, it was obvious that a lot of the bigger ones were in the area; the odd flank breaking the surface and revealing a fleeting glimpse of bulk. Since then, he'd put that corner on his daily patrol route, and although they hadn't been present in the same numbers as that first day, it was obvious that this was an area that the carp would visit regularly over the course of the summer. Oh, just a little bait there, on the edge of the sandy patch. And one over there, where the willow overhangs the last reed stalks. The frustration was immense, and on most days he left in a darker mood than he'd arrived.

The building work was moving on apace, and the first boats were being brought to the slipway in readiness for their maiden voyages. By early June, the slipway would be complete, as would most of the moorings, and it would not be many weeks after that that the clubhouse would be opening its very expensive doors to its new, wealthy patrons.

Sitting on the stump, by the snags, Stan's mind wandered from poachers to poaching, and he had to admit that, had he been in their position, he could quite understand their desire to catch such a fish, legally or illegally. Gamekeeper turned poacher.

What did Ted have in mind? He was deep, that bloke, and spoke in riddles most of the time, although Stan was getting to work most of it out, and he knew that, deep down, he just had a love of the countryside and everything in it. With a final, fruitless glance, he walked away from the snags and back to the Estate. Work to do before supper, then a bit of telly before tomorrow's adventures began. Bloody hell, I'd love to be fishing here again, he thought. Oh, well, you never know. Maybe one day. Tomorrow, I just gotta stop someone doing what I can't. Poor buggers.

Chapter Four
A Hero's Return

'et me down! Get me down, you bastards!'

The night echoed to the plaintive cries of a trussed poacher, and Stan just stood there, hands on hips and head shaking in bewilderment and amazement. When Ted had shown him what he was planning, with ropes and bent saplings and all that Rambo stuff, he thought it was a wind-up.

'What d'you think this is Ted, bloody Hollywood? Me Tarzan, you Indiana bleeding Jones!'

Ted just smiled, enigmatically, and gave the stake holding down the sapling one last tap with the sledgehammer.

Now, a dozen hours later, with one of the guys hanging upside down from a tree, like a loud, pendulous pear, and the other nursing a potentially broken ankle, Stan just had to grin. Ted had been perfectly right, tonight was indeed the night, and having watched carefully over the previous weeks, they knew the exact route through the woods that the pair would take so, to be honest, the laying of the traps was remarkably simple; it was just the traps themselves that had taken some time to set – and accept. But they bloody worked! The mournful pair groaned and whined and complained, whilst Ted and Stan awaited the arrival of Simon, John and the local police boys.

Tackled up rods, landing nets and two huge sacks containing bait were scattered around the small clearing, and although it would have been much better to have caught them in the act, the chance that one or more of the fish might be injured by leaving it until the 'red handed' stage had made up their mind.

The job was done; they may get a fine, they may not, but a message would be sent out, loud and clear. Stay away from the Mere, you have no idea who you're messing with. And Stan would be the first to admit that he felt exactly that – he had no idea who he was messing with, but he meant to find out, no matter how long it took him.

'There you go, Stan, get that down your neck.' John plonked another brimming pint of ale in front of him, and Stan began to think that being a hero was going to be quite an interesting occupation. He'd not brought a pint all night; the story of his and Ted's antics having spread through the local community like wildfire, swelling to epic proportions in the telling and retelling. The last he'd heard, they had single-handedly apprehended twelve gun-toting poachers, using just some rope and a load of guile. A load of bullshit, more like, thought Stan, but he wasn't about to put the record straight, not yet. He gazed blearily across the bar and caught Ted's eye. They raised a glass to each other and smiled, drunkenly but most definitely enigmatically. Tomorrow was going to hurt, thought Stan, but tonight I'm a bloody hero, and that'll do for me.

'Ohh, my bloody head!' groaned Stan. It had all seemed like such a good idea at the time, but then it always does, at the time. Now, many hours later, being a hero didn't seem to be all it was cracked up to be. He wondered whether Superman and Spiderman ever suffered from hangovers after a particularly successful rescue of a plane full of school children about crash into a mountain, or a runaway combine harvester that was about to mow down a line of ducklings. No, it was more likely that Die Hard bloke who would have the hangover. Or any Bruce Willis hero, for that matter. Or Clint; he liked a drink or two at times.

As this meaningless drivel bounced around in his head, he knew it was just him putting off the inevitable – the raising of the head from the pillow. A bleary eye picked out the blurred digits on the clock, and he was sure that the first one was an eight. Oh, shit! From horizontal to vertical was swift and remarkably painful, and he had to close his eyes to stop the room spinning, and to quell the need to evacuate his stomach. A few gulped mouthfuls of orange juice did little to help, and he was a sorry sight as he eventually made his way from the bathroom to the kitchen.

'Oh, dear,' said Jean, in mock sympathy, 'still feeling heroic, love?'

'Nngh,' was all he could manage, and the next twenty minutes were spent drinking copious amounts of non-alcoholic liquids and forcing down anything edible.

By midday, the headache had almost subsided, although wielding a hammer and an electric drill had not been ideal therapy for his complaint. But now it was time for his daily tour of the area, and after a rapid check of all the houses and surrounding gardens, he strolled down to the boathouse. Although not yet complete, it was rapidly nearing that status, and was just the '..u..s..e..' away from being able to be called a 'boathouse'.

The slipway, to the left of it, had been completed a little while ago and a few small craft were now moored close by, and even on this Thursday lunchtime there were a few pseudo-sailors faffing about in the rigging. It brought to mind a Sex Pistols tune, *'Friggin' in the Rigging'* and he whistled it cheerily as he walked close by to the would-be seafarers.

But there were more pressing things to concern himself with, so he strode off towards the reedy corner beyond the boathouse to see if there was any activity. June wasn't quite flaming, but it was warm and he knew that the carp would soon

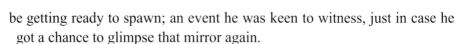

be getting ready to spawn; an event he was keen to witness, just in case he got a chance to glimpse that mirror again.

A southwesterly breeze was blowing, so the corner was flat calm, and with his Polaroids on he could see much of the lake bottom. A few roach and perch darted about, and off to the left a couple of tench busied themselves with some tasty morsels in the silt, but of carp there was no sign, so he moved on. He was thinking of turning right round and going back the way he'd come, but he'd been taking the full tour for the past two or three weeks, and had always found something of interest, so off he went again.

The southwest corner of the lake was now cloaked in lily pads, and looked truly gorgeous, and although he'd only seen a couple of small commons beneath the leafy shelter, he thought that at some point over the summer much larger fish would use this corner for quiet contemplation. From a lofty perch on the west bank he adjusted his glasses, and peered into the lake's depths. Nothing was visible, and after a few minutes he decided to move on. One last look saw something dimple the surface, then disappear. Curious. He sat for a few minutes more, when a similar thing happened slightly to the left and closer to the bank. He carefully descended, then hung out over the water as much as he dared, just as a small, amphibious head poked through the surface film, took a gulp of air, then disappeared beneath a lily leaf.

Ah, a newt. He got out his binoculars and scanned the area closely and there, just on the edge of one of the pads, he could see a tail and two legs poking out. It was quite a large specimen, much larger than a smooth newt or a palmate. Could it be a great-crested, he thought? They were very rare, nowadays. Back when he was a kid he remembered going over Tooting Bec Common, and up to the Rookery on Streatham Common, and watching their activities in the shallow waters. The big, crested newts were quite prolific back then, but not now, and if these were they, he knew he had to let the EA and English Nature know. The chances were that they might well be aware, but if not it could be important news.

He strolled on along the south bank, gazing across at the boathouse almost a quarter of a mile distant. The water between looked fairly uninviting, to be honest, but he had no idea what lay beneath, and would probably never get to find out.

Standing beneath Quill's Tree, he was slightly saddened at the changes that had been made to the lake. From this tree, a year ago, he'd witnessed great carp cruising along the edge of the reeds that flanked the large bay. Now it was a mere dimple in the bank, although the reeds were still present in front of him. The point had been left untouched, as had the pads to the right, but apart from the odd squabbles between moorhen and coot, everything was quiet.

He stood in the East Woods, vaguely cursing the events of a couple of days ago. But his demeanour was false because, by now, his head had cleared, and, if truth be known, he was quite chuffed at how things had turned out. Emerging from the woods with the island to his left, the wind was much stronger, and he was sure that there would be a few carp mooching around, having a last feast before the spawning rituals began. The water was definitely warm, but whether it was warm enough, only the carp would know. Reaching the top corner, he climbed a tree and sat in the crook of a branch, trying to focus through the choppy waters below. He thought he could see the odd dark shape moving about, but the windswept water could be playing tricks on his eyes. Then a large, golden shape slipped through the waves and flopped back down amidst a spray of water. Yep, that'll be one, then!

The next half an hour saw four or five more such displays, but once again, it only helped to stoke the fire of Stan's frustration. A week hence was that most hallowed of days.

June 16th.

The start of the fishing season. Although many waters and clubs didn't adhere to that date any more, Stan still tried to abide by it. Sure, he and Sid had fished a couple of weeks ago, but that had hardly been serious, and in Stan's eyes didn't really count. Ah, the terrible beauty of double standards.

But that didn't register on Stan's conscience. His only emotions were of injustice, to him and the boys. But as much as he whined and whimpered internally, the fact was that this was a lost paradise, and if he wanted to get himself out of this stupid, black mood, he'd have to do it before next week.

There were a few local clubs around that owned some small lakes, but Stan had visited a couple and they were so far from being what he wanted as to be interstellar. The Ringwood waters were twenty or so miles down the road, and sounded right up his street, but getting a ticket was proving to be difficult, to say the least. His other option was to take Sid up on his offer, but, again, it just didn't do much for him, and so his sullen mood perpetuated.

'Trouble on your mind, young hero Stan?' came the question from Ted.

Stan was becoming inured to Ted's remarkable ability to arrive unannounced, but the voice still made him jump.

'Eh? Oh, Ted. Bloody hell, do you get beamed in, or something?'

Ted looked slightly puzzled, but moved on smoothly. 'No, young Stan, I jus' knows where to step. And where not to.'

Stan shook his head slightly, then became aware that an unanswered question was still hanging in the air between them.

'Troubled? Hmm, yeah that's probably about right, Ted. Got nowhere to fish, mate. A week to go before the start and I've got nowhere to cast a bloody line.'

Stan's bitterness was getting closer to the surface and he realised that it wasn't Ted's place to be taking the brunt of it.

'Sorry, Ted. Didn't mean to sound offish; it just frustrates me to see these fish here and know I can't cast a bloody bait to 'em. Me own fault for taking the bloody job, though, I suppose.'

Ted looked steadily at Stan before answering.

'Be aware, Stan. These great fish still need you. You may not be able to catch them yourself, but there may be greater purpose to your presence here. I know plenty of places you can go to catch yourself the fish of your dreams – but not these fish, not these dreams. Many would give up all to have done and seen what you've seen, be very grateful that you are not in their position.'

Stan was staring, slightly open-mouthed, at Ted, expecting at any moment to be called 'Grasshopper'. It wasn't until much later, when replaying the scene in his head for the umpteenth time, that he realised the whole 'speech' had been totally devoid of accent or inflection.

'Now, I believe that ol' John needs to be seeing you. Bin looking all over for you, he 'as.' With that, Ted turned and walked off towards the snag tree. Stan stared after him for a few minutes, then something filtered through the fog.

'What do you mean, you know places?' he asked, striding purposefully after the old man.

'Smiffy, look. Down there.' Posh pointed at the lily pads below the tree and, as Smiffy followed his gaze, he saw a small, leathery head peeking from beneath the broad, green leaf.

'What is it?' he asked, slightly bemused by the vision.

'Terrapin. Been a couple in here for the past couple of years, but you only see 'em down in this corner every now and then.'

Stan stared intently, hoping for the rest of the body to appear, but after a few minutes they both got a bit bored and were soon descending the tree and moving towards Sutton Woods.

'D'you know what a terrapin's girlfriend is called?' asked Posh.

Smiffy laughed. 'Michelle?' he offered.

'Bloody hell, how did you know that?' whined Posh.

'Blimey, I ain't that bloody stupid, Posh. Anyway, where we off to now?'

Posh was striding off in front, slightly miffed that his carefully crafted joke had been sussed. The weekend was warm and their plans to go fishing had been slightly scuppered when Smiffy's parents had told him that his uncle and aunt were coming for a couple of days. By early Saturday afternoon, however, his sullen mood had elicited a question from his uncle, and when he told of his cancelled fishing trip the general consensus, led by his uncle, was that he should get out in the fresh air and leave them to start the barbeque.

'Back no later than seven, Quentin,' commanded his mother, but the raised glass and a wink from his uncle told him that he'd have an ally should things not quite go according to plan.

Posh had met him near the boathouse half an hour later and, with rods and bait in hand, they were off in search of monsters. Since his capture of the tench, Smiffy had talked non-stop about it to Posh, and anyone else who'd listen, but they'd not been since that day. Posh had been away with his family on a canal boat for the week, at the end of May, and hadn't stopped talking about it since his return. As much as it sounded great, Smiffy had got pretty bored with it, and had started pressing to go fishing again, just to shut his mate up.

'Close season, Smiffy. Can't go until next weekend,' had come the confusing reply from Posh.

'Waddya mean, 'close season'? What's that mean?'

Posh gave him a brief explanation, but he was still confused, especially as they'd only been out a few weeks earlier.

'Yeah, well there's a few places you can go that don't close, but if we want to fish the river again, then that's it. Closed until next Friday.'

And 'next Friday' was yesterday and despite beginning their season eight hours later than anticipated, the excitement was still palpable.

'We'll go through the woods to the far end, that's where the stream meets the river. It's normally a pretty good spot, and not many people fish this side 'cos it's quite a walk to get there.'

Once in the woods, the sun's heat was dissipated, and the noise level increased as the buzz of insects and songs of birds mingled to form that 'woodland' noise.

Their journey wasn't subtle, and the odd squirrel and deer were alerted of the anglers' presence long before they came into view, After ten minutes, Stan almost asked 'are we there yet?' but his breath was precious. Then something glinted through the trees, and they were soon following the contours of the stream towards their eventual goal. All manner of birds flitted hither and yon, across the waterway, but their passing was basically ignored by the boys. Then Posh stopped, and set down his rods and bag.

'What? Is this it?' asked a slightly breathless Smiffy.

'Nearly mate, but I'm busting for a pee!' came the reply.

Smiffy moved on a little, leaving his mate to it, and stared intently into the stream. Small dace darted in and out of the beams of sunlight, and Smiffy became almost mesmerised by their movements. Then, from nowhere, a huge fish lunged into view and a dace was gone.

'Bloody hell!' exclaimed Smiffy. 'What the bloody hell was that?' he cried.

'Pike, mate,' replied Posh nonchalantly, 'there's a few jacks in here. Come on, we're nearly there.' With that he strode on past his open-mouthed friend, rounding a bend in the stream and setting his tackle down once more. Smiffy did the same, and they looked out on the glorious summer scene before them.

The stream spilled into a much larger watercourse, but as rivers go, it was hardly the Thames or the Severn. The far, tree-fringed bank was no more than twenty yards distant, and water swirled slowly along its course to the larger Avon to the east. Even with his limited experience, Smiffy could tell that this was definitely 'a spot' and was in even more of rush to get his rod set up. They were going to be float fishing again, which he was more than happy with. Posh had shown him a ledger weight and told him how to use one, but Smiffy much preferred the tangibility and vibrancy of float fishing, especially on moving water.

In short order, they were both set up and sitting on their backless chairs-cum-rucksacks. They'd brought maggots and bread with them, and it was the former that Smiffy had impaled on his hook, a couple of feet below his float. The red tip was bobbing and dipping as the current took it downstream, but within twenty feet or so, he was retrieving it, fishless. Posh had set up thirty yards to his left, downstream, and had already unhooked a couple of silvery darts, much to Smiffy's chagrin. But he was not to be outdone, so he carefully watched his friend as he flicked the float out and let it settle, then fired a small pouchful of maggots a few yards in front of it. He let the float go further, and further, and further, then when it was just about to disappear beneath a willow branch, the red tip itself disappeared, and Posh's rod took on a significant bend as something larger than the previous silver darts took a liking to the passing offering. The line hummed as it cut through the swirling current, and the clutch actually knew the words and sang briefly but sweetly.

'Get the net, Smiffy,' Posh commanded, and shortly a lovely silvery fish of a pound or so was engulfed by the mesh.

'Blimey, wass that, Posh?' asked an excited netsman.

'Chub,' came the curt reply. 'They love it under the trees. See these ones between us, try trotting a bait down there. Should be a few under there, I reckon.' With that, he returned to the task of re-baiting, and Smiffy was surprised to see him moulding a piece of white bread around the hook.

'You're using bread,' he pointed out, rather obviously.

'Yeah, just using the maggots as groundbait at the mo. But if I was you I'd just put on a big bunch of maggots, or dig up some worms; they're brilliant for chub and perch and that.'

Back at his rod, Smiffy set about filling his size 16 hook with as many maggots as possible, which was about four. He then flicked the float into the current and waited for it to settle, before letting line out from the open spool, as his friend had shown him. 'Leave it as long as you can, then leave for another ten seconds,' he'd been instructed and, as the ninth of the ten seconds ticked past in his head, the float dipped and was gone. He struck with his finger on the spool, then flicked the bale arm over. Although not as alarming as Posh's rod tip, his was definitely bent over, and the surge of electricity coming up the line meant that there was more than just a dace on the end. Within a minute or so Posh was sliding the net under a vibrant, magnificent perch of just under a pound, and at that moment in time, it was the most stunning creation he'd ever seen. The dark stripes contrasted against the green body, the reds of fins and tail, the huge mouth, and the angry, erect dorsal spines were emblazoned on his memory, and would never be forgotten.

As the sun sank behind the willows, the fish continued to feed, and it was unsurprising that Smiffy arrived, fully prepared for admonishment, an hour or so later than he'd been told. It mattered not. A further four perch of similar size and beauty, as well as the usual dace and roach accompaniment, left him impervious to rebukes and reprimands. How had he missed this previously? Sitting in a room with a bloody PlayStation whilst all this had been available to him – how had he let it pass him by? Oh, well, that was then, this is now. Like a man just returned from the desert, it would take great mouthfuls to slake this thirst, if ever it could be slaked.

Chapter Five
Remember a Day

So, it gives me great pleasure to declare the Felcham Mere Sailing Association clubhouse officially open.'

Applause and whistles accompanied the raising of glasses as the sun shone down on the righteous.

Stan and John stood at a distance, warm beer in a plastic glass in hand.

'Well, they got it finished on time, good for them,' said John, sipping his warm brew.

Stan nodded, and knocked his back in one, so as not to prolong the agony. This was a Pimms and Champers type affair, not lager and ale, and that definitely wasn't him or John. Jean seemed quite at home, though, having befriended a couple of the wives of those that would sail.

As they squinted in the early afternoon sun, the first of the boats were being readied for some ticking and tacking, and Stan felt ready to tack off. He caught Jean's eye and indicated with a nod of the head and thrust of a thumb that he was off, and she nodded and raised a glass. She knew this wasn't him, but she could definitely get used to it and accepted, gratefully, another pink champagne.

Stan wandered off towards the snag tree, a few hundred yards away, but doubted if there would be anything to see. Pretty soon jibs and spinnakers, lasers and dinghies would be cutting the water to ribbons, and he was sure that the fish would find a deeper, more secluded hiding place until the tumult died down. Round the island, he felt sure, but doubted whether there would be a sight to equal that of a few weeks previously.

Stan's persistent cajoling of Ted over the few days prior to June 16th had finally paid off when Ted gave him an address and a phone number.

'Tell 'em you know Ted Wright. Tell 'em I said you'd be okay to fish there. Best phone first, ask for Jim Baines.'

The phone conversation had been one of those blunt, one word answer type affairs, and Stan wasn't actually sure where, when or what he was going to be fishing for. The final, 'Meet me at the Wilton Hotel tomorrow evening' was enigmatic to say the least. He could have said he was going to wear a pink carnation or something that would have given him some sort of clue as to what was going on.

Far from being enigmatic and strange, when he met Jim Baines he couldn't have been nicer. He and Ted had served together at some point in the past, and it transpired that Jim was head bailiff on a small, private estate lake. Fishing was allowed by invitation only, but it appeared that the 'who you know, not what you know' culture was alive and well and thriving in tiny villages in Wiltshire.

'Ol' Ted says you sin them girt things in the Mere,' Jim pronounced, after their third beer of the evening. 'Not sin 'em meself, but Ted says they's huge. Big as a pig.'

Stan snorted his beer and sat choking for a minute or two, before replying an octave higher than usual.

'Yeah, I've seen 'em a few times. No fishing on there, though, more's the pity,' he managed, eventually. 'So Jim, what can I expect at Linton?' he pried.

'Oh, nothing loik Ted's dragons, but good fish, nonetheless. Bin in there a good few years, old and wise they are. Biggest, last year, just over thirty pounds. But beauties, mark me, absolute Liz Taylors, Stan, and no mistake.'

The evening ended slightly hazily but amicably, and Stan arranged to meet Jim at the crack of dawn on Saturday, in this car park. That rendezvous was kept just before sunrise, and Stan followed Jim through the narrow, tree-lined lanes the three miles to the lake. Fox and deer were still abroad, and the journey was taken with care and full beams. Then they pulled off the road and onto a small track, shrouded by huge oaks. Jim coasted to a halt a few hundred yards from the road, Stan stopping just behind him.

'Walk it from here, young Stan. Just through those trees. Beautiful morning, you gonna have a good day. Oi'll see you later. Off by nine tonight, okay?'

Stan nodded at Jim and bade him farewell, waiting until the sound of the car had faded before getting his rods from the car. The silence was almost deafening, but the sound of waterfowl, gradually waking, left him in no doubt which direction the lake was.

As he emerged from the cover of the trees, the lake was laid before him, mist rising like ethereal serpents from its surface. He felt as though he had been transported back in time, and he wouldn't have been surprised to see a couple of nuns on the far bank.

'Lake' was almost an exaggeration, but Redmire could have been no larger than this, so who knew what lay beneath the mist-wreathed surface? As he drank in the atmosphere he could almost feel himself slough off the skin of despair he'd been wearing for the past few months. This was heaven, and as if to confirm that, God painted a golden carp above the surface of the lake, not twenty yards from where Stan stood. The bubbles that peppered the surface following its re-entry were marker enough for Stan, and within five busy minutes his sweetcorn offering was entering the water just where the last of the bubbles were popping. A dozen golden kernels followed it, and he laid the rod on the damp grass whilst readying his second bait.

The lake had been fished a little, that was obvious, but not much otherwise there would surely have been other anglers here on this, the first weekend of the season. He would never learn that one of Ted's favours from Jim was to let Stan have that one day to himself, just the once. A favour easily agreed.

What to use on the other rod? Maybe a small pop-up – it's bound to be quite silty here, so a bright little pineapple surprise might not go amiss. Carefully pulling the needle through the bait, he broke off a small twig to use as a stop. Then, rising slowly, he surveyed the lake anew. The sun was breaking through the trees and the surface of the lake was dimpling to the activity of small fish, with the odd patch of bubbles here and there. Surely the margins must produce on such a small water, he thought, so crept along to his right, the woods encroaching right to the lake's edge in places, requiring him to walk behind the trunk of an ancient tree. Thirty yards from his rod and tackle bag, he spied a vortex close in to the bank, just below one of the draping boughs of a willow. Carefully edging forward, he lowered the bait no more than a foot from the bank, feeling the lead stop no more than eighteen inches below the lake's surface. The line fell slack, and he ever so carefully inched backwards, laying the slack line over the blades of grass at the water's edge. Looking round to ensure there was nothing to impede him or the rod, he lowered it to the ground, glancing up just in time to see another vortex, just where he'd lowered his bait.

Then all was a blur.

The water erupted, a foot from the bank, and a bow wave shot off across the lake. At the same time his slack line became exceedingly taught and started fizzing through the damp grass.

The last giveaway was the baitrunner buzzing and spinning very, very quickly.

That'll be a bite, then!

He was here, his net was there, thirty yards and three trees away, and the fish was over there, and getting a lot more over there with every passing second. He eventually slowed it, and managed to gain a modicum of control, but it was far from over, and the fish visited as much of the lake as possible to engender an escape. But, probably ten minutes later, the carp's mouth was gulping on the surface, five yards out. Now was the tricky bit; rod around the tree and grab with the other hand. Good.

Repeat. And repeat.

The carp was well beaten, fortunately, and was soon in the net, and Stan was almost bursting with the joy of it all.

He laid the glorious, dark mirror on the mat and just gawped. Probably twenty, twenty one pounds, but the colours of it. Huge, dark scales covered a quarter of each dark brown flank, and the tail was the size of his hands. Truly beautiful.

He took a couple of self-timer shots, and a couple of the fish on the mat, then slipped it most gratefully back into the lake. What a start to the day. It was barely five o'clock and he felt complete. Time for a brew.

As he sat there, leant against a tree whilst waiting for the kettle to boil, he smiled inanely. This was just what he needed and it mattered not a jot if he caught nothing else for the rest of the day.

The kettle having boiled, he now stirred the tea bag and poured in some milk. The sky was brightening markedly, and it looked like being a sunny old day. On a lake like this he doubted that was a good thing, but the evening might bring another chance.

Hiss! Buzz!

Nope, not bees and snakes, but line and reel. The other rod, which had been almost forgotten, was now demanding attention, and the tea assumed its inevitable trajectory as Stan engaged in another fraught battle. This time, however, there were no trees to bypass, and the net was soon engulfing a cousin of the first fish. A pound or so lighter, it was still stunningly beautiful, and was soon being returned by an increasingly more relaxed angler.

The day was, indeed, quite futile, but as Jim turned up in the early evening, he was in time to witness Stan's third and largest fish of the day. A beautiful linear of about twenty four pounds was the veritable cherry on the cake, and despite coming an hour before Jim's curfew, Stan felt no need to recast, and just sat with Jim for an hour.

As much as Stan would have liked to have been offered a permanent place on the lake, it bothered him not that it wasn't forthcoming. Too much of a good thing, and all that. He knew that he'd be welcome to fish once a month or so, but also knew it would never be like the first time, with the place to himself, but this had been enough. This had been just what he needed, and he realised now that it was no longer about size. If he could wheedle a few more secrets out of Ted, of which there were obviously a few, then he might just turn up an absolute diamond.

As they left the lake behind them, Jim bade him farewell with a parting shot that would resound for many years.

'You needs to be asking Ol' Ted about Beaufort's place, up near Hindon. If you loved these 'ere carp, you'll be besotted by them. You ask 'im.' With that he was in his car and gone, and Stan was mentally filing away that information, for future perusal.

This was their third trip to the river, and with each trip came more confidence for Smiffy. Last week he'd turned up as if he knew everything, but two floats lost in the grasping willow branches had soon taken the strut out of his stride, and it took Posh to give him a little more advice before he actually felt like he was back in control. A couple more of the stunning perch succumbed beneath the willow, then the electric pull and tug of something larger ended in a flapping line and a swearing angler.

'Might have been a pike,' declared Posh, eyeing the severed line. 'Look, see how the lines all grazed?' but Smiffy just grunted, still hurt at the loss.

'Better get used to it,' Posh advised his mate. 'They just come off sometimes and there ain't nothing you can do about it.'

But Smiffy disagreed; he was sure that he could do something about it, and he was determined to right the wrong done to him. So this week his 2.6lb line had been replaced by one twice that breaking strain, and his size 16 hook increased to a massive size 12.

And worms! He'd spent the previous evening with a torch and a fork and had dug up a dozen fine specimens. Now let's see who breaks lines, shall we?

They arrived as the sun was just cresting the horizon, surprisingly chilly in the dawn air. Posh had suggested they move upstream a little, so that they could fish down towards the entrance to the stream, and Smiffy had been quick to get the swim closest to the stream. Posh was unperturbed because he was going to fish the far bank, beneath the willows, with a running ledger and a great big bit of bread crust.

His first cast came up short; his crust gone on the retrieve. His next cast followed suit, and his third almost made the branches, stopped just short by a clutching of the spool by the increasingly frustrated angler. But then it went 'plop', right under the branches and inches from the bank, and he carefully set his rod down on the rests whilst slowly tightening the line. The rod tip was bent slightly, and vibrated almost imperceptibly in the current. He sat back slowly, watching the rod tip, and had barely sat down when the tip jerked violently. He struck whilst almost falling and felt the bang of a big fish, but then it was gone. No hook hold. He cursed quietly and set about cutting another piece of crust.

Smiffy, twenty yards further downstream, was oblivious to this, as he was trying to attach a couple of juicy, wriggling worms to his hook. His first cast was less taxing than his mate's, and he let the float drift slowly down past the mouth of the stream, as far as the tree that he'd sat next to on the previous couple of visits. He repeated this a couple of times without success, so then set about firing in some maggots on each cast. A few tugs and dips revealed the worms being nibbled by smaller fish, but he was determined to persevere, and although the perch were wonderful, he craved something larger. That pike that he'd seen on the first visit, maybe. As these thoughts were meandering around in his head, the rod was nearly wrenched from the rests as the float drifted past the stream entrance. The thumping on the end was frightening, and he wondered what on earth he'd hooked. As Posh responded to his mate's calls, he saw the rod tip bent round alarmingly, and heard the clutch squealing. Bloody hell, what was this?

Smiffy managed to slow the fish just short of the willow branches, then watched as the line cut off to the right, into the flow of the river. Steadily he gained line, then a flash below the surface gave them both cause to gasp. This was a bloody big fish, and it could well have teeth!

Soon it was gliding on its side towards the net, a huge pike of unknown proportions. As it slid into the net, Smiffy yelped with joy.

'Bloody hell, mate, how big is that?' he asked, but Posh already knew that this was easily the biggest fish he had ever seen on the bank.

'I dunno, Smiffy. I ain't got a clue. Did your dad get you those scales?'

Smiffy turned to his tackle bag and extracted the Salter spring balances. 'Yeah, got 'em here. They go up to ten pounds,' he declared. Posh looked at them with some doubt. He wasn't sure if they'd be big enough. Carefully extracting the hook from between the pike's teeth, he then reached for a carrier bag with Smiffy's food in and poured the contents on the floor. Before Smiffy could complain, Posh had slipped the fish into the rather inadequate weigh sling and was hoisting it onto the scales.

'Bloody hell, mate, that's huge!' was all he could say. Smiffy looked at the scales and they read ten pounds. Was that the weight or had they bottomed out? To be honest, he really didn't care. What a fish! What a fish!

The morning, despite thoughts to the contrary, didn't deteriorate. Smiffy caught a couple of perch, the biggest going just over one and a half pounds and, if anything, was more impressive than the pike.

And, just minutes before their midday departure, Posh's perseverance paid off when he hooked and landed a huge chub of just under four pounds. Those two fish would have been a highlight of any trip, but were totally eclipsed by the pike. But that didn't detract from their capture, and the lads knew that things were getting better and better. Soon it would be time to move on, but for now this was just good fun.

'Let's go round past the island,' suggested Posh, 'see what we can see up there. Sometimes see deer between the East Woods and Culvert's Woods.'

Smiffy nodded and followed his mate through the dappled woodland, towards the lake.

Still nothing in the snags – that's weird, thought Stan. He'd been keeping an eye on them for a few days, just to see if that was where they might spawn, but to no avail. He strolled along to the Post Office and gazed out at the island. A light southerly was rippling the surface, but apart from that, the lake looked almost glass-like. He stared intently into the margins, but apart from the ever-present perch and fry, saw nothing of substance. A muted 'splash' brought his gaze upwards, and he scanned the lake before him. Nothing obvious, not in the island margins or down to his left, so he carried on walking, towards the South Westerly. As he neared that swim he heard another 'splash', and another. His pace quickened, and his gaze roamed more and more. He carried on past the swim and moved quickly round the corner, towards Island One. That swim faced one side of the island, and as he entered it he saw a huge explosion in the island margin – so this is where it would take place. He scanned around quickly, then went back a few steps before climbing a thin but effective tree trunk. Once a dozen feet above the ground, he put his foot in the crook of a branch and stared out across the lake, just as a huge carp was heaved from the lake on the backs of some hidden suitors. He gazed in wonder as one after another of the great carp were battered and abused by the smaller males, but still they remained, intent on this annual ritual's completion.

Then below, and to his left, there was another commotion, and the margins exploded with spray as half a dozen carp sped along them, uncaring of bankside vegetation or stones. This was a sight, and that's for sure.

'Bloody hell, can you see that?' came an exclaimed and excited cry from below, and he peered from his perch down on a couple of lads. It was the two from the lake a few weeks back; Dan Becks' boy and young Quentin Double-Barrel (he'd been introduced to his father, Peter, but had totally missed what his name was, so that would do for now).

They had obviously been fishing the river because they had all of their gear still with them.

'Blimey, let's put a bait out there, Posh. They look massive.'

Young Becks said nothing, just continued staring, open-mouthed for sure. Another commotion in the island margins was followed by another great carp thrashing the surface, and the boys gasped in unison. From above, Stan could see a fair way along the margins, and so was prepared for what came next – just. It was The Common and one of the big mirrors, being pursued by half a dozen not insignificant males, and they were about to surface like dolphins right in front of the swim.

And surface they did, in all of their magnificence, and had the boys been aloft like Stan, they would surely have crashed to the ground, stupefied.

Their cries and exclamations were lost on Stan; he just stared agog at the spectacle unfolding in front of him. By the time the carp had been sated, he'd been aloft for almost an hour and had lost most of the feeling in his legs, but it had been worth it. The boys had left a little while ago, desperate to put this all into perspective, and Stan had little doubt that they would be back for another look in the next few days. He thought about giving away his presence, but their unabashed wonder was a joy, so he kept quiet and remained hidden. Or so he thought.

Not very far from Stan's perch, Ted had watched everything unfold. He'd been there since early morning, certain that this would be the place and the time, and he was correct. He'd traced Stan's route from the snags, and had heard the boys long before they even reached the far side of the East Woods. He, like Stan, however, preferred to remain unnoticed, so had kept a distant watch. The time was nearing when that would not be the thing to do, but for now all was well. He just wasn't sure for how long.

Strange vibrations seemed to emanate from everywhere. The carp were confused and sought sanctuary in their old haunts; the island margins, the snag tree. There was noise, confusion and much disturbance, but that would soon become a background noise, and the carp would get used to it, and, although wary, would go about their usual summer activities.

Their spawning excesses were now behind them, and most of the wounds and damage to scale and fin had healed. Once again, the huge females had shed their burden and were down in weight, but still they were enormous. The new larders that had been exposed were doing them nothing but good, and the lack of angling pressure meant that they could just continue to grow at their leisure. Or so it seemed.

This new commotion was disconcerting, and The Common and the bigger mirrors were wary and edgy. But a carp's instincts are just that; instincts. They have no way of reasoning or thinking things through. They had no experience of boats and jet-skis, so, after a few weeks, they became less wary and had no need to fear them.

But when you live by instinct there is only one way to survive, and that is to learn from experience. Sometimes, however, the experience may be just too much.

PART TWO

BEHOLD THE BITTEN APPLE
THE POWER OF THE TOOLS
BUT ALL THE KNOWLEDGE IN THE WORLD
IS OF NO USE TO FOOLS

Chapter Six
Us and Them

They cruised just below the surface, lazily flicking a dorsal fin up to break the lake's surface. The water had been warmed in the summer sun for many weeks, and the sensation was pleasant and comforting.

Of the half dozen carp enjoying this experience, four were huge, and had almost regained the weight they had lost a couple of months earlier during spawning.

The unnatural vibrations they had been experiencing of late were more prevalent today but their instincts were yet to be attuned to them as a threat.

Closer. Louder.

Closer still.

Too close.

Noise; disruption; turmoil.

The Common immediately dropped low in the water, hugging the lakebed as she sought the only sanctuary she could trust, and sped towards the island margin, followed by some of her companions.

But not all of them.

The four carp slowed as they reached the relative safety of the island, three hundred yards away, and steadied themselves below the trees that shrouded that part of the lake.

There was no sense of grief or loss, they were not capable of such emotions. There was just another experience to add to many; another instinct to heed in future.

For now, the abundance and craving for the ample new food sources had to be weighed against this new danger. For now, the food would be ignored and the old, regular larders would continue to be visited.

The new lake was proving to be intriguing but more and more dangerous, but instinct is one thing, memory is another.

As is the need to feed and survive.

The world had changed.

And September of 2001 had brought about the most profound of changes to many people, in many different ways.

'Bugger!' muttered Ted, as he stared at the object bobbing in the waves, five yards away. He and Stan had been alerted to a possible dead fish by one of the sailors a little earlier in the day, and they had been waiting patiently for ten minutes as the wind and waves moved the corpse towards them.

They had been looking at the possibility of coppicing some of the West Woods in the winter when the chap had mentioned something to them about a large fish that was floating out in the lake, and they both immediately feared the worst. And now their fears had come true.

The carp was large, very large, but as Stan stepped into the margins to net it, he could see that, thankfully, it wasn't a common carp.

It hadn't been dead too long, maybe a day or so, so it wasn't in too bad a condition and was easily identifiable by its scale pattern. If you knew what to look for.

'Oh, bollocks!' he muttered, 'It's Buzz's 48.'

Ted asked no questions, just bent to examine the huge gashes along the length of its back where it had obviously been hit by a propeller.

'Must've bin Saturday. One of them jet ski lads said they hit a log that nearly turned the damn thing over, but it weren't no log, was it?'

Stan nodded in agreement and wondered if this was going to be the first of many such casualties.

Having just returned home from school, Quentin was in his bedroom getting changed when he looked out of the window at the lake. There seemed to be a bit of a commotion near the slipway so, quickly tying his laces, he ran downstairs and across the grass towards the lake.

'Blimey, how big is that?' came a rhetorical question from behind.

Stan turned to see one of the lads he'd watched from the tree a few months ago, eyes like saucers and mouth agape. He knew him now as Quentin, his family lived on the Estate and their house overlooked the boathouse – very desirable.

'Oh, it's girt big, young'un' said Ted.

Quentin just carried on gawping as Stan slid it into a large sack, then onto the back of Ted's Land Rover.

'What you gonna do with it?' he asked, as Ted strolled to the driver's door.

'Just bury it, lad. In the woods. Good fertiliser.' With that he closed the door and started the engine. Stan walked to the passenger side, then turned to the young boy. 'That's one of the fish you and Neil were watching. But it ain't the biggest,' he said, then climbed into the cab. As Ted moved away, he leant out of the window and looked back at Quentin.

'Here there be dragons!' he declared, then turned and drove off.

Quentin stared after the Land Rover, watching as it passed the snag tree in the direction of the East Woods, then turned to look back at the lake. Dragons? Blimey, if that wasn't the biggest in the lake then they must be huge. Dragons indeed.

Peter put the phone down, slowly, shaking his head in disbelief.

'What? What is it, dear?' asked his wife, having heard just his side of an obviously upsetting conversation.

'Anil and Beth,' he said. 'They were there, in New York.'

'When? Yesterday?' she asked, knowing the answer before he nodded slowly.

'In the North Tower. Eightieth floor or something. No news about them, but, you know, it's not looking good, is it?'

He slumped into the chair, staring blankly at the TV screen that was showing, once again, the sight of an airplane crashing into a huge tower.

'What were they doing **there**? Business? I mean, what were they doing there?' his wife asked but, once again, the answer was unnecessary.

Their friends worked in the City, much the same as Peter had done until last year, they travelled around the world to huge financial institutions. It was just another day in their life. But there would be no more. Not for thousands of people.

For a while, people's lives were 'put into perspective'. Petty problems and squabbles were seen just as that – petty.

The death of a huge carp, at first distressing, was now almost forgotten as Stan watched the same footage as Peter and Wendy, and millions of other people the world over.

The rules had changed, the fortress was no longer impregnable, time to take stock and rethink.

'Incoming!' screamed Jonesy, and they grabbed their helmets tight to their heads, faces pinned to their chests. The 'whoomph' was followed by a blast of superheated air, then dust and sand, and shards of glass and masonry.

Wiping his face with the back of his hand, Ted did a quick inventory of men and machines. Twelve men, two Jeeps, radio, all weapons. Everyone and everything seemed to be present and unharmed. And well it should be; it was their own missiles that were 'incoming', the knowledge of their imminent explosion being transmitted to Jones' headphones.

'Incoming!' he cried again.

An hour later they walked carefully through the rubble. There should be little resistance left, but it paid to be prepared.

'Halt!' screamed someone from behind and to his left. He turned to see Paddy with his rifle raised, aiming across the wasted land to a small figure in a dress. Ted, his gun already at his shoulder, stared through the scope. It was a child, a boy possibly. Face dirty, eyes wide with shock and fear.

'Hold your fire, Paddy,' he commanded, then carefully made his way through the rubble whilst keeping a constant eye on the frightened and confused figure in front of him.

Six, maybe seven years old, he thought. The boy was incapable of weeping, he was deep in shock, so Ted carefully guided him back across the wreckage of the village and to the nearest Jeep. Just as he reached the vehicle, the unmistakable chatter of a machine gun had him diving to the floor, the child below him and shielded by Ted's body. Return gunfire from his platoon lasted little more than twenty seconds, then the deafening silence was eventually broken by a voice from behind him. 'One down. No movement. Stay alert, there may be more.'

The boy below him whimpered, and Ted looked down into blue eyes so deep he felt he might drown. What now for this kid? No family, no home. What next? Peacemaker or hellraiser? Not his place to worry about that; just hand the kid over to the UN chaps and move on.

Looking at the screen on the wall in The Fox that evening, Ted thought back thirty-odd years. What would that young Palestinian kid be now – peacemaker or hellraiser?

They'd solved nothing really, over all those years, just moved a yard forward, a yard back. They, the pawns on the board, being flicked over one by one. Better King than cavalry, that was for sure.

'Rum old do, that, eh Ted?' said Jonas. 'Them bastards killing all them innocent people. Bad doings, and that's for sure.'

Ted stared at the TV without comment, then picked up his glass and emptied it before slowly rising and heading for the door.

'Not staying for another?' asked Jonas. Ted turned slowly, looked him square in the eyes for a few seconds. 'Nobody's innocent,' he said, then turned and left.

Chapter Seven

Breathe

 month had passed since the earth shattering events of what was becoming known as '9/11'. Stan's world had wobbled a little on its axis, as had everybody else's, but now, away from Ground Zero, things were beginning to get back to normal, if only on the surface.

Toilets got blocked, walls needed rendering, grass needed mowing, and that was a fact. In the month since that day, Stan had seen a growing-together of the Felcham Estate, people who had been insular and curt were now chatting freely to each other, getting invited around for drinks and generally just getting on. Even he and John were not just the handymen anymore. Their opinions were sought, their help asked for, and advice given if required.

Quentin's parents, Peter and Wendy, had been affected more than most, as they had lost two very close friends in the Towers, but most people knew someone who knew someone, and so all felt empathy and loss at the same time.

A chance meeting with Peter, one afternoon, had been quite fortuitous for Stan, and would eventually be the catalyst to his fishing adventures for the next decade.

Peter was sitting on one of the seats near the boathouse, just relaxing and trying to get his world back in order. The boats were out in number on this fine Sunday afternoon, and he just sat there, gazing at them whilst his mind wandered off in search of answers, invariably returning empty handed.

Stan was strolling around the lake, prior to the arrival of his children, Stevie and Laura, for Sunday lunch, when Peter called him over.

'Afternoon, Peter. How you doing?' he asked, slightly nonplussed at this turn of events.

'Stan, I wish I knew. I really do. Just can't seem to get my head round it at the moment. Do you know what I mean?'

Stan knew of the plight of Peter's friends, but had no idea what to say, no answers to give or wise words to take away the pain.

Nodding slowly, he said, 'Fancy coming for a stroll round the lake, probably better than just sitting, thinking.'

Peter looked up, then nodded and rose purposefully. 'D'you know what Stan? I've been here all this time and I haven't yet walked around this beautiful lake. How bloody sad is that?'

Stan smiled and walked off in the direction of the West Woods, Peter strolling along beside him. They talked of nothing of note. The world wasn't changed by their musings, nor did they discover the meaning of the Universe, but their eyes were opened, and they saw things they hadn't previously seen.

Peter saw the world around him, for the first time, through new eyes. Birds and animals, plants and flowers that he assumed were normally the domain of National Geographic or the Discovery Channel.

They startled a doe and her fawn in the East Woods. A kingfisher banked alongside them as they walked the south bank. The birdsong from Sutton Woods was like an aria to Peter's ears, and they saw huge carp basking in the sun beneath the snag trees on the north bank.

This last was what Stan had been hoping for since finding the dead carp, a month or so earlier. Because there, in plain sight, was The Common, Sid's Fish, and the uncaught mirror. They stood there for awhile, watching with varied degrees of emotion, as the carp slowly drifted in the light breeze. Peter was astounded, completely and utterly unbelieving of what his eyes were showing him.

'Bloody hell! Bloody hell! I didn't believe him, and now here they are,' he said.

'Who?' asked Stan, 'Didn't believe who?'

Peter blinked and forced himself to look away from the lake.

'Quentin,' he replied. 'He came home a couple of months ago and told Wendy and I about some huge fish that he and Neil had seen, but it sounded fanciful and preposterous, so we thought nothing of it. Then, a week or so before the Towers, he said that a big, dead fish had been found. And, again I didn't believe him.'

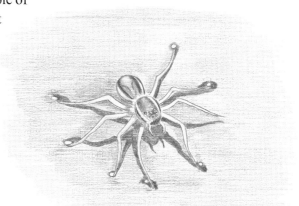

'Yeah, I was there. Both times. He's a good lad, your boy. Looks like he's got some interest in the old angling himself.'

'Don't I know it,' replied Peter. 'Had me down the bloody tackle shop buying rods and reels and all manner of things. Some for his mate, Neil, as well I reckon.' He laughed at that and Stan could sense him relaxing. 'Well, better get back, I can smell a lamb roasting on my behalf.'

'Yep, me too. Got the kids coming over too, so that'll be nice.'

'Yeah,' said Peter, 'nice. Stan, thanks for that. I really mean it. I didn't realise how much I needed to have my eyes opened. To everything. Thanks a lot.'

Stan was slightly abashed at this outpouring, and did his best to pour water on its fire.

'Peter, when all else fails, you just gotta do nothing and talk bollocks. Works every time.'

Peter laughed loudly, and nodded his head. 'Talking bollocks – the cure for all ills! Oh yes indeed.' Still laughing, he shook Stan's hand, then headed off towards the Estate, leaving Stan smiling but slightly bemused. Then he thought of Mick Jagger and started singing to himself.

'We all need someone we can lean on, and if you want it, you can lean on me.'

He carried on humming the tune as he made his way home, stopping halfway as he saw Stevie heading towards him.

'Alright dad, how you doing?' chirped his son. 'Been watching them big old carp again, 'ave yer?'

Stan smiled. Stevie was yet to see The Big Common and her entourage, and it was a source of amusement to the family that this was like James Stewart's six-foot white rabbit, Harvey – only he could actually see them. 'Follow me, lad, and be amazed,' he said, and they strode back to the snag tree.

After dinner, Steve looked at him again and smiled, 'Does Harvey want a drink or something, Dad?' he asked wickedly. Stan glared and smiled, falsely.

'They were there, boy. Me and Peter wassisname both saw 'em, don't you worry.'

'See, you don't even know the bloke's name. Sure you don't need me to wipe your chin for you, Pops?'

They all laughed at that, but they all knew it was just joshing. Of course they existed. They had all seen the photos of Stan and his mates with those huge fish, but since being so close to the lake, it seemed that the only person to actually see the fish now was Stan. Jean regularly took strolls around its banks, but her eyes weren't what they used to be, and she failed to see anything from ground level, and she certainly wasn't about to go scrabbling through brambles, or up trees, just to see a few fish.

'Don't you worry, you lot. One day I'll be holding one of 'em and then you'll be laughing on the other side of your face.' With that he picked up the remote and flicked on the telly.

'Who's playing this afternoon, boy?' he asked Stevie. Jean and Laura tutted, then strolled into the kitchen to begin clearing away the cutlery.

Ted watched Stan and his boy walking back to the houses, laughing and chatting. He'd seen Stan and young Quentin's father watching the carp and now, with the place finally to himself, he sat quietly on a stump and eyed the lake surface. The carp had moved off a ways, but he was sure that they would return, once all was still again. One of the jet skis had come very close to the snags, almost losing control, and the carp had spooked into the deeper water. But Ted could sense that they hadn't gone far. If they were by the island, they probably wouldn't return, but he reckoned that they were in the roots of the sunken island that had been dug away to almost nothing.

As he relaxed by the lake, he could hear distant voices and the buzz of activity by the boathouse. Sunday afternoon. Why couldn't they rest for a while?

With no preamble they were there. Four, five, six carp. Just below the surface, as if they'd just vented ballast and had risen from ten feet below (which, in all probability, they had).

The Common? Yes.

One of the big mirrors? Yes.

Any more? He looked carefully. There was a big carp, but not huge. And there, a slightly smaller one. And what was that, three feet down? Slowly, the bulk of a carp rose, like a submarine. But there were no bubbles to mark its ascent, just a growing sense of wonder.

Then, there it was and even Ted was slightly taken aback. This was almost the size of The Common, surely? Had it spawned or not? He'd seen the activity and it seemed to him that all of the big females had been involved. If that was the case, then this fish could become the biggest in the lake, and beyond.

A water skier came around the corner, towed behind a speedboat, the wake of its passing causing the carp to spook away again, not to return that day.

With that Ted rose and walked off towards the East Woods, and home.

Yes, it could well become the biggest carp in the lake, he thought, if it survived.

Chapter Eight
The Happiest Days of Our Lives

'Bloody hell, it's a bloody snake!' exclaimed Smiffy as he held the line up with one hand. Below his hand, firmly hooked, an eel wriggled and writhed unctuously in an attempt to escape, but being the voracious feeders they were, the hook was probably half way to its gut, and its only means of escape was when Posh cut the line with a pair of scissors.

'Blimey, Smiffy, ain't you seen an eel before?' he asked, slightly baffled at his mate's lack of knowledge.

'Well, no, I haven't, mate. What's the deal with an eel?' he asked, his equilibrium regained now that the offensive creature was gone, and smiling at his little rhyme. Posh just shook his head and replied, 'Better get another hook on there, mate, his big bruvver and sister are probably waiting for you.'

They were in the middle of nowhere, not a building, or car or any sign of civilisation in sight. Apart from their canal boat. After last year's holiday, Posh hadn't stopped raving about his time on the canal, so this summer his dad, Dan, and Smiffy's dad, Peter, had both agreed that it would be a great idea for Smiffy to join them for a week on the boat during the spring break at the end of May.

Dan's rather eccentric brother-in-law, Klaus, owned the boat and had it moored just north of Oxford on the southern stretch of the Oxford Canal. Their route took them through Banbury, up past tiny little places like Cropredy and Wormleighton (where they were now) to Napton, where they would turn around and retrace their steps.

At a maximum speed of three miles an hour, their progress could best be described as sedate.

The 'Protanic' (such a witty name for a watercraft, Klaus had thought) was about fifty feet long and had sleeping room for about six or seven people. Posh's mum and dad had the main bed, Posh and Smiffy slept at the front on the little fold down beds, and Posh's attitude-ridden and hormonal elder sister, Becky, slouched and huffed about somewhere in the middle.

But during the day everyone, bar Becky who had a mood to cultivate, was up on deck. Dan and Maggie sat at the stern doing the steering bit, and Posh and Smiffy occupied the front, trying to spot an ideal spot for a picnic and a bit of angling. The trouble was that around every corner there was 'an ideal spot' and the first day had seen them progress no more than five miles. Dan had been planning on doing about ten miles per day, allowing for locks and the odd pub lunch, so had decreed that they would stop only three times during the day, the last being their mooring for the night.

Initially the boys were a bit peeved by this, but pretty soon realised that there was so much to see that they could have spent hours without fishing and not realised. Which is pretty much what they did.

Mallard and moorhen.

Heron and kingfisher.

A buzzard; two, wheeling and crying high overhead.

All this and more fascinated them, especially Smiffy.

And, of course, they were in charge of locks. The first few miles had been fairly easy, but when they reached Claydon there were five locks in quick succession, and by the end of them the boys were in serious need of some cold lemonade and a little rest. Dan and Maggie laughed and took the mickey, but were secretly very pleased that they hadn't had to perform the feat!

Becky pouted expansively and painted another toenail.

But after Claydon they entered paradise. Miles and miles of unspoilt countryside that seemed to be from a different age, of centuries ago when this canal was brand new. The distant specks of small hamlets and the odd farmhouse were the only sign of habitation, and on many a mile they thought that they could have been the only people left alive.

On their designated stops, which were invariably in the vicinity of a bankside pub, Posh and Smiffy broke out the fishing tackle and either fished from the end of the boat or, if the moorings were a bit crowded, wandered down the canal a few hundred yards where there was, inevitably, an inviting overhanging tree to fish beneath.

Perch and roach were the usual fare, but once in a while the float would dip then cleave away as something much larger made a bid for freedom. The fish was usually successful, but this only made the boys more determined to catch one of them.

The eel had succumbed to a bunch of worms impaled on a size 6 hook, attached to 8lb line, the heaviest they could find between them.

The floats were now much bigger as well, but the eel had been the first thing of any consequence to fall for the heavier tactics.

They were moored beneath a couple of huge weeping willows, and the opposite bank offered similar cover and a cast of a few yards. It was there that both had been casting, but Posh had kept looking along the bank ahead of them, to where a bit of scum had built up in the light current, just past the merest of indentations in the reed-lined bank.

The reeds themselves were moving in the slow current, but, every once in a while, he could have sworn that a couple of them banged and bent in the opposite direction to the flow. After the third or fourth such occasion he couldn't take any more, so took his rod and quietly debarked, creeping carefully along the bank to within five yards of the reed bed.

The worms were still quite lively so he flicked them out and waited until the float was just short of the scum before halting it and allowing the three swan shot to settle on the bottom. Resting against the trunk of the willow, he set his head back and watched as the water lazily moved his float left and right. The insect buzz was not as loud as in Sutton Woods, but it still had the same soporific effect, and it wasn't long before his eyelids were succumbing to the lead weights that had been attached to them.

But one particular insect was so much louder than the others, buzzing and chattering, and he had to open an eye to see if it was settled on his knee or something, so close did it sound.

No insect. Loud buzzing. No insect. Loud buzzing. No float. Loud buzzing.

No float!

Line was hissing through the rings as the clutch buzzed like an agitated dragonfly, and Posh's instincts took over as he grabbed the rod and clattered it into the willow branches.

The clutch still buzzed and the rod was pulled down hard as a fish powered off down the canal. He put the rod way over to the right, with the tip in the water, to try to avoid snagging the bush in front, whilst all the time the fish took more line. Time to stop that, he thought.

Carefully putting a finger on the spool, he gradually applied pressure and felt the fish slow in its flight. He adjusted the clutch a little then applied a little more pressure with his finger. This process was repeated a few times, but no more than a minute had passed since his rude awakening, and suddenly he realised that he might be in control.

The rod tip eased back and he gained a little line. Then again. Then again.

Then something rolled on the edge of the bush, five yards away, and he realised he had no landing net.

'Smiffy! Smiffy!' he called, not daring to look and see if he'd been heard.

'Smiffy!' he called again, thirty seconds later.

'Yep,' came the reply from behind him and nearly made him lose his grip. 'What is it mate, not another one of those bloody snakes?'

'No mate, this ain't no eel. Feels pretty big, though. Did you bring the net?' he asked, still not looking back, but concentrating intently on the water in front of him.

Smiffy raised the net in answer, then swore a little as it got tangled in the drooping willow canopy.

'Language, Quentin,' came Dan's light reprimand. He'd heard the call and was eager to see what his son was battling as well. Dan had fished when he was young, but rugby and work, family and friends had curtailed all of that. He was nonetheless always keen to hear of his son's exploits with rod and line, and was delighted that he had a love of the countryside to match his own.

Smiffy muttered a 'sorry', then moved in front of his mate as the fish rolled on the surface.

The net lowered, Posh tried to ignore the ache in his arm as the fish rolled again, its huge mouth glugging and gulping on the surface.

Then, 'Yess!!'

Smiffy's exclamation announced the fish's capture and they all peered forward to look into the folds of the net.

A thousand golden scales lay before them, the odd beam of sunlight lighting them up like torches.

'Bloody hell, boy, that's huge!' exclaimed Dan, and Smiffy turned and smiled. Dan nodded and smiled back, acknowledging the silent admonishment.

By now, Becky and Maggie were at the prow of the boat, watching the commotion.

'What is it, dear?' asked Maggie.

'A carp, I think. Big'un as well,' replied Dan.

'A fish!' snarled Becky. 'Is that all? I thought it must have been at least a diamond ring!' With that she flounced back down into the cabin to carry on reading how some nonentity was going to cope with the break up of his three-week-old marriage.

'Oh, it's better than a diamond ring,' declared Smiffy, and Dan smiled. 'Mr. Becks, can you hold the net while I go and get the scales?' he asked, passing the handle to Dan without waiting for an answer, then leaping back onto the boat and rummaging through his rucksack.

The Salter scales were still the same ones that had been inadequate for his pike of last summer, but they'd not been required to get anywhere near their ten-pound limit since. However, that may now prove different.

By the time he'd returned with them, the carp had been unhooked, and Dan was holding out a big carrier bag whilst Posh slipped the golden fish into it. As Smiffy hooked the bag handle with the scales, Dan turned to his wife and asked her to get the camera.

Smiffy hoisted the scales, and, with the bag off of the floor, Posh and his dad both bent down to read them.

'Nine… nine and a half, I reckon, Neil,' declared Dan proudly, and his son beamed with delight.

'Ha! Ha!' he laughed. 'A new PB.' Then he did a little jig in celebration.

Maggie returned with the camera, and some very poor photos were taken in the dappled sunlight beneath the tree. Just as Posh was about to release the fish, in full sunlight, Smiffy asked if he could have the camera, then lay down in the grass and took a couple of shots of Posh lowering the carp back into the canal. They turned out to be, by far, the best shots of the lot, and a new talent was unearthed.

By that evening they had travelled a further five or six miles before mooring at yet another quaint, canalside pub. After a hurried meal, the boys left the others to digest fully and made their way back to the boat, a hundred yards or so away. One of the other patrons, a local it would seem, had overheard them talking, yet again, about Posh's carp.

'Fish right next to the boats, last thing at night, first thing in the morning.' He declared, unannounced. 'Nice and quiet then. No boats, no walkers. Carp come in right close, right under even,' he continued. Posh and Smiffy were intrigued so probed and prodded for more information, whilst Mum and Dad sat and enjoyed the tranquillity and Becky practiced her latest withering look.

The advice had been interesting. No floats, just leger right under the boats, and use a big piece of crust. Not flake or paste – crust. The fish were used to people tipping their scraps over the side of the boat, and also feeding the ducks with bread crust, so that was the deal.

But it wasn't that simple. The crust kept coming off on the cast, or would be seen floating to the surface a minute after casting, and as the light began to fade both of the boys were becoming more and more frustrated. Then the purveyor of the knowledge came wandering past to see how they were doing. On hearing of their problems he simply said, 'Got any spaghetti?'

How simple it was after that. The spaghetti went between the hook and the crust to stop it coming off on the cast, then it would soften in the water and come off if they should hook something. The tactic worked well in the short time they had left before the others returned, although the carp that fell for the ploy was merely a quarter of the size of Posh's previous capture. Still, the early morning could be different and they settled down as best they could, but so excited and buzzed by the day's events that it was nearing midnight when they eventually succumbed to sleep.

Just unable to sleep properly, both of them were up and creeping around as the sun slowly crept over the eastern skyline. They'd decided to move along the bank a little to where an old, peeling hulk of a boat was nestled against the bank. It obviously hadn't moved for many months, maybe years, and they were sure that the carp would be used to having this as a roof over their heads. Posh went left, towards the stern, and left Smiffy at the prow end. Mallards and coots were just starting to wake and a few early morning squabbles were beginning to build as Smiffy made his first cast. The lead plopped down a yard short of the boat and he cursed a little. On his retrieval the crust was gone so he quickly cut another piece and inserted the small piece of pasta beneath the hook. His next cast was a little further and the lead 'donked' against the hull, dropping straight down in a swirl of bubbles. Perfect. At the far end Posh had done the same and so they both sat back expectantly. The minutes passed uneventfully. Then some more. Soon they were ten, then fifteen. The crust had not surfaced so Smiffy assumed it was still in position, and he looked along the bank to see if Posh was faring any better. He, however, was absentmindedly nibbling on some crust himself. All was still.

Should he recast? Should he move? He pondered these questions for a moment, but then he saw the line twitch as it entered the water. Then the rod tip pulled down and the clutch screamed. His strike was unnecessary, this was well hooked and the next five minutes or so saw him chasing the fish up and down the bank. Posh had joined him with the net and, pretty soon, oily swirls were appearing on the surface as the rod's pressure began to tell. Then the gulping mouth signalled the final moments of the battle and, pretty soon, another golden prize was engulfed in the waiting net.

'Blimey, that might be bigger than mine, Smiffy,' said Posh as he peered into the net at the beaten carp. They'd had the foresight to bring the scales with them this time, but they needn't have bothered. This fish was beyond their capabilities by a couple of pounds, and once again Smiffy wasn't able to find out the exact weight of his 'new PB'.

It mattered not. They whooped and laughed, then Posh took out the camera he'd also had the presence to bring and took a couple of shots of Smiffy cuddling a carp.

With the return of the fish came something else – hunger. Smiffy was starving, and knew that he couldn't continue without some food. But it was no later than six in the morning and he didn't really think he should be disturbing the rest of the boat, so had to follow his friend's lead and started wolfing down the bread. Posh had recast, but Smiffy felt like moving, but then realised that he had hardly any bread left, so went to see what Posh had. His supplies were equally as low, but he did have something unexpected in his bag.

'Sweetcorn?' said Smiffy, somewhat perplexed, 'What you got that for?'

''s a good bait for tench, and what wiv that bloke saying about people tipping their dinner over the side, I thought it might be worth a go.'

Smiffy eyed the tin, then asked, 'Got a tin opener?'

Posh rummaged in his bag and produced the item, handing it to Smiffy who proceeded to cleave the top from the tin.

'Right, let's see how right you are,' he declared, walking off with tin in the direction of the other boats. He impaled three grains on the hook, then cast the offering towards the far bank, between two moored craft. He knew these were occupied and didn't think that the occupants would enjoy the sound of an ounce of lead hitting their hull at this early hour, so opted for the gap between the two. He catapulted a few grains in the area, though to be fair at least a third of them landed on one or other of the boats. Oh well, better than a lead, he thought.

No sooner had he set the catapult down than the little indicator on the line lifted to the rod and he struck in a panic. Something nipped this way and that, and pretty soon a lovely, olive green tench was sliding towards him. Then the hook popped out and he cursed quietly. Not a carp, but he did love tench so was a little miffed at its loss. His next cast followed the first, and pretty soon his second tench was making its way to the net, successfully. The next hour passed in a blur of olive green and dark brown as half a dozen tench followed the first to his net, all around two pounds in size. Posh had followed suit with the sweetcorn, having blanked quietly with the bread, and also managed three similar sized fish before his dad was walking down the towpath towards them, to find out how they'd fared and to tell them that breakfast was almost ready. The latter had them reeling in immediately, suddenly realising that they were about to die of hunger.

So it was that, less than a year after casting his first ever line, Smiffy was chatting about catching fish in excess of ten pounds, and the tactics required so to do.

The three-day trip back to Oxford was as peaceful and beautiful and full of fish as the previous three days. More carp came their way, although neither of them managed to land anything as large as previously, despite almost certainly hooking fish of that size.

The tench were also plentiful, but outgunned by the tackle the boys were using, so not as sporting as usual. But they didn't mind; they'd had the holiday of a lifetime. One they wouldn't forget and hopefully one they could repeat next year.

But time moves on, things change, and adolescence loomed larger and larger. As did GCSE's and the like. Things would definitely change, but for now it was an idyllic time, and the summer was ahead – who knew what surprises that may hold?

Chapter Nine
Coming Back to Life

As Stan's car rolled slowly to a halt in the muddy car park, he recognised the other two cars.

Sid and Rhodie already here then, he thought. Nothing changes. Opening the door let in a cold blast of wintry air, and he quickly slid into his thermal jacket to combat it.

The trees were December-bare, the lake's surface stirred by a cold, northerly wind. Yep, this'll be winter then, he thought.

Leaving his gear in the car, he walked briskly away from the car park and towards the only two bivvies on the lake, wisely set up on the north bank. As he neared the first, he could see two pairs of thermal boots jutting from its entrance, and hear the sound of talking and the odd laugh.

'Is that bloody kettle on, or what?' he called. 'And you better have some bloody biscuits left as well, Rhodie!'

The boots retracted, then reappeared balancing two thermal-clad figures, woolly hats almost hiding their features.

'Quill, you old bugger, how the devil?' replied Rhodie, strolling forward with hand outstretched. Stan shook it warmly and gave his mate a quick hug.

'Alright, boy. Doing alright. What about you?'

But before Rhodie could answer, Sid was amongst them and shaking Quill's hand warmly.

'Quill, you alright, boy? Looking a bit slow, bit jaded. Don't be expecting any special treatment now, will yer?' With that he did a little shadow boxing, a quick shuffle, then stood there, grinning hugely.

'Forget that old bollocks, Sid,' replied Stan, 'just get the bloody kettle on. Some of us have been working y'know?'

Sid put his hands up, palms facing Stan as if to say 'okay, you win', but Stan knew that was far from the truth, and girded himself for a night of verbal attack and parry.

He loved it.

Slipping quickly in front of Rhodie, Stan sat down in the low chair and crossed his arms.

'So, what's been happening, boys? How many have you had?' he asked, knowing full well the answer. Rhodie glared down at him, but then utilised Sid's absence in search of water to grab the other chair.

'Not been here long, mate,' he replied, ignoring Sid's glare, 'rods've only been out half an hour or so. Not much been out recently has there, Sid?'

Sid feigned indignation at the lack of a chair for him, but a well-aimed thermal boot soon elicited a response from him.

'Steady, Rhodie. You're not too big to take a spanking, y'know?' he declared as he spun round, then continued, 'Nah, last one out was at the beginning of December, what's that, almost four weeks? Not many people been down though, maybe one or two a weekend. This is my first session for about three weeks.'

Stan stared out at the grey lake and contemplated the next couple of days. Even though they were spread far and wide, they still tried to get together around Christmas time and, much the same as last year, they were all going to be able to manage it.

Last year, due to Buzz being off somewhere very hot and returning just after Christmas, they'd met up early in the new year, a couple of days into 2002, and had fished a day ticket water near Oxford. As good as it was to meet up, it was quite busy and time had been tight, so they'd only managed one night together. A lot of the talk had been about 9/11, initially, but then had moved on to carp, and especially Felcham. They'd all grilled Stan about the chances of fishing it, and, eventually, had taken his word that nothing was happening as of yet. His news of the death of Buzz's 48 had left them in sullen mood for a little while, especially as another couple of fish had been found only a month prior to their winter gathering. They had both been upper-twenties, one of them recognisable as the fish that Sid had caught from the pads at the beginning of their first season.

But then the wine had flowed, and things deteriorated rapidly into bonhomie, playful banter and mates generally being mates.

This year, almost twelve months further on, they were on 'Sid's lake'. This was the lake Stan and Sid had fished many months ago, and one that Stan had revisited on a couple of occasions since. There were no monsters in there, although any one of them would have been happy with one of the dozen thirties that the lake held. The reason they called it 'Sid's' was because, somehow beyond their ken, he had been made head bailiff and so had managed to get them permission for an après-Christmas get together.

'When's the big fella getting here, then?' asked Stan, after a gulp of warming tea. Sid had pulled up a bucket and was squatting on that, waiting for one or the other bladder to fill to overflowing.

'Said he'd be down late afternoon, maybe just after dark. He's been up to his mum's in Shropshire, so it's a bit of a trek,' he replied, then rose to put the kettle on again.

'Where you going then, Quill, next to me or next to Rhodie?' he asked, whilst refilling the kettle.

'Hmm, difficult to choose really. There's a nice bar that runs in front of that swim past you, but the kettle and food is up here. Decisions, decisions.' With that he took another gulp of tea and winked at Rhodie. 'No rush, though, mate. Got a good couple of hours before dark. Think another cuppa will be required before the final decision is made, don't you?'

Rhodie smiled and raised his thermal mug, and Sid just muttered to himself.

By the time Buzz arrived, just at dusk, Stan was set up and cast out in the swim beyond Sid, so Buzz just plonked his gear down in the swim nearest to the car park and demanded tea – after the usual bone-crushing hand shakes and blokey banter.

By early evening, all were fishing, although the rapid drop in temperature gave them little cause to think they would be required to utilise any of their gear that evening.

As the beer and wine flowed, they laughed and joked, and, despite trying a few serious 'so how's work going then?' conversations, were soon returning to the well-trod path of toilet humour, smut and innuendo, and carp fishing.

The last took its usual course; from what each of them had been doing, what they'd been catching, 'did you hear about so and so?', and eventually reaching their usual destination.

'So, Quill, what news of the big pond? Any more deaths?'

Stan had many tales to tell. Of huge, spawning carp. Of dickheads on jet skis. Of deer and badger and buzzard. But, fortunately, none of dead carp, not this year.

''spose we've been quite lucky, or maybe the carp have sussed it out a bit,' he said only slightly slurring. 'Seems that, in the summer, they stay in the old lake, by the snags or the island. Sometimes see them up in the top corner by the reeds, past the boathouse, but that's normally when the lake's been quiet for a couple of days.'

They talked of sessions past, of huge mirrors and commons, then one by one, tottered off to curl up in huge sleeping bags and pray that they had no action at all during the night.

Stan could hear some commotion - people talking excitedly, the odd shout or exclamation – so carefully opened his eyes and peered from beneath his bag. It was light, so probably at least eight o'clock. His rapidly filling bladder had been waking him fitfully for the past couple of hours, but now it was demanding attention, so he slowly rose, then quickly grabbed his jacket as the cold penetrated. Slipping his boots on, he got up and walked to a nearby tree to relieve himself, and the talking and laughter got louder.

'Quill!' shouted Sid, 'Buzz has had one, mate. The big fella's bagged himself a winter carp, and it's a good'un.' This news stirred him a little so, rubbing his face, he wandered off past the other bivvies towards Buzz's swim.

The other three were gathered around the net and peering in, so Stan strolled up and joined them.

'What ya got, Buzz?' he enquired.

'Big fat mirror, I reckon, Quill,' came the beaming reply.

'Nice one. Time for the kettle then, is it?'

Sid tutted. 'Weighing and photos first, mate. Then celebrations,' he decreed. Rhodie already had the scales and sling prepared, and pretty soon Buzz was grinning widely at the cameras as he held up a 31lb winter carp for inspection.

'Just melted off,' he related, a little later as the bacon sizzled in the pan. 'It was the one I chucked down the margin on the pineapple pop-up,' he continued. Must have taken about thirty yards of line before I could stop the bloody thing. But then it was all over, really. By the time you got here, Rhodie, it was almost done, weren't it?' Rhodie nodded, whilst manoeuvring the bacon around the pan with a wooden spatula.

'Probably three minutes max, after that first run, but I'm not bloody complaining, boys. Reckon I might need to pop down the shops a little later, just for a celebratory bottle or two. Waddya think?'

Sid and Quill looked at each other and winced, but they knew the score on these sessions. The first night was always mad, over the top, full of drink and bullshit. Then the second night was invariably much more sedate and, inevitably, much earlier to bed.

Early afternoon found all four of them back in their own bivvies, all having a little siesta, and despite being quite weak, the sun's warmth was still such that they were all soon dozing on their respective beds. Stan had barely closed his eyes when a 'bleep' on his right hand alarm caused him to open an eye and peer at the rod. Fished about sixty yards out, to the bottom of the bar, his first thought was that the tufties had found his bait, even in twelve feet of water. Another 'bleep' had him raised on one elbow and still staring out. No birds. He swung his legs round and, with elbows on knees, continued staring at the rod tip. It moved very slowly to the right and the alarm issued another 'bleep'. He slipped his feet quickly into his boots and was soon standing next to the rods. The indicator was tight against the rod and quivering slightly. Oh sod it, he thought, and lifted the rod with a flourish, feeling the immediate thump of something on the other end. The fish carried on moving slowly to the right, and Stan just kept the pressure on, gradually gaining line as the fish kited towards the bank.

'Got one on, mate?' Sid asked as he strolled into the swim. 'Thought I heard an alarm bleeping away.'

'Yeah, feels like a good'un, too,' replied Stan, gradually gaining more line and keeping an eye on the rod tip. 'Just a couple of single bleeps, then I saw the line pulling to the right. Ooh! Shit, thought I'd lost it, must have been the bloody dorsal.' The fish was now no more than fifteen yards away; the swirls giving away its presence, so Sid bent to take up the net. A minute later the large mouth of a carp was gulping on the surface, and Sid leant forward to slide the net cord beneath it and engulf it with the mesh.

'Yehay!' shouted Stan. 'Big fat mirror!'

It was Buzz and Rhodie's turn to enter the swim whilst rubbing their eyes, just as Sid was lifting the net onto the unhooking mat.

'Well done, boy,' said Rhodie, 'another winter whacker!'

Stan beamed at him and nodded, then watched as Buzz and Sid took charge of the weighing.

'Bloody hell!' grunted Sid as he hoisted the scales. 'This is a bit of a lump, Quill.' The scales confirmed that estimate as they spun around to just an ounce under thirty four pounds.

'Yes!!' cried Stan. 'Bloody YES!'

Back pats and 'well dones' followed, then the photos of a large-framed, grey mirror were taken, accompanied by a smiling captor.

'How many bottles did you get, Buzz?' he enquired, and Buzz indicated with both fingers. 'No need for that, fella,' said Sid, and all was well with the world.

Despite renewed enthusiasm, and recasting and everything, no further carp fell foul of the quartet, but this had been their best winter session yet, and they all congratulated Sid on his appointment as head bailiff of such a fine pond.

The evening wasn't quite as bad as the previous one, and the chat was a lot more about the individuals' present circumstances.

Buzz was being called away more and more, and although very lucrative, his fishing was suffering badly. 'I've got to take the work whilst they're paying this sort of money, but not for much longer. Reckon I've got another year on this contract, maybe a bit more, then I'm looking for somewhere to settle down. Gotta get me some more of these sort of carp. 'Course, once I come back, Quill will have sorted the Mere and we'll all be back on there.'

With that there was a chorus of 'yeahs' and raising of glasses, not least by Stan himself, but he was in no doubt that that would **not** be the case.

Rhodie was well ensconced in Cambridgeshire, with a new house, a new baby, a good job, and surrounded by some wonderful fishing, so he was quite content, despite being left with only a weekly phone call or two to keep in contact with his mates.

And Sid was, well, Sid. Joking about how he was going to get enough money to buy a house close to the Mere, then get a job working with Stan. It was all drink-fuelled bravado, but great fun whilst it lasted.

They left by mid-morning; hands shaken, shoulders hugged and empty promises made, and by early afternoon, Stan was sitting down for a nice cup of tea with Jean.

'How were the lads?' she'd asked when he returned.

'All great, babe. They all send their love. Got a photo of Rhodie's boy. Looks like a baby to me,' he said, as he handed over the small snapshot. Jean oohed and aahed, like they do, and admonished him for his dismissive description, like they do.

'Oh, he's lovely,' she cooed. Then went to put the kettle on.

As he put away his gear into the shed, Stan thought about Buzz's comment, about them all fishing the Mere again, and daydreamed of that happening. But it was just that at the moment, just a dream. Maybe time would tell.

Ooh, I could murder a cup of tea, he thought.

Chapter Ten
Signs of Life

'Ninety seven,' declared the scorer.

Right, thought Stan, nineteens.

Thud!

Nineteen. Seventy-eight; treble fourteen.

Thud!

Double eighteen.

Thud!

'Yesss!'

The crowd went wild. Well, Stan's seven team mates and a couple of dozen supporters went wild. They were in the final, and Stan's arrows had secured their place.

To be fair, their lead had been such that there was no real pressure on Stan; his final double taking them over the winning line with three legs to spare.

'Well done, young Stan,' said Ted, handing him another foaming ale. 'Final next week, then.'

Ah, next week. Now that could be interesting.

The final was at Wilton Rugby Club.

On Saturday evening.

Twelve hours after the World Cup Final. A final that could well include England, if they could overcome the French tomorrow.

Yep, it could be very messy indeed – hopefully.

'Swing low, sweet chariot,

Coming for to carry me home!'

Stan's bellow was lost amongst the cacophony of the victory celebrations – again. Celebrations that had been going on for many hours, now.

'Jonny, Jonny Wilkinson! Jonny – Wilkinson!' rang out a raucous chorus as yet another re-run of 'that' kick was played on the big screen in the clubroom.

The darts final had been long forgotten, maybe to be played another day, maybe not. At this moment all that mattered was that England were World Champions.

'Brilliant!' said Peter, snaking an arm around Stan's shoulder. 'Bloody brilliant!'

Stan raised his glass and grinned in agreement. Peter Double-Barrel was alright. Since their stroll around the lake, a couple of years previously, he and Peter had chatted quite a few times, mainly on one of their frequent sorties to the lake. Peter was enchanted by their surroundings, watching the world gradually change with the seasons, and although he would never be a fisherman, he craved Stan's knowledge and help so that he could help nurture his son's growing love of the pastime.

It was on one of these strolls, in the deep midwinter, a little while after the post-Christmas trip to Oxford, that a casual remark changed Stan's fishing horizons for years to come.

The clouds were laden with snow, yet to fall, and the woods looked bare and skeletal, awaiting their new, temporary, vestments. He and Peter were warmly wrapped against the cold, their breath forming clouds around them. Very little else was abroad in these harsh conditions. Most warm-blooded mammals were huddled in a burrow, sleeping fitfully until the onset of spring; the majority of the woods' birdlife had left for warmer climes a month or so earlier, and even the fish were almost torpid below the solid, icy surface of the lake.

As usual, their conversation wandered and meandered along no particular course, sometimes serious, invariably trite and amusing.

Then, out of the blue, Stan said, 'Peter, you're double-barrelled. You must know a few bods with country estates and the like. Reckon you could get me a nice lake to fish on?'

Peter laughed at the 'double-barrelled' reference, and responded in similar vein. 'Well, you urchin, I may know a Lord or two who may be able to help. Her Majesty has a sizeable lake in her garden where I believe most of the fish are adorned with gold and diamonds. Fancy a go on there?'

Stan laughed, and doffed his cap in deference. 'Well, sire, if Her Maj wouldn't mind a mere commoner having a dangle in her pond, that would be fine. Could we get all the rods in the roller, though?'

Peter carried on chuckling, then turned and stared straight at Stan. 'D'you know, I do know a couple of chaps down here with some big estates. Not sure if they've got any lakes or whatnot, but no harm in asking, I suppose.'

'You serious?' asked Stan, slightly taken aback.

'Deadly, Stan. All I might ask as a favour is if you wouldn't mind taking the boy once in a while.' Although a million miles away from his plans, he could hardly say no, and anyway, the chances were that this would all come to nothing.

So, 'No problem,' was his reply, and then they walked on in search of a roaring fire and a pint of foaming ale.

The first buds of spring were peeking through when, one lazy Sunday afternoon, Stan got an unexpected call from Peter. All of the householders had his and John's numbers, in case of emergency, but it was rare for it to ring, and even rarer to be Peter.

'Stan, how you doing, sir?' was his opening question.

'Err, good thanks, Peter. Got a problem?'

'Well, yes, a bit of one,' Peter began. 'I've had a call from a friend of mine, Lord or Marquis or some such. Anyway, he's got a big old pile a few miles away and is having trouble with the fish in his lake. Apparently, nobody can catch the bleeders and he was wondering if I knew some lowlife who fancied wasting away his days in futile pursuit of them. Anyone spring to mind?'

Stan couldn't quite take it all in at first, then just stuttered out, 'Err, what you saying? Me?'

Peter laughed heartily, 'Yes, of course you, you buffoon! Look, I'm off to town for a couple of days, but when I get back on Wednesday I'll give you a call and explain all. I think you'll be very pleased with the whole thing. I'll phone you later. Cheers.' With that, the line went dead and Stan sat there holding the phone, not quite knowing what to think.

'Who was that, dear?' asked Jean as she came back into the room.

'Errm, possibly the Tooth Fairy and Father Christmas, all in one,' he replied, bemused.

'Oh, right. What time's Antiques Roadshow on?'

Just another Sunday afternoon.

Less than a week later, Stan was staring at a seven or eight-acre lake, nestled in a small, Wiltshire valley. The 'big old pile' was about thirty miles from Felcham, but took less than an hour to reach. The guy that Peter knew was neither Lord nor Marquis, and was in fact not titled in any way. They knew each other from the city, but Stuart Goldsmith had made sure that his wealth had strong foundations, so had bought fifty acres of land in the eighties, near to a small village called Hatch, which seemed quaint. The lake and house were already there, as were the people who tended them, and so Stuart had an ideal place not only to take prospective clients, but any number of young ladies he wished to woo.

Then, suddenly, he'd got snared. Married and a father within a year, and now happy to leave the city behind and work from the ample office at home. But that was of little concern to Stan; he just wanted to know about the lake and its contents.

The house had been built in the late 1700's, as had a lake and gardens. The lake had originally been a square of about six acres but, in recent times, another nodule had been added to the north bank, making it look like a spatula with a stunted handle. This extra bay was about two acres in size, and relatively shallow in relation to the main lake, so being south facing would be an obvious place for any carp to reside in the warmer weather. But were there any carp?

Peter was unsure of this; all he knew was that there was a small fishing club whose members were allowed to fish the place, although the gamekeeper oversaw all activities on the lake and surrounding grounds. It was Norman, the gamekeeper,

who he met on that Friday morning in March. He would have preferred to have gone on Saturday, but it being the last weekend of the season, the lake would be full with the club's members.

Norman was pleasant enough, but he wasn't like Jim Baines at Linton, and he wondered if the fishing wouldn't be the same as there either. He'd been back a couple of times, and, despite not being alone on those occasions, had still had a wonderful time. On both occasions he'd managed to catch carp of stunning beauty, although none were any larger than the twenty-four from his first session.

Now, however, he was fishing a lake that held some pretty decent, but elusive specimens.

'So what's in the lake then, Norman?' was his obvious opening gambit.

Norman acted as if it was the first time he'd been asked the question, which was nice, but his answer was fairly non-committal.

'Well, 'bout fifty carp were stocked in 'ere 'bout twenty years ago. Small 'uns, 'bout three or four pound. Not sure how many survived, or how big.'

Hmm, that's really bloody helpful, thought Stan. Let's try another tack.

'How many get caught in a year then, Norman?'

Norman pondered this a little, but was still as unenlightening.

'Difficult to say really. Them what fishes for 'em don't like to say. Them what don't fish for 'em rarely catches 'em.'

Bloody hell, who is this, George bloody Smiley?

'Oh right, so you don't really know if they're even in here then?' he said, bluntly. This was starting to annoy him and he could see a day's holiday being totally wasted. But that line of attack seemed to stir Norman a little.

'Oh, they're in here, lad. No doubt about that. I sin 'em most years when they's spawning, up in the top bay. Not sure how many. Two, three dozen at least.'

Now we were getting somewhere, and with a bit of careful probing, Stan eked out enough information to at least get his juices flowing.

Of the fish that Norman had seen, most had been 'this big', said with arms splayed wide. Allowing for exaggeration, Stan put that at about low to mid-twenties. But then, a few, maybe half a dozen, were probably 'this much' bigger. That made them in excess of thirty pounds, but then came the caveat.

'Course, you'll never find out 'cos they never gets caught.'

Excellent, that must put off most people, he thought. And indeed it did.

That first session had produced a couple of jet-black tench of around six pounds, and a possible sighting of a carp a few hundred yards to his right. It wasn't much, but he thought that it would probably be worth investigating further, come the new season.

Chapter Eleven
A Delicate Sound of Thunder

Ever so quietly, Smiffy crept through the woods, careful not to break a twig or crunch through the many dead leaves carpeting the floor of the wintry woodland. Posh had a ten-minute start on him, but he was sure he knew which way he'd gone and could intercept him in a short time. His knowledge of Sutton Woods had grown immensely in the relatively short time that he'd lived there, but with the amount of time he'd spent in them, it was hardly surprising. A chill easterly breeze sliced between the bare trees, rustling the dormant leaves and causing Smiffy to pull his coat ever tighter, and his hat lower to cover his freezing ears.

He passed by the banks of the stream, and watched as the water chuckled along beneath a thin crust of ice. Man, it must be cold , he thought, but he didn't need a vision of ice to confirm that, he just had to let the wind hit him full in the face if he needed to ascertain the temperature –'bleedin' freezing!' would have been an adequate description.

He sensed some movement ahead so slowed his pace and crouched a little lower. It couldn't have been Posh; he wouldn't have been so obvious. Then into view came half a dozen deer, slowing to a trot after obviously having made a hasty exit from something. Hmm, spooked the deer did you, Posh? he thought. Bad angling, mate. Bet you're a bit pissed at the mo'. He let the deer pass him by, thirty yards distant, careful not to repeat his mate's blunder, then moved off to the left, from where they'd come – closing in.

Ted returned to his cabin, thankful that he'd left the stove burning before he'd left earlier that morning. Must be his age, but these last few winters he'd really felt the cold, on occasion. Oh well, what did he expect? He'd been to so many bloody hot places in his life it was no wonder that his body was complaining. But he wouldn't give it up for anything, this place and time in his life. Just before returning home this morning, he'd spied young Becks hurrying through the woods, spooking a small herd of fallows as he made his escape from someone. All had been made clear five minutes later when he saw young Smiffy carefully following in his friend's tracks, closing on him swiftly. War games. He thought back to a similar forest, on the other side of the world decades earlier, and in conditions so hot and humid it was almost impossible to breathe. The 'enemy' were 2 Squadron and he and his boys had to find and 'neutralise' them. The rivalry was intense enough to make the exercise more than just friendly, and by the end of the two days, the medics and MP's were working overtime. Fortunately, nobody was seriously hurt, although Doug Black would have an impressive scar across his forehead for the rest of his life. But 'War Games' was such an oxymoron. The words 'War' and 'Game' could never been used in the same sentence.

This was a tough season, he thought, as he stirred a little brandy into his coffee. So much death, but then so much life as well, and the ones that survived were always that little bit stronger for doing so. At a quick glance it seemed as though the woods were devoid of life, but Ted knew where to look to belie that deceit. As young Neil had proved, the deer were abroad in many numbers and were regular visitors to all the woods in the area. But stealth and patience would prove that many smaller mammals were also very active in this most austere of seasons. Stoats and weasels couldn't afford to hibernate; their metabolism just wouldn't allow it, and on a few occasions Ted had witnessed them foraging along the banks of the lake and stream, whilst he quietly rested against an aging oak or alder.

The fox family all needed feeding as well, and the russet coat of the dog fox was often seen contrasting against the grey skyline, or the frost covered fields. But winters weren't what they used to be, and where it once had been true that badgers and squirrels nestled themselves down for a three-month doze, now it wasn't unusual to see either of these rummaging around for food after an unseasonably warm spell had stirred them from their slumbers. The same could be said for the smaller mammals, such as voles and mice, and their abundance meant that the feathered predator's forays were more and more successful.

No, we don't have winters like we used to, but Ted had no problem with that. Although this spell of freezing conditions gave everything a reason not to venture out for too long, pretty soon the watery winter sun would give way to cloud and rain, and life would be stirred again. For now, though, another tot of brandy to shield against the cold. Wonder if Smiffy's hunted down young Becks yet?

'Took yer time,' chattered Posh, huddled behind a large tree trunk to hide both from his pursuer and the biting wind.

'Whaddya mean?' asked Smiffy, indignantly. 'I was with you all the way; I just didn't want to blunder along like a bull elephant and spook the whole wood.'

Posh gave a dismissive grunt, then rubbed his hands together to keep the blood circulating. At first, he'd opted for stealth, but that had just let the cold in, so he decided on all out flight, just to keep warm. He knew that the deer would alert his mate, but he was beyond caring by then. What had at first seemed like a good idea had quickly turned into a bloody bad one, and he was quite happy to concede defeat if it meant that they could return to a warm household, damn quickly.

'Bloody hell, it's bleeding freezing!' stated Smiffy, obviously. 'Whose stupid idea was this, anyway?'

The question was rhetorical, as the idea had been his, and he was more than happy to accept the blame. Very quickly, huddled down against the wind, they retraced their steps and headed for home. If there were any other foolhardy souls about, the boys were unaware, and rushed headlong towards the lakeshore. They slowed a little as they entered the East Woods, where they were sheltered a little against the biting wind, and gazed across the ice rimmed lake. Tufted ducks bobbed in the waves, disappearing regularly beneath the surface in search of food. A coot skittered along the margins ahead of them, complaining stridently, and way over in front of the boathouse a couple of swans occupied the space where, a few months hence, only sails and surfboards would be evident.

Their pace soon increased and practically broke into a run as they neared Smiffy's house. Through the back gate, into the empty conservatory where they dispensed with their boots, and through the sliding doors into the huge lounge.

'Hello, chaps. Bit brisk out there?'

Smiffy just grunted at his dad's question and made his way into the kitchen, leaving his mate to deal with it.

'Hi, Mr. R. Yeah, it's pretty cold. Ice all around the lake, and the stream. Who's playing?' That last referred to the rugby that was on the telly. Although he had no great knowledge of the game, he had a love of all sports, and could just as easily watch a rugby match as football or snooker.

'England – France. Just kicked off, Neil. Could be the start of something, eh?'

Posh nodded, then made his way through to the kitchen where Smiffy was setting a saucepan of soup to heat.

'Where's yer mum?' he asked as he took his coat off and draped it over the back of the chair before sitting down.

'Oh, probably Salisbury, shopping,' replied Smiffy. 'She leaves dad to it when the rugby's on.' As if to underline the reasoning behind that, a stream of invective issued from the living room, directed at some unknowing offender.

Smiffy just raised his eyebrows, then continued stirring the soup. Once heated, the boys busily went about consuming it, after which they retired to Smiffy's bedroom to talk of many things.

The weather had frustrated their fishing exploits of late, but since their canal trip they had ventured out as often as they could. The long summer holidays had seen them try their hands at many venues, but mainly the river, which was easily accessible and, inevitably, quieter and easier than the lakes. Many were the times that they'd return from a river trip with stories of monsters and encounters to astound and amuse. But the two most poignant stories had little to do with the fish they'd caught.

The summer holidays were no more than a few days old when they took off for their first foray to the river, with rods in hand. They'd spent the previous couple of days in the woods, 'hunting' squirrel and pheasant with home made bow and arrows, but mainly walking the banks of the river to see if they could find a 'secret swim', somewhere that looked like it had never been fished before. And yesterday they had found it.

The river wound southwest, along the edge of Sutton Woods, then had cut back southwards and through the woods to the boundary with Culvert's Wood. The trees were thick here, and very little sunlight penetrated, but up ahead they could see shafts of light breaking through the canopy, and the undergrowth flourishing again. They battled through hawthorn and bramble, and on more than one occasion thought about turning back, but the distant tinkle of running water lured them forward. Then, as the thorned bushes thinned out and made passage easier, Posh pointed ahead at the reflection of sunlight on water.

'At bloody last!' he exclaimed. Smiffy stopped to remove a number of bramble thorns from his arm, and wipe his brow. Sure enough, just fifty yards ahead he saw a small section of river gliding beneath the trees. Within a minute or so they were standing by the slowly rolling river, shaded from the sun by willow and birch, and surrounded by birdsong. Many years hence, Smiffy would think back to this time, when he and his friend had, indeed, found Utopia. The banks were pretty overgrown, but some careful 'gardening' would soon allow a couple of fishermen to ply their trade. They picked their way through the bankside foliage until they'd pinpointed three or four likely spots to fish, where the river slid beneath overhanging branches, or around tight bends where the water chuckled and churned.

As they sat for a moment, drinking in their surroundings, they saw the flash of a kingfisher, dashing across the water and disappearing around a bend in the river.

'This is bloody beautiful,' muttered Smiffy, 'but it's gonna be one hell of a walk with rods and that.'

Posh had been thinking the same thing, so, a little while later, they made their way back home with sturdy sticks in hand, to cleave a rudimentary path through the grasping undergrowth. Half an hour later, dripping with blood and sweat, tears in their trousers and t-shirts, they emerged from the woods into bright sunlight. They gave little time to assessing their efforts, they were too intent on getting into Smiffy's kitchen and drinking as much cold squash as possible.

But now they were back, rods in hand and plenty of water in their rucksacks. At this early hour they had no worries about the heat, the sun having barely cleared the horizon, and they crept through a rapidly awakening woodland until, after fifteen minutes, they appeared from the 'dark wood' into the clearing near the river. They both set down their bags and tackle and crept forward, the chuckling water drawing them closer. A startled pheasant screamed its alarm as they passed too close, and its raucous exit nearly elicited two heart attacks.

'Bloody hell! I nearly shit meself!' said Posh, whilst clutching at his pounding chest. Smiffy laughed a relieved laugh, glad that he hadn't actually performed that ignominious accident, and knowing how close he had been.

Their equilibrium regained, they stood by the river and eyed up a couple of potential swims to fish from.

'I'll go here for the mo,' stated Posh. 'Where d'you fancy, mate?'

Smiffy had a hankering for a spot forty yards downstream and so, without further ado, they set about the river. Trotted breadflake saw Posh bag himself a succession of nice roach, to just under a pound, and Smiffy's ever reliable maggot and caster cocktail produced some small perch and a couple of small bream. But after an hour or so, both lads were getting a little restless. As lovely and peaceful as this was, they had encountered none of the imagined monsters, so both decided that it was time for a move. A further hundred yards downstream they came upon a long, sweeping bend in the river where the trees on the far bank hung over the water, dark and mysterious. The far bank was steep and they imagined that it extended as such into the water. A couple of legers, with a bread crust hookbait, were soon cast beneath the far trees, and both sat back in anticipation. After fifteen or twenty minutes, the lack of action was surprising, and Smiffy was just about to reel in and wander up to Posh when, from the corner of his eye, he caught a movement to his left. There, swimming confidently against the current, was a large animal, and he knew instantly that it must be an otter. He'd never seen such grace and beauty before, and held his breath as it passed not thirty feet in front of him before disappearing beneath an overhanging bough and out of sight. He sat and watched for a further minute, but then quickly reeled in and made his way to Posh, fifty yards upstream.

Just as he was about to explode with the revelation, Posh held up his hand and pointed towards the far bank, and there was the otter, sitting on the muddy bank with something in his forepaws. The boys remained still and quiet as they watched the beautiful animal devour a sizeable fish, and then slip back into the flow and disappear off down stream.

'Brilliant!' declared Smiffy, and Posh just nodded. Then they broke out some food of their own and continued to discuss the sighting.

'Wonder if that's why there's no fish up here?' said Posh, around a mouthful of ham sandwich. 'Made pretty short work of that one, didn't it?'

Smiffy pondered this, but couldn't see how one otter could clear a whole section of river of fish.

'Who says there's only one?' asked Posh. 'Families, Smiffy. There'll be at least a mate and maybe some young. Gonna need a lot of fish.'

Again, Smiffy pondered the truth of this and then, as if to affirm Posh's theory, they witnessed the most amazing sight as four of the sleek creatures came porpoising and rolling upstream. The parents were clearly larger and more adroit, but the young were no less agile, and the quartet played and frolicked in front of the goggle-eyed onlookers for a couple of minutes before disappearing upstream.

Smiffy had the wherewithal to take a few shaky shots on his camera, and they would remain as framed photos on his wall for many years to come.

The heat was seeping back into the day, and they doubted that anything of any size was either left in here, or would dare to show its fins at the moment, so they slowly packed away and made their way back through the woods, unencumbered by stories of monsters, but enriched nonetheless.

As they crossed into the East Woods, they walked to the side of the lake and sat against a couple of trees, finishing the last of their hardening sandwiches, and washing them down with warm orange juice.

They chatted about the events of the morning then, for the second time that day, were nearly given a heart attack when a voice spoke up, not two yards away.

'Otters, eh?' said Old Ted, from behind them. 'Where be they, then?'

'Bloody hell!' squawked Smiffy, spilling his drink in surprise. 'Where'd you come from, Ted?'

Ted just walked past them and looked out at the flat calm lake.

'Greedy, nasty buggers, otters. Catches a fish, any fish, and devours it. Killing machines, they be. You watch 'em teach their young 'uns. Just nips a fish to slow 'im down, then lets the young 'un chase 'im and harry 'im. Nasty buggers'

Posh and Smiffy looked at each other, eyebrows raised, then Posh said, 'But they're so beautiful, Ted, you must see that. And they've got to eat to survive, surely? I mean, foxes kill chickens, 'n' owls and hawks and that kill birds and mice; it's just nature.'

Ted nodded, then turned round to the lads. 'Young Neil, you're right. But you need to know the difference between killing to survive and just killing. You find a carp that's been got by 'n otter. It ain't just a skeleton, oh no. It'll just have et a small portion, maybe the gills, maybe the stomach, then it's gone. They kills for the fun of it, whether they'm hungry or not, and rest assured, if they eat all that's in the river, then they'll start looking elsewhere, and this is the closest and easiest elsewhere they needs to look.

'Where'd you say you saw 'em? I think I might take a look myself.'

Posh and Smiffy looked at each other again, then Posh explained where they'd seen the otters. Ted nodded, as if he knew the place.

'You done good to find it – not easy. But it sounds like all the good fishing's gone. Try upstream of the mill, a mile maybe. Fast running river there with some good fish; chub, barbel, good-sized roach. Belongs to a club, but if you're quiet I'm sure you'll not need a ticket.' With that he winked, then slowly strolled off towards Sutton Woods, to get some tools. The otters would not be a problem in Felcham Mere, of that he was convinced.

The upstream stretch had proved as good as Old Ted had suggested, with both of them catching roach and chub of impressive dimensions, but the barbel had proved elusive, and, once they'd been spotted by a club member on their fourth sortie, would remain so for another year. The holidays drifted away in a wave of heat and insects. Sometimes they fished, sometimes took to their bikes and investigated the small lanes and tracks around the area. Once or twice they even went out with their parents to the nearby New Forest but, as beautiful as it was, they both found it a tad popular; too many people for their liking, so declined any further outings in favour of adventures closer to home. Then they decided to go camping.

Their parents were a little apprehensive, but this wasn't London or New York. They were safer here than anywhere else, so a night in the woods would be a bit of fun. They chose Sutton Woods because they knew it quite well; it had some good memories, and the old mill would be a good area to start. So, laden down with tent and sleeping bags, flasks and sandwiches, they made there way into the woods one sunny afternoon. Erecting the tent was a relative disaster, but after half an hour a shelter was before them, and pretty soon their sleeping bags were inside and they were ready for the night. Posh had brought along a lighter, as he had recently decided that smoking would be a cool thing to do, and so they collected some small twigs and dry bracken and soon had a small fire crackling away in front of them. They had nothing to cook on it; all their food having been prepared that morning, but they were camping so they needed a campfire. As evening fell, the clouds gathered overhead, which just meant that the heat stayed below them and the oppressive nature of it made them feel just a little uneasy. The fire had died before dark, but that mattered little. Their flasks of tea and soup were long since empty, and only a few biscuits remained, which would hopefully be untouched until morning. At dusk, an owl called from close by, and they sat hopefully for five minutes, smiles splitting their faces as the silent white hunter glided effortlessly by. The wind was rustling the trees more vigorously every minute, but they had no worries, as their tent would surely protect them from any perils.

Chatter and giggles emanated from the tent until well after dark, so they were unaware of the strengthening wind until they tried to sleep.

'Blimey, it's blowing a bit out there, mate,' said Smiffy.

'Yeah, might be in for a bit of a storm,' replied Posh. Barely had the words left his mouth when the tent was lit up like daylight as a flash of lightning rent the night sky.

They both shot upright, expletives flying, then waited for the thunder. When it came it was a long, low rumble, and Posh said, 'Ten miles away.'

They could now hear the wind, and also the odd 'crack' as small branches succumbed to its power. A minute later, night became day again, and the ensuing rumble followed less than eight seconds behind.

Then again, closer, louder.

And again.

Then – 'flash', 'KERRRACKK!'

'****ing hell!' screamed Smiffy, just as the tent door ripped open. They thought it was the wind, their eyes night blind, then a voice commanded, 'Out! Now!'

It was Ted, and he didn't deserve the moniker 'Old' at this moment in time. They scrambled up and out as another huge flash was followed by an ear-splitting roar. Out of the tent they could hear and see the woods as they struggled against the increasing rage of this sudden, summer storm. Ted surged ahead, head down, and it was all that the boys could do to keep up with him.

'Come on! Quick now,' he shouted, and they obeyed without a word. A loud crack from their left announced the demise of a much larger bough, but its eventual crash to the ground was almost lost in the roar of the wind. Their faces were being whipped by branches and bushes, then the heavens opened and torrential rain stung their eyes and threatened their footholds.

'There,' shouted Ted above the storm's crescendo, and pointed ahead at a dim light flickering through the trees. Then, there was a small dwelling, no more than a wood cabin, but sturdy and, once inside, dry.

He slammed the door behind them, then turned to examine them.

'Alright?' he asked. 'Any damage, lads?'

These were questions that demanded an answer, and both of the boys nodded and shook their heads accordingly.

'Cut your face, young Quentin, y'alright?' asked Ted.

Smiffy put his hand to his cheek, smearing blood across it. Posh looked at him, still quite dazed by the recent events, and saw the small mark.

'Just a scratch, mate. Probably a bramble or something.'

The outside world was lit up again, and the small cabin felt less secure when the ensuing clap of thunder followed, a second or so later.

'Tea,' declared Ted, and lifted a voluminous kettle onto an old stove, then busied himself finding three suitable receptacles for the brew. Two cracked, tea-stained mugs, and an odd little cup were soon filled with the warming brew, and the three of them sat quietly as the storm raged above them, small billows of steam issuing from their cups.

'You boys sleep in the bed; I'll stay here in the chair. Be fine by morning,' declared Ted. The boys walked into a small, dark room, where a single bed took up most of the space. Smiffy was sure that this really wouldn't have been to his mum's liking, but those thoughts lasted a millisecond, and once his head hit the pillow, the extreme tiredness overtook him like a steam train, and he was asleep in seconds.

Posh stirred as the sunlight crept though the thin curtains, and he heard Ted moving about in the next room. Pulling on his trousers, Posh joined Ted, who was sitting at a small table, mug of tea before him, and looking out of the window onto a scene of apparent serenity.

He sat down in the other chair, and put his elbows on the table, chin in hands. Ted rose and went to the stove, returning with a cup of strong, sweet tea, and placed it in front of his young visitor.

'Looks like nothing even happened,' said Posh, cupping the tea in front of him with both hands. 'But it did, didn't it?'

Ted nodded. 'Mother Nature's way, lad. Get rid of the dead wood.'

Posh knew he wasn't just talking about old trees and branches, although his closer inspection of the scene outside the window had revealed a less than serene picture than he'd originally thought.

'Thanks for coming out, Ted,' he said. 'I knew it was getting bad but I didn't know what to do. Scared, I suppose.'

'Oh, we all get scared, lad, believe me. Just that some people deal with it different to others. Do you read, lad?' This last came as a surprise question, and caught him slightly off guard.

'Err, yeah. Sometimes. Like what?'

'Books, lad. Books create worlds in your head, places you could never go to or ever experience in real life. And they inspire –

I must not fear.

Fear is the mind-killer.

Fear is the little death that brings total obliteration.

I will face my fear.

I will permit it to pass over me and through me, and when it has gone past I will turn the inner eye to see its path.

Where the fear has gone there will be nothing.

Only I will remain.'

Ted continued to look out of the window whilst reciting the Litany, and Posh sat in stunned silence when he had finished.

'That… that's errm, wow. That was stunning. Who said it? What does it mean?' he asked.

'Frank Herbert. It means different things to different people, lad. One day you should read the book, 'Dune', powerful book.' With that, Ted rose and opened the cabin door, slowly walking outside. Posh followed him, still running the Litany through his head. Outside, the sun shone and birds sang and the night before seemed like it was a million miles away. As they stood outside, Smiffy came up behind them, rubbing his eyes and scratching his head.

'Blimey, did it actually happen?' he asked, rhetorically. They all looked around and began seeing signs of the previous night's storm. Branches and twigs littered the ground, the odd bird's nest could be seen hanging upside down from a bush. But nothing seemed as bad as it had hours earlier.

'Come on,' said Ted, and made his way slowly towards the old mill. As they neared it, Posh and Smiffy began to see signs of massive destruction. On two or three occasions they had to climb over fallen branches, and off to the left, towards the river, there seemed to be gaps in the trees that weren't there previously. The old mill seemed unharmed, but they couldn't see where they'd put the tent.

'Wasn't it sort of there?' said Smiffy, pointing off to the right. Where he indicated they could see nothing but branches, and a couple of huge boughs that had succumbed to the rage of the storm. Then Ted moved forward and said 'There,' pointing at one of the boughs. And there, pinned beneath it, a small piece of maroon material peeped out from under the fallen limb. The same colour maroon as their tent. The significance was not lost on them, and after a little investigation they found their sleeping bags, pinned beneath the weight of the fallen limb.

'*Only I will remain,*' muttered Posh.

Smiffy said nothing, just stared intently at the sleeping bags, his mind spinning with the possibilities. He turned to Ted, but he was already moving away.

'Back home, now,' he said as he left, 'Parents'll be worried. Be careful as you go, lots of dead wood about, some might not know it yet. Keep an eye up.' With that he was gone through the trees and back to his cabin.

Smiffy and Posh looked at each other, in amongst the devastation, then nodded and made their way home, slowly. Glad not to be dead wood just yet.

PART THREE

Follow men's eyes
as they look to
the skies,
The shifting shafts
of shining
Weave the fabric
of their dreams

Chapter Twelve
Learning to Fly

limey. University!' Posh used the word like he was handling an unknown species of arachnid. 'When did you decide on that, mate?'

Smiffy shrugged and carried on walking towards the Mere. 'Dunno, really. I think it's been in my head for a few years now, like it was just the obvious move after school. Been thinking about everything, y'know, that I've seen since moving here. There's so bloody much and I know so little. I just wanna learn more. You know what I mean, mate; you're the same. This is amazing out here, but it's gradually being eroded, we're losing great chunks and nobody seems to be doing anything about it. Look at my house, five years ago that was fields and hedgerows and stuff, now look at it.'

Posh let his mate have his head. He'd heard this more and more over the past year or so, and as much as he totally agreed with Smiffy, he knew that what his mate was talking about doing was beyond him. He was sharp-witted, clever in an 'okay let's sort out a way to do this' sort of way, but he didn't have Smiffy's intellect, and their respective school results showed that. Smiffy wanted to save the world, but he wanted to save great lumps of it - now! Posh, on the other hand, would be happy to save that hedgehog from that combine harvester. Small steps, a little at a time.

This was the year of the Ashes, the excitement of which they'd caught by osmosis from their parents and most of the men in the village and surrounding areas. Quentin's dad, Peter, knew people who knew people, and had been able to get a clutch of tickets for the First Test at Lords, in a month's time, and the whole place was abuzz. A dozen of them were planning the trip up to London in a minibus, Posh and Smiffy included, as their exams would have just finished, and if the fervour and celebrations following the World Cup victory a couple of years ago were anything to go by, this could be one hell of a summer.

Thoughts of fishing had been far from their minds for the past couple of months as the exam season hove into view, but the previous couple of years had seen them grow ever more competent and confident. They'd managed to officially fish the section of river they'd previously poached, having joined the local angling society, and during the summer prior to the World Cup victory had journeyed there on several occasions, both of them eventually catching the barbel they so desperately craved. Although only half the size of the canal carp they'd caught, the fish had fought like demons, and had elicited great excitement in the boys. But after a few more sessions of roach and perch, and the odd chub, their patience began to wane and they both craved something larger.

As the summer holidays neared their conclusion, the two lads were desperate to fish somewhere different; maybe a lake, with carp. And the solution came to both of the boys, independently.

Smiffy was in the kitchen, reading a fishing magazine whilst finishing off some toast when there was a knock at the door. On opening it, he was greeted by Stan's smiling face.

'Morning, Quentin, how you doing? Is your dad at home?'

Smiffy shook his head whilst swallowing a particularly dry piece of toast. He coughed to clear his throat, then replied, 'Not at the moment, Mr. Peacock, he's taken mum to Salisbury, they'll probably be back in a couple of hours. Anything I can help with?'

'Well, I was wondering whether you'd like to go fishing for a day. Thought I'd ask your dad if it was okay, but it's down to you, really.'

Smiffy was taken aback by this offer, and stood in the doorway, mouth slightly agape. Stan laughed, then carried on. 'It'd have to be Sunday; I've got an invite from Jim Baines at Linton. Nobody fishing that day, and he asked if I fancied a little dabble. I asked if it'd be okay to bring someone along, and he was fine with that, so I thought I'd ask you.'

'What about Posh?' blurted Smiffy.

'Who?'

'Err, I mean Neil. Neil Becks. Would it be alright if he came along, 'cos we were trying to think of somewhere to fish other than the river, and that would be great.'

Stan had anticipated this possible line of enquiry and had already gained permission for all three of them, if required. 'Well, I don't see as that should be much of a problem. Have to square it with his dad, but I'm sure he'll be fine. Early start. It's light by six, so we want to be there by then. I'll pick you up at five, okay?'

Smiffy nodded, still a little dazed, then confirmed it. 'Yeah, fine. I'll get Posh to stay round here and we'll be ready when you get here. What about bait? And line, what line d'you reckon? Should we bring food and drink and that?'

Before Smiffy could launch full steam into a list of questions, Stan put up his hand. 'Whoa there, boy! Tell you what, I'll pop over and see your dad this afternoon, then me, you and Neil can sit over by the lake and discuss tactics. Okay?'

Smiffy nodded, and Stan turned and left. Just as he got to the gate, Smiffy called out 'Thanks Mr. Peacock.'

'No problem. And call me Quill.' With that he left, and Smiffy pondered that last one for a second before rushing back into the house and putting his shoes on. Then he was off, in search of his mate.

Posh was strolling through the woods towards the Mere when he heard his name called. On turning, he saw Ted walking between the trees towards him.

'Morning, young Becks. No fishing today?'

Posh carried on walking, with Ted beside him, and told him of their recent sessions on the river, and their need for something bigger.

'Bigger, eh. What for, boy? Glory or pride?' asked Ted, enigmatically.

Posh was seriously bemused by the question, and stopped to look at Ted.

'I don't know what you mean. Glory or pride? What does that mean?'

Ted smiled. 'Do you want to catch something bigger so that you can tell everyone how good you are? Or do you just want to keep it to yourself, knowing that you've done it?' Although not nearly as enigmatic as the previous, shorter question, Posh still had to think about it before answering.

'Well, yeah, of course I'll tell people if I catch something big, but then I'll also tell them if I catch nothing at all, so that's not glory, is it?'

Ted nodded, saying nothing.

'So, yeah, pride I suppose,' continued Posh. 'But happiness as well, I reckon. How happy would I be if I caught a carp over ten pounds? Man, I'd be over the moon!'

'What about young Quentin? What if he caught one and you didn't? Would you be proud of him, or jealous?' asked Ted, quietly but pointedly.

Posh didn't waiver in his response. 'I'd be well chuffed for him. Really. Yeah, course we have a laugh if one of us catches more, or bigger, than the other, but when it comes to the special fish, then it's different. It's like we've both caught it.' As he answered Ted's probing questions, he suddenly realised how true his answer was. It was nothing that had ever been voiced between them, but he knew that Smiffy would have answered just the same, and that made him proud.

Ted nodded again. 'Good. Good, young Neil. Hold onto that attitude through your life, it will hold you in good stead. Reckon I knows somewhere you lads can fish. Got some big'uns in there too, bigger'n ten pounds as well. I'll speak to my old mate Jim Baines, see if he can help us out.' With that, he patted Posh on the shoulder and turned to retrace his steps. 'I'll let you know,' he called over his shoulder. 'Next day or so, I'll let you know.'

As Posh emerged from the woods onto the banks of the Mere he spied a figure emerging from the East Woods. It was Smiffy and he was moving quickly. Posh couldn't wait to tell him of his conversation with Ted, but it seemed that Smiffy had important news of his own, and it took a couple of minutes before they were able to untangle what was actually happening.

'So, you're saying that Ted is going to talk to this guy, Jim Baines?' asked Smiffy, as a semblance of sanity prevailed. 'The same Jim Baines that Mr. Peacock has got

permission off to fish his lake.'

Posh nodded. 'Seems like that, don't it? I wonder if that means that we'll be able to fish there twice?' This last was almost an aside, but they both looked at each other and raised an eyebrow.

'Now that could be interesting,' agreed Smiffy. By now they had emerged onto the north bank and were walking past the snags. They'd spotted a few carp in there over the summer, but nothing of the size they'd witnessed a year or so earlier. Today, with a blanket of cloud above and a stiff southerly breeze, visibility was at a minimum and they dallied for only a short while before moving on.

A yard or so below the surface, large shapes hung in midwater. The summer had been kind to them; food plentiful and dangers minimal. They had become accustomed to the routes that the motor boats took around the lake, and avoided them for the bulk of the daylight hours, staying mainly in the deep margins of the north bank until sundown, when they felt happier to meander about in the open water. The new lake still held small, unexpected treasure troves of food; small hatches of mayfly and dragonfly that had been previously left fallow. The autumn winds and the drop in temperatures signalled not only the onset of the colder months, and with that the lack of food, but also a significant drop in the above-surface activities. This meant that the carp could utilise every square inch of the lakebed in search of any nourishment, safe in the knowledge that they would be unlikely to encounter dangers from above.

But, once again, prying eyes and plotting minds were abroad, bent on securing a place in history for themselves. There was always danger from above.

Stan and the two lads sat on a bench adjacent to the sailing club and the lake in front of it. The sun had disappeared, and with it had come a brisk wind that had just a hint of the chill that would follow in the ensuing months. A shiver momentarily ran up Stan's spine, and he stood up.

'Let's stroll round the lake, shall we?' he suggested. 'Bit chilly just sitting here.'

With that he strode off towards the West Woods, the two boys in tow. They hadn't mentioned Posh's conversation with Ted as yet; they were just going to wait to see what panned out on that score. Instead, they grilled Stan as to what to expect, and what they should take, and all the other questions that precede a much-anticipated fishing trip to a new lake. Stan's knowledge was sketchy, to say the least, having only fished there the once, but he was sure that even that rudimentary knowledge would be enough to bring them some success. So, after an intense interrogation during their circuit of the lake, he bade them farewell and would see them at five on Sunday morning, two days hence.

Their excitement was palpable, and they found sleep hard to come by on Saturday evening, especially as they were both in Smiffy's bedroom. The alarm barely made

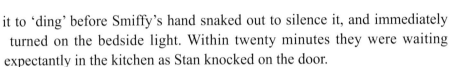

it to 'ding' before Smiffy's hand snaked out to silence it, and immediately turned on the bedside light. Within twenty minutes they were waiting expectantly in the kitchen as Stan knocked on the door.

'Ready to go then, boys?' he asked, unnecessarily. They both babbled inanely, then proceeded to load their gear into Stan's van. The half hour journey through the country lanes was surprisingly quiet, with just the odd question coming from one or the other of the boys, and a low hum coming from the radio. But one question amused him and them alike.

'So, why Quill then, Mr. Peacock?' asked Smiffy, innocently. Posh looked at him, frowning, before Stan replied.

'Peacock. Peacock quill, like the float.'

Smiffy was still perplexed. 'Peacock quill – never heard of it.' Posh snorted at the answer.

'Never heard of it? Bloody hell, Smiffy, you've been fishing for long enough now. It's a bloody float mate – peacock quill!'

'What, like a waggler you mean?'

Stan just smiled as the two lads went at it in the back. Then he interrupted. 'Have you got a float on today, Quentin?'

'Yeah, a waggler,' he replied, glaring at his mate.

'Right, you got a float rubber or is it through the eye?' he continued, ignoring the muttered curses from Neil, behind him.

'Float rubber,' came the reply.

'Okay, when we get to the lake I'll swap your waggler for a proper peacock quill. Bound to catch you one, that is.'

Smiffy just nodded, unsure how this might affect his fishing, but Stan assured him that all would be well.

He'd re-acquainted himself with the route yesterday, which was fortunate as, in the half-light of morning, it would have been easy to pass the turning that led, ultimately, to the lake. The car park was empty, as Jim had promised, and he shut the engine off and just sat for a few seconds, drinking in the silence. Then all was bustle as the boys opened the doors and let in the sounds of a late summer dawn. Waterfowl were the most vocal, as usual, but many of their smaller brethren could also be heard in the surrounding woods.

'Just through there, boys,' indicated Stan with an outstretched rod bag. 'Just grab a rod each for now, might be able to surprise one before they realise what's happening.'

Smiffy and Posh did as they were told, although this had always been part of the plan so their rods and reels were already set up, just awaiting a bait.

Ever so stealthily, they crept through the trees that surrounded the small lake and were soon by its side. A layer of mist hung over its surface, and ripples could be seen below that shroud, created by coot and moorhen.

Splash!

And maybe something below, as well.

Stan motioned them to stand by a large willow, hidden by it from the lake.

'Okay,' he said, in hushed tones, 'let's try sweetcorn at first. Reckon there's a good chance of nicking one out of the margins if we're careful. Quentin, bring your rod over here.' Smiffy offered the rod, and Stan slipped the waggler out and replaced it with a fine, red-tipped peacock quill. He removed one of the BB shot, then handed the rod back to Smiffy.

'There you go, it looks like it's set just over depth, so that should be fine. Just flick it past where you want to fish and gradually tweak it back until just the tip is showing. Look out for…'

'Lift bites,' interjected Smiffy whilst inspecting the new float. 'Yeah, I know.'

'Okay, quietly now. Good luck, see you soon.' Stan stayed by the tree and watched as the boys crept off to his right. He'd give it ten minutes or so before he cast out, just in case one of them got lucky.

The day was gradually brightening, but it was still quite difficult to discern anything in the murk of the woodland. Posh crept forward, ahead of his mate, his eyes flitting from the ground in front of him to the lake's surface, in search of traps or bubbles. After a minute or so he stopped suddenly, Smiffy almost walking into the back of him. Posh pointed at the lake and there, a few yards out, a single bubble rose to the surface, to join half a dozen others that had made the journey a little earlier. Then two more broke the film, a foot to the right, joined immediately by another. Stan had told them to look out for this sort of sign, and here it was, right in front of them. They'd slid three grains of corn onto their hooks, and now was the time to deploy them. Posh nodded, indicating to Smiffy that he should have first cast.

'No mate,' whispered Smiffy, in reply, 'you saw 'em. You have a go.'

Posh shook his head. 'The quill, Luke, use the power of the quill!' He giggled a little at that, then moved back from the bankside and indicated again that Smiffy should cast. The bubbles were still emerging; small, needle bubbles that indicated without question that something was feeding beneath. Smiffy thought of declining again but, truth be told, he couldn't wait to cast at them. He flicked open the bale arm, swung the float back and forth a little, to get the rhythm, then let it sail gracefully out into the lake. It landed with a 'plop' that sounded as loud as the splash from earlier, but the bubbles still rose so he carefully inched it back until the merest redness was visible. As he lay his rod down, the tip rose a little, exposing an inch of red and he thought for a moment that it was a lift bite. But no, it was just the float settling, and now settled, all was still. The odd bubble still broke the surface no more than a foot from the float, and the tension began to rise.

The red tip became the focus of all attention, seeming to glow like a beacon in the half-light. Then it was gone. No preamble, no lift, just gone.

Smiffy had clicked over the bale arm after casting so the next thing to move was the rod as it slid across the damp grass, before Smiffy regained his senses and decided that picking it up might be a good idea!

The tip was wrenched over and the line was pulled, grudgingly, from the reel. It fizzed across the surface like a cheese wire, leaving a stream of bubbles in its wake, and Smiffy suddenly realised that he had **never** hooked anything like this before. From afar, Stan had been keeping an eye on proceedings, but even he was surprised at the speed that this had all happened. Soon standing behind Smiffy, he looked at the rod, listened to the clutch, and was happy that all was well. Posh looked at him and gave a sort of grimace that spoke a thousand words, most of which Stan had heard or thought a thousand times previously. In essence it came down to, 'I hope he doesn't lose it.'

The fish took thirty or forty yards of line, but, like the previous one that Stan had hooked here, that seemed to drain its strength, and pretty soon Smiffy was starting to regain line. The fish moved slowly from left to right, but there were no snags to worry about, so it was a case of taking his time and letting the fish tire itself out. Soon, the telltale vortices could be seen just a few yards out, and Stan lowered the net carefully into the lake. A short burst of strength nearly caught Smiffy out, but the clutch gave up the line just in time and the fish rolled on the surface, five yards out, mouth gulping air and ready to submit. Stan slid out the net, and a bar of gold slid into it, and with it came the whoops and hollers of two elated young anglers.

'Well done, mate. Well done,' said Posh whilst slapping his mate on the back and peering into the net at the same time. Smiffy rotated his aching shoulder and realised that this was a pain he relished. He, too, peered expectantly into the net, and Stan handed him the handle whilst he went back to the car for the unhooking mat, scales and camera.

On his return, the two of them were cooing and aahing as if viewing a newborn baby for the first time.

'Well done, Quentin, that looks like a lovely common, mate.' He lay the wet mat down, then broke down the net and carried the fish to the waiting mat. As he peeled back the mesh, the common glowed at them in the ever-brightening day and Smiffy's eyes lit up.

'Ohh, that's a nice one,' said Stan. 'Reckon that's close to twenty, lad.'

Smiffy just continued to gawp, and it was left to Posh to assist Stan with the weighing, 'Eighteen… Eighteen twelve. Well done, mate, that's a bloody whacker. The power of the quill!'

said Posh, whilst shaking his mate's hand. Smiffy continued to stare gormlessly, but managed to wear a smile when the photos were taken.

'Yeah, the power of the quill! Thanks Quill, I doubt if I'll ever use another float,' he said, after seeing the fish swim away.

'Trust me, Quentin, you won't – ever,' replied Stan, certain of the fact.

Now, we just need to get one for Neil, he thought.

The disturbance had been enough to make the lake look less than inviting now, but he remembered his last trip and how he'd managed one right at the end of the day, so they would persevere.

The morning sped by, with all three of them carefully stalking the margins, but apart from a couple of dark, dark tench to Stan and Posh, they had little to get excited about. They lunched by the big willow, in the early afternoon, and whilst there, Posh stood up and pointed across to the far side of the lake. They'd walked past the reedy corner over there on three or four occasions during the morning, but none of them had been drawn to cast a bait in the area. Now, however, Posh was being drawn towards it.

'I fancy over there,' he declared. 'Don't know why, but I just keep looking over there, like I'm being told to fish there.'

Smiffy snorted. 'Woooo! Spooky,' he wailed, ghost-like, but his mate took no notice, just finished his sandwich and picked up his rod and bait and was gone.

There was nowhere to sit, as such. The reeds were fairly tall and behind them was an oak tree, so it meant just leaning against the tree whilst letting the rod settle onto the reeds. Posh sat for a while just looking, rod leant against the tree. There were no obvious signs, but it just looked like an area that should produce fish. He flicked out a few grains of corn and watched them disappear slowly into the lake. A few more followed minutes later, and by the time he'd decided to cast his float out, three or four dozen grains had preceded it.

The first cast saw the quill tip disappear from view, indicating a slightly deeper area than he'd previously fished, and that gave him a little more confidence. He moved the float up six inches, and once again it disappeared. A further six-inch increment saw the tip rise an inch or two above the surface, but by carefully lowering the rod onto the reeds, and inching the reel handle round, he was left with just half an inch of red tip to watch.

The wind was coming over his shoulder, so the water a couple of yards out was undisturbed, and his float motionless. After ten minutes he heard a commotion from the opposite bank, and saw Stan's rod bent over, the distant squeal of a clutch indicating something more than a tench on the end. He waited until it was netted, then reeled in his float and went round to have a look. On his arrival, the fish was on the mat, and what a fish. Huge scales seemed to have been thrown randomly across its chestnut brown flanks, colours the like of which neither he or Smiffy had ever witnessed before.

'That's incredible, Quill,' he said, stating the bloody obvious. The fish weighed twenty-four pounds and was the largest that either of them had ever seen, and they really, really wanted one themselves. After a celebratory cup of tea, Posh was back to his reedy lair, his float settling once again to its task.

The afternoon moved along lazily, but no one was bored. They had to be away by seven thirty, so they made the most of the time they had. Smiffy had found a small shoal of tench feeding near some dying lily pads, and had managed to snare two of them. He was more than content with his day's angling, but Posh was unfulfilled. He began questioning his choice of swim. He'd seen no sign of fish in the vicinity, and was beginning to feel that he should move, but had no idea to where. As these thoughts were scudding across his brain like the white clouds above, Stan crept in behind him and rested against the trunk of the oak. He said nothing for a short while, just sat there, surveying the lake in front of Posh.

'How deep?' he whispered. Posh extended his arm above the ground to indicate about five feet. Stan nodded. 'What about there, to the left by those mares tails?' Posh looked at the three or four thin reeds, then shook his head.

'Watch them,' suggested Stan.

Over the next few minutes, Posh didn't take his eyes off of them and, sure enough, on two or three occasions they moved as if twanged like a guitar string.

'What do you think?' he asked quietly. Stan shrugged.

'Dunno,' he replied,' but it's something, that's for sure.'

The mare's tails were a couple of yards to the left of the float, and in slightly shallower water, so Posh adjusted the float before flicking it beyond them and coaxing it back, watching it come to rest a few inches from one of the stems. He flicked out half a dozen grains of corn, then leant back against the rough bark of the oak, his back starting to ache a little from the awkward position he was in.

They said nothing, just sat and watched, and for ten minutes the only movement was from one or other of the reed stems, almost imperceptible at times, and leading Stan to think that they might just be small fish, or fry. Then, totally unannounced, a carp's head and gills slid out of the water a yard to the left of the float, and slid back just as lazily. The waves rocked the float and the sight shocked the watchers.

'Bloody hell!' said Stan, beating Posh to the same thought by a second. The float had lifted a little in the waves, and was now sitting at a rakish angle. Posh thought about settling it back down, but was afraid to move for fear of spooking the fish. He just sat and stared, willing the float to right itself.

No more than a minute passed before his wish was answered, but the moment of 'rakish' to 'right' was lost in a blur of thrashing reeds

and screaming clutch. Once again, a stream of bubbles showed the escape route as the fish tore off towards the far bank, and once again Stan made sure that all was fine with rod and clutch before leaving it to the angler. This fish battled longer and harder than both before it, and Stan wondered whether one of the mythical thirties had been hooked. Ten minutes later, with Posh's scream echoing across the pool, and scaring the neighbouring wildlife, he could see that although it wasn't even close to that size, it was still an incredible looking mirror, all scales and burnished flanks. Smiffy had been on hand as the fish had gone into the net, and was almost as vocal as his friend, and he now helped with the weighing, agreeing on a weight of just over twenty-one pounds – a mirror carp of stunning beauty and a captor lost for words – what a great photo that made.

The day ended with one more small double for Stan, and the trip home was so different to the one going as to be from another universe. The talk was of 'big' and 'huge' and 'stunning' and 'scales like saucers', and a thousand other clichés, but Stan knew that these were also like stepping-stones across a particularly turbulent river. They were slippery, and some were small and deceptively unstable, but if you were bold enough to attempt the crossing, the rewards on the far side would be wondrous.

Small steps, a little at a time.

Chapter Thirteen
A Pillow of Winds

As the sun sank lower in the sky, the wind lessened, and soon the lake was flat calm. Stan stood by his rods and surveyed the lake for any sign of feeding carp. Scanning to the right he caught sight of a large bird, silhouetted against the sky, lazily moving toward him and, as it passed just yards from him, he saw the unmistakable outline of a barn owl, a small rodent clutched in one of its talons.

Stan ran to the back of the swim to watch the hunter continue its silent journey for a further three or four hundred yards to a copse on the far side of the field. With that, contented, Stan returned to his swim. Then he thought about it. That wouldn't be the only prey it would seek tonight so, grabbing his camera, he hurried to the back of the swim, just in time to see the ghostly predator silently glide by, not ten yards distant.

Click! Click! Click!

Stan tried desperately to capture the moment on camera, but later perusal would show that his effort was blurred and unsuccessful. No matter, what a sight! If no carp were forthcoming, Stan had still had a session to remember. Bed was beckoning and the experience of that memorable encounter was still with him as he drifted away.

The woods behind him were a cacophony of sound; blackbirds, finches, tits – great and blue – all were joined in a joyous awakening, all trying to outdo each other in the dawn chorus stakes. Stan lay on his bedchair, convinced that it must be too early to be awake but, despite his best efforts, further sleep was beyond him and, as he tried to identify one bird from another, he knew that there was only one sure answer – the kettle must go on.

As he slowly rose, a wren was startled from its reedy hiding place, and complained stridently as it flitted to an adjacent perch. 'Sorry, Jenny,' muttered Stan, 'but tea's tea and that's that.' With that, he flicked the lighter and held it to the gas, flinching involuntarily as it caught. How many bloody times? he thought.

As the kettle slowly heated, he rubbed an eye with the back of his hand and gazed across the mist-shrouded lake. His lines hung limply from the rod tips, just as they'd done six hours previously before he'd succumbed to sleep. He could just see the lily pads, twenty yards away, next to which lay his baited hook and a dozen or so scattered baits. Small ripples emanated from one of the pads, the rings slowly expanding before gradually disappearing. Roach? Tench? Carp, even?

The steaming kettle demanded his attention, leaving such weighty questions unanswered, and he dropped a bag in the cup before scalding and drowning it.

'Beep!'

He looked at the buzzer, the indicator, the rod tip, the line as it entered the water. And then watched as the line lifted. And lifted. And, suddenly, all was a blur.

'Beeeep!'

Indicator 'slam' into rod. Rod tip dragged downwards. Clutch spinning and spilling line.

Hot, weak tea soaking into dew-wet grass. Dew-wet grass soaking into socks as he leapt up to grab the rod in an attempt to steer the fish away from the pads as quickly as possible.

The moments of impasse were minimal, which indicated to Stan that this was no monster, and as the line cut away to the left, away from the pads, he relaxed a little and tightened the clutch a tad. Then all went slack.

Bugger!

Although he knew it was nothing massive, it was still stomach turning when the tension was suddenly gone. And how strange it is that the certainty of moments earlier, that this was 'just a small one', is now replaced with the possibility that it could have been one of the biggies, yet to wake up properly. Oh, the torture.

For the next hour or so the torture was increased as he ran things through his head. What had he done wrong? Should he have tightened the clutch so soon? And on, and on. But the fact was, it happened. We all know that. We never land every one, as much as we'd like to; that's why a fight with a carp (or any other fish, for that matter) is never over until it's over. And we know that, don't we? So why torture ourselves, for God's sake? Who knows, but Stan had to suffer his full hour's worth of self-flagellation before he was ready to go at it again.

Fortunately, an hour later, the same rod produced a similar fight, resulting in a fourteen-pound mirror slipping into the net. No monster, for sure, but seeming much larger than if he'd not lost the previous one – illogical, but true.

It was the beginning of another season, a year since he'd joined the club, and this was an encouraging start. Last year had proved more difficult than anticipated, but that was because he'd not made use of Norman's knowledge. When the head bailiff had told him that 'they don't get caught', he'd assumed that was because the majority of the other anglers fishing on the Hatch were a bunch of Muppets. For the most part, that had proved to be true, but by mid-August, with a couple of low doubles to show for his efforts, he'd been Chief Muppet!

It wasn't a huge lake, the fish were obviously in there because he'd seen them in the close season – some good 'uns as well – but when the starting gun sounded they'd just melted away. The water was perpetually coloured, so tree-top viewing tended to be pointless, and the carp showed themselves so rarely that it was as if they had a tunnel out of the lake, and were spending the summer in some secluded pool, hidden from prying eyes.

But, then, one of the Muppets would hook something large and unstoppable, inevitably losing it, and Stan would analyse the whole event. Where from? What bait? What rig? What time? What weather conditions? The answers were never the same, and it seemed that the carp, just once in awhile, would drop their guard and get careless. The end of August, that first year, saw a change in his fortunes, however.

It was the Bank Holiday weekend. Jean was off to see her mother, who lived in Cornwall, and Stan had promised to join her on Sunday morning, driving straight from the lake. He'd managed to get away from work by Friday lunchtime and was pleasantly surprised to find only one car in the rustic car park on his arrival at the lake. He recognised the car, so went round to have a chat with Bill, its owner.

Bill had been a member for a dozen years, and was one of the few who didn't deserve the epithet 'Muppet'. In his early sixties now, he'd fished for most of his life and had maintained a love of all forms of the sport, being just as happy crusting for summer rudd as he would dead-baiting for winter pike.

Bill knew of the futility of targeting the carp on the Hatch, so concentrated his efforts on the fine tench and bream the lake also held. But he was, nonetheless, fully aware of the larger denizens' activities, and had been instrumental in both of Stan's captures earlier that season.

'Alright, Bill, how's it going?' asked Stan quietly, as he crept into the back of Bill's swim. He could see the orange tip of a float next to a lily pad, ten yards distant, so didn't want to disturb him too much.

'Stan. How you doing?' he replied. 'Going okay, son. Had a couple of nice tench this morning, both over six, I'd say. Bit quiet now so I've fined it down a bit, see if I can't bag a couple of them crucians.'

The crucian carp in the lake were as elusive as their larger cousins; their numbers having dwindled over the years to leave just a couple of dozen in there, but Stan knew that Bill would be the man to outwit one, if anybody could.

'Cup of tea, Stan?' he offered.

'No, you're alright, Bill. Wanna get myself set up before this cloud gets any thicker.' The day had started bright, but the forecast was for intermittent showers over the next twenty-four hours, which was the main reason that Stan had made the effort to go. The previous month had seen little change in the weather, with a stubborn, slow moving high-pressure system over southern England seeing to that. But now things were about to change, with low pressure, southwesterly winds and rain – what more could a carp angler ask for?

'Seen anything of interest then, Bill?' he asked, coming straight to the point. Bill smiled and nodded.

'Well, boy, over by the pines this morning, just the other side of the pads, two big fish left the water. Could have been the same fish twice, couldn't tell, but I went and had a look. Bubbles about ten yards out, little bits of movement, but nothing since.'

Stan absorbed the information and thought it through. That bank was one of his main choices, as the wind would now blow straight into it, and although it was probably only one fish, his close season sightings had shown that the larger fish tended to congregate in groups of five or six.

'Cheers, Bill. That ought to be worth a look,' he said. 'Good luck, mate. I'll let you know if it was one fish or two, later.' With that he turned and left, Bill chuckling behind him.

By early evening he was settled in. He'd seen no sign of fish, but that was par for the course. Any sightings tended to be in the early morning, like Bill's, the only other evidence of a big carp in the vicinity being in the middle of the night, a resounding crash betraying their presence, but invariably unrepeated. The wind had picked up by now, so much so that Stan had set his bivvy up at right angles to the lake and behind one of the large pines. The water was lapping loudly at the bank in front and conditions looked their most favourable for ages. But was that true for here? He had little to go on to form an idea of what constituted 'ideal conditions' for the Hatch, but this was his first session on there in conditions that most would have described as 'ideal'.

All three baits were no more than ten yards from the bank; one being tiger nuts whilst the other two were boilies. It had taken him little time, on his first session, to realise that three-ounce, fixed leads were not the way forward on such a silty lake, so all three rods had light, running leads with nylon hooklinks. The conditions, he thought, dictated a bit more bait than of late, so about a hundred and fifty boilies and a few handfuls of nuts had been scattered around the swim. Now it was back to waiting. The rains came after midnight, stopping an hour later, and Stan pulled on a sweatshirt as the temperature dropped a little. Another shower a few hours later stirred him, but he quickly returned to sleep. A grey dawn did nothing to rouse him; the sun hidden behind a wall of thin clouds.

When the run came it was like an electric shock, dragging Stan from the deepest of sleeps like someone having cardiac paddles attached to their chest to restart their heart.

The right hand alarm was screaming, the spool spinning so fast that a fine mist enveloped the reel. Still technically asleep, Stan's 'carp angler' went into autopilot and played the fish for the first minute or so until Stan, himself, was able to take over. The power of the carp was incredible, and Stan realised that it had been a few years since he'd hooked something like this.

His feet were wet, his mouth was dry and the clutch was still ticking as the carp continued its quest for freedom. He had no idea of the time, nor how long he had been playing the fish, but as he gained control he realised how much he had missed this sort of battle. Soon, there was a sub-surface flat spot as the fish tired. Then it was closer and the net was lowered into the margins. The mouth came up, gulping, the hooklink protruding from it. And then it was in the net and Stan whooped with delight.

Securing the net in the margins, he set about preparing everything.

Unhooking mat. Sling and scales. Tripod. Camera.

Shoes and trousers first, though. Then, as he strained to lift the net with both hands, he knew that it would be close to thirty pounds. But when he laid the carp on the mat and peeled back the mesh, that didn't matter at all.

'Oh my God!' he whispered. 'Oh. My. God.'

There before him lay the most stunningly beautiful carp he'd ever seen. The colours were impossible; dark reds, light reds, a dozen different shades of brown, and an all over sheen of gold. The scale pattern was almost a caricature of everyone's idea of the perfect carp – huge, linear scales ran the length of the body on both sides, with a starburst scattering by the tail, and a perfect row along the back, the length of the dorsal fin. If this wasn't a Leney, then nothing was.

The carp flipped, half heartedly, and broke the trance. Stan didn't even know if he wanted to weigh it, but he did so anyway and it seemed even more perfect that it was just a few ounces below thirty pounds rather than above.

But, a self-take photo of a fish like this? He thought not. He thought about calling Norman, then decided better of it. Who else was on the lake? Carefully sacking the fish in the margins, he walked through the damp grass until he came across a familiar figure. Bill was beneath his brolly, sheltering from the rain whilst concentrating on his float once more. That would do fine.

'Morning, Bill. Any good, mate?' he began.

That capture seemed to be the key to unlocking the lake's secrets, and in the next couple of months, up to the end of October, Stan landed a further half a dozen carp. All were wonderful examples of the Leney strain, with four of them in excess of twenty-five pounds although none exceeding that first, stunning carp. But then, as suddenly as it had started, it stopped, and for the next four months, to the end of the season, he blanked mercilessly. To be fair, from the turn of the year he only ventured to the lake on four or five occasions, and for the most part the weather had been cold and bleak. The last session of the season had seen him eventually break his duck when he landed a small common on the last night. Small, maybe, but that had been enough to spur him on for the new season, as had a couple of close season sorties, when he'd once again seen some much larger carp. But how to catch them?

Of the nine carp he'd caught the previous year, four had fallen to tiger nuts, two of them over twenty-five pounds. Was that a clue? Maybe not, because that also meant that five had fallen to boilies. The lake was rich with natural food and it seemed that a seasonal break in the food chain had caused the carp to search for other forms of nourishment. So, what then, only fish September and October? That sounded silly but it could also be worth considering. Maybe not 'only', but concentrate his efforts in those months and see what transpired. But what about the change in weather conditions, maybe that was significant as well? Oh, bloody hell, he could go on and on. In the end, it was carp fishing and ever was it thus.

One thing that bugged him was the occasional loss of something decent by one of the float or pleasure anglers. They could be just sprightly mid-doubles, of which there were a few, but Bill had lost a fish last summer that, he said, was the biggest thing he'd ever hooked. Stan had every faith in Bill, although as his personal best was a little under thirty pounds, he had to take Bill's point of reference into account. Still, it was something, and further investigation revealed that the few lost carp had all been hooked on sweetcorn. Food for thought, for sure, but also food for tench and bream. Ah, the agony of possible ecstasy.

That evening the barn owl returned but was never close enough to warrant an attempted photo. Instead, Stan just revelled in its silent beauty. By the time that it was too dark to see, the ghostly assassin had provided its family with half a dozen unfortunate rodents to dine on, and would no doubt continue to do so throughout the night.

It was the end of June, Stan's second session, and the failure and success of the morning was a distant memory. He'd tried a boilie/sweetcorn combination on one rod, and that had produced a succession of bream, and one fine tench, but no carp, and he had been loath to continue with that approach through the night. He didn't mind being awoken by a carp in the early hours, but not a string of snotty bloody bream.

The pads once again seemed the obvious spot for his two hookbaits, both boilies, but the third was to be a bit of an experiment.

The right hand margin was bland. No lilies or reeds, just a grassy bank that led straight to the water's edge. The left hand margin was dark and deep, beneath overhanging trees, but he'd seen no sign of fish there, ever. On his last visit to the lake he'd sprinkled a few handfuls of tiger nuts along the lawn bank, and so again yesterday and today, so now seemed just about the right time for his plan. Carefully creeping along the bank for fifteen yards, he lowered feet from the bank, in a similar depth of water. Then, slowly walking back to his swim, he paid out the line from the spool so that everything was slack, finally attaching a small backlead to the line and pinning the whole thing to the lakebed. When an alarm screamed in the dark, a few hours later, he was convinced it was going to be that rod, but he was mistaken. The middle rod, cast next to the pads, was bent round to the left and line was hissing through the rings. The fish was intent on making the heart of the pads, and the impasse lasted much longer than the previous morning's. Gradually, however, the pressure began to tell, and, very slowly, the rod tip eased upwards. Once away from the pads, the fish immediately surged towards the left hand margin, and Stan had to act quickly, dropping his rod tip so as to avoid the overhanging branches. He could hear the fish wallowing beneath the canopy, and pushed the rod tip even lower lest the line caught in one of the grasping limbs. But, once again, the pressure told, and Stan could see faint ripples a mere two yards from the bank. The net was in the water, but the night was so black that he missed twice before eventually bullying the carp into the net. His arm ached like buggery, but it was a good ache because he knew that there was something of substance in the bottom of the net.

When he attempted to lift it from the lake, that thought was confirmed and he carefully walked the dripping prize to the waiting mat. Flicking on his head torch, he peered down to see what the parting of the net would reveal, and it revealed a thousand golden scales. Not a common, but a beautiful fully scaled mirror of handsome proportions. Oh, deep, deep, joy! There was no way that he was using a self-timer for a fish like this, so he set about wetting a carp sack, then zeroing his scales before putting the carp in the sack.

Thirty-five pounds – deep joy, indeed.

'Bloody hell, I didn't think they were that big in here,' he said to himself.

With the carp safely sacked and secured in the margin, Stan sat back and put the kettle on. '3.04' read his clock – what a way to start the day!

He had every intention of staying up for the rising sun, but by the time he was draining the last of the tea, his eyelids were heavy and he lay his head back down 'just for five minutes'.

The sun had been risen for an hour or so when he next opened his eyes, and it took him a few seconds to come round. Had he heard an alarm? He looked at the rods, there were two of them. That was right because he hadn't bothered to recast the rod that had produced the fish. Then he looked again. There were two rod butts but only one rod tip. The buzzing noise that he'd assumed was a host of insects was not. It was the right hand reel, spinning furiously in an attempt to keep up with the carp that had wrenched the rod from the alarm and had then torn off up the lake. With Stan's hook in its mouth.

Eventually working this out, Stan gingerly lifted the rod, which hooped round dramatically, and he carefully put his finger on the still spinning spool in an attempt to slow the fish. But the fish was not for slowing, and just kept heading up the lake, towards the Boathouse Bay. Something had to be done, and soon, so there was nothing for it but to clamp his hand over the spool and hope for the best. The 15lb line was singing under the sudden pressure and Stan watched the rod tip bend ever further, expecting a 'crack!' of carbon or nylon at any moment. Instead, there was a 'crash!' as the fish rolled on the surface, sixty yards away, then kited off to the left and out into the main part of the lake. As is often the way with these things, that initial burst of speed seemed to take its toll on the fish and it soon began wallowing and slowly kiting, shaking its head all the while. Nevertheless, it was still a further ten minutes before Stan was able to ease the carp over the net cord and into the net.

That glorious ache was with him again, and he felt vindicated with his tiger nut plan. Another glorious mirror soon lay on the mat, this one with fewer scales than the first, but equally as stunning in its beauty. The battle had not gone unnoticed, and one of the older members, having just arrived for a morning's tench fishing, came round to see what had occurred.

'Blimey, that's huge!' he exclaimed. 'I saw you playing it, when it rolled I thought it was a bloody dolphin!'

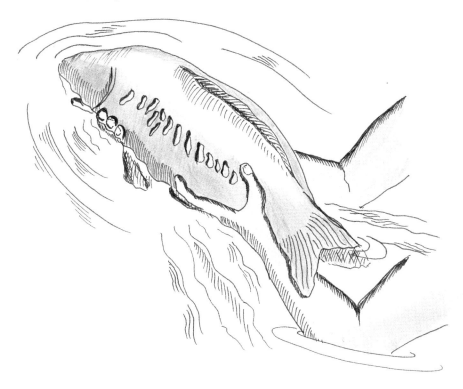

Stan laughed, then hoisted the weigh sling onto the scales. He held the dial for the other guy to read, and had little doubt that his reading of 'bloody hell, thirty two pounds eight ounces!' was correct.

'What you like with a camera, mate?' asked Stan.

'Yeah, alright. What you got? Replied the guy.

'Canon EOS. You used one before?'

The guy laughed and said, 'Yeah, once or twice,' before taking the proffered camera. Stan just had to trust him, and readied the fish whilst the guy inspected the camera, and played with a few settings.

'Just do it on Auto,' requested Stan.

The guy smiled again and said, 'Don't worry mate, just concentrate on the fish.' He then clicked away and oohed and aahed as Stan posed with the fish before slipping it back into the lake.

'Well done, mate,' said the guy, 'lovely fish.'

'Don't go, mate, there's more,' said Stan, who then went and extracted the sack with the fish from earlier.

The early morning sun painted the carp in glorious colours and both captors were speechless for a few moments.

'****ing hell!' said the cameraman, and that seemed to sum everything up nicely. Once the photos had been taken, the guy handed back the camera and shook Stan's hand.

'Mark,' he said, by way of introduction. 'Me mates call me 'The Canon'. Photos should be fine.' With that he left and returned to his float rods, in search of tench. Stan slowly packed away, slightly stunned by the events of the previous few hours. He'd cracked it, or so he assumed, but whether he had or not would become apparent over the next few months. For now, he was on cloud nine and he couldn't wait to let the lads know, Rhodie first. He just hoped that the photos would be okay. 'The Canon', that was a strange name.

The photos proved to be 'fine', so fine, in fact, that they adorned a wall at home for many years.

Chapter Fourteen
Fearless

Ted sat quietly, his back against a tree. The night was black, the new moon phase shedding no light whatsoever, but above him the curtain of night was pinpricked by a million stars.

He loved his time on watch, this time on watch. The middle of nowhere, the middle of nothing. Barely a sound. The distant tinkle of a small stream running across stone and scree, the lullaby accompaniment to his hours alone.

And no foe. For miles, thousands of miles. Another continent away.

A twig broke off to his left and he focused his eyes, now accustomed to the lack of light, and stared at a creeping figure moving towards him. Another twig cracked, closer this time, and he smiled.

'Clumsy,' he declared quietly,

'Jesus!' exclaimed Stan, the voice seeming to emanate next to his head and nearly giving him a heart attack.

'Maybe next time,' continued Ted.

'Bloody hell, Ted, my heart's going like a bloody steam train. Why'd you have to be so bloody… well, bloody quiet?'

'Ain't me that's quiet, young Stan, it's you that's loud.'

Stan stared in the direction of the voice and could just make out an outline of something next to the tree. He stood for a few more seconds before moving forward a little, hand outstretched, until he found a tree to lower himself next to.

'How long you been here, Ted? Thought I was going to be early.'

'You are, boy, just not early enough,' said Ted quietly. He stared out into the blackness and said no more.

Stan's heart rate soon returned to normal and he, too, sat quietly, drinking in the peace. His eyes were also accustomed to the dark, by now, but there was little to discern in the distance, across the lake, just a faint outline of trees on the horizon. This would be a bugger of a night to fish on, wouldn't be able to see a fish to net it unless it was under your rod tip. Nice to try though.

As if to affirm his thoughts, a huge splash rent the silence and caused a couple of coots to complain sleepily.

'Shit!' he whispered. 'That sounded like a good'un.'

Ted nodded, but said nothing. They were there, once more, to repel boarders.

A few months earlier, Stan had been strolling round the lake when he'd bumped into someone he didn't recognise.

'Morning mate, are you lost?' he'd asked, politely.

The guy looked at him blankly, before replying.

'No mate, just walking.'

Stan was immediately on edge; something about the guy's demeanour rankled, so he pushed on.

'No, what I meant was, you must be lost because this is private land. No trespassers, that sort of thing.'

The 'rambler' smiled at him, then from his back pocket produced an Ordnance Survey map. Unfolding it once, he indicated with his finger, 'Bridle path, mate. Public right of way – just exercising my legs, and my rights.'

The smile was becoming sickly and annoying, and Stan was not happy. 'What year is that map, 'cos it ain't no bridle path now?'

The map had already been folded and slid into the back pocket. 'Dunno mate, but that's what it says an' that's good enough for me.' With that, the guy carried on walking towards Sutton Woods, past the East Woods, and Stan stood and watched him go, quietly seething inside. They'd had no walkers down here for a couple of years, and the only horses that had been ridden past, belonged to neighbours or occupants. Something wasn't right.

The guy was definitely not your normal rambler-type and Stan smelt a rat.

Back at the office, he pored over existing maps and by-laws, and found that the public right of way was still in existence, it just wasn't used by many, if any, people. Oh well, maybe the guy had just rubbed him up the wrong way, no point dwelling on it. So, The Orchards had a bit of a plumbing problem, better go and get that sorted out, didn't want to upset Peter in any way.

'Yeah, got a bit of a tug, but he's gone now. Probably won't get away with leaving the footpath if he's watching, but I can see enough from here. Yeah, looks just like Jake said - lovely. No, no sign of any at the moment, but the cloud's starting to break, sun'll be out soon. Might see some then. Yeah, okay. Talk later.'

With that the guy clicked 'END CALL' and put his phone back in his pocket. Unwittingly, he was standing in exactly the spot that Buzz had parked his car, a few years earlier, prior to capturing the 48. The summer sun was trying to break through the cloud cover, but Dave knew that he had to get close to the lake if he was going to be able to see anything. Retracing his steps, he walked back past the East Woods, and once convinced that he was hidden from view, walked into them and towards the lake. From the footpath to the lake was about a hundred yards, and he crept quietly and carefully through the dappled grass, keeping one or another tree between him and the lake, until he was no more than ten yards away. Then, he edged himself as close as possible, his back to a tree trunk to hide his silhouette, his camo jacket and trousers hopefully blending in to make him look like a real tree. A southerly breeze was blowing, so the water in front was lapping lazily against the bank. The reeds growth was gaining momentum, and would soon form a considerable barrier along this bank of the lake. The sun was behind him at the moment so he was happy to remove his binoculars from his inside pocket and survey the lake, knowing that reflection from the lenses would be minimal. At this hour, on a midweek morning, there were no sailors on the water, although he could see a little activity near the boathouse; just the general preparations for the day ahead. He scanned right and stopped as his eyes picked out the snaggy corner of the old lake. Little to see from this distance, and so open to view from the houses that it was pointless thinking about. The traps would need to be set further away from prying eyes.

Scanning back to his left he peered into the very far corner, and could just make out the odd lily leaf flipping up on the surface. The woods on that west bank came very close to the water's edge, and the plan that they'd begun to hatch whilst looking at the map was now beginning to take some form. Okay, time to be bold.

With that, he stashed his binoculars, then left the woods and headed south, towards Sutton Woods. He carried on around the lake, nonchalantly looking at plants and trees, and let his meandering course take him all along the south bank towards the far lily bed. Nobody challenged him, which he found surprising, and when he reached the pads he was able to melt into the woods and peer out over the water. The pads covered about ten square yards and looked very inviting. There was cover enough that two people could safely remain hidden but still use a couple of rods each, but that was many months ahead. This plan, unlike Jake and Ken's, would be meticulous, not just a case of doing a bit of baiting and turning up one night to see if they could bag one.

But now, the next bit was crucial. He continued on his circuit of the lake and was soon strolling casually towards the boathouse. As he thought, there were no sailors about as yet, but just a few young guys who obviously worked in the boathouse and kept everything shipshape.

'Morning,' he said to one of the guys, who was in the throes of doing something with a whole load of rope.

'Morning,' came the reply. 'You sailing this morning?'

Dave laughed, 'No, not me, I'm afraid. I prefer to see the water from the land, not vice versa. My brother's the sailor, bloody loves it, he does. Got a boat down at Lymington. Loves going to the Isle of Wight when he can.'

The other guy nodded whilst looping the rope, 'Nice. What boat's he got?'

'Blimey, not sure. A Westerly, would that be right?'

The guy nodded, 'Yeah, nice boat. Speedy on the Solent I would think.'

Dave stood with his back to the boathouse, looking across the water. 'What's the deal here? Is it private, or do they have outside members?'

The guy had stowed the rope and was wiping his hands on a small cloth. 'Well, it started out private, a couple of years ago, just for the residents of the new houses. But so few of them actually did much sailing that they opened it to non-residents as well. Think there's a waiting list, they don't want too many members.'

Dave almost shouted 'Bingo!' but instead said, 'Oh, you don't know who he'd need to speak to, do you? Just that he fancies some winter sailing, for some bizarre reason, but The Solent's a bit hairy at times. Got a Laser he wants to try out. He only lives the other side of Salisbury, and I've told him about this place, which sounded great.'

By the time he had left the Estate, unhindered, he was on the phone to Tony.

'Yep, got a name and number, just need to get Norman up here to do his bit, drop a few names, and I reckon we'll be sorted in the month. This is definitely a 'who you know' sort of place, I reckon.'

As he left the way he had come, along the bridlepath, eyes were on him all the way. Ted stood with his back to the island, on the north bank, and watched the rambler leave. He'd spied him earlier, casually walking past the point on the south bank, and had followed him from a distance. He'd seemed just a walker, but then had spent an inordinate amount of time hidden in the southwest corner, by the pads. His subsequent discussion with one of the boat boys had seemed to be the final part of his 'walk' and he'd then left, trying desperately not to look in the snags, as far as Ted could see. Something to think about.

That evening, just as Ted was leaving The Green Man, Stan was popping in for a quick meeting with John. Stan stopped him and told him of his encounter, earlier in the day, and Ted recounted his own findings.

'Interesting,' said Stan. 'Maybe just a bloke whose brother is a sailor, but it might be worth keeping an eye out. Oh, by the way, Dean's not going to Lords for the Test, gotta be somewhere else. Ticket going if you want one.'

Ted nodded, 'Yeah, maybe. I'll let you know very soon. Thanks.'

With that he went out into the late evening sun and took a slow walk home.

It had been a strange month or two. He'd sat in the lounge of The Green Man, last month, watching a programme that had brought home so many memories. It began with two balaclava'd figures on the balcony of a London town house. The explosion that ensued, after they had thrown a device through the window, suddenly declared to the world, 'We are the SAS.' Something that the vast majority of the populace had not known up until that point. Now, twenty five years on, the Iranian Embassy siege was being 'celebrated'.

Ted had watched the whole thing, not from a house or on a TV set, but from a mess room in Hereford, on a flickering screen, with a camera position that was very different from that shown by the BBC. He felt calm, assured. Confident that his lads would perform the task with precision and, ultimately, success. He called them 'his lads' but they weren't, as such. He was a year or so away from retirement, but his input was still much sought after. He knew, however, that everything was about to change. These were dangerous times. Hi-jacking and kidnap seemed to be on the increase, and the element of surprise was always the main weapon in a government's armoury when trying to achieve a satisfactory outcome. But now they knew, everybody knew. Now the surprise was gone, or that particular surprise. They had many, many more tricks up their sleeves, and as technology moved forward they would need them.

The screen showed some familiar faces; old friends, young upstarts, some still with us, others not. The words meant little; they were for the majority that didn't know, not the minority that did.

He left before the end of the programme, not letting on to anyone else his much deeper knowledge than that being rolled out to the masses. Of the snipers hidden from view, but with excellent vision. Of the surveillance team just a wall's width away from the hostage takers. Of the need for speed, accuracy and surprise. All of which were achieved, and then some.

The rest of the week had left him feeling somewhat hollow, and when Dan Becks had told him of a trip to Lords to see the cricket, he had declined the invitation. Not that he didn't like cricket, just that he didn't feel the urge to share that pleasure with 20,000 other people.

Since then, however, he'd calmed a little, and just last week a chance encounter with young Neil had made him feel a whole lot better with himself.

He'd been checking a few of the trees in the West Wood, after a particularly windy night, and had spotted a few limbs that would need to be severed. He'd get hold of Stan to help him with that, and a couple of the chainsaw boys from the village. If he went directly to John there'd be all sorts of 'health and safety issues', and hard hats and the like. No time for that; just competent people doing the job well, that's all that would be needed.

As he peered up at a large oak branch, he heard young Neil coming around from the boathouse.

'Morning, boy,' he said, without taking his eyes from the faltering branch above. 'All alone? Where's your mate?'

Neil turned towards the voice, then walked between the trees towards Ted. 'He's gone up to London with his parents, to see his nan and grandad. Thought I'd just come for a stroll, have a look at the bluebells.' Sutton Woods was a carpet of blue at the moment, covered in that most English of springtime plants, and it was nice to hear one of today's youth speaking of them with such regard. Ted turned to look at him, and was just about to reply when he heard a deep, groaning crack from above. Looking up he saw, in slow motion, the branch of the oak tree finally succumbing to its weight and falling earthwards, with him right below it. As he prepared to move, the wind was knocked out of him as something heavy caught him in the side, and he skittered across the forest floor, just as the severed limb crashed to the ground where he'd just been standing. He gasped for breath for a few seconds, then felt Neil release him and get up, brushing leaves and detritus from his hair and clothes.

'Blimey, Ted, that was close. Are you all right?' said Neil, looking down at him with some concern. He eased himself up onto one elbow and eyed the tree branch. Then turned to his 'assailant'.

'Fine, lad. Guess that makes us even.' He smiled, then winced as he got to his feet, rubbing his side where Neil had hit him. 'Should take up rugby, lad – some tackle you got there.' With that, he brushed himself down, then looked once again at the offending branch. 'Oh, well, one less we need to cut down, I suppose. Come on, lad, I reckon we needs a cup of tea.' Neil nodded, and followed him through the woods.

The bluebells were a riot of colour on their journey, and Neil studied them intently, despite his mind still whirring at what might have happened if he hadn't passed by. Ted was thinking much the same thing, whilst trying to convince himself that he would have been looking at the branch and would have been able to avoid it if necessary. But, deep down, he was unsure. Young Becks had acted quickly and surely, and before Ted knew it, a plan was being hatched in his head.

As the tea brewed, and Neil stood in the doorway looking at the early summer woodland, Ted ran over in his head a conversation he'd had with his boss, young Daniel, a week or so ago. The jist of it had been that Old Ted would not go on for ever, and wouldn't it be a good idea to start training someone as an assistant, someone who could take over when Ted felt it time to retire. Daniel was being as diplomatic as possible, and Ted as stubborn as possible, but both knew that it was a sound idea; it was just a case of who would crack first – Daniel by demanding, or Ted by admitting.

And now Ted could see the solution before him.

'There you go, young Wilkinson, nice cuppa for your troubles.'

Neil smiled at the reference to a national hero, and took the incredibly strong, sweet tea from Ted, setting the cup on the table. 'You sure you're alright, Ted? I didn't mean to hit you that hard, just didn't know how close the branch was gonna be.'

Ted flicked a hand as if to dismiss an irritating pupil, slurping on his tea before carrying on. 'No harm done, lad. Not to worry. You acted good and fast – quick thinking. I like that.' Neil nodded and tried not to grimace as he took a mouthful of the slightly sickening brew.

'Now, young Becks, this your last year at school?'

This was a strange turn in the conversation and caught him slightly off guard. 'Errr, well, yeah. I s'pose. I could go to college if my results are okay, but I don't really fancy that. Had enough of school, I reckon. Time to earn some money.'

Ted eyed him closely, didn't seem like he was sure one way or the other.

'Good plan, lad. Got any ideas? Work with yer dad, maybe?'

Neil shook his head, as if unsure of both questions. His dad was a car mechanic, had been for years, and although it would never make him a millionaire, there were always plenty of customers to keep him busy. Trouble was, Neil wasn't really one for cars, and certainly didn't fancy working for his dad.

'Not sure, Ted. I'll have to start looking pretty soon, but if the worst comes to the worst, I'll just have to do college for a couple of years until something comes up.'

Ted mused over this for a few moments, trying to work out how to approach the subject, then carried on.

'You love these woods, don't you lad?' The question was rhetorical, but it seemed to Neil as if the subject had changed again, so he nodded his affirmation of the statement.

'Yeah, Ted, I wouldn't want to be anywhere else at the moment. Those bluebells were stunning, weren't they?'

'They were that, lad, but they still needs tending. Looking after. Same as those buggering branches. And the deer 'n' badger. And pheasant 'n' grouse. All needs nurturing, and tending. That's what I does, for the most part. Nurturing and tending these woods, keep 'em strong and safe.'

Neil looked at Ted, and realised that, up until that very point, he'd had no idea at all what Ted actually did. He'd assumed that he must be retired, and the fact that he was always around, somewhere, was just because that's what he did – just walked around.

'What, you mean it's, like, your job? I mean, you actually get paid for it? No, I don't mean it like that, well, yeah I do, but. Well, what I mean is, errm…'

Ted laughed out loud, like a bark from a large dog, and slapped his hand on the table.

'Young Becks, you've come over all kerflummoxed! Haa!' Another bark of laughter hit the ceiling, and another slap on the table rang out like a gunshot. Neil could feel his face reddening, and tried to think of something else to say, but opted, instead, for silence – it was safer.

Ted's mirth subsided a little, and with a slight chuckle, he continued. 'Yes, young Becks, I do get paid for doing 'this',' he waved his hand expansively, to encompass everything. 'I guess you could call me the keeper, of the woods. Yerss, the keeper, that would just about cover it. I keeps everything ticking along. I keeps everything safe. I keeps my eye on things; many things. Things that you don't even know's there. But you could, boy. Ain't always gonna be here, keeping my eye on things. Gonna need to be someone else, maybe soon, maybe not. But gonna need to be someone. Young Stan, he's a good man, very good man. He sees things, he learns, he knows. Lot to learn, but he's a good learner. Won't be able to do it alone though. Me, I got Stan if'n I needs him, but who's Stan got?'

Neil listened intently and didn't realise that Ted had finished with that last question. Was he awaiting an answer?

'Err, well, no one, Ted. I don't s'pose he's got anyone. Has he?'

He looked at Ted, and watched Ted looking at him. Seeing the dawn rise in his eyes. Watching the meaning filter down, like raindrops through a forest canopy. He watched Ted watching realisation flower across his features. He watched Ted smile, as he himself smiled at what Ted was suggesting. It was like looking in a mirror.

'Oh, you mean… You mean that I… I mean you're saying do I want a, errrm, a job?'

Ted smiled more broadly and cocked his head to one side.

'Well, do you?' he asked, finally.

Neil didn't quite know what to say. An hour ago he was wandering aimlessly around, with nothing particular to do, and since then he'd saved someone's life and been offered a job. The first job he'd ever been offered. The first life he'd ever saved.

'Well, errrm. Yes. Yes! Yes, I bloody do! Oh, mate, wait 'til I tell Smiffy. When do I start? I mean, I leave school in two months, so do I start straightaway after that? Or now, shall I leave now?'

The words gushed forth like water through a sundered dam and Ted had to hold up his hands to stem the flow.

'Whoa, lad. First things first. Let me discuss things with young Daniel, he'll want to have something to say as well. And your dad, I'd like to talk to your dad as well. But I reckons you finish your schooling – always gonna need schooling, lad. Then, maybe we start in the summer, when things are a bit slow. Nice and easy. I'll talk to young Daniel on Monday, and if I sees your dad, I'll talk to him as well. Now you be getting on, lad, I got things to do, we'll speak again very soon, that's for sure.'

With that, he rose from his chair and took both cups over to the sink. Neil was still in a state of shock, and stood in the doorway, unsure of what to say.

'Off you go, boy. I'll see you very soon,' said Ted whilst rinsing out the two cups.

'Oh, and thanks, lad. Good work, although I knew it was coming.'

Neil walked off into the woods, unsure whether the last was a compliment or not.

No matter, this had been a good day; a very good day. He couldn't wait to speak to Smiffy.

A week later, Ted sat, ashen-faced, in front of the telly at The Green Man. No one was saying a word. The screen showed a horror scene. A London bus in a London street, its roof peeled back like a can of beans, its contents spilled across the blackened, cracked pavement. Smoke and sirens filled the air.

Here, thought Ted. Here, again.

Decades earlier he had witnessed similar scenes, in London and Guildford, in Birmingham and Warrington. Smoke and sirens, death and destruction. But that was somehow different.

These were fanatics, the worst sort of enemy. They would die for what they believed in, in the certain knowledge that they would be accepted into a better place. They had no fear; just conviction.

The others, the Provos, they were cowards. They spoke of 'a cause', but they were just common criminals. Thieves, extortionists, murderers. They dealt out terror like Satan's croupiers. The house always won.

But these ones, they were not cowards. They were not criminals, not in the usual sense of the word. Their crime was their fanaticism. They did it for no other reason. Not to fund drug cartels, or money laundering schemes, or arms trafficking.

The others you could beat, did beat. These? They were a whole different ball game. Bus, tube, aeroplane, train. School, shopping mall, underground station. All were a weapon. All were a war zone.

And in two weeks 'his boys' were going to Lords. The centre of London; the middle of the war zone.

An hour later, as the conversation picked up, and the harrowing scenes were no longer occupying the TV screen, Ted walked over to Dan Becks.

'Dan, tell me. You still got that spare ticket for Lords?'

21st July '05

LORDS!

This could be some day. Left at 6.30, Gus driving. Should be at the ground by 10. Depends on security getting into London. Weather looks okay, should swing a bit. The Toss!

Bloody HELL! What a morning! When Harmy whacked Langer in that first over, the place went ballistic! Who'd have thought 90-5 at lunch?

Got good seats in the Mound Stand, well done Pete! Bit of lunch and a beer or two. Went into Lords shop, got Panama hat and a shirt. Looking sharp!

Just waiting for the players to come out. Excited!

Oh my god, don't know if I'll be able to take this all summer. Brilliant bowling, Harmy, Freddie, Hogg and Jones. ALL OUT 190!

But then, whack whack, four down for 35 at tea. Need to steady the ship a bit, see how Pietersen does.

Tired now. Should be home by 9-30. Brilliant day, pity about the end, 102-7. Not good. Pete's had a great day, he looks a bit tottery, bit of champers on the coach too. Pity some of us have to work tomorrow. Great day.

Chapter Fifteen
Let there be more Light

The day after Dave's visit to the lake, and his acquisition of a phone number, Norman had called the number and had managed to get a meeting with the commodore. The following Saturday he had met the man and, within a short space of time, had parted with the £750 required to ensure his membership of Felcham Sailing Club. The rules were outlined to him, and were pretty standard, but the one he had expected wasn't there.

'Great, so I'll bring the boat over in the next couple of weeks to give it a try. Standard charge for storage?'

'Yes, £180 for the year. £100 for a second boat, if you need one.'

'Fine, no problem,' said Norman. 'Alright to bring a guest along once in awhile?' He said it like it was standard practice, which in some clubs it was, and the commodore treated it as such.

'Yes, that's fine. £30 per day for guests, preferable if you use just the one car, though.'

Norman had no problem with that, and shook the man's hand, before walking outside and having one final look at the lake. He wasn't an angler, but he was Dave's brother-in-law and was more than happy to play his part in the big plan. And the plan seemed to have worked perfectly.

A week later, he and Dave were unhitching the trailer from the car, then they slid the boat down to the lake, under the supervision of one of the boat boys. Once the car and trailer were parked, they then took to the lake for a few circuits. Dave hadn't been totally truthful on his previous visit, as he was a fairly competent sailor. But fishing was his first love so he rarely got to sail much any more. After a few, leisurely circuits of the lake, Norman deftly guided the Laser towards the pads, tacking into the wind to slow them a little and allowing the boat to slide effortlessly past the pads. At the same time, Dave leant casually against the side of the boat, thus hiding the tube that was extending from within his life jacket and into the water. His jacket was full of boilies, maybe a couple of kilos, but after two or three passes they had all been deposited in the vicinity of the pads. No one said a word back at the boathouse about their pads excursion, and after a quick beer they left with a hearty, 'Cheerio, see you soon.'

They repeated this tactic half a dozen times over the next couple of months and, whilst Stan and Ted were enjoying their day at Lords, Dave took the opportunity to walk around to the pads corner to initiate the next part of their plan. The lake was quiet, with only Norman's and one other boat on the lake, so a couple of the boat boys were having some fun windsurfing. Dave crept a little deeper into the woods, sure that he was invisible to any who would look, then got out a compass and started to head northwest. The map showed a small track about three hundred yards in that direction, which led subsequently to a road about half a mile distant. Once in the woods he took out his phone and hit REDIAL, then waited for an answer.

'Dave?'

'Hello mate, you there yet?' he asked, whilst continuing to walk slowly forward.

'Well, I'm at the end of the track in the woods. Not sure if it's the one, though. Where are you?'

'I should be about a hundred yards away,' Dave replied. 'Hold on, just coming through these trees. You should be over there.' He carried on walking, scanning left and right, then caught a glimpse of sunlight on metal.

'Right, think I can see you. Look over to your right,' he said.

He took off his hat, which he then waved above his head.

'Gotcha!' came Tony's reply.

The plan was coming together.

Their baiting campaign continued regularly, although not so much that it raised suspicion, but Norman's presence at the lake was soon just normal and little attention was paid to him. If they went at the weekend, it would normally be quite early, when few people were about. And if they managed a weekday trip, there were fewer people anyway. But sometimes, there is always somebody capable of seeing.

'Right, I reckon we give it a go after next weekend,' declared Dave. 'There's a regatta on Saturday, and a bit of a do afterwards, which will probably put the carp off a bit. But then it'll be quiet next week 'cos most of 'em are off to Cowes Week.' He and Tony were sitting in his kitchen, an Ordnance Survey map spread out on the table in front of them. They'd been discussing tactics in depth; cutting down on tackle, no bivvies or chairs, a couple of rods each. They didn't plan on fishing for long, maybe just four or five hours of darkness, then away before dawn. The first couple of trips would just be recces, to suss out the logistics of moving the carp. If they caught one of the biggies, that would be a huge bonus, but they would get what they wanted with the minimum of fuss. The midweek sortie also coincided with a new moon, and a bit of cloud cover, so there would be minimal light.

Norman dropped them off at the end of the track, then disappeared off up the road to park up and sleep for a few hours. The walk along the track was straightforward, but then it became tricky when they had to cut through the woods to the lake. The compass helped, but the journey was slow and fairly hazardous, with a number of trips and stumbles for both of them. Eventually, however, Dave recognised the outline of a double-trunked tree that he had stood by, a week earlier. He stopped next to it and rested his rods against it. They'd had some eight-foot stalking rods specially made for this; strong rods that could be easily transported. Dave and Norman had been sailing the previous day, and had deposited the best part of five kilos of bait into the lake, so they felt that all they would need at this time would be single hookbaits, in the hope that the carp would still be visiting the area in search of food.

The night was dark and still, but below the surface life continued. The Common and its two large companions moved easily along the margins of the lake, preceded by a dozen smaller carp. This area was where there was most activity in the daylight hours, but after sunset all was quiet, and they felt no danger. A few items of natural food were soon snaffled by the marauding lead group of carp, then they continued on their slow circuit of the lake. They were headed for an area that had, of late, been bountiful with food. Although not their normal diet, the smell and taste were just as enticing and there seemed a plentiful supply.

As they moved along the margins, towards the pads, all of the fish had picked up the scent of the food, and were beginning to search diligently. The three, large matriarchs began to surge forward, anxious to sate their appetite, but there was a commotion ahead and the leading group of carp scattered wildly. The larger three followed, unsure as to what had happened, but sure of their need for safety.

Maybe they would return on another night, when the memory had dimmed.

'Shit, I'm in!' Tony's hoarse whisper sounded deafening, as did the buzz of the baitrunner, and Dave shushed him to calm down.

Calm was not something that Tony could do very well at that moment, however – who knew what might be on the other end?

'Can't see a bloody thing,' he said, needlessly, and crept closer to the water's edge to lower the net in. The carp battled for ten minutes or so, but in the heightened excitement of the moment it seemed to take forever. Eventually, however, oily swirls were just visible on the surface, and Dave pushed the extending net handle a little further. Then it was in and he felt the carp bucking against its captivity.

'Bloody hell, Dave, we done it,' said Tony, excitedly.

'Shush! We ain't done nothing yet. This ain't one of 'em. Even I know that and I weren't playing it.'

With that, he raised the net from the lake and laid it on one of the sacks. He couldn't risk a head torch, but his arm told him that this was barely twenty pounds. He moved his hand along the flank, and up to the mouth to remove the hook, then raised the fish for Tony to see. He could make out its silhouette, and agreed with Dave.

'Yeah, low-twenty, maybe. Bloody hell, that pulled like a donkey, god knows what the big'uns'll be like.'

Dave slipped the fish back into the lake, then broke down the net. Looking at his watch, he could see that it was barely two o'clock, but they weren't staying, that had been agreed. Within ten minutes they were walking back along the track and phoning Norman. They would be home by dawn.

Everything was working out fine. They'd keep the bait going in for another few weeks, then return on the next new moon, at the end of August. But next time they'd have the van, fully equipped and ready for the biggest of cargoes.

Ted didn't realise that he'd noticed something amiss until a little later. He'd decided to walk the West Woods to check on the badger set, up in the northwest corner and, at first, the odd broken stem here and there hadn't seemed too unnatural, probably deer or an errant dog. But when he'd got closer to the track he'd noticed a trampled area of bracken and had gone for a closer look. Sure enough, where the damaged bracken met the track he could see evidence of a vehicle, the tyre tracks still faintly visible in the dirt. Carefully following the signs, he walked all of the way back to their source, which brought him out to the southwest corner of the lake, by the pads. As he stood there, shielded by the trees, he noticed a sailing boat manoeuvring thirty yards out in the lake, then turning and moving away. Of the two occupants, one was at the sail, whilst the other continued to look at the pads as they moved away from them. As the wind caught the sail, he threw something back into the lake and it landed with an audible 'plop', near the pads. Then he turned back to the other and away they went, back to the boathouse.

Ted stood in the shadows for a while, giving the whole thing some serious thought. Were the tracks just an animal's? Was the sailor just flicking a pebble? And what about the tyre tracks, could they have just been one of the ranger's cars?

Ted was uneasy when the questions outnumbered the answers. But sometimes, no matter how many questions, there was just one answer.

This was a puzzle that could well be worth persevering with.

'So, that's it, we're all ready, yeah?'

Tony and Norman nodded at Dave in acknowledgement. He had planned this with military precision, and knew that nothing could go wrong. The van had been kitted out with two large tanks, both with a separate aeration system. He'd got a couple of huge camouflaged nets and sewn them together, to drape over the van whilst it was waiting for the call. The rods and reels had been tested out on a private lake, owned by a mate, that housed some whacking great French carp, and they'd hooked half a dozen of them over the past month, just to test the equipment. The fish were huge, but they weren't 'real' in Dave's eyes. They weren't proper, English carp.

He'd gone for another walk around to the pads a few days after their only visit to the lake, just to reacquaint himself with the area in daylight. All seemed fine, so he'd just kept the bait going in regularly, the last introduction being yesterday afternoon. He'd chosen a midweek night again, knowing that being the last day of August a lot of people would be having their final week's holiday before the end of the school holidays. The new moon was due in a couple of days' time, but would only be a thin slither when they made their move, so it should still be as dark as hell.

'Right, Norm, we'll see you at eight. Should be there by half ten, plenty dark by then. Out by five, or earlier hopefully. If not, we go again.'

That was another reason for the midweek choice, if they were unsuccessful they would go again on the next night, and then on the following Monday, which would still be almost moonless.

Dave and Tony left Norman's house, and then drove round to Dave's. All of the gear they required was laid out on the lawn. Four rods and reels, spooled up with 25lb mainline. Two collapsible, extending landing nets, the handles specially reinforced for their other use, as the two poles that would go either side of the canvas hammock they'd had made. In this they would transport any carp they caught, once secured in one of the three extra-large carp sacks they also had. The hammock would be like a sedan chair, but instead of carrying the handles, they would put them on their shoulders, onto special foam pads they'd made.

And bait. Just the smallest amount, half a kilo each, but enough to entice the carp a little.

That was it, they were ready. The van was ready. The carp's new home was ready, a couple of hours away and very secluded. Now they just had to wait.

Black, black night, the sky peppered with stars. On any other night Dave would have just stopped and gawped at the sight, but he had only eyes for the dark path in front of him. He had toyed with the idea of getting some night-vision goggles, but the cost was ridiculous, so he just had to trust his own night vision. They moved very slowly, taking care with every step, but pretty soon he saw the double-trunked tree and made straight for it. Everything had been planned to perfection. Tony took the rolled hammock from his rucksack and unrolled it, laying it out flat on the small piece of clear ground to the left of the tree, then put the rucksack back over his shoulders. Dave removed the carp sacks and bait bag from his own sack, then moved towards the lake. The rods were made up, rigs baited, and they both knew where they were going to fish, so moved quietly into position. The merest of 'plops' signalled the baited rigs entering the lake; the leads having been dropped down to below an ounce. A few baits were thrown out in the area of the hookbaits, then they sat back to wait.

As usual, the carp's nightly patrol of the lake took a very similar route, their knowledge of the lake and its food sources having been ingrained into them over many years. The usual gaggle of a dozen smaller fish preceded the three large females, but there was food aplenty, and none were going hungry. They skirted the concrete of the sailing club jetty, then moved on towards the reedy corner, where a recent hatch of dragonfly larvae had been a welcome addition to their diet. But the larder was bare, lasting no more than a night or two, so they moved on, towards the pads, where there was always food. Amongst the 'smaller' group were two or three fish that would have graced any anglers net, anywhere in the land, and they were the size they were because they always got to the food first. One, a particularly fine and healthy linear carp, sensed some food to its right, close to the margins, and moved swiftly to devour it, lest its equally eager cohorts got there first. There wasn't much, so in a couple of mouthfuls it had been consumed, but as the fish moved away it felt a strange, sharp resistance in its mouth, shaking its head angrily to remove it. But it would not go, so the carp did, in fright.

Dave's baitrunner suddenly buzzed into life and the rod tip bucked as something had fallen for his trap. Picking up the rod, he let the baitrunner spin for thirty seconds before putting a finger on the spool to slow the carp. As excited and apprehensive as he was, he appeared outwardly calm, and Tony stood by his side wondering if his mate had a single nerve in his body.
'What d'ya reckon, Dave?' he whispered, but got no reply, just a hum from the line as the fish left the sanctuary of the pads, which at this time of year were no sanctuary at all; another reason for starting their campaign now.
After what seemed a dark eternity, they heard a wallow on the surface, and saw ripples lapping back towards them. Tony extended the net handle fully and lay it in the water. His first attempt was really a stab in the dark, and he missed completely, hearing a hiss of annoyance from his mate. The second time, however, he felt the net fill with angry carp, and almost screamed in relief.
They lifted the carp from the lake, and although it took two of them to walk it to the hammock, they knew it wasn't one of the real biggies. However, they could just about make out the beauty of it, and estimated it to be over forty pounds, so decided that this would be a fine acquisition for their new lake. A sack was wetted in the margins, the carp then being secured inside it. They broke down both of the nets,

and slid the handles through the reinforced loops on either side of the hammock. The rods were also broken down and laid in the hammock, along with the carp. They then hoisted the hammock up, carefully, and settled the handles onto their shoulders. The regime was simple by now, because they had practiced it many times in Tony's garden, using his six-year old son as the carp!

'Norm, we're coming back with one. Be there in five minutes.'

'Okay. Is it one of the biggies?'

But Dave had clicked off after 'okay' so had not heard the question. They moved slowly and carefully and, within five minutes, were lowering the hammock carefully onto the floor of the open van. The buzz of a pump could be heard from within, and so they lifted the sack up and lowered it into the waiting tank. Once the lid was on the tank, they quickly closed the back of the van, after removing the camo netting, and jumped in the front. Norman moved away slowly, without lights, until he came to the end of the track, then he put on the lights and turned right, towards home.

'Yess!' shouted Dave and Tony, and Norman smiled a huge smile. This was like shooting fish in a barrel.

They had been meticulous in their planning. Nothing had gone wrong; they'd left nothing behind, no sign that they'd even been there. Or so they thought.

'Mornin', young Stan. 'How you'm doing today?' Ted had to remind himself to be a yokel, sometimes, but Stan was long past wondering what was going on with the accent. He just accepted Ted for what he was.

'Doing fine, Ted, thanks. Had a nice break with the missus so I'm feeling fine. What a finish to the cricket, mate. Did you see it?'

Ted smiled and nodded, and they dissected the finer points of the Fourth Test before Ted put a halt to it.

'Tonight, Stan. Can you get over here with me? It'll be late, maybe all night, but I think we might have a bit of a poaching problem.'

Stan stopped and looked at Ted, then nodded firmly. 'Yeah, sure. What makes you think that, though?' he asked.

Ted explained about his sighting of the guy at the lake, a few weeks earlier. He'd been keeping an eye on the area since then, but had seen nothing else until that morning. On walking around to the pads he'd noticed a bit of trampled ground by one of the trees, so had investigated a little further and, sure enough, a rough path led through the bracken to the track at the far end of the wood. Tyre tracks were, once again, evident and there, squashed into some mud, was a small object.

He handed it to Stan, who looked at it, then smelt it. 'It's a boilie,' he stated, with certainty. 'Bet if you look you'll find a few more, as well. Bloody hell, what d'you reckons happened, Ted? You don't reckon they've got one, do you?'

Ted shrugged. 'If they have, then I reckons it's only one. And one won't be enough, that's for sure. But I don't reckon it's one of the big'uns. They tried to be very careful covering their tracks. If I hadn't bin looking, I wouldn't have spotted it. Just think that, if they'd gotten first prize, they wouldn't have cared, 'cos they wouldn't have been coming back.'

Stan nodded at the wisdom of this, but felt aggrieved that even one of the carp from here had been taken. 'So, what's the plan then, Ted?'

'Well, have you ever heard of a stinger?' he began.

Half an hour later they parted, arranging to meet back there after dark, a plan in place.

Food aplenty. The carp were earlier this night. The usual natural larders were beginning to dwindle as the summer ended and winter loomed, so the fish made their way to the only constant supply that they were sure of, beneath the pads. The previous evening's disturbance was already a distant memory, and so, as the sun painted its final strokes behind the trees, the carp moved easily beneath the dying lily leaves, grazing on the replenished supply of food items. The Common and the two large mirrors allowed the lead group of carp to feed undisturbed for half an hour or so, no hint of danger in their minds, then moved amongst them to feed equally as confidently. Food aplenty. They would spend the next few hours casually moving back and forth, eating when they felt like it, storing energy for the cruel months ahead. Every now and then, a small surface disturbance alerted them to possible danger, but within a few minutes all appeared fine so they carried on feeding. Oblivious.

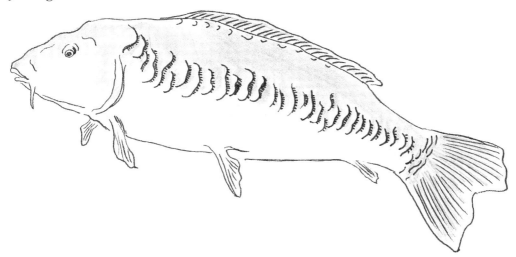

Same time, same place. Like clockwork. The carp that they'd caught yesterday had been a stunning mirror of forty two pounds and had surged away strongly when they released it into the lake earlier that day. Now they were back, to add to that with something much larger, they hoped.

Like clockwork, everything went as easily as yesterday, and by eleven in the evening they were both back in position. Norman and Dave had paid another visit to the lake during the afternoon and had put out another few kilos of bait, sure that the rest had been consumed, and now they added to that with a few handfuls of their own.

The night was even darker, so when the barn owl silently passed over Tony's head it was like an electric shock and he screamed inadvertently. Dave nearly jumped out of his skin and would have gone and given him a slap if he was closer.

Thirty yards away, two pairs of eyes stared intently into the dark, watching as the ghostly wings disappeared into the night.

As silence and calm returned to the night, Dave settled back and thought about what might be. He'd convinced himself that he wouldn't be greedy, that just one of the two biggies would be enough, but on seeing their prize from the previous night, he realised that, with some stealth and careful planning, they could end up with one of the best stocked lakes in the land.

His thoughts wandered, the silence broken occasionally by a distant waterfowl, or a successful night-time predator. He didn't feel his eyes close, but the next moment a buzzing sound slapped him back to life, and he dropped his hand to the reel, feeling the line fluttering against his skin. In again.

Unlike the fish of the previous evening, this one just moved away slowly and steadily, but unstoppably, and he knew that this could well be what they'd come for. He applied some pressure to the spool, lifting the rod a little higher, but it did nothing, and he grunted as loudly as possible to attract Tony's attention. He too had nodded off, and it wasn't until the third 'Tone!' that he stumbled awake and down to his battling mate.

'Good 'un, Tone. Real good 'un,' said a much more talkative Dave. 'Been on for five minutes and I haven't gained an inch.'

The slow, ponderous battle went on. And on. And the two distant observers watched intently, ready to put their plan into action.

Slowly, so slowly, Dave began to gain line, and his aching arm began to beg for a swift end to this battle. But it just plodded on. And on. Almost an hour had passed, with Dave's arm now screaming for forgiveness, and the first inky swirls were visible to the two miscreants. Another five minutes, and something the size of a hippo seemed to be wallowing just out of netting range. Another huge, wallowing splash, and then Tony screamed. He couldn't help himself, but he knew it was in the net, and the slap round the head made little difference to his excitement.

Dave massaged his arm, whilst Tony readied the sack and the hammock. He broke down the rods, and slid one of the poles into the loops, whilst Dave held the other in the margins. When they tried to lift it they both grunted with the exertion, and the classic, 'Is it caught on a branch?' was uttered by Tony. Both taking two handholds, they heaved it up and staggered to the hammock, unbelieving of the weight. The French fish that Dave had caught recently had been in excess of fifty pounds, but had felt nothing like this, and Dave began to shake with excitement. He so wanted to turn on his head torch, but daren't. They were so close, they couldn't bugger it up now.

Sliding it into what had appeared to be a huge sack earlier, they realised that it would fit this carp like a body stocking, so just had to hope it would suffice until they got to the van. Once in the tank, all would be fine.

The phone call made to Norman, they tried to hoist the hammock, but it wouldn't budge. They tried again, with an equal lack of success, so Dave stood and thought. 'Tone, only one thing for it. Reckon we'll have to carry it, mate. Have to be careful it doesn't scrape on the ground.'

Tony nodded, despite the fact that Dave couldn't see him.

'Right, ready?' said Dave.

'Yup, let's go,' replied Tony. 'One, two, three, hup!'

With that they both lifted and, with Dave slowly leading, made their way to the rendezvous point.

A few trees away, Ted and Stan moved steadily and quietly to their own rendezvous point, the glasses that Ted had 'acquired' lighting the path as if it were daylight.

The walk back to the van was like a silent torture, the sinews and muscles in their arms and shoulders screaming for mercy, and they had to stop on a number of occasions for a small respite. Eventually, twenty minutes after making the call, they reached a very agitated Norman.

'Where you bin? Bloody hell, I thought you'd been nabbed. Why didn't you answer your phone? I bin bloody kacking myself!'

Tony and Dave carefully lowered their precious cargo to the floor, before Dave slowly eased back up, rubbing his shoulder, his back, his neck.

'Norm, it's okay mate. This thing weighs a bloody ton, and it's taken us ages to get it here. But we bloody did it!' With that, he slapped Tony across the back and gave him a big, one armed hug. 'We bloody did it, mate!'

Tony just beamed, then nodded down at the very inadequate sack. 'We better get that in the tank real quick, I reckon.'

Norman was slowly taking in what they were saying, and as the penny dropped, he let out a small yelp. 'Waaa! You've got one. You've got one of the biggies.' Then everyone was smiling.

It took all three of them to raise the huge bulk up onto the floor of the van, and then all three to lower it into the oxygen enriched water of the tank. They watched it for a minute, ensuring that it was none the worse for its battles, then closed the lid, shut the back doors and got into the cab.

'Right, real slow and careful until we get to the end of the track, Norm. Can't afford any mishaps,' advised Dave, unnecessarily.

Norm eased them forward, slipping into second gear and taking it carefully along the Stygian black track.

'Bang!' 'Bang!'

'What the **** was that?' exclaimed Dave. The van juddered, then two more similar sounds emanated from behind them, and the van shuddered to a halt.

'Oh, shit, what's happened?' said Tony rhetorically, then opened the passenger door.

As he and Dave jumped out, a voice came from the left.

'Good evening, gentlemen. Having a spot of bother?'

They could see nothing, but sensed that the voice came from about ten yards away.

'Who's that? Who the bloody hell is that?' screamed Dave, phlegm spraying from his lips.

'Lights,' said another voice, and the night suddenly became day as the main beams from the two police cars further along the track lit up the scene. The three poachers were temporarily blinded, shielding their eyes with their arms. Expletives filled the air, but to little effect, and the police officers took them by the arms and led them towards the cars.

'What we done? Eh, what we done?' demanded Dave.

'Oh, I'm sure we'll think of something, sir. Now, mind your head. That's it.' Sliding into the back seat, Dave looked out of the front window, at the stricken van with four remarkably flat tyres, and thought about its cargo.

'Bollocks!' he said, quietly, then sat back as the car reversed slowly up the track, followed by the other. In the headlights he saw two people emerge from the undergrowth and walk towards the back of the van. 'Bollocks!' he muttered again, then they were turning and heading off along the main road, never to return.

The big mirror felt the lake's water envelope it, the slowly lapping waves rocking it back and forth whilst it was being cradled in the margins. Then, a burst of strength and realisation – freedom. It's huge tail flicked twice and it surged away from the cradling arms, heading straight towards the snag tree to its right, below which it lay for the rest of that testing night.

Stan dried his hands on his trousers, then turned to Ted.

'Bloody hell, Ted, how big was that? It was huge, bloody huge. Probably as big as The Common.' Shaking his head in disbelief, he looked at Ted. 'Good plan with the spikes, Ted. And the glasses. They were the nuts!'

Ted smiled in the gradually awakening morning. 'Good plans nearly always work, Stan. Nearly always.' He then turned away, and walked off towards his Land Rover, with the improvised tank on the back. 'Time for some sleep, I reckon. Well done,

Stan, you did good.'

Stan stood and watched as Ted drove off around the lake, the sound of sloshing water just audible above the engine noise.

Sleep, you've gotta be joking, he thought. How big was that carp?

Oh, please. Someday.

CHAPTER SIXTEEN
Childhood's End

They sat very quietly, allowing the tall, swaying grass to hide them from view. The wind was blowing from their right, so their scent shouldn't be a problem either. As the tall strands swayed from side to side, rustling and hissing, the deer came into view, not thirty yards away. Smiffy and Posh were just on the edge of the wood, and the deer were grazing in the cornfield in front; ten of them in all. Mainly does, but a couple of young bucks were strutting around, getting ready for the autumn ritual a few months hence.

They'd been walking back through the woods after an afternoon fishing the river, and had noticed the deer through the trees, so, leaving their tackle and taking only a camera, they had crept as close as they could. Then, obligingly, the deer had moved slowly towards them until they were almost within touching distance. Their spotted hides were a good camouflage in the dappled sunlight of the woodland, but not so in open pasture, but despite their natural paranoia, the deer were still unaware of their admirers.

Smiffy tried to get some shots through the grass, but the camera was unable to focus, and he was woefully unsuccessful. This was to be their penultimate fishing trip before the end of the holidays, and the beginning of new and diverse lives for the two of them. This trip was almost an afterthought. Smiffy and his parents had been away to Greece for a week or so, but a bout of gastroenteritis for his mother, and the prospect of an extra day's cricket for his dad to watch, had meant they'd returned on the Friday morning, rather than the planned Saturday evening. After an hour of sorting things out, getting the doctor over to see his mum, and generally tidying up, Smiffy had then phoned Posh and they'd met over the Mere for an hour in the afternoon. One last, quick trip to the river had been planned, and very enjoyable it had been as well. But, alas, no last great barbel graced their nets, and they left with the usual chub and roach bag at the end of the day. This unexpected deer sighting, however, had been all the bonus they had needed, and Smiffy soon gave up on his poor camera work and just enjoyed the moment.

The sun was setting to their left, and it would soon be time to move, especially as their buttocks were becoming decidedly numb. The timing of their departure was, however, chosen by a late arriving doe and her fawn. She strolled casually from the trees, just to the left of where the boys sat, and it was difficult to say who was the more startled. Posh caught a movement out of the corner of his eye and flinched. The doe caught the movement of Posh flinching and leapt in the air as if having been stung. She let out a startled cry and all of a sudden the herd were a blur of movement, not stopping for a quarter of a mile.

'Bloody hell, nearly shit meself,' exclaimed Posh. Then rose and began massaging some life back into his buttocks.

'Mate, that was great, wasn't it? They didn't even know we were there. Brilliant!' said Smiffy, adopting the same massaging method as his mate.

'Ain't gonna be seeing anything like that up in Leeds, Smiffy. Maybe a few stag do's, but not a lot else.'

Smiffy moved back into the wood to retrieve his fishing tackle, then walked alongside his friend, through the long grass towards home.

'No, probably not, but I think there'll be a certain amount of wild life up there,' he replied smiling. Posh looked at him and laughed.

'Yeah, I'm sure there will, mate, and I bet you'll tell me all about it,' he said. They both laughed and carried on walking, absent-mindedly swishing the long grass with their fishing rods.

'So,' said Smiffy, 'one last hurrah.'

Posh nodded. He was referring to the trip they'd planned with Stan to Linton's, on Saturday. It would be their fourth such trip since their initial sortie, a couple of summers ago, and they were both hoping for similar results. On each previous trip they'd both managed to catch beautiful carp, both increasing their bests by a few pounds, and this last trip, they hoped, would see them both achieve a similar feat. They'd searched out some carp pools of their own, as well, as the Linton trips were few and far between, but their searches had revealed nothing close either geographically or aesthetically. A couple of small pools, a few miles away, held fish to low-twenties, but they were muddy-banked and open to the elements, and the bulk of the fish were stunted and scabby. They caught a few, but, after their fourth or fifth session, decided that there was more to it than just catching carp.

To be fair, the last year had been tough for both of them; Smiffy striving towards a University place, and Posh just trying to get the best results that he could. This had impacted greatly on their fishing time, and the rods had been indoors much more than out over the previous twelve months. Of course, things like girls also seemed to have an impact on their free time, and given the choice between a cold riverbank in search of pike or a warm bedroom in search of flesh – well, what's a poor boy gonna do?

So, as they were returning from Lords in the minibus, they were more than happy when Stan slurred out an invitation to fish Linton's one last time. It had taken a little longer than anticipated, what with exams, holidays, oh, and girls, but the last weekend of the holidays seemed like a perfect way to end their freedom.

Stan picked them up just after five, and they headed off down the bumpy track. They knew they wouldn't have the place to themselves this time, as Jim had told Stan that a couple of old boys were due to fish for the weekend, but they thought an early start might afford them the chance of an early fish – and how right they'd been. There were no cars there as they quietly closed the doors and stretched in the half-light of dawn, the sounds of the lake and its inhabitants drifting through the trees to greet them. Splashes and squawks, whistles and chirrups, the wood was gradually coming to life, and there was no time to waste.

As usual, Stan took his time whilst the other two eagerly scurried through the trees to the water's edge, eyes scanning for movement or bubbles. As usual, within minutes they'd spied some telltale signs and were off in pursuit. Unlike their very first trip to the lake, however, there was now no sign of any gentlemanly conduct; it was each man for himself so they strode off in opposite directions, in search of carp.

The first of the morning fell to Smiffy, when his trusty quill float disappeared, reappearing five minutes later next to a fine eighteen-pound common. No sooner had Stan slid the fish back for him than he was required at the far end of the lake, where Neil was doing battle with something more ponderous. The fish took an age to succumb, but when eventually it slid over the net cord, Stan knew that this was one of the fabled 'big'uns'. He took his time with everything, wetting the unhooking mat, zeroing the damp sling, before helping Neil lift the fish from the lake. Neil was slightly dumbfounded, and just sort of stared as the net revealed yet another of the lake's wonderful inhabitants.

Stan slipped the hook from the rubbery bottom lip, then slid the fish into the weigh sling. This is gonna be close, he thought, but when the scales read a mere twenty-eight pounds and ounces, he was sure that it mattered not at all. It certainly didn't seem to matter to Neil; he was like a headless chicken, and once the photos were done, and the fish safely returned, he just mooched around the pool for an hour.

Stan had to admit to being just a little envious. That was a stunning, old carp; deep, deep brown with huge, old scales along its flank. Jim Baines had told him that the original stock had been introduced into the lake in the late fifties, and this was surely one of them. He was sure that Neil wasn't yet aware of the significance of that, but he'd attempt to impress it upon him as much as he could.

That would surely be it for the day, or so he thought. The other anglers turned up a little before nine, and set up nearest to the car, so Stan and the lads moved over to the other, more open side of the pool, and decided to have a little tench match.

There were just a few remnants of pads on the surface in front of them, but enough to attract a few grains of corn and a quill float. Within a few minutes, Stan was slipping his net under a small, feisty male, unhooking it in the net and letting it slide back into the deep water. Another followed next cast, and by the time Neil had opened the lads' account, Stan was four to the good. The banter was lighthearted and fun, and Stan felt pleased that this last session of theirs was going to end on such a note.

The sun remained hidden behind high cloud for the rest of the morning, which seemed to keep the tench feeding, and by lunchtime they'd taken a baker's dozen between them, with a couple knocking on the door of seven pounds. Stan still held the lead, but only by one over the improving young duo.

They sat back against a couple of trees and drank lemonade to wash down the rolls they'd eaten, unconcerned and unhurried.

'So, boys, what's the plans, then?' Stan asked.

Neil lay back on the grass, eyes closed, and muttered, 'Just make it to the end of the holidays. Then, get ready for the big, wide world.'

Quentin nodded, 'Yeah, me too. But I reckon Uni' will be a bit easier than working with old Ted.'

Stan laughed, and took another swig. 'Don't you worry about Ted. I reckon he's got some stories to tell, and some knowledge to pass on, too. Neil'll be fine. You just watch out for all those University chicks, Quent. Keep your mind on your studies and off of everything else.'

'Yeah, like he's gonna do that,' snorted a prone Neil. 'He's only gotta see a bloody bitch on a lead and he starts shaking.'

Stan laughed along with Neil, but Quentin just shook his head, a rueful smile on his lips.

'Don't you worry chaps, I'll be fine. The only anatomy I'll be thinking about will be dead ones.'

He'd decided to major in biology, knowing that it would be a huge move towards the path he wanted to take, along with English and sociology. As much as his friends derided him, he was genuinely concerned about the future of his planet, but rather than sit cross-legged in front of the Houses of Parliament abusing hapless policemen, he preferred to take a more positive step to help. As yet, he was unsure which route it might take, but he felt that he wanted to be 'out there, doing it', as Stan would say, rather than sitting in a lab or an office, theorising about it.

'Right, come on Posh,' he said, 'let's give the old boy a tonking.'

The afternoon was slower, but none the less enjoyable, and when Stan hooked a lively double figure carp on his light, tench tackle, the derision was directed firmly at him. After many minutes, and the total destruction of the swim, Neil netted a lovely, dark mirror of about sixteen pounds for him, and it seemed a fitting way to end the trip.

As they packed the gear away in the car, Neil asked Stan about the poaching incident, a couple of days earlier. Stan gave them a brief synopsis, explaining how some 'friends' of Ted's were able to furnish them with night-vision goggles and something called a 'stinger'. It basically unrolled like a mat, to lie across the road, but had hundreds of sharp, metal spikes that would render even the toughest tyre useless and shredded.

'What about the carp, Quill, which one was it?,' asked Quentin.

'Well, it wasn't The Common. One of the big mirrors. I couldn't see it that well because it was so bloody dark, and we wanted to get it back into the lake, but it was huge. Really big. I'm sure it was as big as The Common.' He seemed to be talking to himself by now, almost unaware that anyone was listening.

As he'd thought, sleep had been almost impossible to come by. He'd held in his arms one of the biggest carp in the land, how was he expected just to forget about that? Sleep eventually came as the sun rose, and a few hours later he was by far from in the best of moods. By evening he just needed to rest, and sat on the chair, in front of the telly, miles away.

'I got it, by the way,' said Jean.

'Mmm? What? Sorry, what did you say?' he gabbled, unsure of the words he'd just caught.

'I said I got it. The job. I got it.'

'You got it? Oh, babe, brilliant! I'm sorry, I forgot. I'm sorry. But you got it, oh that's brilliant. When do you start?'

Jean had decided that working at home was no longer for her, and so had embarked on an entirely different career path. An Open University course had reinforced the idea that she could teach, and so she had applied for a job as English teacher in the local junior school. And now she'd got it.

He let her tell him all about it. The interview, the wait outside, and then the swift decision. He was really pleased and knew that she would be great. As they lulled back into the telly, the phone rang and Stan snaked an arm out to answer it.

'Hello.'

'Hello, mate, how ya doing?' said the unmistakable voice of Rhodie.

'Rhodie! Bloody hell, mate, I thought you'd died. How you been?'

'Oh, you know – ducking and diving, bobbing and weaving. Bloody working, mainly. Ain't stopped in the last month or so. China, Singapore, bloody Brussels. It's all go, Quill.'

Stan laughed heartily and settled back for a welcome chat with his long-distance mate. They'd seen little of each other over the previous year or so, what with the distance involved, but that had been exacerbated when Rhodie had got a job, out of the blue, that entailed him being away from home a great deal. This had affected not only his social life but, more especially, his fishing, and the frustration was evident on the few times that they talked.

Now was little different, and he had Stan chuckling away with his stories of Oriental culture and Far Eastern cuisine and transport.

'Mate, they eat some shit out there, I tell you,' he began. 'Balls and cocks, eyes and ears, the lot! We went to this big do, way out in the middle of China. Massive city that you've never even heard of, I bet. But to get there, and it's, like, a three-hour flight, you're in a tiny little plane, with a prop. About thirty seats and six windows. It was like something out of the bloody Wacky Races. I expected Dick Dastardly to be at the controls and Muttley serving drinks!'

Stan was chortling away by now, acutely aware of his friend's decided 'uncertainty' about flying.

'Quill, I tell ya, at one point the thing was shaking, and the engines were revving and I'm looking out of the window and there's lightning and rain, and I thought, "This is it, boy. Stick yer head between yer legs and kiss yer arse goodbye!" No kidding.'

Jean tutted and adjusted the volume on the telly to compensate for Stan's near hysteria, but still it continued.

'Then, when we eventually get there, after being driven to the hotel by Michael Schumacher on angel dust, we're told we're going to this special reception, just for us. In the bloody mayor's official gaff. You know me, Quill, I ain't up for all that poncey stuff, but the boss says we gotta go, so I get togged up, then we're in the bloody loony mobile again. Luckily, it's only ten minutes so my life only flashed before my eyes three times. Then, we get to this right posh gaff. All marble and fantastic carpets and we're led into this massive bloody dining room that must house a thousand. There's about forty-odd people in there when we arrive and we're shown to this table with the mayor and his missus. Then they start bringing the food round and suddenly I realise I'm bloody starving!'

Stan's hysteria had subsided a little by now, but his stomach was aching and he knew there was bound to be more to come,

'You know me; I love a bit of foreign grub, so I have a bit of this, and it tastes like chicken, then I have a bit of that and it tastes like fish. Then a nice, spicy something, and I'm loving it. Drop of sake to wash it down, and suddenly the day don't seem so bad after all. Then the waiters clear away the stuff, before I've really started, and the interpreter says that we have a 'velly special dish.' Okay, I think, lets be having you, I'm 'ank Marvin. Well, they bring out these silver platters and on each one is, like, a silver egg cup with a lid on. It gets set down in front of us and I'm thinking, a bloody big chicken better hatch out of this. Anyway, we sit and stare, then the mayor lifts his lid and reveals what looks like a black egg.'

Stan is off again because he can see exactly what's coming.

'Yeah, you're way ahead ain't you, boy? Well, we all follow suit, then he taps the shell with his little silver spoon, so I do the same, then use the little silver knife to lift the top and inside is this stinking black mess. Mate, the stench hit me like a bloody fist and I thought I was gonna chuck! I've never smelt anything like it.'

'Hundred-year-old egg,' said Stan, barely.

'Exactly, mate. And it bloody smelt like it, and I thought, there's no bloody way that is going near my mouth. But then I look at my boss, who is sitting opposite, and he's staring at me as if to say, 'Eat!' I looked at the others, and they were all having a little nibble, so I thought, sod this, if I've got to eat it, I'm gonna do it in one. So I dug the spoon in, took a deep breath and just whacked it straight in. In seconds my mouth was full of liquid, you know, like when you're just about to chuck up, and I really thought it was chunder time. But I just closed my eyes, swallowed and just willed my stomach to stay where it was. When I opened my eyes I had tears streaming from 'em, my gag reflex was on time and a half, and I just grabbed the jug of sake, poured out a huge glass and whacked it straight back.'

Stan's hysteria had returned in bucket loads, and Jean had abandoned the telly and had retired to the kitchen to do a bit of washing up.

'What happened?' he managed between gasps. 'What about your boss?'

'That was it, wasn't it, the bastard. He never even put a bit to his mouth. Everybody was watching me convulsing and turning green, so he got away with it. I looked at the mayor, and he was smiling at me, as if to say, 'Ha, stupid Engrish man, you fall for old egg tlick.' I excused myself a minute or so later and chucked the whole lot back up in their very posh toilets. Didn't eat another thing all night. Bloody heathens.'

After that, Stan was incapable of speech, and just whimpered a little.

'Anyway, I'm off to Germany tomorrow, so at least there'll be some decent beer. I'll call you when I get back, at the weekend. We need to sort out some bloody fishing. Talk to Sid; he's on a new lake or something, ain't he?'

'Yeah, apparently,' said Stan, slowly recovering some semblance of equilibrium. 'I'll talk to him and see what the crack is. Enjoy Germany; don't mention the war.'

'Yeah, that'll be just my luck. See ya later, boy,' and 'click' went the phone.

Posh and Smiffy laughed along with Stan when he related the story, but they weren't nearly as amused as he was, and it took little time before Posh returned to the original question.

'So, how big d'you reckon, Stan? Forty? Fifty? How big is 'really big'?'

Stan knew. Stan had the perfect yardstick – The Common. He knew how much that weighed six years ago, and was sure that it was even bigger now. And he'd held the big mirror in his hands, had seen it alongside The Common on numerous occasions. He knew.

'Yeah, possibly fifty pounds, Neil. Really big.' He stared at the road ahead and seemed to drift off, and the two boys looked at each other and shrugged. As they entered the village, Stan seemed to snap out of his trance, and turned to his passengers.

'Well done, boys, that was a good day's fishing. What a way to end the summer, eh Neil? That was a very, very special carp, mate. Very special. I know it's your biggest, but believe me, size means very little with a fish like that. Be proud. And good luck with Ted.'

'Cheers, Stan, I'm sure it'll be great,' he replied.

'Yeah, cheers Stan, that was a great trip,' agreed Smiffy.

'No problem. And Quentin, you do good things, mate. I know you can, so do your mum and dad. Enjoy yourself, and when you pop back maybe we'll get another trip in.'

He then pulled up outside Smiffy's house, and they took out their tackle and bits and bobs, then waved Stan goodbye, thanking him again.

'Right then,' said Posh. 'This is it, mate. First day of the rest of our lives.'

'Not yet, Posh, that's tomorrow. Fancy a quick go on the PlayStation?'

Posh smiled, then led the way to the back door. One last time, before it was time to go out and meet the world.

Ted sat quietly by the snag tree, watching. The previous night had been successful, but had also been fraught with danger. It was a hostage situation, and he knew only too well how wrong they could go. Speed. Accuracy. Surprise. Once again it had worked, but it hadn't always.

Things can go wrong; people can get hurt. Accidents can happen. Difficult to avoid, sometimes, impossible to forget.

His mind drifted, to a smoky room, full of sound. Screams, shouts, banging doors, barked orders. Another stun grenade dimmed the view, dulled the senses. Eyes stinging, throat rasping.

But not yours. Mask on tight and breathing normal. The room a confusion of terror and fear. Gunshots ringing out, a muzzle flash to your left. Identify target. Short burst of automatic fire, deafening within the small enclosure, inciting more shouts and screams. Target nullified. Time to move, fast.

All occupants PlastiCuffed and dragged out of the building, hostage and terrorist alike.

Three fatals; all hostage takers. It happens.

But later, it turns out that one wasn't. A taker. One was a hostage, forced to hold a gun. In the smoke, and the noise, and the muzzle flash, impossible to tell. Only one solution.

Final.

Deep, deep down, he sensed movement. Something substantial, moving large amounts of water in its passing. Leviathan. To his right, a movement caught his eye, and four or five small carp sidled into view. He'd not seen anything this small before, maybe less than a pound. They must be from last year's spawning, one of the few successful ones he can remember. Careful observation reveals another couple, then a bigger one moves amongst them. Twice the size, almost a couple of pounds. Surely not the same year? But, he'd seen nothing last year, nor earlier this year. This was good news, and unsurprising. Unsurprising that from such a tree, fruit so bountiful should grow.

As it flashed on its side before diving deeper, he saw its flank. A common.

Ted smiled. Nothing to worry about, now. All would be well in the end.

Chapter Seventeen
Wearing the Inside Out

Stan peered from beneath his brolly into the damp gloom.

Is it drizzle? Or light rain? Or mizzle? With nothing else to occupy him, these weighty thoughts were allowed to wander unfettered across the wasteland of his mind.

Whatever it was called, it had started at dawn and had continued unabated for the next dozen hours. Dusk was premature due to this enforced gloom, and Stan pondered the possibilities. He'd arrived twenty-four hours earlier, relatively confident after having a couple of successful sessions in the previous month. But now, that confidence was gradually being washed away and all he could think of was how comfortable that sleeping bag looked – but not yet. It was barely seven o'clock and he'd yet to have any dinner, delaying that event for as long as possible. The radio muttered and hummed in the background, and he caught a hint of a melody that he recognised. Turning it up a little, he smiled to himself, mentally patting himself on the back for spotting Tom Petty's 'Breakdown' from the merest clue. He hummed along, then joined in the chorus with Tom. Just as the song faded, another more jarring note rang out and he looked at the mobile phone on the bedchair. The screen announced 'SID' and he picked up the phone and answered straight away.

'Sid, you old dog, how are you mate?'

A throaty chuckle came back in response.

'Hey, hey! Quill! How's it going, buddy? Are you out there doing it?'

'Yeah, mate, you know the flavour, can't let the bastards grind you down. What about you?'

'Oh yeah, Quill. You know me, out there battling the elements. Been bagging any?'

Stan told his distant mate of his recent successes and concluded with, 'Nothing this weekend, though. Looks bloody shit at the mo'. Bin raining all bloody day and I haven't seen a thing.'

'Drismal, that's what it is, fella,' Sid declared, and Quill smiled – a perfect description.

'What about you, Sid? You been having any, boy?'

'Well, as it happens, I bagged meself one a little earlier,' he replied with that trademark chuckle. 'A lovely twenty nine pound mirror. Reckon I might have a chance of some more, as well. Just seen a fish head and shoulder near my right hand rod.'

'Where are you? On that new lake?' asked Stan.

'Yeah. Lovely lake, about forty-odd acres and hardly anyone here. You should pop over for a session, mate. It's really lovely.'

Stan furrowed his brow a little. 'What's the deal, then? What's in there?' he asked.

'Well, apparently there's three or four forties and about a dozen thirties. About sixty, seventy fish in total. I've seen photos of a thirty-eight common and a forty-two mirror. Thing is, the club have come up with some bizarre rule where you can't drive your car round the lake any more. Gotta park in the car park by the sailing club, so to get to the far side of the lake is about a fifteen-minute walk.'

Stan nodded. 'Same old story. Where you fishing, then?'

'Fifteen minute walk from the car,' replied a chuckling Sid. 'No other bugger's been over here for about a month. Been popping over after work, once or twice a week, to put a bit of bait in. Seems to be working, eh?'

Stan smiled and was suddenly slightly envious.

'Where is this lake then?' he asked.

'Other side of Andover, towards Newbury; 'bout forty minutes from me. Dunno, maybe hour and a half from you. Fancy a bit of winter fishing with yer old mate, then?'

Stan peered out at the thickening gloom, listening to the hiss of rain on the water and the brolly.

'Yeah Sid, I might just fancy that. Tickets easy to come by, then?'

Sid chuckled, 'Oh, yeah, mate, you just leave that to… SHIT!'

Stan heard a faint buzzing from Sid's end of the line, and what with the expletive, was quickly able to put two and two together and come up with 'run'. He listened for a few seconds, hearing a faint, 'Call you back' from Sid, then hung up, smiling. A text came through, twenty minutes later to explain: 'LOW BATT. 22.04 C. CALL YOU TOMORROW.'

Hmm, that hadn't been in his plans at all, but all of a sudden it loomed large in his future, and he could think of nothing else for the rest of the evening.

He'd been fishing the Hatch for a couple of years, now, and had been fairly successful – hugely so, compared to previous records on the lake – but he was now getting a high percentage of repeat captures and that made days like today depressing and hard to take. The previous couple of winters had been totally fruitless, and he saw no reason why this one should be any different, and to be truthful he probably didn't anticipate doing more than half a dozen sessions between now and the end of the season. The clocks changed in a couple of weeks, and this wasn't the sort of lake he relished arriving at in the dark on a Friday night.

And fishing with someone again, that would be cool. Since the Mere closed he'd rarely spent any sessions with anybody for company but himself. The odd, fun session with Neil and Smiffy had been a pleasant interlude, but the Hatch was a quiet lake, with no other serious carp anglers, and he found the company of the pleasure anglers testing at times.

Then, as if to cement his thoughts, he caught the opening bars to a favourite song of theirs. Reaching over to turn up the volume, he sang every word of 'The Boys are back in Town' with Phil Lynott. That nailed it then, time to move on.

The last time he'd bellowed out that refrain was a month earlier, with Buzz, on their way back from the Oval.

It was the second day of the fifth and final Ashes test, and Peter found him on the far side of the Estate, up to his waste in mud.

'Gosh, Stan, that looks like enormous fun,' he said, smiling.

Stan smeared some mud across his face as he wiped away a drop of sweat from his brow. 'Oh, its bloody lovely Peter, couldn't think of anything else I'd rather be doing. What's happening in the cricket? Last I heard we were all out for 373.'

'31 for nought at the moment, bit cloudy. Sure you'd prefer to be down there than at the Oval, though, eh?'

'Oh yeah,' snorted Stan, 'what I'd give to be there, Pete.'

'Hmm, I wonder what you would give, Stan my lad. Eh, what would you give for two tickets for the Sunday of the last Ashes test at the Oval?' Peter stood there, smiling, whilst watching the play of emotions and thought processes on Stan's face. He loved playing these games, knowing that he always came out a winner.

'What are you saying, Pete? Have you got tickets, mate?' Stan still wasn't sure what was going on, but his heart had started to beat a little faster.

'Stan, I have two tickets for the Oval on Sunday. I and a friend were due to go, but he's just been taken ill and I, I'm afraid, have to accompany the good lady to her parents for some god-awful function. Can you bloody believe it? I'll be about five miles away and will have to watch the whole bloody thing on TV, and believe me, I will.' Peter was quite animated, but Stan had lost the whole lot after 'two tickets'.

'So, what you're saying is, that you have two tickets, you can't use them and you're offering them… to me?'

'In a nutshell, that is exactly what I'm saying. What do you think?'

'Yo, Quill, how you doing, mate?' A big voice answered his call on the second ring.

'Buzz, I'm doing bloody great, buddy. Now, I have a question for you. What you doing Sunday?'

11th Sept 2005

The Oval!

Result! Pete couldn't make it to the Oval today. Had 2 tickets in corporate so me and Buzz are off there. Meeting Buzz at Clap June 10.00

This could be a tricky day — 277-2 overnight. They both look set, need an early wicket — cliché. Coming through Surbiton, should be there in twenty mins. Bright sunshine at the mo, but rain later, maybe.

WHAT A MORNING — FREDDIE!!

Met Buzz at Clap J then straight to ground for a bit of breakfast. Saw Aussies getting off coach, they look relaxed. We're in the new stand, all food and drink laid on — pukka. Jerusalem was incredible, shivers up the spine.

Freddie bowling like a train. & Hoggard. The roar when Hayden went was deafening. 6 wickets down and still not reached our total yet. Bit poncey here, most people are here for the food, not the cricket — not us.

YOU BLOODY BEAUTIES!

What a day, what a day. Freddie is a bloody God! Most incredible atmosphere I've ever known — sod the football, this was brilliant. That hour after lunch was just the most wonderful hour of sport I've ever seen. Rain came at the right time. We could bloody do this! May have to call in sick tomorrow, need to watch this!

Fat chance.

Perversely, Stan's first session on Brampton pit was undertaken alone. He'd had to work at the weekend, and so had Monday and Tuesday off instead. Sid, sadly, had to work so Stan arrived mid-morning, on his own, but in a car park that already housed ten cars. His initial apathy was soon washed away when he realised that all but one of the cars belonged to the sailors that were already on the water. The day was bright and breezy, and the small sailing craft were skipping across the waves with some gusto. These guys were obviously much more competent than those that graced the waters of Felcham Mere.

After a few moments of quiet admiration, he closed the car door and set about a circuit of the lake. Sid had been fishing the far end of the lake, but Stan was open-minded on this first session, and would see where his fancy took him. After no more than a couple of minutes walk he came across the owner of the only non-sailing car, and stopped for a quick chat. The guy was set up with three rods, and with his bivvy firmly placed, looked like he was there for a day or two.

'Alright, mate, how you doing?' he enquired as he stood at the back of the swim. The guy turned in his chair and shielded his eyes from the low sun.

'Yeah, alright mate,' he replied, shortly. Stan knew what it was like, being confronted by a complete stranger and unsure of what was expected of you.

'Any good?' he continued, in time honoured fashion.

'Nah, only got here an hour ago,' came an equally short reply, and it was obvious that the guy was not going to be effusive about things, so Stan brought proceedings to a rapid close.

'Oh, well, good luck, mate. See yah,' and with that he turned away and continued on his circuit.

Despite the time of year there was still quite a lot of vegetation about, and the trees had yet to shed all of their leaves. The southwesterly wind was rattling through the trees, though, and Stan was sure that the foliage wouldn't resist for too much longer. A few hundred yards beyond the mute angler, Stan came to a large bay, with a point of land shielding it from the southwesterly wind. Standing in the swim at the end of the point, he surveyed the water in front of him, watching a couple of boats scudding past fifty yards or so out into the lake. The wind was coming from his right, and the sheltered bay to his left looked quite inviting in the late autumn sunshine. He stood for a few minutes, unsure of what was below the surface, but, as this was a gravel pit, convinced that there would be features aplenty.

Continuing his tour, he soon came to the swim right opposite the car park, sure that this was where Sid had been concentrating his efforts. Since their phone call, a couple of weeks earlier, Sid had managed to catch another couple of low-twenties and was confident that more, and larger, were to follow. Stan could see the attraction of the swim. The southwesterly was blowing almost straight into the swim, but the trees to the right of it offered shelter from the stronger blasts. Although unable to see for himself, Sid had told him about a shallow plateau at sixty yards, as well as a couple of gravel bars that crossed in front of the swim, closer in. Yep, this certainly looked like a good area, but he'd decided already that he wasn't going to fish the swim. When he and Sid were able to fish together, he wanted to be happy in his own swim.

And within a hundred yards he found what he was looking for.

The point that he'd stood in earlier was opposite, separated by a couple of hundred yards of windswept water, and the swim he stood in now was completely different. There seemed no obvious reason to fancy it, but something told him to sit and ponder. 'Should have brought a plumbing rod,' he muttered to himself, whilst watching the white horses chase each other towards Sid's swim, to his right. Then, something turned over, forty yards out, and he was all attention and staring eyes. He'd not seen the fish, but it wasn't small, and when it rolled again he was staring straight at it and saw the golden flank of a carp disappear beneath the waves. That'll do me, he thought, and was soon striding purposefully back to the car. Going that way round took only ten minutes to walk back to the car, and within half an hour he was back, panting and sweating despite the time of year.

His first priority was to deploy the marker float. It was still quite early, with little chance of rain, so the bivvy could wait until all the rods were in place. After half an hour with the plumbing rod, it was evident that the area in front of him was fairly devoid of features, apart from two very obvious ones. To his right, starting at about sixty yards, and extending for a further thirty, was what appeared to be the end of the plateau that Sid fished from his swim. This was obviously a very large feature, and one that didn't really fill him with confidence, and he realised that this couldn't be the main focus of his fishing or baiting.

The other feature, however, was much more encouraging. At first he thought he'd found a gravel hump at about fifty yards from the bank. Further investigation showed it to be a couple of yards wide, which was fine, so he cast twenty yards past it to see how deep the water was behind it, and his lead landed with a 'donk'. Dragging it slowly towards him, he could feel it bumping and bouncing along the bottom, and on letting the float rise, he measured a depth of seven feet, the same as the gravel hump. The penny didn't take too long to drop, and by his fourth or fifth cast he had established that it was a gravel bar that was running almost straight towards him. In fact, it was running from '11 o'clock' to '5 o'clock', which meant that he could put two baits on it; one at the nearest point to him, and the other off to the left a little and anywhere between ten and fifty yards further out.

Time to put the plan into action.

The wind from his left made baiting up a little tricky, especially for the furthest rod, so that dictated the maximum distance he would fish, making it easy to bait up in most conditions.

A couple of hours after leaving the car park, and just after lunchtime, all three baits were settled. He scattered a bit of bait around all three rods, using the spod to get the bait to the furthest mark, and was quite happy, for now, with his morning's work. A couple of tufties were bobbing in the waves, a hundred yards out, and he hoped that they weren't going to invite their mates over for a party during the night. A few seagulls wheeled overhead, which had made baiting up a bit tricky, but he knew that the bulk of the bait had made it to the bottom, he just wondered what it would be like later in the year with those flying, bait-snatching vermin.

An hour later, as he was putting the finishing touches to his home, 'Light my Fire' rang out on his phone, and the screen announced SID.

'Hello boy, checking up on me, are ya?' he said, by way of a greeting.

'Heh, heh! Just wanna make sure you're not doing any poaching, Quill.'

'Nah, just moved straight into your swim, save any disturbance with the plumbing rod. Nice, innit? Lovely plateau out there. Where you been baiting, mainly?'

Sid paused for a second or two, then chuckled again.

'Don't be shitting me now, Quill. You know what'll happen, mate. I'll have to come down and put some manners on you.'

Stan smiled and thought about continuing the subterfuge, but decided against it. They could be there for hours and, as amusing as it would surely be, he just couldn't afford the battery life on the phone.

'Oh, okay you scary man, I'll come clean,' he said.

'Best you do, fella. So where you fishing? What you caught?'

Stan was staring out at the rolling lake, watching another boat sail past a hundred yards out. He explained the carp sighting, the plumbing revelations, and his subsequent baiting.

'Don't you be casting too far to the right now, Quill. My water, mate.' As jokey as he made it sound, Quill knew that there was a certain substance to it, and filed that away for later.

'Yeah, yeah. My water at the mo,' Sid. Anyway, got two baits on the bar, sixty and ninety yards, and the third one on the end of the plateau, not quite sure how far along.'

Sid just went, 'Hmmm,' then continued. 'I'm gonna pop over this evening, put a little bit in. D'you want me to bring you a nice fish 'n' chip supper, mate?'

Despite being well supplied with food, Sid's offer made his mouth water. 'Bloody hell, yeah! Cod 'n' chips for me, mate. Loads of salt and vinegar. If you're a good boy I might even make you a cuppa.'

'Bloody right you will! Right, I'm off. Somebody's gotta be doing some work around here. I'll come straight from work, so I'll see you about seven. Good luck, mate, bag a whacker,' and with that he was gone.

A phone conversation with Sid was always a verbal jousting match, and invariably you did well just to stay on your steed. A cup of tea was definitely in order after that.

As the steam rose from his cup, the bobbin on the left hand rod dropped a fraction. The wind was fairly brisk, but not enough to disturb the bobbin. A few seconds later it dropped a little more. Then again, and he had that sinking 'bream' feeling. On picking up the rod and starting to reel in, he felt something on the end, but it could have been a lily leaf or plastic bag for all the resistance it put up. As it flipped across the surface, close in, he saw the unmistakable shape of a small bream, skimming along on its side. Bugger! He hand-lined it to the bank and unhooked it in the margin, letting it lie on its side until it realised it was actually still alive. Insipid bloody creatures.

He'd lined up a particular tree on the far bank, and had put a marker on the line, but it took three casts before he felt the lead land with a thud. That could be tricky in the dark, he thought. By the time darkness was upon him, however, another couple of bream had fallen to the same rod, and he pondered the wisdom of spodding out pellets with the boilies, earlier on. He just hoped that they knew about pyramids in this lake.

Sid arrived just after dark and announced himself in typical fashion.

'Right, stand by yer beds. Lovely grub, lovely grub. Probably the only fish you'll see this week, eh?'

Stan had seen the car pull into the car park ten minutes earlier, and had assumed that it was his meals on wheels, so had put the kettle on in preparation.

'Come on, Quill, I'm bloody gagging. Where's me…' Stan handed him a steaming mug of tea to put paid to any further abuse. 'Good man, Quill. I don't care what the others say about you, mate, I think you're alright.'

'Cheers, Sid. Now, where's that lovely grub?'

They ate and chatted, and Sid tore into him when he learnt of the three bream.

'Oh, I'm glad you're gonna be fishing here, Quill. That'll keep the snotty bastards away from me, heh, heh!'

Stan took little notice, and just put the kettle back on. An hour later, as he was leaving, Sid demanded results. 'Call me, tell me how big. No shirking, now, buddy. Talk to you soon. See ya.' Then he switched on his head torch and walked off towards his swim, to deposit a kilo of bait. Stan could hear the 'swish… plop' as Sid wielded the throwing stick for the next half an hour. Then he heard a faint, 'See ya Quill, good luck,' as the task was completed.

It was barely midnight when he woke, and wondered how long the mole that was trying to burrow out through his belly button had been in there! The sharp, stabbing pains were coming every minute or so and he felt like he was about to give birth. Something was very wrong in his stomach, and it seemed that his body was trying to decide which end it should be ejected from. The decision process took another couple of hours, but when it came, Stan was out of bed and on his hands and knees within seconds, heaving and retching as the command to 'be gone' was eventually given. Liquidised fish and chips spattered to the ground on a wave of tea for the next ten or twenty seconds, but that wasn't all of it and he stayed down, elbows on the floor, kneeling like he was waiting to be beheaded. Another wave of bile preceded a further evacuation. Then another.

That seemed to be it, but he stayed in position for another minute, clammy sweat covering his body.

'Bloody Sid!' he muttered whilst dribbling onto the floor.

When, eventually, he was able to return to his bedchair he felt little better, but knew that the worst was past. Sleep eventually came after half an hour of small aftershocks, only to be interrupted an hour later by the left hand rod, indicating another drop back.

He left it for ages, but the insistent beeps that came, like his stomach pains, every minute or so could not be ignored forever, and so eventually he dragged himself out of his bag and unceremoniously winched in the slimy culprit. This was a slab of a bream, way over ten pounds, but he cared little and unhooked it in the water, like its predecessors. He then just dropped the rod on the ground, and crawled back into bed.

A watery sun lit the inside of the bivvy when the next electronic beeps awoke him. He peered, bleary eyed, at the remaining two rods but nothing had moved and no lights were on. He then looked at his phone and could see the envelope that indicated he had a text message. He slowly clicked it on and unsteadily read the words.

BLOODY ILL. POXY FISH. U OK.

It was from Sid, obviously, and at least it gave an answer to his night-time ailments. He lay there for a further minute or so before sending a garbled text back.

NO. SHIT. CHUCKED AL NITE. U WANKER

He pressed SEND and lay back down. Boy, did he need a drink. Could he risk it? As these thoughts fumbled around for an answer, the middle alarm just screamed into life, the rod tip bouncing and spool spinning. In a jumbled heap he left the bivvy and grabbed the rod. The baitrunner was still on so he clicked the bale arm round and felt the fish surge on the other end. It kited off to the right, but was nowhere near the other rod, so he let it go. For a few minutes it stayed low in the water, the line cutting through the relatively calm surface. His mouth was very dry and his head ached, and although this was obviously a carp he wasn't really enjoying the moment.

After five minutes he saw a vortex twenty yards out, and the carp was just below the surface. Another vortex, ten yards closer, and the game was almost up. Then the lead flipped out of the lake and plopped back in, a yard closer. The bloody hook had pulled, and his feeling of wretchedness was multiplied a hundredfold.

'Bastard!' he screamed, and threw his rod to the floor, turning back to the bivvy and disappearing beneath the sleeping bag.

When he awoke, a few hours later, he felt a lot better, but not great, and it didn't take long for him to decide that enough was enough. A nice hot bath, then a warm bed, was only a couple of hours away, and by midday he was gone. The trek back to the car park had seemed like an assault on the north face of the Eiger, and his journey home probably took ten minutes longer because he didn't have the strength to push down the accelerator.

Later that evening, after Jean had woken him and he had declined dinner, he called Sid. He had also been rough all day, and had stayed at home in bed. The fish was the obvious culprit, and they both vowed to burn down the shop later that week.

'Still up for the weekend, mate?' asked Sid. Stan didn't exactly feel like it at that moment in time, but confirmed anyway, saying that it would probably be Saturday morning when he arrived. After the call he slumped back in his chair, knowing that bedtime was beckoning, and thought about the prospects for the winter. He'd seen a carp. He'd hooked a carp. If he'd stayed another day maybe he would have landed a carp. Would this be a good winter water? At that moment, feeling as he did, it just seemed like a jinxed water. Time would tell.

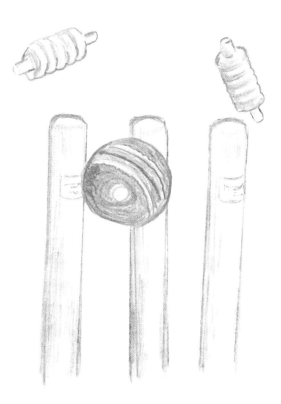

PART FOUR

WINTERTIME IS A RAZORBLADE
THAT THE DEVIL MAKES
IT'S THE PRICE WE PAY
FOR THE SUMMERTIME

Chapter Eighteen
Comfortably Numb

Stan slowly packed away his tackle, stopping every couple of minutes to rub some warmth back into his hands. Once again, winter had flicked its tail and a cold blast was sent across the March countryside, sending animals and people alike scurrying for cover and warmth.

This was his last session of the season, and although there were still two weekends left on Brampton, which closed at the end of March, he and Jean were scurrying for cover and warmth – to the Indian Ocean - the freezing cold of the day seeming to justify that move a thousandfold. And the prospects when he returned were beyond his wildest dreams.

The winter had been hard in many ways. The pre-Christmas run-up had brought torrential rain and serious, property-damaging floods, which in turn had made many lakes and rivers unfishable. Brampton had suffered quite badly, and the swims that he and Sid had earmarked for their winter campaign spent most of November below the waterline. Then, after a brief post-Christmas respite, the rains had returned, followed by freezing weather that had, once again, made many lakes unfishable.

Then Jean's dad had finally succumbed to a long illness, and the winter had seemed even bleaker.

This holiday was just what they both needed, and he couldn't wait. Ten years ago he couldn't have imagined even contemplating missing the final two weeks of the season, but now his perspective had changed; close friends had fallen seriously ill, out of the blue, and it brought home to him that life really should be taken by the throat and enjoyed in the moment. No more, 'Oh, maybe next week, next month, next year.'

Then, to sprinkle just a little fairy dust on the bleak landscape, he learnt that he was going to be a grandad, and everything came perfectly into focus.

The fishing that he'd been able to do over the previous few months had been relatively fun, in Sid's company, but not too successful, and despite managing a couple of fish on the session following the 'Fish 'n' Chip' incident, things had gone downhill from there. The floods had put paid to most of

November, and when they'd returned for a couple of sessions prior to Christmas, the lake had just turned off, and they ended the year on a blank.

Rhodie had returned from another sojourn, at the end of November, and had demanded that they go fishing in the very near future, before he went totally insane. Stan had, therefore, contacted Buzz, who was also on one of his away trips to a foreign clime, but would be back just before Christmas. That was it, then. They would meet after Christmas for a couple of days and whether they caught any carp was incidental, they just needed to get back together for a few days, chew the fat, put the world to rights, and generally talk bollocks – what a perfect recipe.

This Christmas, Stan and Jean had managed to get their children, Stevie and Laura, to come down for a couple of days, so they would have a houseful on Christmas Day once again. It would be a bit cramped, but that was no bother, and what with Stan managing to rent a two-bedroom cottage from one of the estate managers for a couple of days, at a very reasonable price, it looked like it would be a fine time. On top of that, Peter and Wendy were having a bit of a do on Boxing Day, and they'd all been invited over, so that took the strain off of Jean and Laura, who would be in total control of Christmas dinner.

The festivities went perfectly, especially as, unbeknownst to them, Jean's dad was with them for his last Christmas. Bellies were filled, bottles were emptied, and charades was once again a hilarious fiasco. But at the end of a very long day, Jean was in her cups and very, very chatty.

'Was it alright, babe?' she asked for the fiftieth time, still concerned that dinner was below par, as she did every Christmas.

'Babe, it was brilliant,' Stan assured her. 'Absolutely lovely. Like it always is.'

'Yeah, I know, but, you're not just saying that, are you?'

'No, babe. It was lovely, really lovely.'

'My dad doesn't look well, does he?' she continued, a catch in her throat.

'No, babe, he doesn't, but he had a great time. He's still as sharp as a tack. When he was winding your mum up about Titanic, I thought that was great. She didn't have a clue, and he was just chucking in the odd little line, with that cheeky old grin of his. No, he had a great time.'

Jean mumbled into his shoulder, 'Yeah, he did, didn't he?' She fell quiet then, and Stan knew it wouldn't be long before there was a soft snoring sound coming from her.

'It was alright, though, wasn't it?' she muttered, almost in her sleep.

'Yeah,' he said, smiling, 'it was great.'

The following morning had been slow and quiet, with many heads in need of nursing. Jean looked tired, and even went for 'a little lie-down' just after midday. Everyone else took a little time to come round, but by late afternoon there was a bit of life showing here and there. Jean's mum and dad had decided to stay in, rather than go to Peter's, and although Jean complained at first, Stan convinced her that it was for the best.

'I'm not drinking much tonight,' stated Jean, still a little the worse for wear. Stan looked around at Stevie and Laura, and their partners, and raised his eyebrows. They just smiled, then looked up as the door was opened by Peter.

'Stan! Jean! Lovely to see you, come on in.' Introductions were made, directions to the drink and food given, and 'Make yourself at home' commanded.

Twenty or so people were already present, mainly family Stan surmised, but there was enough to feed the whole village, so he assumed more would be arriving. He spotted Quentin, back for his first holiday from University, and raised a glass, knowing that he'd be able to have a chat later. Jean looked a little worn, but within an hour or so, and with a couple of glasses of rose inside her, she was full of life and having a good chat with a few of the other wives.

As the evening wore on, and with a few beers inside him, Stan was also feeling fine, and had been chatting with Quentin about University. Then Neil Becks had arrived with his parents and Quentin excused himself. Stan smiled at people, chatted genially, and generally had a pretty good time.

'Stan. Stan. We need to speak, old chap. Need to introduce you to someone. Old friend of mine, bit of a wag. Likes a bit of the old outdoor pursuit. Huntin', shootin', fishin' type thing.' Peter snaked an arm around his shoulder and guided him, unsteadily, across the room to a small group of people. Amongst them was a man of about late fifties, casually dressed, but in that sort of casual way that only people with great wealth or tramps can get away with.

'Dickie! This is the chap I was talking to you about. Stan, Dickie. Or should I say, Richard, Duke of Beaufort.' Peter performed an exaggerated bow, then came back up, smiling and a little tottery.

'Stan. Nice to meet you,' said the Duke, extending a very steady hand. 'Pete's been extolling your virtues over the past few months. Do a bit of fishing, I believe?' Stan shook the firm hand, and suddenly realised that he really shouldn't be as drunk as he felt.

'Err, yeah. Love a bit of fishing, but haven't really had the time of late. Lot of work on here and, to be fair, not many places around here I'd really want to fish.' Richard picked up his whisky glass and took a sip. 'Really? I thought that there were quite a lot of places in the vicinity that offered some good fishing.'

'Oh, there are, but they're too busy for my liking. And too, err, what's the word? Too commercial. I love fishing, but not just to catch fish. Too much else to see to just be sat around a bowl, waiting for something to happen by.' Stan was in the full thrall of his ale, and his tongue moved freely. 'I've caught big fish, bloody big fish, but the best fish I've seen for ages was one that young Neil over there caught. From Linton's. Stunning old warrior of a fish, probably fifty years old. Didn't matter what it weighed. I would have loved to have caught that fish. D'you know what I mean?'

Richard nodded, smiling. 'Yes, Stan, I know exactly what you mean. I'm not a coarse angler myself, prefer the old trout and salmon, but to catch a trout from one of those bloody reservoirs instead of a little chalk stream. The difference is incomparable. No, I know exactly what you mean, and it's refreshing to hear such an attitude in this era of instant fame; biggest is best. Not my cup of tea at all.' He took another sip of whisky, then asked, 'Where are you fishing at the moment, then?'

Stan was trying his utmost to stay focussed, and used a chair to steady himself. 'Well, I belong to Stuart Goldsmith's syndicate, on the Hatch,' he began.

'Stuart! Hah, the old rogue. We used to be at Rothschild's together, ooh, must be twenty years ago now. Good lad is Stuart. We do a bit of hunting now and then. Haven't seen the old boy for a few months, now. Must give him a call.'

Stan didn't know what was expected of him next, so he just carried on. 'Yeah, the Hatch, which is a lovely water with some lovely fish, but I've caught most of them, now, and I really don't like the recaptures. Been over at a big lake near Newbury for a month or so, but I'm not sure it's the one for me. Maybe it'll be different in the spring, but now it's just cold and windswept.'

Richard looked thoughtfully at him, then took another sip of his drink, before continuing. 'Hmm. Well look. I've got a little lake on my land, out near Tisbury, got a small syndicate of good chaps on there. Few carp, old 'uns, been in there for as long as the Linton fish because I believe they came from the same source, at the same time. Few of the landowners, my father included, bought a batch of 'em from some farm in Surrey. Put 'em in the lakes to keep the weed down. Been there ever since.'

Without thinking, Stan just said, 'Leneys.'

'What? Actually, yes, that was the name of the chap. Seen it on the old records. Leney. David, or something.'

'Donald,' corrected Stan, who was suddenly starting to sober up. 'Donald Leney. The Surrey Trout Farm.'

Richard stared intently at him. 'That's it. The very fella. D'you know him, or something?'

Stan shook his head. 'Not personally, but I know of him. He bred the most wonderful carp up until about 1970, I think. Stunning fish, wonderful strain.'

'Interesting, because the last recorded stocking record is exactly that – 1970. Fifty fish. Might have been a closing down sale or something.' Richard laughed at that, but Stan was trying to evaluate the benefits of grovelling over begging, and whether sobbing would help.

'So, Stan, you seem to know a lot about these 'wonderful fish', how d'you fancy fishing for 'em?'

'Morning dear, cup of tea?'

Jean's voice cut through the fug, and he grunted in the affirmative. His head ached, and his mouth was dry, despite the copious amounts of water he'd obviously drunk during the night.

Something important was knocking on the door of his memory, but at that moment in time, there was nobody to let it in.

Jean arrived with the tea, and a couple of slices of toast, and sat back in bed.

The something was now shouting through the letterbox, trying to get somebody's attention.

'That was a nice night, wasn't it?' she said. 'Some lovely people there. You seemed to be getting on very well with that Lord, or whatever he was. What was his name?'

'Ah, come in. I've been expecting you. Sorry to keep you waiting.'

'Don Leney!' he shouted, sitting bolt upright and spilling a drop of tea on the duvet. Jean looked a tad startled, then just took a sip of her tea.

'So, it's full of Leneys and, for some bloody reason, he's letting **you** fish it?' Sid sounded less than impressed, but was, more to the point, just a little jealous. 'How the bloody hell does that happen, eh?' He looked around for support from the other two, but Buzz and Rhodie just grinned and raised their glasses.

'Fill yer boots, boy, that's what I reckon,' said Buzz, and Rhodie nodded in agreement.

'You're just bloody jealous, Sid,' he said. 'You'd be the first one to be crowing about getting a chance like that. Why don't you just let the old boy enjoy the moment; he might not get too many more at his age.'

Stan smiled, and raised his glass, and Sid just growled. It was a couple of days after the fateful Boxing Day conversation, and Stan and the others had met up earlier that day on one of the many lakes just outside Oxford. The weather was very wintry, and they anticipated very little carpy action, but were just glad to be out in the fresh air with their mates. They'd all turned up during the morning, and had spent most of the daylight hours drinking tea and exchanging Christmassy tales. Then, as they'd settled down for a huge turkey curry and some wine to wash it down, Stan had regaled them with the tale of his late night ducal conversation, and they were now all abuzz with the possibilities.

'So, do you know what sort of size they go in there?' asked Buzz. 'Fifty years old don't necessarily mean they're gonna be whackers.'

'Yeah, but that's the point, Buzz, they don't have to be whackers, they're bloody

Leneys,' said Sid, still sounding a bit too disgruntled.

'Yeah, exactly,' agreed Rhodie. 'Don't matter how big those babies are; they'll be stunners. Well done, Quill. You go and teach 'em a lesson, don't you worry about the old green-eyed monster over there.'

Stan was chuffed, Sid just huffed and they spent the next hour goading him with comments so barbed they would have been banned on certain waters.

They were only able to do the one night, with other commitments getting in the way for once, but it was still a nice break. On the way home, however, Stan reflected on how their lives had changed over the past half a dozen years, and wondered what would have happened if Felcham Mere hadn't been taken from them.

Would Rhodie have still moved to the other side of the country? Would Buzz have taken on as much work as he had done? Would he have carried on travelling a hundred-odd miles each way, through shit traffic, to get to the place?

Sid was always just an hour away and, despite their present winter campaign, they'd not really fished together much since the Mere had closed.

It seemed like the Mere had been the cement that bound them at the end. Would that cement be laid again, he wondered?

But then his mind found its way back to more joyful things – the prospect of fishing Beaufort's lake. Richard was firm in his offer, but told Stan to call him in a day or so to confirm everything, so Stan was still not counting his chickens.

But what did it hold? Richard had said that it had 'some good fish' in there, but had not expanded on that, but like Rhodie had said, it really didn't matter; he just wanted to get on there and have a look at it. He'd give the Duke a call this evening, and hope to God he wasn't out of his face at Peter's and had forgotten all about it.

'Hello, this is the Beaufort residence. I'm afraid we're out at the moment, but if you'd care to leave your name and number and a brief message we'll… Hello? Hello?'

'Err, hello?' stuttered Stan.

'Hello, sorry about that. Forgot to turn the bloody thing off. Just got back from taking the dogs for a run. Sorry, this is Richard, who's that?'

Stan was suddenly very dry-mouthed. 'Errm, Stan. Stan Peacock. We met at Peter's on Boxing Day. Night. Boxing Night, err…'

'Stan! Oh yes, the carp man. How are you? Hell of a do. Old Peter does love the post of host, doesn't he? Does it all with such… panache. So, Stan, how are you? What can I do for you?'

That was exactly what Stan had been dreading, the bloke **had** been pissed and he'd forgotten the whole bloody conversation. Before Stan could formulate a reply, however, Richard continued.

'Oh, yes. Bloody fool! The lake. We spoke about the lake and a syndicate place, didn't we?'

'Yes, sir. You asked me to give you a call in a couple of days, so I thought…'

'Yes, of course. Bloody stupid of me. Sorry Stan, completely forgot. Right, I'll have a chat with my head bailiff, just to make sure we're not overloaded at the moment, then I'll give you a call back. Is that okay?'

'Fine, sir. That'll be great. I look forward to hearing from you soon. Thanks.'

'Righty-ho. Talk to you soon. Gotta go, bloody dogs are chucking up something rotten. Bye!'

The phone line went dead and Stan was totally baffled as to what was happening. Was he in? What was that about being overloaded? Oh. Bloody hell, I knew it couldn't be that good, he thought, and went out of the back door to go and check on the drainage plant.

'Hello dear, you look freezing,' said Jean when he returned, a couple of hours later. 'Nice cup of tea?'

'Yeah, not half. Blimey, it's bitter out there. That wind's got razor blades in it. I was gonna go over and see Old Ted, make sure he was alright, but there he was, strolling round the lake as usual, in that same old coat. Looked bloody toasty.' He shucked off his big fleece, and rubbed his hands together in front of the fire.

'Oh, somebody called for you. Richard? Said he'll call back later.'

Stan cursed to himself. Now he'd have to go through the whole painful waiting process again.

'Did he say anything else?' he asked.

'Said he had some good news and some bad news. That was all. What's that about then?'

Stan had almost given up on a call that night, and was just preparing to watch the ten o'clock news, when the phone rang, and he nearly leapt out of his chair.

'Hello?' he said.

'Hello, is that Stan?' came a brisk voice.

'Yeah, how you doing?'

'Stan, it's Richard. Yes, I'm fine. Sorry for the lateness of the hour but we've had some friends over for a couple of days and they were supposed to leave this afternoon, but, you know how it is. Time marches on and all that.'

Stan was fully aware of the march of time, but had to bide his for a few more minutes.

'Anyway, spoke to Jackson about the syndicate. Only small – twenty members – and we don't want to expand it anymore. Thing is, we're full at the moment, but one of the chaps is off to Canada in April. For good. So, I reckon that you're the man to take his place. Is that okay?'

Stan was more than happy with that, sure that the coming few months would be totally the wrong time to start on a new lake anyway.

'That'd be great, sir. Brilliant. Any chance I could pop over sometime before just to have a look around the lake?'

'Most definitely. I'd want you to meet Jackson anyway, prior to starting. So, yes. Give me a call in a month or so, when the weather's a little more clement, and we'll arrange a meeting. All the best and, oh, a Happy New Year for tomorrow.'

'Yeah, you too. Bye,' said Stan. Then put the phone down.

'Was that the good news or the bad news?' asked Jean.

'Oh, yeah, that was good news. Very good news. Where's that Ordnance Survey map?'

Chapter Nineteen
A Saucerful of Secrets

The old barn creaked and groaned in the stiff breeze. It held no warmth any more, was less than waterproof, but was a fine hiding place.

Ted looked along the iron sights of his rifle, safety disengaged, and he tensed his trigger finger a little.

'Target acquired,' he said quietly. There was no reply. The sights continued to divide the head into two halves.

'Target acquired,' he repeated, unhurried but keen to complete the job at hand.

'Roger that… Wait. Out,' came a crackling reply. He continued to watch the figure, chatting with two others next to the car.

Armagh. A war zone if ever he'd seen one.

The trio continued chatting, smoking and priming their weapons for a couple more minutes. Then it seemed as if they had come to a decision. One of them opened the driver's door and climbed in.

'They're going to move. I still have the shot.' The head was moving, but he still had it square in his sights.

'Hold your fire. Hold your fire.' The message surprised him and he nearly took the decision upon himself, but that could never be right.

Then the man joined his two cohorts, and the car drove away. The most wanted man in Northern Ireland, and he could have finished him. He was angry, so angry, and he got back onto the radio to vent his spleen and demand an answer.

'Ted, you will follow orders, that is all. Do you understand?' came the barked reply.

'Yes, boss!' he snorted back, as sarcastically as he could. That was ignored, and they were told to make their way back to Base.

Later that night, a man was brutally murdered in front of his family. By three men, one of whom was identified by the deceased's distraught wife as the most wanted man in Northern Ireland.

The bitterness still stung Ted when he thought about that night.

But the stag was moving out into the open and he had a clear shot. Neil was lying next to him, watching the stag through binoculars. He glanced over at Ted, knowing that now was the perfect shot, but instead Ted slowly lowered the rifle.

'Not today, old boy,' he muttered, then lay the gun down. 'Okay, young Neil, we could have had him then, but there's plenty of time, lad. He'll be on show for a few more weeks. Maybe you should have a look for him next time, what d'yer think?'

'Okay,' said Neil, still a little perplexed at Ted's inaction, but more than happy with the prospect of culling the great beast next time.

It was the middle of winter; a chill January day, and Ted and his young protégé were wrapped against the elements, walking the woods to check that all was well. As much as they would never interfere in Mother Nature's grand design, there were occasions when just a little help might be required. A few weeks ago, a day or so after the New Year's celebrations, they had been walking the West Woods and had seen a fallen birch lying across the entrance of the badger's sett. There was no way that the incumbents would be able to escape, come the spring, so Ted, Neil and Stan had returned with a chainsaw and had cut the tree into manageable logs, thus removing it from the entrance. Survival of the fittest is all well and good, but sometimes, even the fittest need a little help.

Now, however, they were working for the other side. The deer population was growing larger, again, and all of the surrounding woods needed to be culled prior to the spring. The pregnant does were obviously left alone, but there were still many that could be taken. It amounted to very few, in wider terms, but was still a part of the job that Ted was uncomfortable with. He'd seen enough needless death in his life to want to have to continue it now. That's where young Neil would help. He knew that he was competent with a rifle and shotgun, and that would hold him in good stead in the future. Now, however, Ted would just have to take it carefully, didn't want any unnecessary accidents.

'Right, young Neil, I reckons we should head back now. Getting a bit cold, and looks like there might even be some snow coming in.'

They looked up at the leaden sky, and Neil knew that he wasn't wrong.

That was handy. He'd give Smiffy a call and pop over to see him. They'd not had much chance to catch up since Boxing Day, and there had been talk of a piking trip before Smiffy returned to Leeds. The weather wasn't great for it, but if it snowed it would be lovely to be out by the river. Might at least bag a chub or something.

'Okay, Ted. Think you're right. Hope it clears up tomorrow. Me and Smiffy are going down the river for a bit of piking.'

Ted looked skywards again. 'Wrap up warm then, lad. Gonna be cold after this lot.'

They walked off towards the frozen Mere, then Ted carried on towards Sutton Woods and his cabin, running over in his head how many logs he had stacked outside. Neil went off past the empty boathouse, and on to Smiffy's place.

The fall of snow was exactly as Ted had predicted and, by the morning, the land outside was hidden beneath a four-inch thick white blanket. Darkness was when the bulk of it had fallen, but there was still the odd flurry in the air as the sun revealed a true winter wonderland.

The phone rang and Neil knew who it would be.

'Neil, Quentin's on the phone,' his mum called up the stairs, and he walked onto the landing to pick up the call.

'Smiffy, alright? White enough for yer?' he said.

'Oh, yeah, mate. Don't it look fantastic? What d'yer reckon, still up for it?'

Neil was looking out of the window and weighing up their prospects. He'd normally either walk or cycle the mile or so to Smiffy's place, but that looked like being quite a task. Then he heard a big old diesel engine rumbling up the road, and had an idea.

'Mate, give me ten minutes. I might have a plan. I'll call you back.' With that he replaced the phone and ran downstairs to the front door. Quickly pulling on some boots and a coat, he ran outside and towards the engine, which happened to be housed in Ned Brown's tractor. He got alongside and shouted up to him, and Ned stopped.

'Where you off to, Ned?' he asked, slightly breathlessly.

Ned was well wrapped against the cold, and pulled down the scarf that hid his mouth. 'Just off to the Mount. Gotta make sure the sheep are okay, take some hay for 'em.'

'Brilliant!' declared Neil. 'Any chance of a lift?'

Smiffy was standing by the boathouse, shielded from the northerly wind and looking out over the frozen lake. In the lee of the building, and facing the watery sun, he felt decidedly tropical and had even taken off his scarf, but he knew that wouldn't last. Posh came around the corner, all steaming breath and crunching feet, and stood beside his mate.

'We must be out of our blooming minds,' he said, whilst clapping his gloved hands together to instil some heat. The tractor ride had saved his feet, but it wasn't exactly fast, and there was no heating, that was for sure. Smiffy laughed.

'Yeah, mate, but what else were we gonna do? Watch another re-run of 'The Sound of bloody Music'?'

Posh nodded, then shucked up the rucksack on his back. 'Right, let's go then. I feel a certain futility in the air but, as you so rightly say, my learned friend, what else we gonna do?' and off he trudged.

They went east, past the snags, which protruded white and dead, like bones in a parched desert. The snow was virgin; not a sign of life anywhere, and their footprints were the only ones to break the white blanket that morning. As they entered Sutton Wood, the silence was almost deafening. There was no sound. Nothing, bar the crunch of their feet in the snow. The woods were almost eerie in their stillness because, even in the depths of the coldest winter, there always seemed to be something. A crow. A robin. Even a startled deer. But today there was nothing. It was as if this was just one frame in an old roll of film. Nothing moved; everything was still, but once the projector clicked forward, all would be motion and sound. The walk warmed them, their thermal clothing reflecting back their body heat and keeping them free from the cold, but they knew that once they stopped moving, the cold would creep into their bodies like a thief.

'Look', said Smiffy, pointing ahead. A quarter of a mile distant, a thin pillar of smoke rose skywards, almost lost amongst the white trunks of the trees. 'Ted's,' he stated, unnecessarily.

'Hmm. What you thinking, mate?' asked Posh, just as rhetorically.

'Well, I just thought we might pop by, see how the old boy was. You know, no problems, roof still intact, that sort of thing.'

'What, and whilst we're there maybe just a quick cup of tea?' said Posh, on exactly the same wavelength.

'That's the idea, mate. Just be neighbourly. Old folk in winter and all that.'

No more words were needed, and they picked up speed as they moved towards Ted's surprisingly inviting cabin. Ten minutes later, as they were within fifty feet of it, the door opened and Ted stuck his head out.

'Come on then, kettle boiled five minutes ago. What kept yer?'

They glanced at each other, and Posh shook his head, before trotting forward and into the beautiful warmth of the cabin, followed shortly by Smiffy and a closing door.

Once inside, the lads took off their thermal coats and scarves, and sat down at the table.

'Still fancy a bit of piking do yer, lads?' asked Ted as he poured the steaming brew. The twinkle in his eye was not missed by them, and Posh replied.

'Oh, yeah, Ted. We just thought we'd pop in to make sure you were okay. Y'know, check that your fire hadn't gone out and that.'

Ted looked at him sideways on, then plonked the two cups in front of them. 'Very kind, I'm sure. But I reckon I should just about be able to muddle through.'

He sat down opposite them and stared out of the window. 'Gonna be a few in trouble today, mind. Pity you're off piking. I could do with a little help. Just make sure all's well with the wood folk.'

Posh looked at Smiffy and pursed his lips, as if to say 'Yeah, why not.'

Then Smiffy said, 'Yeah, why not?' and Ted nodded.

They finished their tea, having been warmed sufficiently by the brew and the stove, then donned their thermal jackets, scarves and hats and made their way back out into the cold, white wood.

'We'll head down towards the river for now, seeing as you was going that way, anyway. Just want to check out a couple of small dens, see if foxy's around,' said Ted. 'Then we'll head back towards the West Woods to check on the badger sett.'

There was no sound, barring the crunch of their boots in the virgin snow, and talking felt almost an intrusion in this silent world.

After a few minutes, though, Smiffy felt compelled to break the silence, and his question came from way out of left field.

'So, Ted, what did you used to do?'

Posh looked at his mate, but the surprise on his face was hidden by scarf and hat. Ted, however, took no such umbrage and answered simply.

'I used to take orders, lad. And carried 'em out as best I could.' As usual, and unsurprisingly, the answer was enigmatic and begged a thousand questions.

Smiffy looked at Posh and could just make out the raised eyebrows beneath the woollen cap. Unperturbed, he pressed on.

'Take orders? So, what, you were in the Army or something like that?'

Ted trudged on slightly ahead of them, not bothering to turn his head, and replied.

'Yes lad. The Army. Or something like that.' His answers were going off the end of the enigmatic scale, and Smiffy could tell that, to pursue this conversation, they'd need to be sitting somewhere warm and comfortable, and have a **lot** of time on their hands. They walked a few hundred yards in silence, then Ted stopped and looked about him, getting his bearings.

'Just down there, I think,' he said, indicating a small dip in amongst some skeletal birches. They walked slowly forward; the cold beginning to insinuate itself into their boots, and then Ted stopped again. Below a larger mound of snow they could see a dirty, brown hollow and Ted bent low and ran his hand across the ground in front of it. He stood and nodded. 'Yep, reckon they're okay. Snow's not got down there. Be warm as toast in there, I reckon. Right, let's see if the sett's in the same condition,' and off he went, with the boys trudging along behind.

An hour later, they were stamping their feet outside his cabin, clearing their boots of snow before they went back into the warm. As usual, the huge copper kettle was sat atop the stove, and it took little time before the steam indicated that it was ready to produce more strong, hot tea.

They sat at the table, talking about the badger sett and the tracks outside it. Then Ted said to Smiffy.

'So lad, what makes you so curious about an old fella like me?' He cupped the mug of brew in both hands and peered across the brim at Smiffy. Almost caught off guard, Smiffy took a gulp of tea to compose himself, then went straight for it.

'Well, Ted. Nobody seems to know much about you. Rumour is you were born here, before the war. Then after the war you left, left for a long time. And I think you came back about twenty-odd years ago. But what did you do before you returned here?'

Ted stared out of the window, then turned to look at Smiffy and Posh, who were assuming they were just about to be asked to leave. Smiffy had discussed this subject on many occasions with his mate, but Posh was happy to leave things as they were, content to have a job and not wanting to rock the boat. Now, he thought, the boat's practically under bloody water!

'Why would you want to know anything about me, lad? I'm just Old Ted, always have been, always will be.'

Smiffy pressed on. 'But Ted, that's not all you are. You know things, loads of things. We've learnt so much from you without you even trying to teach us. There's loads more. Loads. We just, well, y'know, we just want to… know.'

Ted sat still, thinking, saying nothing. He stared out of the window, then back at Smiffy. Then Posh. Then stood up.

'More tea, lads?' he asked. They both said, 'Yes' and Posh got up and took the cups to the small sink and rinsed them under the tap. He looked straight at Smiffy as he sat back down and furrowed his brow deeply, as if to say, 'What are you bloody doing?'

'Army,' said Ted, out of the blue. 'Got conscripted, after the war, then just sort of stayed. Tried leaving for a year but it didn't work. Army was like a family to me, gave me direction. Fed and watered me. Took me places I'd never been before, physically and mentally. 'Specially mentally. Stayed for a few years. Then a few more. Could have left after twenty-two years, but where would I go? So stayed a bit more.'

He set the two mugs in front of them and plonked a biscuit jar in the middle of the table, taking out a digestive and dunking it in his tea.

'I learned things, many things. Saw lots as well. Stuff you've never seen, stuff you'll never wish to see. Been to places so beautiful they would take yer breath away. And places so horrific ain't enough tears in yer eyes to cry for 'em. You think you learnt stuff from me without me trying. Wrong, lad. You learn stuff from me because you knows how to learn. Both of you. And I saw that in you years ago. The lessons are all around you; you just got to be willing to attend. You think you're the only one going to University, Quentin? You be so wrong. Young Becks is at the best University in the world. He'll learn just as much as you, just won't have any letters after his name to let people know. But then, if you've got knowledge, only you that needs to know, anyway.'

Posh and Smiffy were staring, wide-eyed, as Ted continued his diatribe.

'You both got something to give. Something big. I can tell that in you. You care about things, proper things. Not none of them telly soaps and all that contrived rubbish. You care about the world around you, and that's good. I didn't used to care, didn't used to know. But things happen in yer life, make yer see things differently. I seen many things made me see things differently. Death and poverty. Sin and hatred. Wanton apathy and sickening greed. Out here, in the woods, it's just plain life and death. No envy or enmity, just the need to survive. To make one generation survive the next. You ask what I'd done, lad. I did things that many wouldn't or couldn't do. Never questioned orders, just did what I was told, and, in the end, that's made me who I am. No choice in that. Made my choice many years ago; nobody to blame but me, if blame were needed.'

'But don't you get lonely here, all alone?' said Smiffy, intrigued.

Ted pondered the question for a few seconds, then replied.

'Everybody's alone, lad. But they only get lonely if they're not happy with the person they're alone with.' Ted looked straight at Smiffy, took a sip of tea, then said, 'So, is that helpful, lad? Does that tell you who I am, because that's all there is.'

Smiffy nodded slowly. 'Yes, Ted. It does. I'm sorry for asking, it's just…'

'No need for apology, lad. No law against asking. No law to say I have to answer. Just look at it this way. I am a University, I have much to teach for those who wish to learn. And that's that. Now, anyone for some rabbit stew? Managed to bag a couple before the snows came, damn tasty if I say so meself.'

On their way home through the silent woodland, Smiffy and Posh said very little, just concentrated on moving carefully and quickly, the temperature falling quite rapidly as the light bled out of the day.

When they were eventually warmly ensconced in Smiffy's kitchen, Posh addressed the subject they both had on their mind.

'You do realise he never told us a bloody thing, don't you?'

Smiffy smiled and nodded. 'Oh yeah. But he certainly did it in a powerful way, didn't he? I mean, what the hell has he seen in his life? D'you reckon he's, like, killed people?'

Posh looked out of the window into the deepening evening gloom. 'Dunno, mate. Not sure he'd ever tell you, well not directly. He might hint at some, I dunno, pain or memory or something, but I can't imagine him out-and-out saying that he shot someone. Can you?'

Smiffy shook his head. 'No, s'pose not, really.' He stood up and went to the cupboard, where he grabbed a chunk of Christmas cake that had been left over from the celebrations. 'Bit of cake, Posh? S'lovely. Me nan makes it.' He took a bite himself, then lay the rest on a plate and put it on the table between them.

'Well,' said Posh, grabbing a slice for himself, 'looks like you ain't the only one going to University.'

Around a mouthful of brandy soaked fruit cake, Smiffy mumbled, 'Nnh, looks that way. Mmph. Errm. Cor, that was lovely. Cup of tea, I reckon. Err, so, what about them pike then, mate? Reckon it'll be better tomorrow?'

Posh wiped his mouth with his hand, then said, 'Yeah, I reckon it could be. Try to get to the river this time, eh?'

Ted sat in the one armchair in the room, reflecting on things. Those boys, good boys. Got a good head on their shoulders, both of 'em. Seen their like many times. Too many times they didn't have a chance to make something of their lives. Ted was one that did have the chance. What had he made of his life? Had it been worth it? Would the big book at the pearly gates have more ticks than crosses against his name? In the long run, he reckoned he'd fall on the side of 'good' rather than 'bad'. No point in dwelling on it, not long left to change things now. Probably only time for one more tick. In the meantime, did he stay in his cabin or did he brave the cold and make the twenty minute journey to The Fox? Big old log fire'd be roaring away in there. Nice bit of Mabel's pie and tatties would go down a treat. Might bump into young Stan, see how the lake's doing under all that ice. Oh, and nice pint of Doombar to wash it all down.

Hmm, might just be worth the effort.

Chapter Twenty
On the Turning Away

Stan could hear the shouting coming from the lake, but he just thought it was the usual boisterous crowd of youngsters who used the jet skis, so carried on checking the wiring. A few minutes later, when he'd extracted his head from beneath the staircase, he walked to the window and looked out through the back gate towards the boathouse. There were a lot of people milling around; a few running back and forth to the boathouse, and he sensed that something wasn't quite right.

It was the middle of May, quite warm for that time of year, and a few of the lads were dusting off their dry suits and fancied a go on the Mere, before it got too busy. When they arrived, with their four jet skis, there were a couple of small dinghies out on the water. Perfect. A few circuits of the lake, just to warm up. Once more round the island, for fun. The trees obscured the far side of the island, hiding the capsized dinghy from view until very late. Almost too late. The jet ski veered to the right, avoiding the craft by inches, then hit something hard and almost flipped on its side. What was that? Oh my God, what was that? Turning a full circle, he sped back towards the stricken craft and saw an orange life jacket in the water. And a dark slick of something. Something red. Oh my God, what is that?

Following a frustrating winter, Stan was almost glad to reach the season's close. The few sessions he'd managed with Sid at Brampton had been almost totally unsuccessful, until the penultimate weekend of the season had produced a couple of doubles and a nice mid-twenty for Sid. The last session saw the usual reappearance of Jack Frost, for one last performance, and had ended in a cold blank. He and Jean, however, cared little of Sid's plight. Their main concern was which cocktail to choose prior to strolling along the sandy beach to the restaurant – Utopia was quite tricky at times.

But that was then. Now he had much more to look forward to. Having once again contacted Richard, barely avoiding calling him 'your dukeship' on more than one occasion, because that title had been drummed into him by Sid in the previous couple of months. The amusement that had caused was forgotten now, and he was dreading letting it slip and, thus, a place in the Beaufort syndicate. Richard had been quick to assure him that all was on course for a ticket at the beginning of May, and had then arranged a meeting with the head bailiff, Jackson. Hence, at the end of March, an early morning drive across country for almost an hour before arriving at the outskirts of the estate.

The skies were grey and the wind still held a memory of winter, so he knew that these were not the best conditions to be walking around a new lake, but he also knew that if the lake grabbed him at this time of year, what would it be like in full bloom in a month or so? He drove slowly along the long track that led towards the house, then veered off to the left, as instructed, a hundred yards before the substantial dwelling. In the strengthening early morning light he could pick out a number of windows, three or four large chimneys, and at least three different levels of roof. Yes, a seriously substantial dwelling. But that was of little consequence at the moment; his attention was being pulled further left. Through a small copse he emerged at the top of a hill and slowly coasted down. A small herd of deer were startled by his silent approach and bounded off into the wood to the left. Then as he rounded a corner, he caught his first sight of the lake, at the bottom of the hill. Despite the dreary early morning light, the water sparkled and beckoned through the trees. It was surrounded on three sides by trees of many varieties, and he was sure that a similar descent down the same hill in a couple of months would reveal hardly any of the lake, as the trees' full, green crowns hid it from view.

As he reached the bottom of the hill, he saw a Land Rover parked next to a small, wooden cabin, so coasted up next to it and cut the engine. Standing next to the slowly ticking engine he heard a distant coot, and a few mallards, but other than that, nothing. Perfect.

'Morning,' came a gruff greeting. 'Stan Peacock, I presume.'

Stan turned to see a huge bear of a man stooping to miss the top of the cabin as he left it. A mop of grey hair protruded, hither and yon, from beneath a dark green, peaked cap. The face below was ruddy and wind worn, but the bright eyes betrayed a soul full of life. A well-worn barber jacket did little to hide the bulk of the man's frame, a well-over six-foot frame, Stan thought.

'Err, yeah. Then you must be Jackson.'

The man offered a paw and Stan looked at the deep lines in his palm, that looked like they had actually been carved by a flint axe or something. He'd seen a paw like that before, in a car park like this, next to a lake. He knew what these paws could do to the unsuspecting recipient of a handshake. But he'd had practice. He knew what to expect. And he was right. Just. The grip lasted an eternity, or so it seemed, but Stan just held there and looked straight at the man, smiling.

'Pleased to meet you,' he said, as his temporarily ruined hand was returned to him for CPR and physio. Jackson looked at him and smiled.

'Pleased to meet you, Mr Peacock. Care to take a stroll?' he asked, then ushered Stan forward through a small arbour that opened out to reveal a corner of the lake. To his left was the requisite dam wall, and about fifty yards to his right was the bank of an island, no more than ten yards from the right hand bank.

The dam wall had some huge trees along it, a couple of which looked in danger of toppling so far forward that they could sunder the dam. Jackson obviously caught Stan's concerned glance and motioned towards them.

'They gotta come down. Storms this winter were too much for 'em so we got a team coming in tomorrow to cut 'em down. Real pity, probably been here for a couple of centuries but we can't allow them to damage the dam. It'd be bloody disastrous.'

Stan nodded in agreement with all the sentiments, then followed as Jackson took him past the island. The channel between the bank and the island was only about ten yards wide, the island itself about forty yards long, and crowded with trees.

'Bet they get along this little channel, don't they?' he suggested.

Jackson nodded. 'Oh, yeah, but very few people even give it a glance. More inclined to fish the back of the island from the far bank. Eighty, ninety-yard chuck, and invariably at least one set of tackle ends up in the trees each weekend. Yeah, good little margin this is, much neglected.'

Stan made a mental note of that as they emerged from the cover of the island and saw the full expanse of the lake for the first time. He'd found it on a map and had estimated it at about twelve acres or so, and, seeing it now, he thought he might have over estimated it by an acre or two. The bank they were on was relatively open, with the odd stand of willow or birch acting as a division between the half a dozen swims along that bank. At the far end of the bank the lake narrowed and became clogged with reeds. There was one swim at the end that was obviously popular, the well-worn bank as yet not recovered and re-grassed.

'Looks like a popular swim,' said Stan, looking across to the far bank where the semicircle of reeds ended and formed a small bay that would just have to have a bait cast into it.

'Yeah, it is. But when the lilies come up it's a real tricky one to fish. They cover half of this bay, and that little spot you're eyeing up, over there, is totally un-fishable.' Stan looked at the bailiff, who smiled back at him. 'No matter, though, still plenty of lovely swims to fish. Come on, we'll walk down the dam wall and you can have a look at the Boathouse Bay – reckon you'll like that, too.'

An hour or so later they were sitting in the cabin drinking tea, and Stan was in the middle of an interrogation.

'So, you've fished quite a bit for carp then, Stan. Had any good'uns?' asked Jackson. Stan held back a smile. Oh yeah, he'd had some good'uns alright, but that was for him to know. 'Well, if you mean bigguns then, yeah, a couple. But good'uns? I've had loads of good'uns, and very few of them that big. Had a couple of stunners from a lake not far from here. Incredible linears that most people would die for. Really lovely fish. That's what excited me about this place. When Richard said that the fish in here were Leneys, well, that was music to my ears. Don't matter how big when they're that sort of quality.'

Although he was laying it on a bit thick, he did sincerely mean it; he just hoped that Jackson got that from him as well. But before the bailiff had a chance to respond, Stan was starting his own line of enquiries.

'But, tell me,' he began, 'you reckon there's about ninety to a hundred carp in here at the moment. Any recent stockings, or are they all originals, Jackson?'

'Call me Jack,' said the big man, to which Stan nodded, then he went on. 'We've got a small pond, 'bout an acre or so, up beyond the big house. We've been keeping some of the spawnings from the past few years in there. Been pretty successful, so we've been dropping a few back in here for the past few seasons. Probably about twenty or so introductions in the last five years. Reckon there's about twenty true originals in here; big, dark fish. Stunning. The others were stocked up to about thirty-odd years ago and have grown on from there, with a few survivors from previous spawnings. About three generations I'd say.'

Stan was soaking all this up like a sponge. 'Big, dark fish'. That excited him and over the next ten minutes he gleaned as much as he could about the lake, before asking the most important question.

'So, Jack, am I in?'

Jack smiled at him, then extended his huge hand again. 'I reckon you are, Stan. I reckon you are,' he confirmed, whilst slowly crushing the life from Stan's hand again.

The journey home passed in the blink of an eye and a rush of blood to the hand. He was in and he was truly excited by the prospect. It appeared that the oldest fish were not the biggest, with a couple of their number topping mid-thirties normally. But of the others, there were at least another thirty over thirty pounds, and a couple in excess of forty pounds. As much as size didn't matter with fish of this quality, when Jack had shown him some photos, the one that blew his mind was of a black, big-plated mirror that bounced around the forty-pound mark. It wasn't one of the true originals, but Jack had photos of the fish from thirty years earlier when it weighed a mere twelve pounds, so was probably eight to ten years old at the time, and there was every chance it was from the final stocking from Don Leney's farm in 1970. The thought sent shivers up his spine. Time to get serious.

The first of May was Bank Holiday Monday, so Jackson had decided that the season could start a day early, at midnight on Saturday. Of the thirty members, eighteen had turned up on the Saturday afternoon, and Stan was a little chagrined to see such a number. He'd been led to believe that this was a quiet water, but it was early days, and in a month or so he'd invariably be sharing the lake with no more than three or four others.

They'd had a barbecue on the south bank, and he'd met a few of the members. It didn't take long to suss out who he'd be seeing again, and who'd he'd have forgotten about in a matter of days. They had a draw for swims, and for once he didn't come out last, just second to last! Amazingly, however, by the time it came to him, the channel behind the island was still free and he thought that, with the barrage of lead that the rest of the lake would see, the fish would surely seek refuge behind the island.

Two days later, as he slowly packed away his very dry landing net, he decided that the fish knew nothing, and would need to be taught a lesson! A dozen had been caught over the previous couple of days, although most were recent arrivals, and none topped the thirty-pound mark. On a walk around the lake he'd been on hand to net a beautiful, golden mid-twenty common for a guy called Lee, fishing the Boathouse Bay swim, but apart from that he saw nothing. Oh well, that was the mayhem out of the way, let's see what the rest of the season had in store.

Four days later, as he coasted to a halt in the car park, he couldn't believe his eyes. Just two cars were already there. On a Friday afternoon in May. Maybe there'd been a bomb scare or something. He loaded his barrow and pushed it to the end of the dam wall where he left it before walking around the lake to see what he fancied. He found Lee in the Boathouse swim again, and stopped for a quick chat before moving on. Lee had only been there for an hour or so, and had caught nothing as yet. He couldn't see the owner of the other car but was sure that he'd be in the Reeds swim at the end of the south bank. Standing in the Willow swim, half way along the north bank, he looked across at the island margins, eighty yards distant. It certainly was enticing, and was almost as popular a swim as the Reeds, he gathered, but during the week only a couple of recent stockies had been caught from there, so he was unsure about setting up there. A glint of sun on metal caught his eye, and he looked up as another car cruised down the hill towards the car park.

Still no rush, but he was unsure of what or where. He'd passed a swim at the beginning of the north bank that would have afforded a cast back into the Boathouse Bay, if not for a bed of lilies that was in between, and he'd stood and stared at the lilies for some time, willing one or two to twitch. They'd remained frustratingly motionless in the calm conditions, but he felt sure that carp would visit them at some point.

He continued his walk along to the reedy bay at the end of the north bank, and stood in the last swim. The lilies were twenty yards to his left, and extended across the lake towards the far bank, forming a bay that the opposite swim had a nice easy cast into. Sure enough, a bivvy was already set up in there, and the two rods were both pointing into the bay. He could see a guy sitting in the mouth of the bivvy, but when he waved across at him there was no response. Oh, well, sod yer, thought Stan.

Decisions, decisions. This swim looked good, as did the Willows. Then there was the other lily swim, and of course the island channel that he'd fished last week. He'd scattered a kilo of bait liberally behind the island on his departure and had decided that, even if he didn't fish there this time, he would keep the bait going in until he thought it was right.

The new arrival was walking along the south bank with determination, and Stan felt sure he was about to be deflated when he saw his destination occupied. But he stopped a couple of swims short of that and set his barrow down in an innocuous looking swim flanked by some thin birches.

Right, what to do? He looked at the lilies, then walked back to the Willows, then further to the Boathouse lilies, then back to the Willows. Oh, bloody hell, you've got a whole bloody season; just pick one for now and see what happens! He knew it was going to be this bank, so went and retrieved his barrow and lugged it round to the north bank, settling finally in the Willows. He'd devised a plan, of sorts, on his way back, and that was to fish the Willows, but to sprinkle some bait in the Boathouse lilies and just keep an eye on them. That decided, he had a couple of exploratory casts with a lead, and found silt, silt and more silt. It was doubtful that gravel had ever been present in this locale, and definitely not in this lake, but that was pretty much the same for the Hatch and Linton's, so he wasn't too concerned. The island margins looked lovely, and pretty soon he had both baited hooks nestling beneath the trailing branches eighty yards away. A throwing stick dispensed a few hundred boilies along and onto the island, then it was time for a brew and a brolly. The sun set off to his right, over the dam wall, and pretty soon he was thinking about bed, but just as he shucked off his shoes, the right hand alarm gave a single bleep and he looked straight at the indicator. It sat there quivering, a couple of inches below the rod, then twitched up a little as the alarm gave off another bleep. There were no birds in the vicinity as far as he could tell, so when it sounded for a third time, he whipped up the rod and struck hard. Something was on the end, but he couldn't quite tell what it was, but pretty soon he was certain it wasn't a carp and was shortly unhooking a small, male tench. Fortunately, he'd marked the line, so was able to recast with confidence, but by the fourth tench of the night to the same rod he decided to drop it ten yards short, just to get some sleep. The ploy worked well and the early morning sun woke him just after seven.

The lines hung limply from the rod tips as he swung his legs over the bedchair and ran his fingers through his sleep-ruffled hair. Stretching expansively, he rose, then walked to a nearby tree to relieve himself. As he looked across the lake, he saw a flash of something, then focused enough to see the guy opposite bending to net a fish. It obviously wasn't just a whim, then, his swim choice, thought Stan. He peered through binoculars as the fish was lifted from the lake and onto the waiting mat. Difficult to gauge from this distance, but it looked to be around the twenty-pound mark. Nice.

The right hand rod needed attending to, so that was the first order of the day, and within five minutes he was happy with the recast, so then put on the kettle. The steam had barely left the spout when the right hand alarm bleeped once – not again! Being light now, he was able to watch the rod tip so saw the line moving very slowly left. Another single bleep announced the dropping of the indicator, and two and two suddenly made four. He wound down fast, then lifted the rod tip high, which hooped over with a sudden thump. Maybe not a tench, then. Once away from the island, the fish moved slowly left, then right, then left and continued the zig-zagging movement all the way to the net, and, five minutes after casting, Stan was removing the hook from a beautiful, scaly mirror of about twelve pounds. Obviously one of last year's stockies, it was still a nice start to his campaign, and he took a couple of quick photos of it on the mat, to show Jackson later.

The brolly was full of steam, so he turned off the gas before recasting to the same spot, hopeful of an instant repeat, but by the time he was ready for his third cup of tea of the day, clouds had gathered, the wind had got up, and he was unsure whether these conditions were conducive to a bait at the back of the island. A quick bacon sandwich followed, then he wound in both rods and went for a stroll.

The pads at the mouth of the Boathouse Bay still looked very inviting, with the wind rippling into that area, but he stood there for ten minutes without seeing anything, so moved on. Lee, in the bay swim, had hooked two during the night, landing a low-twenty mirror and losing the other in the pads. The fish were obviously in and around the area, and Stan gave that some serious thought as he carried on his circuit. Someone had set up on the dam wall early that morning, but was just float fishing in the margins and had accounted for three tench and a couple of bream, which he was more than pleased about, and regaled Stan with every tail flick and olive green roll, before Stan had to feign an urgent toilet requirement to escape.

Walking along the back of the island, he sprinkled a few handfuls of bait in the channel, then stood still as he heard the piping call of a kingfisher from his right, watching as the bright blue bird banked and dipped on its way past him to a further perch. As he carried on, smiling to himself at the sight, he heard something wallow and splash beneath one of the island trees, and peered into the enforced gloom to search out the source. There were moorhens and coots aplenty on the lake, as well as a pair of grebes, so they could quite easily be the culprits. But coots tend to bob straight back to the surface, and one hadn't, so he scanned for a re-emerging grebe but, after a minute or so had seen nothing. Intriguing. He stood attentively and scanned along the island margins for a further five minutes, but nothing else occurred so he moved, pensively. Could have been a vole or something, plopping into the water when he spooked it. Could have been a pike, or even another kingfisher. Unconvinced by his counter-arguments, he carried on to the swim of that morning's captor.

'Morning, mate. Alright?' he said as he entered the swim. The guy was sitting on a lowchair, drinking tea, and turned round to look at his visitor.

'Hello, mate. Yeah, good. You?' He stood and walked around the back of the bivvy to talk to Stan.

'Oh, not bad,' replied Stan. 'Had a little'un a couple of hours ago, nothing since. Saw you landing one first thing, any good?'

'Yeah, twenty-three pound mirror. Bloody stunner it was. I'm well chuffed with that. Wanna cup of tea, err, sorry, what's yer name?'

'Stan. Yeah I'd love one. What's yours?' Stan replied.

'Bob. Pleased to meet yer,' he said, extending his hand. He was quite a small, rotund type of chap, and Stan couldn't help thinking about Lord of the Rings when he looked at him. He was unsure which category Bob fitted into, but with the addition of a beard and an axe he was sure that he would have made a passable Gimli.

They chatted for a while and Bob filled Stan in on what he knew about the lake. He'd been a member for a couple of years, but only tended to fish one-night sessions during the spring and summer. Winter fishing wasn't really his bag, although he had heard that the lake fished quite well in the colder months. He'd had a few out in his time on there, with the best being a twenty eight pound mirror; one of the old originals. He showed Stan a crumpled photo of the fish, and even in that state he could see that it was one that he definitely needed to catch. They chatted for a little longer, then he moved on to the end Reed swim.

The guy there couldn't have been more different from Bob. Short, sharp, one word answers left Stan in no doubt that his presence was an imposition, and he was soon back at Bob's swim.

'Bloody hell, he's a miserable bastard, ain't he?' he said.

Bob laughed and his eyes sparkled. 'Heh, heh, heh! Yeah, shoulda told yer really, but thought you should find out for yerself,' he said, still chuckling. 'Ol' Smiler ain't one of the most chatty of people. Once he gets to know yer he'll maybe grunt in yer general direction. 'Part from that, stay clear.'

Stan nodded, than waved a hand as he made his way back to his swim. A brief stop at the island channel revealed no further movement, so that made his mind up for him – the pads it was.

By early afternoon he was settled. One bait was no more than a couple of feet from the bank, thirty yards to his right, and the other had been cast to a similar distance, but about ten yards from the bank and into a little bay in the lilies. Fifty or so baits had accompanied that hookbait, whilst he'd broken and crumbed up a similar amount of boilies and sprinkled them along the close margin. The wind was gently pushing into the Boathouse Bay to his right, and the cloud cover meant that there was still a bit of nip to the wind, so a fleece jacket was a necessity. The afternoon passed uneventfully, apart from the sighting of a small herd of roe deer in the woods behind him, and pretty soon he was thinking of dinner and maybe a final cast before nightfall.

Darkness brought the sounds of owls hunting, and small creatures being hunted, successfully. A couple of loud splashes to his right filled him with confidence but, a few hours later, in the dark early morning, he was yet to receive the merest of indication, and dozed back off to sleep, slightly troubled.

The run, as usual in those situations, was blistering, as the right hand margin bait was picked up and the fish tore off for the sanctuary of the lily pads. Being early in the year, however, the roots were yet to achieve their full strength, and pretty soon Stan had guided the fish back out into the open water to his left. There was no zig-zagging with this fish, just steady, plodding power, and he felt certain that this was a much better fish than the previous morning's double. The grey, pre-dawn light afforded just enough visibility for Stan to see the oily swirls of the fish, five yards out, and it was not long after that it came, gulping and splashing, to the net. Stan gave a small, grunted, 'Yes!' then went about getting everything ready for the unhooking and weighing of the fish. Lifting it from the water, he realised that this was, indeed, a much better fish, and he struggled with it over to the unhooking mat.

The sun was just beginning to brighten the eastern skyline, but not enough to negate the use of a head torch, and in its beam he could see the line of scales running the length of the fish. This was a big old linear and he knew, straightaway, that this would be worth the £600 fee alone. The light from the torch gave it a washed-out look, but he was sure that the flanks would be dark and burnished in the light of the sun, so slid it straight into a sack and into the margins. The weighing could wait until he had a photographer, but he was sure that it was in excess of thirty pounds and was delirious with this, his first proper carp from the lake.

A couple of cups of tea, a couple of text messages to the usual suspects, then it was time to wind in the rods and go round to request Lee's assistance with weighing and photographing. He had no idea of his ability with a camera, but there was no one else close enough, so he just had to hope that he was cool.

As he lifted the sack from the water, it felt even heavier, and he stood there for a few moments to let the water drain from it. Once on the mat, he carefully unzipped the sack and slid back the green material, to reveal the most stunning, chocolate brown flank with a line of almost perfect linear scales along it. They both stared, open-mouthed, before Lee uttered an appropriate expletive, and Stan replied in kind.

'Bloody hell,' said Lee as he looked at the dial, 'thirty-six pounds… six. Thirty-six, six. Bloody hell! That's the biggest fish out of here for about a year or so, I think. Bloody hell!' He was shaking his head in disbelief, and Stan had the feeling that this was the biggest carp he'd ever seen. Although that was not true for Stan, it was certainly one of the most beautiful, and as he posed with it in the early morning sun, he prayed that Lee was not too awestruck to be able to use the camera.

As the fish slid back into the lake, Stan just gazed after it, slightly numbed. If this was what it was going to be like, then he sure was gonna like it here.

A few days later, he was preparing his tackle for tomorrow's departure. He tended to finish early on a Friday afternoon, so liked to be ready for a quick getaway, and his Thursday evening ritual had changed little over the years. Just need to get the baits out and leave them soaking in water overnight, then all would be ready for tomorrow. He had a bit of admin to do, then a little rewiring job over at the Pearson's place, but once that was done he'd be away, probably just after lunch. Lovely. What could go wrong?

Chapter Twenty One
One of These Days

'rack!'

The gunshot made Ted flinch, but through the 'scope he could see that the aim was true. The target shuddered and fell, twitching, to the floor. He looked across to his right, at the sniper, and nodded. Then they rose and steadily walked towards the patently dead body.

Steam was rising from its flanks, but the large, pink tongue lolled from the side of its mouth and the antlers held the head at an unnatural angle.

'Good shot, Neil. A nice, clean kill. That's good to see, well done.' Ted took the rifle from his young charge and let him look over the animal, making sure that it was all over. This was their sixth of the week; more than enough to keep the herds in check, and Neil's third successful kill. His first few attempts had been a tad clumsy, but his confidence was building, and Ted was happy with his progress, but this had been only a small part of their tasks since the turn of the year.

The winter had been a harsh one, and Ted feared that quite a few creatures wouldn't have made it through. He and young Becks had been kept busy, after the thaw, retrieving a few carcasses that had not survived beneath the ice. Mainly bream and roach, there were also three or four carp that had succumbed to the winter's foggy freeze, and although not large, Ted had no doubt that they would have survived a few dozen winters before this one.

Stan had been on hand one day, when they found a bloated carcass in the corner behind the big island, and initially the size of it had given them cause for some concern. But, once the stinking corpse was extracted from the lake, it was evident that although it was a common, it had probably never exceeded twenty-five pounds in weight.

Stan dreaded the next month or so, just in case something considerably larger turned up, but by the time that he'd begun his Beaufort's campaign, no further corpses had been found, and the worry had passed for another year.

Ted and Neil had spent the last few months tending to the woodland; removing dead wood, fallen branches and the like. Checking on the dens and setts to make sure that they were unobstructed and undisturbed, and generally getting ready for the onset of spring and the abundance of life and vibrancy. The work had been hard, and sometimes tiresome, but Neil was enjoying it hugely; the added bonus being things like the deer culling. As much as he wasn't keen on seeing anything killed, if it had to be done, then do it well, that's what he thought.

He'd had little time for fishing, and when the close season had suddenly been upon him, he managed just a quick afternoon session down on the river before the three-month closure. If only Smiffy had been with him because, at last, he'd managed to catch one of the river's small head of large barbel.

He'd been trotting maggots down beneath a float for a few hours, and this had accounted for half a dozen decent sized perch and a suicidal chub of about three pounds, but as the evening loomed, he decided on a bit of trundling, so changed the float for a small leger, and the maggots for a huge chunk of luncheon meat. He knew that the stretch he was fishing held a few barbel at certain times of the year, but was unsure as to whether this was one of those times. After the third or fourth run he felt a little pull on the line, then saw the rod tip twitch, and flicked it back instinctively, totally unprepared for the reaction of the fish on the end, which tore off into the middle of the river, then headed off downstream. The reel positively buzzed as the line was stripped from it, and it was all he could do just to hang on to his rod. The battle raged for about ten minutes, but with nobody else around he could do little but hope that it would soon be over. Eventually, the fish tired, and he saw it slide to the surface, ten yards downstream. Carefully lowering the net, he slid the fish into it and knew, instantly, that this was the one that he and Smiffy had been striving for. Laying the torpedo frame of the barbel on the small mat, he stroked away the streamer weed to better feast his eyes. What a fish! Huge, rubbery lips opened and closed as the fish strived to regain its strength. It was long; very long, but he had no scales to weigh it, so could only lie it next to his rod and reel and take a couple of photos of it. After all this time, he didn't know how big it was! But it mattered little; it was still a beautiful fish, and one that he would relish texting Smiffy about.

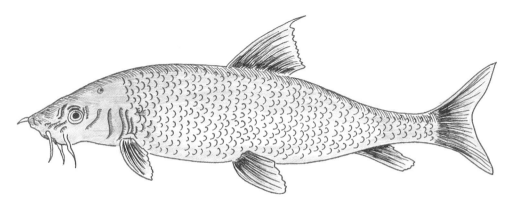

He held it in the water for a few minutes until he felt its muscles tense, then, with one flick of the tail, it was out into the current and gone. The sun was barely visible through the trees, so he packed his gear away and made off back through the woods, towards home. He was going to call in on Ted, to let him know of his success, but it was getting late, and the telling would be just as sweet tomorrow. Dinner beckoned, and he was suddenly famished.

Since that epic capture, he'd had little opportunity to get the rods out and the combination of a close season on the rivers, Smiffy's absence at Uni, and girls, had meant that fishing had been pretty far from his mind.

The spring had been slow in coming, but the animals of the woods and fields had taken no notice. The sun had risen to a certain height in the sky, and to Mother Nature's hordes that was like a starting pistol in the race for life. The water was alive with fowl of all shapes and sizes, and it wasn't long after Neil's barbel success that male coots and moorhens were vying for the attention of their female counterparts. The mating rituals were raucous and invariably quite vicious, and within a month small clutches of scrawny chicks could be seen bobbing along behind their mothers.

The woodland was as alive with the sound of young birds as the lake, and some mornings it was almost impossible to tell one hungry mouth from another. Pigeon, thrush, blackbird, woodpecker, jay, all were in competition for food for their growing young, but fortunately the woods' insect population had also quadrupled in size, and there was food enough for all.

As the days lengthened and warmed, the woods became a riot of colour, and as the first bluebells poked their heads through the mulch, Ted and Neil were about their business. Two of the woods' three main mammals were also now with young, and the cubs of the foxes and badgers were all starting to venture out of their burrows and into the big, wide world. April and May was one of Ted's favourite times in the wood, when the young began to overcome their initial fear, and would roll and tumble outside the entrance to the dens or the setts. Both would become fearless as they grew older, but, for now, they still relied on their parents, and aunts and uncles, to offer protection. Ted had long since been accepted by the badger clan in the woods, and he spent more and more time watching over them during the late spring. On a couple of occasions Neil accompanied him, and was open-mouthed with delight at the sight of the frolicking cubs. Never had he been so close to these strangely unobtrusive creatures, and he vowed to learn all he could about them

The foxes were a little more wary of the presence of humans, for obvious reasons, so to view them they had to take into account wind direction, sound and vision, hence most of their viewing was through binoculars, but wonderful just the same. The female deer of the woodland were moving into heavy pregnancy, and it wouldn't be too long before the newborn fawns were blinking in their first early morning light, but they would be just as difficult to see up close, and, invariably, Ted tried his best not to disturb them or their mothers until early August, when they would be more confident and capable of flight.

The winter had, once again, been hard, and the carp had lain almost torpid at the start of the year. The cold winds from the north and east had prevented the surface of the lake from freezing just after Christmas, but the New Year had brought snow and plummeting temperatures, and the lake's surface had remained frozen for many days.

Following the thaw, further cold winds had kept the water temperature unnaturally low, and with few places to hide from the chill, some of their number had eventually succumbed.

But then the light levels began to change; life returned to the silt and the weed and the margins, and the carp began to move freely around the lake once more. The surface was quiet for now, save from the squabbling, splashing waterfowl, and the carp had little to fear. Soon it would be their turn to enjoy and endure their annual mating ritual, but for now they sated themselves on the eggs and minute young of the lake's other aquatic inhabitants, feeding at will and building up strength for the coming months.

'Sounds like we might need to take a look at the lake, Neil,' said Ted. He could hear a distant buzz from that direction, which indicated that the lake was, once again, host to a variety of watercraft. 'Them jet ski chaps are back, by the sound of it. Best go and make sure they don't disturb no young'uns, eh?'

They strolled off through the wood and emerged on the south bank, opposite the boathouse. A lot of people were milling around near the water's edge, and Posh peered intently across the lake, trying to make out what the commotion was all about.

'Something queer going on, young Neil,' said Ted, as he made off to the left. 'Lot of agitated folks. Something don't look right.'

Ted had seen and heard it all before. Scared people, confused people, shocked people. Running around, not knowing what to do, whom to talk to, where to go. He cut straight through the milling crowd to the centre of their attention, and knew instantly that all the shouting and running around would do nothing to resolve this situation.

Stan was one of those trying to help, a phone to his ear whilst he gave directions to some emergency service or other. All thoughts of an early departure to Beaufort's forgotten. So much blood. He'd never seen so much blood. People were trying to staunch the flow by wrapping towels around the guy's head, but they were just soaking it up, turning bright red in a matter of seconds.

'Too late, I'm afraid,' said Ted, from behind him. 'No life in those eyes, Stan. Lad's gone.'

Stan barely heard it amongst the clamour of voices, but it registered deep down, and when he looked closely at the prone body, cradled in someone's lap, he knew Ted's statement to be oh so true. The lad was gone.

Chapter Twenty Two
The Show Must Go On

The sign read **'Closed Until Further Notice'.**
Strange how something so devastating can be summed up in just a few cold words, thought Stan. Ted had been right, the lad was D.O.A. at the hospital, and the whole community was in a state of shock. The blame-merchants had been at it straightaway, and the pitchforks and flaming torches had been wielded mercilessly. It had been an accident; nothing else, and the driver of the jet ski needed nothing further to make him feel worse than he already did; a feeling that he would never be rid of.

The obvious reaction was to close the lake, if only out of respect, but that situation would remain for many months. The residents committee had convened a few days after the tragedy, when their little community was once again devoid of police and reporters, and had decreed that the lake should remain free of waterborne craft for the foreseeable future. That had been a few months ago, and there seemed little chance of the ban being lifted for the rest of the year.

Stan, initially shocked to his core, had gradually got his world back into its usual orbit, and within a week was back at Beaufort's lake, but despite the peace and tranquillity, or maybe because of it, he was unable to shake the vision of the bloodied head cradled in someone's lap, and his session drifted by without incident or concern.

A few days later he was standing by the snags, on the Mere, peering into the wind-rippled waters to see if he could get his first sighting of the year. As usual, Ted's arrival behind him was unheralded, and caught him by surprise.

'All in mourning, I fear, young Stan.'

Stan looked at Ted, standing off to his left a little, and nodded. 'Yeah, seems that way, don't it?' he said, then looked back into the lake in front of him.

'Never get used to it, sight of a dead body. Still hard to accept an end of a life, 'specially one so young.' Ted seemed to be talking to nobody in particular, just voicing some inner feelings, and Stan felt disinclined to join in at that moment.

'Hard to forget, too. Sits at the back of yer head, quietly, then emerges when you least expect it. But… you gotta carry on, Stan. Nothing you could do. Can do. Dead and gone is a true fact.'

Stan continued to stare, then said, without turning, 'You seen many, then, Ted? Dead bodies, you seen many?'

Ted nodded to nobody in particular. 'Too many lad, too many. And I remember every one. But if I mourned every one, I'd be with them by now. You wanna live, you gotta remember their life, not their death.'

Bloody hell, thought Stan; that was profound. 'But I didn't know him, so how can I remember him?' he asked.

'I gotta ask, then, if you didn't know him, why you so mournful? Is it 'cos of a life passing, or the shock of seeing a dead body? Feel that that's what's expected of you, or something? Ain't no bandwagon worth jumping on, mourning the unknown dead, lad. Believe me, you'll have time enough to mourn those you know. For now, get on with your life, don't waste it.'

Stan stood for a moment, and let the words sink in. He thought about how he'd felt when his father-in-law had died – how could this recent death bear any comparison? As usual, Ted's quiet wisdom hit home hard, and Stan nodded.

'Yep, you're right,' he said, turning away from the water to look once more at Ted, but he was too late. There was nobody there but him, and as he looked across the lake he just caught a glimpse of the old guy through the trees of the East Woods, as he made his way back to his cabin. Stan nodded again and carried on talking, 'But you know you're right; you don't need me to tell you. Thanks, mate.' He then turned around and walked purposefully back past the houses towards home.

Ted had looked down at the prone figure, emotionless, or incapable of emotion, he wasn't sure of the difference. The blood was now slowly seeping out of the wound, no longer pulsing; the heart that had pumped it around the body now stilled, lifeless. The lad was young; eighteen or nineteen, probably the same age as Ted, and the bullet that had found him could quite easily have found a different, random target. Don Sanders, the first dead body he'd ever seen, many lifetimes ago; one he would never forget.

He sat by the old mill and waited for Neil, aware of his approach from the odd snapped twig or rustled leaf mould. He knew how Stan felt, but he also knew that there was no gain in pointless grieving. Neil saw him and walked over.

'Alright, Ted?' he asked as he sat down on the mossy brickwork of the mill wall.

'Yes, lad. Fine. Got a bit of work to do today, over by the river. Couple of trees getting a bit top heavy. Need to have a look, see what can be done.' He remained sitting, staring into the woods, and Neil sat quietly next to him. They'd already discussed the tragedy on the Mere a couple of times, but Neil felt there was no more to say, and knew that there was no more for Ted to say. So he sat and waited. From the corner of his eye he caught a movement, and looking to his left saw a bird zig-zagging through the trees.

'Ted!' he whispered, then pointed just as the hawk banked through a small stand of alder and flew off in pursuit of something fractionally less agile. As they were almost out of sight through the tightly packed trunks, the hawk swooped and the kill was made.

'Wow! Exclaimed Neil, eyes wide.

'Merlin,' said Ted. 'Beautiful.' The sight seemed to stir him and he rose with purpose. 'Right lad, no more dawdling, work to do. Let's go,' and with that he set off towards the river. Yep, thought Neil, Merlin, performing his magic.

'That bloody Ronaldo, cheating bastard!' said Bob, as he entered Stan's swim. 'Did you see it, mate? Got Rooney sent off, din't he?'

'Yeah, but we still missed the bloody penalties again. How much are they paid a bloody week? Can't even knock one in from twelve yards, for God's sake.'

The same argument had resounded across the land, but the outcome had remained unchanged – another World Cup, another penalty shoot-out, another England exit.

'Yeah, I know,' agreed Bob, 'but sod that, how was Roger Waters?'

Peter Double-barrel had come up trumps again for Stan, and had managed to get him a couple of tickets to see Roger Waters perform the whole of 'Dark Side of the Moon' at Hyde Park. Unfortunately, the Portugal game had been on the same afternoon and a large percentage of the Hyde Park crowd had watched, with growing dismay, the events unfold on the big screen. But a few hours later, all was well again, and as the sounds of the ticking of a clock and the ringing of a till drifted across the gathered throng, Stan and Sid stood mesmerised, smiling, unbelieving, entranced.

'Stunning, mate, absolutely stunning,' he replied to the wee fella's question. 'Every bit of 'Dark Side', then stuff off of 'The Wall'; and 'Sheep'! Bloody hell, I never thought I'd see that performed live, but it was worth the bloody wait. Brilliant mate, just brilliant.'

Bob smiled widely, then plonked his cup on the ground and sat down next to it. Stan took the hint and fired up the cooker, setting his own cup next to his visitor's bucket-sized receptacle.

It was the second Saturday in July and he was set up in the Boathouse lilies swim again, the scene of his capture of the thirty-six. Since the Mere incident, almost two months previously, he'd only fished three times, and had managed just a couple of small stockies, but this was the first time he'd been able to get back into this swim. The Boathouse Bay had been an area that the fish were obviously happy to be, and a further three thirty-plus mirrors had come from there since Stan's success. Bob had found himself in the Boathouse Bay swim the previous week, just prior to the football and the concert, and had managed to catch his largest from the lake in the shape of a dark, heavily scaled mirror of just under thirty-eight pounds. When Stan had seen the photos his jaw had nearly hit the floor, and he was certain it was the fish that Jackson had shown him a few months earlier. Bob was obviously elated, and replayed the battle many times for any who were within even distant earshot. Stan vowed that he would not be leaving this lake until that particular fish was nestled in the bottom of his landing net, no matter how long it took.

Being a shift worker, Bob's times at the lake varied, and he'd just arrived, straight from work, to undertake a two-night session. But first, people needed to see photos. After an amusing chat, and another cup of tea, he bade Stan good luck and set off back past the Boathouse in the direction of the south bank, where he would settle for that night.

Stan settled back for a bit of peace and quiet, but pretty soon decided that a recast was in order. His visitor was a lovely chap, but not the sort you wanted in your swim when your bait was only a yard out. On reeling in, he thought better of an immediate recast, so set the rod back down, and went for a stroll, in the same direction as Bob. The pads were strangely lifeless, and it was no surprise that the guy in the Boathouse Bay swim was also blanking. The weather had been really warm for a few weeks, but was now set to break, and Stan wondered if the deeper water might be worth a bet. He walked the length of the dam wall, passing only one other angler, but he saw no sign of carp so dallied only a few minutes.

As he neared the back of the island, along the south bank, he knew instinctively that this was where he had been heading all along. On the few occasions he had been down he had continued to scatter bait along the channel, but since the very first day of the season, had not fished the area. Now, however, as he neared it and peered into the tree-shrouded channel, he just knew that this was where he needed to be. As he stood by the oak at the mouth of the channel, the sight of a huge vortex in the margins was barely a surprise, and when a carp slipped out of the water and back in with barely a splash beneath the overhanging island trees, he casually turned and strolled back towards his swim. Outwardly, he was just out for a nice stroll in the sunshine, but inwardly he was sprinting like a hundred-metre champion, and the walk back to his swim was torture. Once there, however, he was a blur, and in very little time the guy in the bay was looking very quizzically at him as he huffed past with a brisk, 'Time for a move.'

He set his barrow down at the far side of the channel, having walked behind the trees to avoid any bankside disturbance. He then crept to the end of the channel and stood by another oak, at the opposite end. The channel was only about forty yards long, but because of the trees it was not possible to fish the whole length of it from one swim. The obvious ploy was to put one bait in the close margin, and one to the island margin, but the disturbance caused by the latter could quite easily empty the channel of fish in short order. Stan decided, therefore, to carefully place one legered bait a yard from the bank, but twenty yards down the channel through a gap in the trees. He'd set that up on an alarm, turned up loud, and leave it to fish quietly, on its own. His other rod would be used to float fish at either end of the channel. An hour or so at one end, and if unsuccessful, then the same at the other end. The plan was to fish like that until the early evening, when he would set up camp and finally put a bait out by the island.

As he lowered the bottom bait into the margins, ripples came back from the island, indicating that there were still fish present. He'd had the foresight to sprinkle some baits in the area the previous evening, so was happy just to break up three or four baits and drop them around his hookbait. Setting the alarm fairly loud, he crept back to his other rod, at the far end of the channel, and slipped a couple of grains of sweetcorn on the hook before flicking the peacock quill five yards out into the lake. Once the line had been mended, the red tip of the float was just a couple of yards out, just beneath the leaves of the oak, and he settled back against the trunk to wait.

A splash from his left had him peering out to see where the ripples were coming from, and they weren't too far from his other bait, which filled him with hope. He was so certain that he was going to get a bite he almost wanted to scream, but he concentrated on the float and tried to calm himself. The tip was wobbling and dipping ever so slightly, but he put that down to the attentions of the shoals of small rudd that the lake held. Was sweetcorn the right bait? Should he switch to a boilie? Should he run maniacally through the trees to quiet that screaming alarm?

Yes!

The baitrunner was singing, and he carefully applied pressure to the spool as the fish tore off towards the far end of the island and out towards the dam wall. Due to the trees there was no way he could follow it down the bank, and the margins here were at least three feet deep, and pretty silty, so he didn't fancy a dip. The only answer was to hang on and hope for the best. He had to keep the rod tip low because of all the grasping branches, but the grating sensation coming back down the line did not fill him with confidence, and he knew that the fish was past the end of the island, and using it as a very abrasive fulcrum. Harsher tactics were required, so he clamped his hand over the spool and tried to get the rod tip as far to the left as possible. The grating continued, but he felt the tip pulling round, then it pulled down hard and he had to give a little line. The tactic seemed to have worked, as the grating sensation was no more, and the fish appeared to be heading further into the corner nearest the cabin.

Slowly, so slowly, Stan eased the rod back, gaining line two or three turns at a time, until he could see dark swirls in the shadows beneath the bankside trees. A long, lazy roll showed the fish to be ten yards away, and Stan scrabbled around behind him for the landing net, cursing as it caught in some brambles before being wrenched free and settled into the water. It was very difficult to raise the rod above head height because of the branches overhead, and he knelt down as low as he could to help bring the fish under control. Three or four times the line caught in one branch or another, and Stan swore profusely on each occasion, whilst flicking the rod tip madly to get the branch to release its hold. Eventually, however, the fish was there, and with one desperate swoop he bundled it into the net and gave a small whoop of delight.

He had no idea how big it was, but the success of his tactics was reward enough, although he was sure that this was no boisterous double. On lifting the net from the water, that became a certainty, and when he laid it on the unhooking mat, his eyes sparkled and his heart raced. This was so far removed from a double as to be from another planet. The length of the fish was immense, its mouth on one side of the thirty-six inch mat, and the tail hanging over the other side. It was huge; surely the biggest carp he'd caught for many years, and he didn't know whether to laugh, cry or do a strange dance. In the end, all three seemed quite appropriate.

He'd obviously made some noise because Bob was suddenly standing over him.

'Bloody hell, Stan, that's massive. Bloody massive. Looks even bigger than my one. Where'd you have it from? Down there? Didn't even see you move. Kept that a bit quiet, din't you?'

All of this was just white noise to Stan; something else that he had missed for the past few years, and something that was so satisfying and… right.

Even without its length, the fish was another of the lake's dark brown jewels, and Stan was almost shell-shocked as he peered down at it. Not a perfect linear; a few scales missing along that line, but that made it even more perfect as far as Stan was concerned, and he really, really, didn't care how much it weighed. It was the fish of a lifetime, and he'd had a few of them in his lifetime, so he should know.

He voiced his opinion, but the gnome-like Bob would have none of it, and growled like his Lord of the Rings counterpart, insisting on a weighing. Stan conceded, and let Bob take control, wetting the sling, zeroing the scales, but when it came to putting the carp into the sling, there was only one man for that job. They hoisted the scales and Stan held them as steady as he could, the landing net pole helping with that.

Chapter Twenty Two

'****!' Bob stared at the scales and swore.

'What?' said Stan. 'What's up?'

'I can't believe it,' said Bob, with a slight shake of the head. 'It ain't a forty. You sure these scales are alright?'

Stan was unconcerned and just told Bob to read off what it said.

'Thirty-nine pounds exactly. Can't believe it, could have sworn it was well over forty.'

Stan just smiled. That made it even better. The fish was now not wonderful because of its weight, but because of the fish itself. Its length, the size of its fins and its tail, its imperfect linear scaling, its chocolate brown perfection.

That was all that Stan needed, and it would stand him in good stead until something better came along, which, as far as he was concerned, could be quite a while. Perfect.

Chapter Twenty Three

Time

asking in the summer sun, the carp were semi-dormant. Not awake enough to burn up unnecessary energy, but not so asleep that they could not react instantly to danger. A dozen or so fish hung in the water at different levels, glorying in the warmth of the water around them. The summer was moving lazily on and, for the first time in many seasons, the lake was quiet. No unnatural sounds and vibrations had been evident for many months, and the carp were becoming more confident as they moved about the lake, day or night.

It seemed that, with every passing year, the lake was becoming more and more fertile, and the carp were showing signs of that fecundity. As well as the three large females there were at least four other carp that had increased massively in weight and had more than doubled their twenty-odd pounds in the last three or four years. Coupled with a few of the old originals that had maintained a steady, but unsurprising, weight gain, the number of carp in the lake that more than exceeded forty pounds was into double figures, and there seemed nothing, barring old age and infirmity, that would change that. The basking carp were all in that group, and the sight would make many mouths water.

The summer drifted slowly towards autumn, and the lake thrived.

'Good to see yer, mate,' said Posh as he warmly shook Smiffy's hand and gave him a little hug. His friend had arrived the previous day, and was planning to stay for a few weeks before a quick Spanish holiday, then back to University.

'Yeah, you too, mate,' he replied. 'All been kicking off here, then?'

'Not many, Smiffy. Place was in a state of shock for a few weeks, nobody knew what to do or say. Like we were in limbo. 'Course, Old Ted just got on with it, seen it all before I s'pose. But, to be fair, that's what it needed, I think. Stan was a bit upside down for a while, then I think Ted had a word and he was okay again. Bin catching some good fish, as well. Wait until you see the photos of his thirty-nine – bloody incredible.'

They walked across the field from Smiffy's house to the now abandoned boathouse, and sat in front of it, basking in the sun and looking out over the calm waters of the lake.

'What about you, mate, you been doing much fishing?' asked Smiffy, whilst pulling a baseball cap lower over his eyes.

'Not much, to be fair. Had a little dabble on the river a couple of times but didn't have much; just a few chub and perch. Then went down to Yasgar's Farm for a bit of tench fishing. Lovely fish, had four up to six pounds, but the lake was a shit hole. 'part from that I've been pretty busy. Man, you should have been here a couple of months ago. Just after the boat accident, Ted decided to leave the Mere be for a few days, let things settle down a bit, so we went off through Culvert's and out the back, towards the forest. Bit of a trek, but it was real nice to see different bits of the wood. Then we hear this screeching, and up above, in one of the big pines out that way, we saw a nest, real high up. And there were these two heads poking over the side.'

Smiffy feigned interest, although what he was more interested in, at that moment, was sleep.

'Right. What were they then?' he asked, drowsily.

'Buzzards, mate. It was a buzzard's nest, and as we stood there one of the parents came back with a dead something in its talons. Rabbit or squirrel or something. Bloody amazing.'

Smiffy knew he should have shown some interest, and was indeed quite excited by the story, but the late night before he left, then the six-hour train journey, via London, had really knocked it out of him.

Posh continued on, unaware or uncaring of his mate's apathy. 'Ted reckoned they were probably ready to fledge, so we returned for a couple of days and then, amazingly, we got there one morning just as the first one took off. It was brilliant. We watched for about an hour, whilst the four birds circled overhead.' Posh looked over at his mate for a reaction, but could see that nothing much was happening under the cap, so continued to himself: 'Then this elephant flew alongside them and did a little dive, like the Red Arrows, and all of them held hands and bowed as the otters and foxes applauded. It was amazing.'

'Mmm. Sounds great,' slurred a recumbent Smiffy, and Posh just smiled, then stood up and walked to the water's edge. The bank was raised and concreted here, to allow boats to come alongside in deeper water, so he was a few feet above the waterline and had a great view across the lake. Off to his left, towards the fateful island, he saw a few insects flicking on and off of the lake's mirror surface, then scanning round he saw a couple more just in front of him. Looking closer, however, he could see that they were in exactly the same place every time, and concentrated a little harder. They were no more than forty feet from the bank, and there seemed to be half a dozen or so. Then another flicked up and below it rose a broad scaled back, and Posh's mouth dropped open and he quietly swore. They weren't insects, they were dorsal fins.

Standing quietly and adjusting his glasses a little better, he began to make out the shape of the carp just beneath the surface, and his first estimation seemed to have been wrong. He counted eight, ten, twelve. Twelve of them and, to his eye, they all seemed huge. This was no time to be sleeping.

'Smiffy,' he said, in an exaggerated whisper. 'Smiffy!' louder this time.

'Mmm. What, yeah, flying elephants, very funny,' his mate mumbled, so he went over and shook him.

'Smiffy, come on mate – sleep when you're dead and all that. You gotta see this,' and, with that, he turned back and walked carefully towards the lakeside. Smiffy joined him a minute later, rubbing his eyes and stretching hugely.

'What? What have I gotta see?' he asked, somewhat indignantly. Posh hushed him with a wave of his hand, then pointed to the basking monsters. Smiffy took a few seconds to focus, then became fully awake as he realised what he was looking at.

'Bloody hell! Bloody hell, there's, what, ten of 'em?'

'Twelve, I think, and they're all bloody huge. Can't quite see them at this level, sun's at the wrong angle, but I think those two over there are The Common and The Poached Mirror. Hold up,' he put his hand up slowly, then pointed carefully to his right. Along the margins ambled a mirror carp of fairly impressive proportions, and as they stood stock still, trying to make like a couple of trees, it swam slowly past, no more than four feet from the bank, and they could see every scale on its back.

'Shit!' whispered Smiffy, now ultra-awake. 'That's massive. Is it the other one? The one that Stan calls Sid's Fish?'

'Dunno, don't think so,' replied Posh. 'Looks a bit smaller than that, but… bloody hell!' The last exclamation was in response to the mirror letting them know its exact identification by slowly rolling on its side and rubbing against the gravely lakebed. A line of linear scales ran the length of its body, from gill cover to tail root, and when they later described it to Stan he would know exactly what fish it was, as would Rhodie.

They stood, enraptured, for the next half an hour as the carp hung almost motionless in the water; carefree and content. Frustratingly, most of them were just far enough away that their admirers couldn't quite get a good enough look at them, but the odd sighting of a broad, be-scaled back here and there was enough to convince Smiffy and Posh that they were in the presence of many hundreds of pounds of carp flesh. Their one final, precise sighting came when one of the 'smaller' carp seemed to decide that sunbathing was over for the day, and a large common carp slid up out of the water and fell back with a resounding splash, just like a whale. It was almost as big as the linear, as far as they could tell, but on its re-entry, all the others suddenly became alert and within minutes had faded from view.

'Time for a beer, I reckon,' said Posh, and Smiffy nodded, then followed his mate as he made tracks, by way of the West Woods, to The Green Man.

The early morning mist was rising from the waters of the Mere as, forty-eight hours later, they made their way past it towards Sutton Woods and the river beyond. The hour was early, but the world was gradually waking, and the calls of waterfowl could be heard, getting louder, as they passed into the woods. Here, the day was taking a little longer to register, and the creatures of the night were still abroad. A small herd of deer spooked as they heard the boys approaching, and the two of them watched as they bounded off between the trees and were soon out of sight.

A hundred yards further on, Posh put his arm across his mate's chest and they stopped still. Through the trees, Smiffy could see a ghostly white shape moving easily, and the unmistakable sight of a barn owl drifted past silently, ten yards in front of them and paying them no heed.

By the time they had reached the river, they were both highly charged, and had seen the owl as a good omen – this was going to be a good day. They began where Posh had caught his barbel from, a few months earlier, but after the usual fare of chub and perch in the first hour, decided to move upstream a little. It was still only a little after six o'clock, and they doubted that anybody would be on the river on a midweek morning, so a little 'guesting' would surely be harmless. Posh had dabbled on the private stretch a couple of times, but usually only in the colder months, which had proved the wrong time for the better fish. Now, the river looked resplendent in its summer finery, and they were confident that success was just around a leafy corner. Posh was first to feel the pull of a barbel, and was soon netting a fine fish of about six pounds. Although not the monster they were hoping for, it was an encouraging start, and they fished on with more confidence. Another of a similar size followed within half an hour, and they were both sure that a shoal was present, in amongst the streamer weed that Posh was rolling his luncheon meat past. Smiffy was pleased for his mate, but really wanted to get in on the action, so took himself a little further upstream to see what he could find.

The woods ended after a hundred yards and opened out into a glorious water meadow. The river here was lined with sedges and rushes, and the bright yellow of marsh marigold gave the whole area a wonderful, summery feel. Smiffy hunched down and crept carefully through the sedge and long grass, trying to keep out of sight of fish and members alike, but still needing to see the river for signs of fish or potential fish-holding areas. After a short while, he came to a small opening in the reeds and crept into it, and there in front of him was just what he'd been looking for. The river ran from his right to left, and just to his left he could see clear, clean gravel beneath the long, sinuous streamer weed. The gravel ran for twenty yards or so downstream, and he could almost smell the barbel beneath the weed. He settled himself down on the bank, hidden from prying eyes by the rushes and sedge, then opened out his landing net in readiness. A few swan shot gave him some casting weight, although the square of luncheon meat would probably have been weight enough, and carefully flicked it all out to the edge of the weed, letting it settle down, and slowly trundle along the gravel run. A few pieces of broken meat accompanied the hookbait, and he sat very still, watching the rod tip and feeling the line with his thumb and forefinger.

Nothing on the first pass, nothing on the second, but just as he was about to retrieve the bait for a third time, he felt a pluck on the line. Then another, and he struck forcefully, the rod tip pulling round, then down as a fish made off downstream. The reel screeched as the line was torn from it and as he raised the rod, the weed hung from the line like slimy, green washing. The line hummed as the fish held tight to the far bank, thirty yards downstream, and Smiffy debated whether to walk down to meet the fish. The problem was, there was nowhere further down where he could easily get to the bankside, and it might cause more of a problem than solve one. Steady pressure soon began to tell, and the Avon rod began to gently ease upwards, moving the barbel away from the weed and into the middle of the river. This in itself didn't help, as it gave the fish the assistance it needed, and once again the reel complained bitterly as five yards of line was given up.

The battle seemed to last an age, and Smiffy felt like he must be glowing brightly to anyone who would look. But no indignant shouts were forthcoming, so he just battled on, sure that once the fish was netted he wouldn't give a damn about his own capture.

With the fish almost spent, and five yards away, he thought that his fears had come to be reality when he heard movement behind him and a voice speak his name. He daren't look round, but just concentrated on the fish. If he at least landed the thing then he would have caught it, and that was that.

'Smiffy!' came another urgent call. It was Posh. Bloody fool, it was Posh. How would anyone else have known his name, for Chrissake?

'Yeah, over here,' he replied, then heard the sedges rustle as his mate slipped down behind him.

'Got one on, mate? Good man. Is it a good'un?' asked Posh.

'Feels it, mate. Been on for about ten minutes or so, arm's aching like buggery. Ooh, here we go, here we go. Nice… and… easy. Yes!'

As the fish went into the net, Posh slapped Smiffy on the back and they both peered into the net at an inordinately long barbel.

'Bloody hell, Smiffy, that looks bigger than mine,' declared Posh.

'How big was yours, then?' said Smiffy, as he brought the net towards him and knelt down to extract the hook.

'Dunno,' replied Posh, 'it's still in the net!'

Smiffy turned and beamed a huge smile. 'You old dog, Posh! Well done, mate. Least we brought the scales this time, and the camera.'

Posh grabbed the rod and tackle bag, whilst Smiffy hoisted the net and fish, and they quickly made their way back to Posh's swim, where the net was lowered into the steady flow of the river.

Once all was set, they worked out a quick plan.

'Right,' said Posh, 'we'll do yours first, while it's still tired. Then you hold it in the water until it's ready to go. After that mine, same thing. Bish, bash, bosh!'

Smiffy's fish was beautiful, and the golden flakes of sun that came through the trees and were sprinkled on its flanks made it even more so. They couldn't believe the scales when they spun around to just under thirteen pounds, but a subsequent re-weighing of the sling and the fish gave them the same result. Posh's fish was a pound or so lighter, but wonderful just the same, and he reckoned it was probably bigger than the one he'd had earlier in the year. All in all, a glorious morning's fishing, and they packed away and strolled back through the very awake woodland, chirruping like the birds around them.

Ted had seen the deer spook earlier on, so was aware of someone's presence in the woods just after dawn, and it hadn't taken a genius to work out who it was. Likewise, he was prepared for a visit at sometime during the morning, and when the lads came through the door, they were equally unsurprised that the tea was on the table, along with half a dozen slices of freshly buttered toast.

With crumbs flying hither and yon, the lads gave Ted the full story of their morning's exploits, and he smiled back appreciatively.

'Well done, boys, two really good fish. But I wouldn't go shouting about 'em too much. Most folks around here know that the big barbel stay up near the meadows, in the private stretch, so it might look a bit, shall we say, strange that you both managed one from the lower river, if you get my meaning,' said Ted.

They both nodded slowly, Posh replying for them. 'Don't matter. We know we caught 'em, got the photos to prove it. Don't need to be shouting about it too much.'

'Gotta show Stan, though,' said Smiffy, whilst gulping down the last of his tea. 'He's a good old boy. He won't say anything to anyone.'

With a mouthful of tea and toast, Posh could merely nod. Then nodded again as Ted lifted his empty cup to indicate a refill.

'Yeah, cheers Ted,' said Smiffy. 'Any more toast?'

Ted looked over his shoulder and glowered, but picked up the knife anyway and started carving a few more doorsteps from the loaf.

'Oh, we didn't tell you Ted,' continued Smiffy, unabashed at his earlier request. 'Saw a shoal of huge fish over the Mere the other day, didn't we, Posh?'

Posh nodded, and swallowed, he coughed to clear his throat, and then took up the story.

'Yeah. Out in front of the boathouse on Monday afternoon. A dozen biiiggg carp.' He then went on to describe their sightings, especially of the linear and the leaping common, finishing with, 'I reckon they were all over forty, Ted. I could just make out The Big Common, and The Poached Mirror, and they were a lot bigger than the rest, but that's only 'cos they're bloody huge, innit?'

Ted stood by the stove, thinking about that last from Neil. Yes, they were considerably larger than the rest, but that didn't mean to say that the rest were 'small'. He'd seen two or three different groups of carp in the past few weeks, each group consisting of anywhere between six to twelve fish, but there had been no more than three of the really large fish in amongst them, and the majority were probably less than thirty pounds in weight. But now it would seem that the carp had finally split into peer groups, and if that was so, he, Neil and Stan would have to be extra vigilant. It wouldn't take much for one of the residents to see a group of huge fish like that and go charging into the pub to tell everyone who would listen. Definitely a mixture of good and bad, this news from the boys.

Stan stood with them, by the boathouse, and discussed the future. Smiffy was due to leave for Spain tomorrow, and on his return would be returning to Leeds, in preparation for his second year at University.

They'd met here a couple of times in the past fortnight, in the hope of a repeat sighting of the shoal of monsters, for Stan's benefit if anything, but they'd been unlucky. The weather had changed, bringing clouds and wind, and they'd seen nothing, barring a couple of long-range rolling carp. Today, however, the weather was a bit more clement, the wind having dropped to a light westerly, and the sun regularly breaking through the sparse cloud cover.

The three of them sat by the boathouse, and soaked up the intermittent rays.

'So that's good, then, Quentin,' said Stan. 'Already got an idea of what you want. That's good mate. How d'you reckon you'll go about it then?'

Smiffy had told Stan and Posh about a meeting he'd had with one of the tutors, and the subsequent discussion about the conservation work that the National Trust do, all over the country. He'd obviously been aware of the Trust, having the New Forest right on his doorstep for the past few years, but wasn't aware of all of the backroom work and research that was continually going on.

'Well, I'd have to get a distinction in biology, which is fine, then I'd have to go for a doctorate in ecology, which is another two years. But then, it's also fieldwork so I'd be posted somewhere to get to know the full scope. There's so many ways to go, from warden to research chemist, but I really want to be a bit hands on, y'know. It's early days yet, but I must admit, it's pretty exciting. And they've got loads of lakes all over the country!' He laughed at this, but he knew that there was every possibility that the Trust had access to waters that nobody else did, and who knew what they might hold?

Stan stood up and stretched. 'Good for you, lad. Don't forget your mates if you find any secret lakes now, will yer?' He turned and winked, then turned back towards the lake.

'Hello, what have we here?' he said as he walked slowly to the water's edge. Posh and Smiffy both jumped up and followed him, but what they saw, although fascinating, wasn't what they'd expected. A grass snake slid easily across the surface of the lake, moving away towards the reeds to their right, and the two of them walked slowly in that direction, to see where it would make landfall. A few minutes later they returned, but Stan was out of sight so they carried on walking, sure that he'd be round by the snags. As they rounded the corner he was about ten feet above ground, in the crook of a large oak tree, peering down into the lake below. He saw them below and pointed out into the lake, but they could see nothing from ground level, so both shinned up the tree to join Stan at different levels.

His mind went back, to a different century, a different tree, but the same lake. And there below were probably the same fish. The Common was hugely evident, ten yards out, as were the two big mirrors, but they had been joined by three or four good-sized carp, and all were meandering around slowly. He had some Chum mixers in a pocket, an essential part of his everyday walking kit, so flicked out a dozen of the floating morsels to gauge the carp's reaction. Initially, the food was totally ignored, but after a few minutes, one or two of the fish began to move more purposefully. Then, with a slurp, a mixer disappeared. Then another. By the time that Stan had emptied his pocket, the larger carp had been joined by half a dozen smaller fish, and the lake surface was all ripples and bubbles, dorsals and lips.

All three of the watchers were agog, as a huge mouth came slowly to the surface and hoovered up a line of mixers, like a baleen whale sifting krill. The cessation of food brought about a slow cessation of feeding, and soon all that was left were a few small swirls and some unforgettable memories.

At the bottom of the tree the usual 'bloody hells' and 'how bigs' followed. Then as they walked slowly back towards Smiffy's house, Stan just said, 'Somehow, boys, we've got to fish this bloody lake. In the meantime, sights like that just can't be bought.'

He bade Smiffy goodbye and good luck, then made his way back past the boathouse, stopping briefly to look in the reedy corner.

This place was getting more incredible by the minute. Needed something to take his mind off it. Oh well, back to Beaufort's. Wonder if they've seen much Chum mixer?

PART FIVE

ICY WIND of NIGHT BE GONE
THIS is NOT YOUR DOMAIN

Chapter Twenty Four
Round and Round

'Fifty bloody years!' said Buzz. 'How the hell have you survived that long, Quill?' He swayed a little, pint glass in hand, and looked down at Stan. Rhodie and Sid were close by and were quick to join in the verbal assault.

'Yeah, you old bugger, you ordered that Stannah stairlift yet, or is that Jean's surprise present for you?' quipped Sid, before taking another mouthful of beer.

'That and the incontinence pants,' added Rhodie. 'Be like Billy Connolly later, sloshing around on the dance floor.' He accompanied this with a visual parody, and Sid nearly choked on his beer, spluttering a lot of it over Buzz. The big man growled a little, but Sid's mirth was infectious, and pretty soon Stan was being mercilessly dissected by his friends' wit, but he cared little. It was great to see them all, and the fact that it was at his fiftieth birthday bash mattered not a jot.

Jean had organised the whole thing, but as much as she'd tried to keep it a surprise, in such a small community that had proved almost impossible, so eventually she'd just enlisted Stan's help with sorting out the hall and the beer, whilst she dealt with everything else. The village hall had been perfect, and when she'd asked some of the mums at the school if they knew of a band or disco, Neil Becks' mum, Maggie, had suggested her brother. It had been his boat that Smiffy and Posh had gone on a few years earlier, but he tended to pop down to see her and Dan fairly regularly, and had a weird but wonderful disco that he sometimes brought out of the cobwebs.

'Kensational! Why that?' Jean had asked. 'I thought his name was Klaus?'

Maggie had smiled a sort of embarrassed smile that family members the world over smiled. It said, 'Don't ask. He's the one we don't talk much about. Perfectly harmless, just a little strange.'

Maggie, however, said, 'Yes, Klaus Fabianski, but his name is actually Ken Pertwee. Hence, Ken-sational!' Jean frowned, and was about to ask more when Maggie just said, 'Don't ask. Just trust me, he'll be great, he always is.'

That sorted, Jean had just concentrated on getting as many people as she could to attend on the day, and looking at the hall, brimful with bodies, and reverberating with music, laughter and the constant buzz of voices raised in conversation, she reckoned she'd done pretty well.

As Stan moved away from his character assassination, the other three fell into a familiar round of chat and questions. Buzz was still involved in some major dive projects, and earning a pretty penny for the privilege. Rhodie was now a dad, like Sid, and was settled in his job, although the travelling was a bit gutty at times. And Sid was, well, Sid. He'd taken to fatherhood with ease, probably due to his mental age being closer to his son's than his wife's, and had just plodded away with his job on the motors, never complaining, and looking on the bright side of everything. Naturally, the conversation soon became pinpointed on the one subject common to all three, and Buzz bemoaned his lack of fishing, as usual.

'Oh yeah, I can swim with the bloody things all day long; bleedin' big'uns as well, but I can't remember when I actually went fishing for carp. Probably the last time we all got together.'

Rhodie nodded, 'Yeah, I'm a bit like that at the moment. Zipping all over the bloody place, then of course, when I get home there's the wife and kid to sort out. Managing about one night every couple of weeks at the mo. Doing my crust in, it is.'

Sid, however, felt no sympathy, and went for the jugular. 'Ah, blessums! I'm weeping into me beer here. Listen to you two! Now you know how it was for me and Quill for all those bloody years, knowing that one or both of you bastards would be at the lake well before us, and invariably have bagged a couple before we'd even left work! Well, my heart bleeds, boys, but I'm loving it at the mo. Get out almost every weekend, and sometimes even manage to nick an overnighter during the week. And I'm 'aving loads! Two thirties in the last two sessions; thirty-four pound common the best, and even Quill's getting amongst 'em. Still, can't complain, eh? Whose round is it?' They both glared at him, and he suddenly realised it must be his, so wandered off to the bar, chuckling away to himself.

Smiffy had just walked inside, and saw Posh chatting to a couple of girls, so wandered over and casually stitched himself to the edge of the little group. A laugh here, a murmured agreement there, and pretty soon all four were chatting away. When the girls went off to do that nose powdering thing, Posh said, 'Blimey, you smoothed in pretty swift there, Smiffy. Slid through the door on a wave of cool, or was it a snail's trail?'

Smiffy laughed. 'Can't let you be keeping it all to yerself, Posh. I mean two's a bit greedy, innit?'

Posh smiled back, then looked around to see whether the girls were returning. But no, that would be much too quick; they probably had loads to talk about, so he changed the subject.

'So, mate, how's Uni doing? Made your mind up yet?'

Smiffy took a sip of beer and nodded. 'Yeah, been looking into that National Trust thing. Mate, it ain't just the work they do, which is just what I'm looking f it's the bloody lakes as well. I mean, some serious waters, dotted around the place. I found out about this one, out west somewhere, not sure

Well, this bloke I'm chatting to, one of the tutors, he's into his carp fishing a bit and he tells me that there's this lake that some bloke called Don Leney used to use as a holding pond when he was moving fish out west. You heard of him?'

Posh frowned a little. He'd heard the name, he was sure, but couldn't remember where. Then, just at that moment, Stan wandered up and raised a glass.

'Stan, just the bloke,' said Posh. 'Don Leney. I'm sure you've mentioned his name before. Who is he?'

Stan was taken slightly by surprise by the question, but carried on nonetheless. 'Don Leney? Yeah, some people call him the father of modern carp fishing. He imported top quality fish back in the thirties and stocked them in lots of lakes, mainly in the south of England, but a few other places as well. You know that lovely twenty-eight you had from Linton's?' Posh nodded, then realised where he'd heard the name before. 'Well, that was a Leney, and so are a lot of the fish I'm fishing for at Beaufort's. Why'd you ask?'

Posh looked at Smiffy, who shrugged, then told Stan the story.

'Bloody hell, Quentin, best you be learning a bit more about that lake, like grid references and the like!' exclaimed Stan. Smiffy nodded, then turned to look at the two girls who were walking through the crowd, giggling and whispering. Stan followed his gaze, and realised that the conversation was over, so strolled away and let nature take its course.

Ted stood quietly in a corner of the hall, glass of beer in hand and a contented look on his face. Everybody was happy, laughter vied for supremacy over the music, and people danced with gay abandon, unconcerned about ability or vanity.

'Good old do, Ted,' said Jake as he joined him in the corner. 'That old Stan, he's a good old boy, and his mates.'

Ted nodded, more to himself than his recently acquired audience of one. He had a lot of time for Stan; a lot of time. He had a smart head on his shoulders and knew how to use it. A good man, was Stan, and he'd known enough bad'uns to know the difference, that was for sure. He'd been in smoky dance halls before, filled with hormones and testosterone, and it was a dangerous mix. Blood, bottles, knives and worse. Too many times for him to care to remember. Stu Gutheridge, Manny Tiler, wee Sammy Dalgish; all gone, not from an enemy hand but from a bloody stupid brawl over something trivial, fuelled by alcohol. But not now, not in this place. These were all good people, and he was happy to be a part of this.

'Alright, chaps?' said Stan. 'Fancy another?'

Jake looked at Ted, and they both looked back at Stan. 'Don't mind if we do, young Stan,' replied Jake, and he and Ted drained their respective glasses before handing them to the host.

Good people, thought Ted, happily.

'Stan, a quiet word.' He looked round to see Peter standing next to him, and wondered if he was going to enquire as to his son's intentions.

'Yeah, sure Peter. What's up?'

Peter looked around furtively then motioned Stan to follow him, and walked through the open doors to the field outside. Darkness had fallen an hour previously, but there were plenty of lights on, so they walked to a quiet corner at the edge of the field.

'You all right, Peter?' he asked as they came to a halt. 'Got a problem or something?'

Peter took a sip of his ale, then wiped the back of his hand across his mouth.

'The death, a very bad thing. Tragic, and we'll never forget that,' he began, and Stan knew that he wasn't just stating the obvious. Four months had passed since the accident, but the memory was still quite vivid in many people's minds, and it was still a constant source of conversation in the local pubs. He took a sip of his beer and allowed Peter to continue.

'Bad, very bad. The blackest of clouds,' he went on, 'but every cloud, even the blackest, well, you know what I mean, I'm sure.'

Stan wasn't sure if he did, but if Peter had continued, would he have gone on the way Stan thought? Would he have actually said 'silver lining'? Once again, he just nodded, whilst taking another swallow of beer.

Peter seemed stuck for what to say next, so took another deep draught of ale, as if to strengthen his resolve.

'The thing is, well, I think that boating of any sort is off the menu for the foreseeable future. Understandably.' Stan had already heard this from John, so it was no big surprise. Then Peter continued: 'I, and a few others on the residents committee, were thinking that, with the proper supervision and such, well, we thought that now might be the time to propose that fishing, once again, be allowed on the Mere. As a source of revenue as well as a much less, errm, well, less fraught with danger type pastime, you know.'

The words took a little time to filter through Stan's drink-induced torpor; he hadn't been expecting this at all, so it was the classic double-take.

'I'm sorry, can you run that past me again, Peter?' he asked, as calmly as he could.

Peter swallowed another mouthful of beer before continuing, seemingly much more in control of his emotions now that he'd actually voiced his feelings.

'Fishing, Stan. We thought that we could start a fishing club. Exclusive. What do you call it?'

'A syndicate?' offered Stan.

'Syndicate, that's the fellow. Small, maybe fifty or so members. Heard Quentin talking of such a thing recently. Similar to Richard Beaufort's place, I assume. And I know that Stuart's happy with his. But we need someone to run it. Wondered if you fancied it? We know you've got quite a bit on your plate, but thought you might have a few ideas on how to organise it and such. What do you think?'

Stan was dumbfounded. Totally stunned. This had not entered his mind at all, not in the slightest, and now here it was, huge and bright and staring straight at him.

'Peter, I'm a bit, well, stunned to be frank. I mean, yeah, of course I'd love to head up a syndicate but, well, isn't it a bit soon? I mean, it was only a few months ago, y'know.'

Peter nodded, as if that was all very obvious, and needed no mention. 'Quite, Stan, but we're not thinking of starting tomorrow! However, it may well be worth getting things moving, and then we thought that we could open at the start of next spring, maybe the first of May. What do you think?'

A lot of thought had obviously already been put into this, and Stan was sure that he was just a minor detail. If he declined there would soon be someone else who would accept. But why on earth would he decline? Not in a million years had he thought that he would once again cast a line into the Mere, and now here he was, being asked to be the bloody head bailiff! He'd get to vet all potential members, and he could think of three in very close proximity that would go straight on the list.

'Peter, of course I'd love to do it, you know that. You've seen the bloody fish, so you can imagine how I feel about fishing it. Of course I'll do it, just let me know what you need.'

Peter smiled broadly and raised his glass in a mock toast. 'Brilliant! I had no doubt that you'd agree. Keep it quiet for a while, wait for the dust to settle. I'll talk to John shortly, then we'll have another chat, see what we need to do to get things moving.'

Stan nodded and was just about to ask another question when Jean called to him. 'There you are! We've been looking all over for you. Come on, time to blow out some candles, love.'

Stan looked at Peter, who winked, then they followed Jean into the hall, amid catcalls and applause.

After the candle blowing there was a brief stuttered thank-you speech from Stan, which ended with the command, 'The bar's open until midnight, so get it down yer necks!'

Klaus, aka Ken-sational, was all that Maggie had promised, and there was never a moment when the dance floor was empty. A selection of velvet jackets seemed to appear and disappear behind the decks, and the ruffed collar and cuffs of his shirt gave him the appearance of a nineteenth century gentleman thief.

He was a parody of the parody that was Smashie and Nicey, and the evening was punctuated with 'Now then, now thens' and 'Does a lot of work for chara-dee, doesn't like to talk about it' and 'Get ready to roll with the queen of soul.'

By the time that the velveteen voxmeister declared, 'And now, one of the greatest records of all time... Ladies and gentlemen, please bow before the Lords Bachmann and Turner, and the Duke of Overdrive – You ain't seen nothing yet!' the assembled throng were more than happy to do his bidding, and 'B-b-b-b-baby, you just ain't seen nothing yet!' rang out raucously across the sleepy, Salisbury countryside. The evening was a great success, and all present reckoned it was the best night in the old hall since Charlie Dean's wake, which was mighty praise indeed.

Chapter Twenty Five
Dark Side of the Moon

A month had passed since the party and, more importantly, since his brief but startling meeting with Peter, and Stan was still none the wiser. The revelation that the Mere would, once again, be open for fishing had shocked him, but that shock soon turned to elation when he realised that, not only would he and his mates be able to renew their quest for those magnificent carp again, but also that **he** would be in charge. Over the next few days his mind was full of what, and who, and where, but as the days became a week, then a fortnight, and he'd heard nothing further from Peter, he wondered whether it was just a drunken ramble.

By now, as October moved inexorably towards November, he'd all but erased the idea from his mind, and was concentrating solely on his fishing at Beaufort's. Prior to, and since the party he'd enjoyed a bit of success, and a couple of sessions were memorable in very different ways.

It came as no surprise to Stan that, following his success in the island channel, he was unable to get back in there for a couple of weeks. He'd added a twenty-two pound common to the thirty-nine, later the same day, and it doesn't take long for an unfancied swim to become the most popular on the lake, once someone's done the initial hard work.

It was no surprise, either, that only one more fish came from the channel in the ensuing weeks; the word 'stealth' obviously not a part of the vocabulary of most of the Beaufort's members. Bivvies were set up at either end of the channel, and large leads splashed hither and yon, leaving the carp in no doubt that they were being targeted. Oh, well, ever was it thus, but Stan knew that, pretty soon, the channel would be seen as a 'no carp' area and he would be able to return, and begin his autumn baiting campaign. In the meantime there were plenty of other swims to fish, and one that he really fancied just happened to be the furthest from the car park.

He'd decided to fish a few of the less popular, more neglected swims, and one such was the one at the far end of the north bank, with the lilies to its left. It was a half-mile trek from the car, but, once you'd made it through the pain barrier, you were totally secluded from the rest of the lake. The swim to the right was almost a hundred yards away and separated by willow and alder, and the Reeds swim, opposite, was almost in a different lake, with a green jungle of lilies in between. Initially, it didn't seem to be as productive as that swim, but it soon became apparent that anybody who fished there tended to put their baits as close to the lilies as possible, giving themselves very little chance of stopping a carp from escaping into the jungle of lily roots and stems.

Stan had fallen foul of this tactic on his first session, and had lost three carp in quick succession, one sunny afternoon, so he had to make a decision: abandon the swim and never return, or work out a different method of fishing it to give himself a fighting chance of landing any hooked fish. The latter was always going to be the way forward, and so he eventually came up with a couple of possible solutions. The problem with using a bite alarm was that you tended to let it fish for itself, but when a run came it was so blisteringly fast that, in the time it took to react, the fish was already five yards into its sanctuary and the game was already lost. So, to give himself a better chance, he decided to float fish during the day. The indication was immediate so the initial strike should catch the carp by surprise and give Stan the advantage he would need.

Then, for the nights, he would fish two baits in the close margins, no closer than five yards to the pads. This may cut down the amount of action he received, but any that he did get would have a better chance of being converted to a carp on the bank. The beginning of August gave him the first opportunity to implement his plan, and the conditions couldn't have been better. A warm westerly was blowing up the lake, into the pads, and the cloudless sky foretold of a very warm weekend. He'd normally be champing at the bit to get away as early as possible on Friday afternoon, but this time he was in no rush. He'd decided to arrive just before dawn on Saturday; that way he'd be wide awake and raring to go with the float, rather than turning over for just five more minutes' shut eye.

The grass was damp with dew, and a light mist hung above the lake surface, and even though he'd cut down his tackle as much as possible, he still arrived puffing and blowing into the swim. He passed three other anglers, all sound asleep, and assumed that the owner of the fifth car in the car park was in the Reeds, opposite. He'd prepared everything, even the depth of the float, so all that was required was to scatter a few handfuls of hemp and tiger nuts, followed by the float with its tiger nut hookbait, to the edge of the lilies. The float nestled down perfectly, but he hoped that the sun wouldn't be too long in rising above the surrounding trees, because the red tip was difficult to make out in the half-light of dawn.

Coots and moorhens began their daily arguments, and a pair of grebes appeared, here and there, searching out breakfast for their insistent young. As the sun rose, Stan could see the odd lily leaf being nudged from beneath, and he drifted back a few decades, to Old Bury Hill lake with Perky. The float had nestled next to the lilies back then, and the ensuing take from a carp had left him quivering and fishless. The memory was not painful, though; it was one of the reasons that he had chosen this particular path, and it made him smile.

This float, by these lilies, was suddenly animated.

It twitched, ever so slightly, then lifted a fraction. Rings were emanating from the pad next to it and Stan guessed that a tench, or carp, were very close. The red tip lifted a fraction more, then dipped and was gone.

Stan struck forcefully and the rod tip bent alarmingly as the fish was taken completely by surprise. The battle would be won or lost now, in these first few seconds, and with the clutch wound up tight, 15lb line and a good rod, Stan knew that he had the upper hand. The water churned and boiled as the fish realised its mistake, but Stan kept the pressure on and, amazingly, within no more than a minute had bullied the carp into the waiting net. The fish thrashed and foamed, but to no avail – the battle was lost, and Stan gave a little whoop of delight at the immediate success of his tactic. Don't you just love it when a plan comes together?

The carp was no more than eighteen pounds; a beautiful mirror probably stocked within the past couple of years, and Stan took a couple of shots of it on the mat before releasing it. Brilliant!

The swim was going to be a no-fish area for another half an hour or so, so he sat back and made a cup of tea, and ran the short battle through his head once more. He wondered how successful the float tactic would be with a fish of twice that size.

An hour later his float was nestled next to the same lily pad, amongst another scattering of hemp and nuts. He'd thought of casting a little further, but that would give the fish a better angle of escape, so he continued with the same spot, no more than four yards from his rod tip. As well as the baiting pattern, he'd also thrown individual nuts into the gaps in the lily pads, to entice the carp to search out more, and within ten minutes of recasting was bundling another, similar sized mirror into the net. This was great fun, and by early afternoon his arm ached from playing two more carp, both commons, into the waiting net. The largest had been just over twenty pounds, and, although he was delighted with the action, he was starting to crave something larger.

The sun was very warm by now, almost uncomfortably so, and Stan was beginning to feel drowsy after his early start, so spread out his bedchair in the shade of the trees and lay down for a few minutes. As he drifted slowly away, the accompaniment of birdsong and insect buzz put him in mind of one of his favourite Floyd songs, Grantchester Meadows, and he ran the song through his head a few times, until sleep eventually put paid to another chorus.

Hear the lark and harken to the barking of the dog fox,
Gone to ground.
See the flashing of the kingfisher dashing to the water.
And a river of green is sliding unseen beneath the trees,
Laughing as it passes through the endless summer,
Making for the sea.

He slipped in and out of sleep; the odd raucous cry from an agitated waterfowl dragging him back from that realm, closer to wakefulness. An hour or so passed, and beneath the brolly it was warm and airless, so Stan woke a couple of times for a drink of water. Four in the afternoon, still a bit early for the float, back down on the pillow.

'Alright, Stan?' said a familiar voice. 'You having a little nap, mate?'

He peered around the corner of the brolly and was greeted by the scary sight of Bob's knees.

'Well, not now, Bob,' he murmured. 'You got a licence for them?' he continued, pointing at the offending items whilst reaching behind him for his sunglasses.

'Hurr! Hurr! Yeah, they're a bit dodgy, in't they?' said Bob. 'See you had a couple then, Stan. Any good?'

Stan emerged from beneath his brolly and ran a hand through his hair.

'Nah, biggest was a twenty-pound common, what about you?'

'Had a couple of doubles yesterday, then a twenty-four pound mirror this morning. Happy with that,' replied Bob. Stan eyed the mug in his hand, so bent to light the cooker and fill the kettle.

'So, Stan, you're being a bit coy, mate. How many d'you have? Sure I saw you playing two or three.'

Stan thought for a second or two, then decided on the truth.

'Four in total, all on the float, but please don't say anything. You've seen what's happened with the channel, won't be able to get back in there for awhile. I'd like to keep this quiet for as long as poss, just to see what might come along.'

He'd taken Bob's cup and dropped the tea bag into it, as well as one into his own, and was now filling them from the kettle.

'Nah, definitely not, mate,' replied Bob. 'I know what you mean. Don't you worry about me, I'll keep stum, you can be sure of that.'

Stan nodded, and said, 'Cheers,' then handed Bob his tea.

They sat and chatted for half an hour, Stan gleaning as much as he could about the lake from Bob. This was his second season, and the thirty he'd had from the Boathouse Bay was his second from the lake. For all that they spoke of, Stan learnt little that he didn't already know, and pretty soon he was willing Bob to leave. A further ten, dry minutes passed before Bob took the hint, took his mug, and took his leave, wishing Stan good luck.

The sun was beginning to lose its sting, so Stan prepared for another few hours of float fishing, before resorting to bottom baits for the night. Firstly, though, it was time for food.

Half an hour later he was replete with curry and a glass of wine, so readied the float rod and flicked the float back to its spot next to the pads. The evening was different from earlier in the day, and the float remained motionless for an hour or so. As Stan's concentration waned, his gaze wandered and he watched a number of swifts as they skimmed the surface of the lake, picking the last of the summer's insect hatches from it.

Suddenly, the rod was wrenched from the rests and the tip splashed in the water. The clutch was wound up tight, so no line was forthcoming, and Stan just about grabbed the rod butt before the whole thing disappeared into the lake. As he bent into the fish the rod creaked and he saw the lily leaves fold down to show the route the fish had taken in its escape bid. Even before it happened, Stan knew that he'd blown it, and pretty soon he was extracting his hook from a thick lily stem.

There was probably half an hour of light left, and although he fancied there would be another chance on the float, he decided to get his rods ready for the night. Both were dropped a yard out from the bank, one five yards to the right of the pads and the other a further fifteen yards to the right of that, and he wondered how far the carp would venture from the pads under cover of the night. In the early hours of the morning he thought he had the answer, but the right hand rod produced a dark tench rather than a golden carp, and nothing further disturbed his sleep.

His journey home was a good one, and he was happy that part of his plan had worked. The guy in the Boathouse Bay had caught a couple of twenties, but the one fishing the channel had blanked, and Stan knew that it wouldn't be long before the channel was, once again, left alone, and his winter baiting campaign could commence. For now, though, he needed to see if any of the better fish could be enticed from the pads on the float.

The following weekend was his last for a few weeks, as he and Jean were going away with the kids and their families to Cornwall. He hoped he could repeat his success of the previous weekend, and have something to bore Stevie with. Once again he arrived very early on Saturday morning, and with only four cars in the car park, was pretty certain that his swim would be free, and he was right. The weather was similar to the previous weekend, although strong wind and rain was forecast for later in the day, which might just be perfect.

Everything fell into place as before, and within no more than half an hour, another double-figure mirror was nestled in the mesh of the landing net, Stan unhooking it and releasing it without a photograph. Although pleased, he was beginning to feel that this might just be a small fish tactic. As the float settled again, small wisps of mist dancing around the red tip, Stan barely had time to place the rod on the rests before it sailed away and another hard fighting carp made a bid for safety. He'd been caught slightly off guard and the fish made the sanctuary of the pads before the test curve could prevent it, and a few seconds later the float plopped lifelessly to the right.

Normally he'd have been annoyed at the loss, but a sight of the carp's flank was enough to show a similar sized fish, and Stan sat back and put his chin in his hands. What to do? The tactic was working, very well, but where were the larger carp? He wasn't even sure if they were in the lily bed, although logic dictated that this was the only real sanctuary they had, and the odd capture of a larger specimen from the Reeds, opposite, strengthened that viewpoint. What to do? What to do? Over a cup of tea he mulled the problem. There were obviously larger fish in the pads, it was just that the smaller ones were getting to the baits first – the classic baiting pyramid. Okay, so let's build a pyramid!

He dispensed with a float for the rest of the day, flicking a lead down the right hand margin just so that he had a bait in the water. Then, every half an hour, he catapulted out hemp and tiger nuts to the edge of the lilies. As the evening drew close he put out a few boilies with each baiting; not many, just half a dozen each time, but as the sun started to sink a little lower, he dispensed with the hemp and nuts, and put out a few dozen whole and broken boilies, followed by a float fished one.

Within minutes he watched the float sink, then held on hard as a carp of low-twenties did its best to avoid capture. This was the largest carp he had landed from the swim, and although encouraging, he was still hoping for better. Half an hour later, with dragonflies dancing above his head and feasting on the pillar of gnats and midges there, he hooked a much larger specimen. He winced as the rod bent so far round as to almost form the letter 'C', but still held on tight and gradually felt the rod tip easing back towards him. He kept moving the rod to the right, not touching the reel, which was wound tight. Then, unexpectedly, the fish made for the open water to his right and he had to frantically loosen the clutch to let it have some line. Now the battle was fully joined, and he let the fish go as far right as it desired, hoping that it would tire itself out enough that it couldn't make it back to the pads.

Bats had replaced dragonflies, but the feast was still the same, as he eventually led the long, dark fish into the net and, no matter what its weight, Stan was elated that his plan had worked. Looking at it on the mat, Stan knew that it wasn't close to thirty pounds, but he also knew that it was probably one of the oldest carp in the lake, and drank in the sight of it as the sun finally sank behind the trees. He took half a dozen photos of the carp, laid on the mat next to the scales, then quickly weighed it, recording a weight of just under twenty-eight pounds. No monster, but a fish that he would be rightly proud of for many years.

A holiday beckoned, and after that he was pretty sure he'd be back in the channel, but that was fine. The fish would be here next summer, and he'd be targeting them much earlier in the season, so would surely get a chance of one of the lake's larger specimens. For now, though, everything was going just fine.

On his return from holiday he'd managed one more session before the party. He'd been able to get back into the channel, which had, inevitably, been left alone, and Stan's capture of the thirty-nine seen as just one of those things. He realised that the session could be a little futile, but wanted to keep an eye on the area and begin trickling a little bait in there, so fished to the right hand side of the swim. This enabled him to fish his left hand rod in the margins of the channel, his middle rod to the island, and his third rod to rove around a little. From September 1st three rods were allowed on the lake, which seemed a little stupid to him. Two rods were ample, as far as he could see, but the previous season's rule of three rods after November 1st had been changed to suit a few members who thought it might make them better anglers. Sadly, it didn't.

Jackson strolled round on Saturday morning, not long after Bob had popped in for his customary chat and mug of tea, and the three of them sat and chatted for an hour. Stan had the photo of the twenty eight to show Jackson, and he was delighted with it.

'Beautiful, Stan, just beautiful. Definitely one of the old originals,' he confirmed, and Stan was equally as delighted. 'Gotta be over fifty years old, that one. Think it last came out a couple of years ago, same sort of weight. Lovely fish. Where'd you have it from, Stan?'

Stan looked at Bob, who raised his eyebrows as he took another swig of tea. Stan looked back at Jackson, then slowly answered.

'Jack, please don't say anything to anyone. You saw what happened when I caught that fish from here; it won't take seconds for someone to jump in the swim and destroy it.' It was then Jackson's turn to raise his eyebrows, so Stan hastily continued, and told of the plan, and the float, and the success.

Slowly, Jackson's eyebrows lowered and he just nodded a couple of times. 'I see where you're coming from, Stan. No problem, they'll hear nothing from me, but I would like to put the photo up in the lodge – a bit of extra ammunition when the ones that can't catch see that there are still carp in here!'

Stan smiled, and Bob sniggered and nodded, knowingly. After they'd left, Stan gave some thought to the whole thing. He'd probably not be making the trip to the far swim again for a few months, and when he did it would offer a totally different challenge. So what if he told people where he'd caught it from; he'd just leave out the float fishing bit, and maybe the other carp that were caught. Let 'em sort it out for themselves. The session ended with the capture of a couple of fine looking tench from the channel, but nothing carpy, so he left on the Sunday morning after depositing a kilo of bait along the channel.

He'd had a word with Bob, who'd readily agreed to do a bit of baiting for him over the next couple of weeks, as Stan wouldn't be back until the very end of September. Due to his job, Bob would be back on the following Thursday, and then ten days later, but that would be perfect, so Stan gave him a couple of kilos of bait, which he hoped **would** find its way into the channel, and not into Bob's swim. He had every faith, and Bob duly repaid that faith over the next couple of weeks.

The nights were drawing in, and when Stan arrived on the Friday evening, he knew he had little time to get everything settled. He'd called Bob a couple of days previously, who told him that he'd seen a couple of fish rolling in the channel the evening before he left, three days ago. This filled Stan with some confidence, but Bob couldn't confirm that they were definitely carp, and after the tench that Stan had caught last time… oh well, no point in stopping now.

He set up at the far end again, but this time planned on employing all three rods in the channel. The margin bait was walked down thirty yards to his left, weaving around trees and bushes and eventually being dropped a couple of feet out amongst a scattering of whole and broken boilies. The middle rod was cast about fifteen yards out, to the middle of the channel, this time with just boilies thrown around it, and the right hand rod was cast out to the edge of the island, beneath the canopy of trees. He fished this one with a popped-up tiger nut bait, and it was just close enough to fire half a dozen 'pults of tigers along the island margin. It was barely seven thirty when he'd finished, but the light was almost gone, and once his brolly was up, and everything set out as normal, darkness had fallen completely.

The autumn chill was very evident, and the clear sky gave warning of a cool night to come. The moon was halfway through its phase, and half of the silver orb could be seen rising over the far hills. He settled down, and was pretty soon enjoying a nice chilli and a bottle of wine, with the sounds of the radio in the background to accompany it. An owl, probably a tawny, called from the wood to his left, behind the dam wall, and continued for five minutes before an answering call could be heard off to the right, beyond the boathouse. Stan sat back and put on his headtorch, picking up some pulp fiction he'd bought earlier. A couple of splashes had him putting down the book and peering into the darkness, but nothing else occurred, so it was back to the book.

A little after ten he got up for a pee, turning off the headtorch before walking a short way from the brolly. The moon was halfway across the sky, now, over to his right, and a few clouds were dulling its glow, but he could still see it reflected in the broken panes of glass in the boathouse windows. It was slightly eerie to watch, because as the clouds passed in front of the moon, it appeared that someone was moving over at the boathouse. He watched for a short while, but then a thicker cloud totally masked the glowing moon, and the broken panes returned to black. Still, it made him shudder a little, and he quickly turned his headtorch back on and returned to his brolly, where a candle softly glowed. Soon be time for bed.

He awoke, drowsily, and stared at the bobbins, glowing brightly in the dark night. His bladder was calling again, but he did his best to ignore it, as usual. The sleeping bag was warm and cosy, and he was reluctant to give that up at the moment. As he lay on his side, willing himself back to sleep, he heard a sort of sploshing sound, and pretty soon realised what it was; a pair of oars on a rowing boat. It seemed quite far away, over the other side of the lake, and he peered out to see if there was any reflection to help, but all was dark. Who'd be out in a boat at this time, and why? There were no snags to speak of, no weedbeds, and the lilies were dying back rapidly, so why would someone need a bloody boat? Although faint, he could still hear the slow, easy strokes as someone pulled themselves across the water. They definitely didn't sound in a hurry, which would surely have been the case if a fish had been snagged up. The moon had obviously appeared from behind its cloud curtain, because he could once again see its light reflected in the boathouse windows, like a shadow show behind a white sheet. After a few minutes he realised that he could no longer hear the boat, and then the moon was gone and so the shadow show. He couldn't put it off any longer, so got up and quickly relieved himself before snuggling back under the sleeping bag. It was only then that he realised that the sky was full of stars, totally cloudless – and totally moonless. It had obviously disappeared beyond the horizon, so what had lit the window panes opposite? A shiver ran the length of his body, but not from any cold, and he pulled the bag tightly around himself. What the bloody hell was all that about?

Pulling the bag over his head he tried not to think about it, and willed himself even more forcefully to sleep.

His feet were wet from the dew as he blinked in the early morning sunlight. He lowered the net into the water and carefully eased the carp into it. The island rod had produced the take, five minutes earlier, and had wrenched him from a deep sleep. The carp had sped around a bit, so he was sure that it was one of the recent stockies, and as the net engulfed it he could see that he was right. But that was fine. It was a start and he was sure that more would follow.

5:54 read the clock on his phone; a fine way to start the day. He took a quick photo of the fish, which he estimated at about seventeen pounds, then slid it back into the slightly steaming water. A recast landed pretty well, followed by another few 'pults of tigers, then it was time for the kettle.

As he sat there, wreathed in the steam from his cup, he thought back to the night's events. He must find out who was in the boat, and why. And also why someone was walking around in the boathouse with a torch. He'd thought about that a lot, and it was the obvious answer to the lack of moonlight, not some silly, ghostly apparition. An hour later his left hand margin rod screamed for attention, and pretty soon another mirror of similar size to the first was being photographed on the mat. That was equally as fine, the baiting pyramid was in action and he was sure that his next capture would be in excess of twenty pounds.

It was, in fact, about one hundred and fifty pounds, and brought its own mug with it.

'Morning, bro, how's it going?' asked Bob as he plonked himself down in the lowchair. Stan had just put the kettle on, which was probably not a coincidence, and took Bob's mug.

'All right, mate. Had a couple of doubles this morning, which was nice. Just waiting for the big fellas to make an appearance. Baiting go alright?'

Bob nodded, 'Perfect, mate. Put a bit in on Sunday when I got here, then the rest when I left Tuesday, looks like it might have worked.'

Stan handed the steaming mug to his visitor, then sat back down with his own. 'Yeah, cheers for that Bob, I reckon you're spot on there.'

'How was the party? Good?' asked Bob.

'Yeah, brilliant, really great. Had a great time, got a bit here and there, like you do, but it was cool.' He was just about to mention the conversation with Peter, but thought better of it. Nothing had been confirmed; in fact Peter had been conspicuous by his absence, so Stan wasn't at all sure what was going on. Instead, he veered the conversation in another direction.

'Here, Bob, is there a boat on here?'

Bob looked at him thoughtfully before answering. 'I don't think so,' he said, slowly. 'You'd have to ask Jackson. Why, what d'you need one for?'

Stan went on to explain about the events of the previous night, including the lights in the windows, and Bob smiled a sinister smile.

'Whoooooo! Spooky, Stan,' he said, raising his arms and wiggling his fingers in an apparently scary manner. 'D'you reckon we got ghosts, mate?' He laughed at that and took a final swallow of his tea, plonking the mug down forcefully to indicate that a refill was required. Stan couldn't remember much tea being drunk by the dwarves in Lord of the Rings. Ale yes, but not tea. Maybe this was a trait of the Somerset dwarves; the lack of mountains and caves diminishing their ale drinking ability so that they needed copious amounts of caffeine instead. He smiled to himself at the thought, and could imagine a conversation between himself, Sid and Bob. Now that would be something to behold.

Bob suggested that they pop round to the guy in the Boathouse Bay a little later to see if he'd heard anything, so, after a third cup of tea, and no visible sign of carp in the area, Stan reeled in his rods and joined Bob as they made their way towards the dam wall. They'd just come out of the trees at the far end of the channel when they saw someone pushing their barrow along the dam wall, towards the car park, so moved to intercept him.

'Alright, mate, any good?' asked Bob, but the guy looked flustered and just carried on. 'Mate, you all right?' called Bob, after the retreating figure.

'No, mate, I bloody ain't,' came the gruff reply, and Stan and Bob looked at each other with furrowed brows, before following the departing angler into the car park. He'd settled his barrow by his car and was searching through his pockets for the keys.

'Blimey, slow down a bit, mate,' began Bob. 'What's happened? You like you've seen a ghost.' Bob winked at Stan as he said the last, and a wicked grin flitted across his face. Hmm, a beard and an axe, thought Stan. Definitely.

The other angler stopped dead at that comment, then slowly looked round. 'You wouldn't believe me if I told you,' he said, his eyes glistening a little.

'Try us,' said Stan, feeling the start of a shiver at the base of his spine. The guy looked around, as if he was being watched, then turned to face the pair.

'I was in the Boathouse Bay; got there yesterday afternoon. Looked good, so I plonked 'em out and had one about seven. Small common. Then, dunno, sometime after midnight I had another, bit bigger, so I took a couple of shots and slipped it back. Put the kettle on and had a cup of tea.' Stan and Bob said nothing, just waiting for the story to unfold, but Stan thought he knew what was coming, and so did the shiver at the base of his spine, readying itself for action.

'Well, I'm sitting there and was just about to get back into bed when I heard this noise.' The shiver had its running shoes on and was standing at the blocks, awaiting the starting pistol. 'It sounded like someone in a rowing boat, sort of just out into the bay to my right, and I thought that couldn't be bloody right. Anyway, I put on my bivvy light so that they would see me, but the noise just continued, real slow. I stood up and looked out, but there was no moon so I couldn't see anything, just heard it.'

'Why didn't you put on yer headtorch?' asked Bob, not feeling quite as wicked now.

'Well, silly as it sounds, I didn't want to shine a light across the water in front of me in case I spooked the carp,' replied the guy.

'What, like a boat rowing through yer swim weren't gonna disturb it too much!' snorted Bob.

The guy nodded, 'Yeah, stupid eh? But, anyway, that's what I thought, so I called out, not too loudly, to see if I'd get an answer, but there was nothing. I could tell that the boat was going towards the boathouse, so I thought, "I'll get yer, you bastard." I grabbed my headtorch this time, and walked off towards the boathouse. It's a bit broken down, but I've been in there before, so knew it was just round the back and straight in to the mooring platform. As I came round the corner I switched on the torch, and there was the boat.' He stopped then, and wiped his hand across his forehead. There'd been a false start, but the shiver was once again on its blocks. 'What,' said Bob. 'What was it?'

'The boat was there, next to the platform, but there was no one there. I walked over to the boat and shone the torch on it and… bloody hell! There was nothing. I mean boat, there was no boat. The floor of the boat had totally disintegrated and there was mud oozing up through it. One oar was in the mud, rotted away, and there weren't another one. No way was that boat capable of being rowed anywhere. Then as I stood there I heard another noise.' He stopped and Stan and Bob remained quiet. 'It was the sound of somebody walking across the floor above, but when I looked up, there weren't no floor, it was all rotted away.'

On your marks. Get set. Go! The shiver ran the length of Stan's spine, and completed a decathlon of events in record time, whilst Bob looked straight at the guy. 'You are pulling my plonker, in't yer?' he growled. 'You don't expect me to believe that old shit, do yer?

'Believe what you bloody like, mate, but I ain't fishing this place again, and that's a fact.' With that he inserted the key in the car boot and proceeded to load up his car. Stan looked at Bob, and they just walked away.

'You don't believe that old tosh, do yer Stan?' asked Bob, as they walked along the dam wall. Stan ran over in his head what he'd seen and heard, and what the guy had just told them. It all sounded so similar, but he was sure there must be a logical explanation. They walked past the swim and into the boathouse. Sure enough, there in the mud at the front was the rotted carcass of an old rowboat, an equally rotted oar lying at an angle across where the seat would have been. The floor above was, indeed, mostly missing, but something caught Stan's eye, and he moved to one side to get a better look. Yes, just over to the right, leaning against a wall, something glistened. It was an oar, almost brand new, and still slightly wet from a recent dip in the lake. Bob looked at it, looked at Stan, then shrugged and walked away.

Stan wasn't sure whether to stay another night, but Bob convinced him that it was rubbish, and nothing would happen. That was the second of the truths that were borne out that night. The first was that he would catch a fish in excess of twenty pounds, and the twenty-nine pound common that he took from the margins confirmed that prediction as well.

All in all, one hell of a session that would linger long in the memory. He just wondered if there would many more like it, or whether fate would intervene once more.

Chapter Twenty Six
Any colour you like

Walking slowly past the empty boathouse, Ted thought about his recent conversation with John. A fishing club, on the Mere. Ted could see the merits of the idea, but also the pitfalls. He'd spent many years looking after things - people, places, ideals - but first of all you had to look after yourself, and Ted could feel the years slowly seeping into his bones.

Stan would be the right man for the job, if it happened, and young Becks would ably assist, of that there was no doubt. But Ted had been there from the start. From the first morning, as he'd watched that beaten up old van chug off down the lane, its cargo given over to the Mere for safe keeping. And he was the one who did the keeping, whose care the cargo had been given over to.

He'd not seen the fish on that first morning, hadn't even known that they were even fish, he just knew that something had occurred, and he was certain that consequences would be attached to it. A week or so later he'd spied them, four of them, moving cautiously along the margin behind the big island, close to where they'd been dropped into the lake. They were big; bigger than most in the Mere at that time, and since then he'd kept an eye out for them.

He'd seen them thrive and grow. Then he'd seen other eyes watching, drinking in the sight. Four pairs of eyes, eventually. He'd watched them, tested them out, tried to spook 'em. Big as a girt pig!

He smiled at that, and had smiled even more when he'd seen the big man at Stan's party. Buzz, was it?

Then he'd watched them catch and lose and, overall, care. And they'd caught her, The Big Common, and although he wasn't sure which of the four anglers it had been, it hadn't mattered, not to him and not to them. They all cared; they were all proud, not vain.

Then, a reprise, of sorts, and it had become easier, to an extent. But now, here we were again, and this would be the worst of all, because people knew now, the poachers had proved that. If they had been able to find out about the lake's desirable treasures, then others would as well, and now it would be legal, he would have no recourse at all.

He stood, once again, by the snags. What would happen when they were found in here? Not by him, or Stan, or Neil but by someone bent on one thing – fame and glory. Would it be a fish at all costs? He'd seen a lot of that, seen the carnage and suffering that trying to achieve something 'at all costs' could bring, and it mattered not whether it was the scaling of a mountain, the breeding of the perfect specimen of cat, or the capture of an indiscriminate tract of desert, the outcome was always the same. Someone would have to pay, dearly.

This late in the year, with the sun lower in the sky, it was difficult to see below the surface, but he sensed that something was close, and content, and at peace. Unfortunately, it would seem that the peace and contentment would last only a short while longer before the battle for survival was undertaken once more.

'Can you see anything, Ted?' Neil's voice gave him a start, but he didn't let on. He just stayed where he was, leant against the tree trunk, and shook his head.

'They're down there, but deep, staying out of sight for now. Be up and about soon, though. Last big feed before the cold weather sets in. What you been up to, Neil? Been over to the West Woods to check on those fences?'

Neil nodded, 'Yep, done that. Just a couple of 'em needed tacking. Probably a few deer going through, I s'pose.'

Ted stood up, then walked to the water's edge. 'Aye, there'll be more of that over the next few weeks. Them old stags were making a heck of a racket last night. They're ready to see who's boss, that's for sure.'

The rut was always an exciting time in the woods, and the big stags spent many hours declaring their authority and defending their harem of hinds against all comers. Ted and Neil had been out a few nights earlier and watched through the 'scope as the big males paraded in the fields behind the West Woods, the sound of their clashing antlers resounding around the natural arena. It was an exhilarating sight and one that Neil couldn't believe he'd been so close to all these years, and not actually witnessed.

'So we'd better have a look at all the fences, then,' said Neil.

'No harm in it, that's for sure, but they'll mainly stay close to the edge of the woods. Also need to take a look over past Culvert's pretty soon. Old Jake reckons he's heard of some wild boar over there. Be a new one on me, but I know there's been talk of 'em in the forest over the past few years. Escaped from some zoos or something like that. Shy, though, so difficult to spot. Not sure if old Jake has seen too much of the bottom of his pint glass.'

Neil chuckled at that, but hoped that Jake's sightings weren't drink-induced. Wild boar, that'd be something to see. Have to Google 'em later and see what he could find out about them.

Stan stood up and rubbed his back. These old bones are starting to show a bit of wear and tear, he thought. He'd almost finished clearing out the ditch, and was looking forward to a soft chair and a cup of tea.

'Stan, how are you, sir?' he turned to see Peter walking towards him and couldn't stop himself.

'Blimey, I thought you'd either been abducted by aliens, or you'd emigrated to some Turkish hippy commune!' he said as he dragged himself out of the ditch. Peter laughed and waved his hand in a 'never mind all that' sort of fashion.

'Sorry, Stan, been ridiculously busy of late, then one of Wendy's aunts died so we had to go up country and help sort that out. Many apologies, really wanted to get everything sorted out after our little chat, but I needed to talk to a few people first, make sure we weren't, you know, barking up the wrong tree and all that.'

Although slightly chagrined that it had taken so long, Stan was at least pleased that he hadn't imagined the whole damn thing.

'That's okay, Peter. I was just a bit, well you know, dangling carrot and all that?' Peter smiled at the turn of phrase, catching the obvious jibe, but chose to ignore it.

'Quite. Anyway, I've spoken to the residents committee, and then John, and everyone seems to be of the same mind, and that is that we open the Mere up for fishing next spring. We need to have a serious chat about how we move this forward, so I was wondering what you were up to this evening?'

From nought to sixty in three-point-four seconds, thought Stan. He wiped his hands on his overalls before answering.

'No problem, Peter. I've obviously been giving it a lot of thought, and I've got a few ideas, suggestions, call them what you will. What time, where?'

'Say eight thirty, Green Man. I'll speak to Tommy shortly, see if we can get the back room to ourselves. Good, that's settled. I'll see you later then, Stan,' and with that he gave a little wave and walked back towards the houses.

This was it then. He was almost bursting with the need to tell someone, but he'd avoided that up until now, another night wouldn't hurt.

'So that's it, then. Fifty to start with, at £600 each.'

Peter sat opposite Stan, with John and Simon, from the residents committee, sitting to their side. They'd spent an hour or so going over things and had come to a pretty satisfactory conclusion.

Stan would oversee all that went on with the lake, recruiting whoever he felt necessary to assist him. He'd vet the possible members, but Peter and Simon would have the final say as to whom they wanted to join. John would help Stan, where necessary, to ready the lake for the start of the season, at the beginning of May. Creating swims,

clearing areas that might require it, and generally tidying up. The boathouse would be converted into a sort of rudimentary clubhouse, but would not be as well equipped as the boating fraternity had seemed to require it.

Stan had made his feelings known on a couple of points. Peter and Simon felt that, if there were fifty members, then there would need to be fifty swims to accommodate them, but Stan had to assure them, quite vociferously, that there would never, ever, be a situation when all members were at the lake at the same time. It just didn't happen. Some people worked during the week, so fished weekends, others like Bob worked shifts and were able to move their fishing time around. And others just bought the ticket because they could afford it, and would fish once or twice a year, and be very content at that. He was certain, also, that within a few months, the men would be sorted from the boys, because he knew that it wouldn't be easy.

He'd also had something to say about the membership fee, which had originally been set at £900.

'That's a ludicrous amount of money, Peter. Some of the best lakes in the country don't charge that sort of money,' he said.

'Yes, but look what's in the lake, Stan. Surely that's got to be worth a whole heap of money?' John and Simon looked at the two of them, not sure what they were referring to, but Stan used them and carried on.

'**We** know, Peter, but who else does? John, Simon, any idea what's in the lake?' Simon shrugged. 'Fish?' Stan smiled but Peter looked at John.

'Nope, no idea. Carp, tench, bream, pike I suppose. And some other stuff.'

'See?' said Stan, 'They live here and they don't know. Why should anyone else? And to be honest, I don't want the world and his wife to know because we'll have another bloody poaching incident when someone decides either that they can't afford nine hundred quid, or that there are no tickets left but he fancies having a go anyway.'

Eventually, Peter saw sense, but only after Stan suggested that they should allow guests on the lake at a cost of £25 per twenty-four hours, and that in a bid to stop the membership being increased to seventy-five.

'Right, one more for the road, gents,' said Peter, not asking but offering. They all accepted and went out into the half empty bar. As they left, Peter offered Stan a lift, and on the short drive home got serious.

'Stan, this is more than just about fishing, you know that, don't you?' he said.

Stan nodded. 'Yeah, Peter, I know. Gotta cleanse the lake, sort of thing. Get people back together. But if I'm gonna do this, I'm gonna do it properly. I'm not sure if you'll understand this, but those fish, they mean a lot to me. And to a few others; your boy for one.'

Peter stared ahead, the full beam lighting the wooded lane and picking out a deer fifty yards ahead.

'Got to be so careful at the moment. Been a few crashes involving the deer of late, have to take it slow and steady.'

He stopped to allow the deer to cross, and waited whilst another half a dozen followed, then moved slowly forward.

'Stan, I know exactly what you mean. I may not have my son's knowledge or enthusiasm for everything in the natural world, but that doesn't make me an unfeeling barbarian. This move to the country has been the best thing I've ever done, and I wouldn't go back for anything, but it's not just for the country. It's the sense of community, and I feel that that was somehow tarnished a little after, well, you know, the tragedy. But now, we can bring it back together. Ah, here we are, Stan, home sweet home.' The car slowed to a halt and Stan opened the door.

'Thanks, Peter. Been a good evening, in many ways. Talk to you very soon,' and with that he got out, closed the door and waved Peter off.

Well, well. Here we go, he thought. Jean first, obviously, but then who? So many phone calls to make, and it was so late at night. He was fit to burst, and it wasn't just his bladder this time.

Chapter Twenty Seven
Wish you were here?

Just run that past me again, Quill.'

The initial response had been almost the same for all three of them, although a variety of expletives and invective had been liberally added to the general tone. It had been one of the most pleasant tasks he'd had to undertake for quite some time, and he revelled in his role of ultimate provider.

That had been six months ago, just prior to Christmas, and the same question had been asked more than fifty times since. Stan had his ideas of whom he'd like to join the syndicate, as had Peter and the others, but that had amounted to no more than twenty, which left quite a hole to fill, so they'd had to go public. Initially, they advertised in a few of the local rags, and that brought in a small selection of hopefuls, but by March there were still more than a dozen places to fill, and Stan's flippant 'might as well advertise in the Angling Times,' had been taken much more seriously than he'd intended. Those last dozen had been the hardest of all to fathom, and Stan was still unsure of a couple of the lucky applicants, but only time would tell.

Of the few that Stan had asked, both Sid and Buzz had leapt at the offer, but Rhodie had been much more reluctant. For him, the issue was not just the money, but the amount of time he'd be able to dedicate to a water that was over a three hundred mile round trip from his home. That scenario Stan had anticipated well in advance, which was why he'd suggested the 'guest ticket' system, and Rhodie was more than happy to go for that.

A couple of the others were more recent friends, and both had the time and money to consider the offer worth taking. Bill, from the Hatch, was delighted to be offered a chance, and even more delighted when he heard of the monster bream and tench that the lake held. He was just the sort of member that Stan wanted; someone who wasn't a carp fisherman and who'd probably only ever fish a dozen or so times a year – lovely. The other had been the dwarvish Bob, and he'd leapt at the offer. Stan had regaled him with a few tales of the Mere over the previous season, and now his natural scepticism could be put to the test. The rest of the 'locals', as Stan regarded them, were more in Bill's camp than Bob's, which suited him just fine. The only two that he knew would really put some time in, and get the relevant rewards, were Neil and Quentin. Peter knew that his son would want to fish the lake, if only during the holidays, and was toying with the idea of offering half the required money for the ticket, but Stan had a better idea. He was going to need a lot of help getting everything ready for the start of the season, and there was no doubt that he would have to employ the brains and brawn of Ted and Neil. He also knew that when Quentin came home for the holidays he'd be more than willing to help, so as repayment for that, he was sure that they both deserved a ticket. To clinch the deal he also had the idea of appointing Neil as bailiff; a perfect candidate, who would willingly relish every opportunity to be by the lake.

Now, here we were, just two days before the start of the season, and Stan was feeling pretty nervous. They'd worked like Trojans through the winter and early spring, he and Ted, Neil and John, and Quentin when he was around. Even Peter had lent a hand on a couple of occasions, although he was more used to wielding the whip than feeling its sting. Initially Stan had just gone with the flow, and started felling trees and clearing shrubs to make way for swims, but then he rebelled. It had to be natural. It was a big lake; there was loads of room for everybody. Sure, some people would like a nice manicured swim, but those swims would sort themselves out over time. Invariably, those sort of anglers didn't venture too far from the car, so the most comfortable swims became those closest to the car park, just by regular use. He'd originally thought of having just the one car park, next to the boathouse, but the clamour of disagreement was deafening, so he relented and cleared a small area in the southeast corner, where Buzz had parked all those years ago and then caught a forty-eight pound carp. It would be called the 48 car park, simple as that.

The south bank was all pretty new, and quite open, so little gardening was required along there; the banks either side of the boathouse likewise. The West Woods encroached along the west bank just enough to create three or four swims, and in the end Stan was confident that the lake could comfortably accommodate forty anglers. He never foresaw that occasion arising, and he wasn't wrong, although the first weekend was the busiest he had seen for a few years, but would never come close to being repeated.

'Ready for the off then, young Stan?' said Ted the Stealthy. Stan had gone beyond surprise at the old guy's unannounced arrivals many years ago, and just let his heart sort itself out.

'Dunno really, Ted,' he replied. 'Strange to say, but I feel a bit nervous. Does that sound stupid?'

'No, lad, not at all. Feel a bit like that meself. Been looking after this old girl for many years now. But now she's being courted anew, by many suitors, and I don't know half enough about any of 'em.'

Stan stood quietly, looking out at the lake, and the boathouse in the distance. The sun was shining, there was a light breeze blowing up the lake and he felt like a god.

Surely this was what heaven was like? Amongst the many waterfowl abroad on the water, a pair of grebes were busily hunting in front of them.

'Bloody hell, don't they ever stop, poor bastards?' he said.

Ted shook his head. 'Still feeding one of the old brood. She'll soon be gone though, be another clutch on the way soon. Gonna have to keep an eye on 'em, though.'

'Why's that?' asked Stan.

'More 'an two in a clutch, smallest one gets killed by the other two. Survival of the fittest, for sure, but brutal nonetheless. Soon as she lays I'll have a look. More 'an two eggs and I'll have one away. Harsh but fair, Stan.'

Stan pouted his lips and nodded, whether in agreement or acknowledgement he wasn't entirely sure, but he'd never had reason to doubt any of Ted's previous actions, so he sure wasn't about to start now.

'So, are we ready then, Ted? Bound to be a few arriving early tomorrow, having a good look around. Wanna make sure there's no sneaky angling going on before the off. Alright to have Neil doing the rounds?'

'No problem,' said Ted. 'Probably be having a stroll round meself, once in a while. Gotta make sure all's well, know what I mean?'

Stan knew exactly what he meant, and as they strolled along the edge of Sutton Woods, towards the west bank, he wondered who would be first to feel the adrenaline rush in the coming days.

Unsurprisingly, because the start of the season fell on a Tuesday, not many people turned up, and of those that did, most were gone by the following morning. The start had been at nine in the evening, giving people just enough light to cast out by, and within an hour or so Stan had heard a bite alarm scream. He was just going to do the night, mainly to ensure that he was on hand if anything major should occur, and had set up next to the boathouse. It wasn't a swim he'd ever fancied, and would probably never fish it again, but for now it was comfortable and convenient. Peter had popped over for a chat and a cup of tea and seemed to love the atmosphere, although the emergence of some early mosquitoes soon had him making for the hills. After that, Stan had sat, wreathed in citronella candle smoke, and drank in the sounds of the lake. It was strange; he'd fished pretty much constantly since last casting a line in this lake, but this evening just seemed to be… different. A resounding crash echoed across the lake, coming from his right, and he could hear the excited chatter from a couple of guys who were fishing the pads in the far corner; the Poachers' Pads, they'd dubbed them, for obvious reasons. Now, an hour later, that was the direction that the run had come from and he wondered whether he should take a walk round to see that all was well. They'd seemed pretty competent when he'd walked round for a chat earlier, so he left it for now. He'd asked all of them to let him know if they caught anything in excess of forty pounds, and handed out plastic cards with his mobile number on, just in case. He watched the head torches dance, and heard the splashing and talking, but no call was forthcoming, so he assumed it had been just a small one. A camera flashed half a dozen times, a lead splashed into the lake and, pretty soon, all was quiet.

The fish turned out to be a twenty-eight pound common, and was the only one of the night, although a few bream and tench had made their presence felt. By midday, there were just three anglers left. Not for long, thought Stan, and he wasn't wrong.

It had been so quiet, so peaceful. The winter had been its usual, demanding self, but the majority had survived, and with the spring came warmth and food. And noise. Along the banks, much commotion. Trees falling, boats rolling and splashing along the margins, noise and pressure.

The carp moved confidently, aware but unfazed by the extra activity. Soon, the sun grew warmer, the food more abundant, and hither and thither, small pockets of new, tasty morsels. Warily these new food items were eaten, but no harm was forthcoming, and so the carp grew confident and greedy, and careless.

Thursday was the start of it, and a few cars turned up during the day, brimming with tackle, bait and confident anglers. They spread themselves out and the lake still appeared quiet, but by midday on Friday Stan counted twenty-six cars in the two car parks. Suddenly, he feared that Peter's request for more swims should have been heeded, but the peak was reached on Saturday morning when the thirty-fourth angler arrived. After that, a few were on their way, and the banks of the Mere never saw more than twenty anglers at one time from that day forward.

Stan was uncertain how many carp the lake now held, especially as the stock of old pike lake was a total mystery, but from his many sightings over the previous few summers, and chats with Ted about his encounters, he estimated there were between fifty and seventy carp in the Mere. In a lake of seventy acres that would seem a light stocking, but he also knew that a high percentage were in excess of thirty, and of course there were at least two, huge, succulent cherries on top of that cake. Therefore, he wasn't overly surprised that only four carp had been hooked by the Friday evening. The two guys in the Poachers' Pads had hooked another the following evening, but had lost it after an epic battle, the line eventually parting when the fish had found a hitherto unknown snag. When Stan talked to the angler the following morning he was still in a bit of a state, and declared that he'd never hooked anything with such power. The two of them, Ben and Chris, had been angling for a fair few years and had caught some pretty decent fish between them, to over forty pounds. They'd also been on a few French trips and had accounted for two or three fifty pounders between them, so they were no strangers to big carp. But this had been different, and Stan knew that he'd be seeing a lot of them over the coming season. They were two of the members who had answered the Angling Times ad, and when he'd first met them he knew straight away that they'd be fine. They had to travel over from Sussex, which was about a two-hour journey, but they were keen for something new and big, and unknown. But now they knew, and they would be back for more.

The other two carp had been hooked and landed from the old lake. A twenty-four pound mirror that Stan didn't recognise had been landed from the Post Office, on the north bank. He and the others had named it that due to a letterbox shaped slot in the tree there, and it had provided some, errm, interesting results for them. He'd made that the last swim before the snags, which were a good one hundred and fifty yards along the bank, thus allowing the carp some sanctuary. He also didn't want people fishing in amongst the fallen trees there, very aware of the losses that could occur.

The other fish was an old friend, and Stan was unsurprised that the 19 had been amongst the first to slip up. It had been taken by another old friend, Bill the float angler, who had turned up at first light and set up in one of the swims in East Woods. The carp had been in the net within ten minutes of Bill casting out, as the sun was still below the trees behind him, and as pleased as he was, he was unaware of the significance of the fish, so had slipped it back after taking a couple of quick snaps of it on the mat. After that he had taken three or four tench of average size, and a bream of just under double figures, a much more pleasing result for him.

By Saturday morning the lake was awash with anglers, and Stan had to tell Sid that a visit was probably futile. Sid was working until lunchtime, and phoned to find out the score, so was not too happy with the news.

'Bloody hell, Quill, I hope it ain't gonna be like this every weekend, mate,' he whined.

'No, you know the flavour, Sid. They all get excited at first, but then when reality strikes they'll be back to their comfy waters. Already had three or four whingers asking if there're any carp in the lake. It'll be fine, mate.'

Despite that, Sid was unsure, but despite even that, he turned up just after two and found that half a dozen had left, and a couple more were packing up. One of them was in the pads, near the 48 car park, and where he had landed a stunning twenty-eight pound carp from in the last century – that would do just fine. By the time of his Sunday afternoon departure, Sid had managed to sneak out a couple of nice tench and, amazingly, a small common of about twelve pounds. He and Stan had a good look at it and were certain it wasn't the little nine-pounder they'd previously caught, so assumed that it was from the pike lake. If this was the stamp of fish that the lake had held then Stan was a little unsure what the reaction of the anglers might be. Still, it was early days, and who knew what surprises might turn up?

So, the first weekend had been and gone, and Stan, Ted and Neil sat by the boathouse, teas in hand, and ruminated over the whys and wherefores. A total of nine carp had been hooked, seven landed, the biggest being Ben's twenty-eight pound common and they were all fairly certain that, apart from the 19, all were from the pike lake. The bigger, old lake denizens had been more circumspect, although the fish that Chris had lost definitely sounded like one of the biggies.

'What d'you reckon then Stan? Do you think that most of the pike lake fish are small commons?' asked Neil. Stan looked out across the lake, towards the Poachers' Pads, and could have sworn he saw a fish stick its head out. He said nothing about that, but replied to Neil instead.

'Well, that mirror that the guy had from the Post Office looked pretty new to me, but I get your point. Yeah, they may all be of a similar size, I mean, that twenty-eight might have been the biggest in there, but, after all this time? I doubt it. It's early days; there's no way the lake will experience that sort of pressure again, no way.'

'I bloody hope so,' said Neil. 'Got stuck in a poxy swim over there and didn't see even a roach all day.'

'No, like I said yesterday, there're already people having a moan 'cos they didn't catch anything. They won't be rushing back. There's also a few who are just here for the bream and tench, like Bill from the Hatch. They'll probably only be doing the odd morning here and there. Trust me Neil, by the middle of next month you'll practically have the place to yerself.' Neil remained unsure but said nothing, instead, Ted joined in, from left field as usual.

'Wonder what was lost, from over there?' he said, nodding towards the pads opposite.

'Yeah, I was thinking the same thing,' said Stan. It was obviously an area that the carp found attractive, hence the poachers' success last year. It could well have been the same fish. 'We'll have to keep an eye on the snags, see if we see anything sulking in there.'

As they stood up and turned to leave, Stan caught another glimpse of movement by the pads, and vowed to return later that day to have a little dabble.

Along with the introduction of new, *a l l u r i n g* food items, the lake was also resounding with noise and vibration. The carp were, once more, wary but relatively unfazed, and continued to explore their usual haunts. As darkness fell, a dozen of them moved easily through the layers of warmth and cold; the odd one leaping clear of the water and revelling in the sensation as its massive body crashed down onto the lake's surface. The lily pads were just breaking the surface, but below was a veritable jungle of roots and rhizomes, amongst which were many tasty morsels, natural and unnatural. The Common browsed easily, unhurried and contented, sucking in mouthfuls of food, water and general detritus, and expelling the unwanted items through its gills. Every now and then a hard root or stone would catch on its huge, rubbery lips, but the sensation was not painful, just a dull ache that faded fast.

One dull ache, however, failed to fade, and it shook its head to try to rid itself of the sensation. Vibrations sensed along its flank indicated movement close by, above the surface, then it was suddenly wrenched back from its course. A distant memory was triggered, and flight seemed to be the only answer.

It left the pads at speed, all the while feeling an increasing tugging sensation in its mouth, which caused it to exit even faster and further. The flight covered a hundred yards or so, but the tension on its mouth caused it to slow, then move off towards the middle of the lake. This seemed to last for a long, long time, and the great carp was gradually losing strength, allowing itself to be eased back from whence it came, then employing a short burst of speed in an attempt to escape this increasingly alarming feeling.

As its strength faded, it dove once more towards the bottom of the lake, and felt its flank running along something sharp and hard, losing scales and blood in the process. Then, suddenly, the pressure was gone, and it made its way slowly across the lake, the dull ache still in its lip, and trailing a length of line along behind it. The overhanging trees of the big island would be its refuge for the next few hours, and then the snags. In that time it would recover, learn a lesson once again, and be much more wary over the coming months.

Until the next time.

Ted stood by the snags, peering into the inky blackness. He thought he could see movement down there, but was unable to discern shape or size. He felt sure that it would have been one of the three largest carp in the lake that had fallen for Chris's trap in the pads. The previous couple of evenings he'd spied a couple of good fish leaving the water in and around the area, and he'd been certain that at least one of them had been The Common.

Time to be vigilant, he thought. You've made one mistake; you need to take care now. They've returned.

Chapter Twenty Eight
Astronomy Domine

'How you doing, young Becks?' asked Ted, as he walked quietly into the swim. He'd purposefully coughed lightly at the back of the swim, so as not to startle the lad. As much as he enjoyed arriving at someone's side without prior warning, he knew that there was a time and place not to surprise the unsuspecting, and whilst relaxing by a lake on a fine, summer's evening was definitely high on that list.

Neil turned and smiled at Ted. 'Yeah, good, Ted. Had a couple of nice tench earlier on the float, but I'm after one of them there carp now. Cuppa tea?'

They sat quietly, drinking tea and watching the moon slowly rise off to their left. Neil was set up on the end of the point, on the south bank, and had almost a quarter of a mile of bank to himself. It was the first Monday in June and, just as Stan had predicted, the lake had quietened considerably. Three other anglers were present; two of which were either side of the boathouse, and the other in the East Woods, way off to his right – it was glorious.

After a while, Neil broke the easy silence. 'Look at that sky, Ted, it's bloody amazing.'

'Yeah, lad, truly so. Seen many a starry night like this, told me many a story to keep me from sleep,' said Ted, in his usual enigmatic way.

'Waddya mean, Ted, "told me a story"?' asked Neil, adding 'Shooting star!' as he pointed up, but it was gone in the blink of an eye. Ted just smiled.

'Well, you see the Plough?' asked Ted, pointing out the constellation.

'Yeah, I know that one, and Orion,' replied Neil.

'Right, well if you take the top two stars of the saucepan, then trace a line upwards, you come to the tail of the Little Dipper, see it?'

Neil looked hard, not sure what he was looking for, then exclaimed, 'Yeah! It's like a smaller Plough, upside down.'

'Exactly. Well, see the star at the end of the tail that your line took you to? That's Polaris, the North Star. That stays in the same place all year round, so it's what sailors, and many others, use as a starting point if they ain't got a compass and the like.'

'Blimey,' said Neil. 'Have you ever had to use it?'

'On a few occasions, lad, on a few occasions. Now, see the moon? It's a crescent.'
Neil looked up and 'ah hah'ed'.

'Well, take a line from the top point to the bottom point, then down to the ground. That's due south. Also very handy to know, but not too helpful when it's a new moon!'

Neil was becoming fascinated with this influx of knowledge, and just lay back and drank it in.

'You mentioned Orion,' continued Ted. 'Well, d'you know his story?'

'Err, he's a hunter, isn't he?' replied Neil.

'Yep, but what's he hunting?'

'Dunno,' said Neil, shrugging his unseen shoulders.

'Well, there he is over there,' said Ted, pointing west. 'You see his belt, and above it that bright star, that's Betelgeuse, that's his right armpit.'

'Betelgeuse! Never heard of it,' said Neil.

'Yeah, well you probably know it as Beetlejuice,' which Neil acknowledged with a laugh. 'Anyway, above it is a column of stars, see 'em?'

Neil couldn't at first, so Ted suggested the use of binoculars.

'Oh, right, yeah I see 'em,' said Neil.

'Well, that's his club. Now, look to the right of his belt and you'll see a crescent of stars, like a backward C. Got 'em?'

'Yep.'

'Well, that's his shield and do you know what he's fighting?'

Neil shook his head, then said, 'No.'

'Look a little further right and you'll see a bright star, should look a bit red.'

'Err, a bit red. No can't… oh, no, got it. Yeah, sort of orangey,' declared the young stargazer.

'That's the one. Well, that is the red eye of Taurus the bull, and its horns extend out before it. That's why Orion has his shield up, to protect himself from the horns.'

Neil was utterly enraptured, and for the next hour or so, Ted told him stories of Perseus, and Cassiopeia, of the Twins, Castor and Pollux, of the winter triangle with Sirius, the brightest star in the sky at its base point.

Eventually, when Ted bade him goodnight, a little before midnight, Neil felt that a whole new world had been opened before his eyes, and before the week ended he would spend hours on the Internet, gleaning more and more information.

In the meantime, there were carp to be caught, and with dreams of bulls and rams, hunters and fish flooding his head, the early morning run was like a thousand volts running through him. The right hand rod was bouncing in the rest and the alarm screaming, and his margin bait was getting progressively further away from the margins by the second. The line cut up through the water, heading off towards the East Woods, where the faint light of a dawn sun was beginning to limn the trees. The carp, for carp it obviously was, continued its headlong charge towards the far bank, and Neil felt as if he had hooked a train. There was nothing that he could do to even slow it, let alone halt it, and suddenly his mouth was dry and he felt very alone. The fish took yards and yards of line - thirty, forty, fifty – and still it continued. Neil heard something huge wallow out there, in the deep, dark lake, and he imagined a mythical sea-monster, fleeing from Poseidon's trident. As the sun slowly rose, the carp slowed a little, then wallowed again, before moving away to the right, towards the pads. Lifting the rod tip to clear the bankside bushes, Neil followed it around the corner, and played it from the right hand swim, which looked straight across to the pads, and the 48 car park. The line continued to cut through the water like a cheese wire, and soon a grating, rubbing sensation was coming back up the line – it had found the pads.

Suddenly, all went solid, and they were at an impasse. Neil could only assume that the size 8 hook had found a firm hookhold, and that the 15lb line was undamaged and remained strong. The fish had found the sanctuary of the pads, and had buried itself as deep into that jungle as it could. But the pads were still quite young, and the line was, indeed, like a cheese wire so, one by one, they floated to the surface, having been sliced clean through by the nylon. Neil held on steadily, now and then feeling the rod tip buck a little as another pad gave way, and a few inches of line were gained.

After ten minutes his arm was beginning to ache, ten minutes more and his shoulder was on fire, but still there was no obvious conclusion in sight. He walked back along the margins, to stand at the spot where the fish was initially hooked, and tried to get a better leverage on the fish. At first this seemed to have been futile, but then the rod tip came back a few inches, wind down. Then a few inches more, wind down. Then, with an almighty explosion of water and severed lily stems, the carp erupted from the water and headed back out towards the middle of the lake. By now, the sun was above the eastern trees, and Neil could see all that was happening, so watched as a line of bubbles showed the trail that the carp was blazing. Once more it rolled, but this time it was less vigorous, and was no more than fifteen yards away.

He lowered the net, but dare not think of the consequences of that, of the sequence of events that had to occur before he could lift it.

Splash! Roll! Splash! Gulp, gulp, gulp!

'YESSSSSSS!!'

The events were now just a blur, merely history. What was in the net was all that mattered, and for a moment he dare not look, but look he did. It was huge, enormous, a creature from Greek mythology, surely. And he had vanquished it.

He had no idea what to do next, his mind was blank. He carefully secured the net in the margins, then pulled over the unhooking mat, which began to look woefully inadequate. Carp sack, need a carp sack. And scales. No, sod the scales for now, there was no way he was weighing this on his own.

Stan. Phone Stan. What was the time? Five fifteen. Oh well, he said anytime, and this was any time.

Ring! Ring! Ring!

'Nngh? Yer?'

'Stan, it's Neil. I've had one!'

'Ungh. Errm, right. Yeah, good. Err, what time is it?'

'Just after five, mate. You said to phone if I had a good 'un, well I think I have.'

He could hear Stan slowly waking, shuffling of body against sheets, and a muted word from his wife – 'who is it?'

'Aaaaarrrr!' yawned Stan. 'Right, a good'un , you reckon. How big?'

'Not sure mate, still in the net, but big. A mirror. Took me about half an hour or so to land it. At first it just went…'

'Yeah, right. Save that for later. Get it in a sack and make sure it's secure in the margins; you know the score. I'll be there in ten minutes. Where are you?' By now Stan was in the bathroom and splashing some water on his face.

'In the point. Oh, better bring some big scales, not sure if my Avons will be big enough,' he joked. Stan, however, was already thinking of that, and said goodbye as he made his way to his tackle shed.

Neil felt a bit calmer now, so wet the biggest sack he had in the margins and lay it next to the mat, before returning to the tethered net. He heaved it up and grunted at the load. This was the biggest thing he'd ever seen on the bank, let alone landed, and he wished that Smiffy could be here to see it. As he slid it from the net onto the mat, the sun painted it golden and he was open-mouthed.

'Need a hand with that, young Orion?' asked Ted, as he walked into the swim. He'd heard a cry from someone as he sat with his first cup of tea of the day, and he didn't need to be a genius to work out what had occurred.

'Ted, I've had a bloody whacker. Look at it.' Ted didn't need to be told where to look, it was all there before him, and he had to agree that it was, indeed, a whacker.

'Can't argue with that, lad. Come on, let's get her in the sack for a moment, give her a chance to recover. Best phone young Stan, as well.'

'Yeah, I've done that, he'll be here in a minute,' said Neil, whilst he bent over the carp and stroked its shimmering flank.

'Here we go then,' said Ted, as he opened up the damp sack for Neil to slip the carp into. Once safely inside, he carefully zipped it up, then hoisted it over his rods and into the margins, securing the cord around one of his banksticks. That done, he walked gingerly back to his bedchair and sat down to dry himself off and put on some trousers. Ted lit the gas and put the kettle on, turning just in time to see the sun glint off of a car windscreen as it moved along the north bank towards the 48 car park. Three cups, then.

Stan walked into the swim to be greeted by a cup of tea and a maniacally grinning young angler.

'Cheers, Ted. Been here long?' he asked. Ted shook his head.

'Five minutes. Just long enough to help young Neil slip her into a sack. Impressive fish, not sure if she's one you know.'

Stan walked over to Neil and shook him warmly by the hand. 'Bloody well done, mate. Brilliant! You bloody deserve this after all the work you've done. Well done.'

Neil just stood there, grinning inanely, before Stan put his tea down on the floor, then slipped out some digital scales from his inside pocket.

'Hopefully these should be good enough. Go up to one hundred pounds!'

Neil laughed as Stan handed them to him.

'Right, got my camera, you got one?' Neil nodded and produced a compact digital camera, which Stan gave to Ted. 'You all right with that, Ted. Picture in the back, here. That's the button, there. Got a zoom on it as well, but you should be fine, just get as close as you like.'

Ted took the proffered camera and said nothing. Then they were by the waterside and Neil was hauling in the sack with its prize. Up and dripping, they carried it to the mat, and Stan felt adrenaline coursing through his body. Safely unzipped, they removed the sack, stopping a couple of times as the fish flipped and flopped. It was a big fish, that was without doubt, but Stan knew it wasn't either Sid's Fish or the Poached Mirror. He didn't recognise the scaling; definitely not the linear that Rhodie had, so maybe a real new one. It had a couple of scales near the tail on one side, then a small starburst of scales near the gill cover on the other side, with a larger, reddened scale along the lateral line. Apart from that, it was a leathery, golden brown beauty.

'Phew! What a fish!' exclaimed Stan, and Ted nodded in ready agreement. 'Well done, Neil, this is an absolute stunner.'

'Cheers. Bloody hell, look at it. I wish Smiffy was here. I'll have to send a couple of photos to him on my phone.'

'Right,' said Stan. 'Moment of truth.' With that he slipped the weigh sling into the lake, before zeroing it on the scales. When all was ready they slid the carp into the sling, then Stan hoisted it up off the mat.

'Whoa, this is a heavy one, guys,' he grunted, as he held it aloft. 'Be quick now.'

Ted and Neil both bent to watch the flickering red letters, waiting for them to still. Then Ted declared, 'Forty seven ten. You happy with that, young Becks?' But Neil was incapable of speech at that moment and just grunted an acknowledgement. With that, Stan lowered the fish back onto the mat and they prepared for the photo shoot.

Much groaning and cooing, sliding and flipping ensued, but pretty soon Neil was standing back in the lake, supporting the great fish as it regained its strength. Then with a splash and a swirl it was off, and Neil let out a cry of delight.

'Can I name it, Stan?' he asked, a little later.

'Err, yeah. Can't see why not. It's not one I recognise, dunno if it's ever been caught before. So, yeah, what you got in mind?'

Neil looked at Ted and smiled. 'Taurus,' he said, simply, and Ted nodded slowly in agreement.

'Cool,' agreed Stan. 'Taurus it is then. Well done, Neil, absolutely brilliant. I'll get those shots over to you later. Now, though, I think I can hear some bacon frying. See you later, guys,' and with that he turned and headed towards his car.

Ted turned to follow, and said, 'Well done, lad. A mighty fine fish that was. You staying on?'

'Dunno, maybe for a couple of hours. Is that alright?' he asked. Ted nodded as he left.

'Yep, no problem, but we got a bit to do this afternoon, so I'll see you after lunch,' and then left the swim.

Neil sat back and let the sun warm him. What a fish. What a fish! Just wait until he told Smiffy. What was the time? Six o'clock, bit too early for a phone call, give it an hour. Man, what a fish. Probably wouldn't be catching something like that for a while, but if he fished on here long enough it surely was the lake to beat it. What a fish!

Jupiter & Saturn

Oberon, Miranda & Titania

Neptune, Titan

Stars Can Frighten

ORION

Betelgeux
(Alpha)

Bellatrix
(Gamma)

Alnilam
(Epsilon)

Mintaka

Alnitak
(Zeta)

Great
Nebula

Iota

Rigel
(Beta)

Saiph

Chapter Twenty Nine
high hopes

It was a real quandary. Almost ten years ago Stan had made the decision to move down here, to be next to the Mere and its wonderful fish, just in case the opportunity should ever arise that he could once again cast a line in here. And now that opportunity was laid on a plate before him, with a salad dressing and all the olives he could eat, and suddenly his hunger was gone. It wasn't that he didn't want to fish there – that couldn't be further from the truth; it was just that he had sort of fallen in love with Beaufort's and the fish it held. But he'd always been a one-water man; if he was fishing a lake he had to give it his full attention. He had never been able to flit from one lake to another; a few days here, a couple of weekends there. He needed to get his head into the water, the carp, try to learn its ways, listen for the change of tone.

Now, he had two of the most desirable lakes a man could wish for, and he had to choose one against the other. It was like having to choose between Marilyn Monroe and Raquel Welch – which one of them would you kick out of bed? The answer came, as it invariably did, from his mates.

Over the first couple of months of the season, Sid had spent a few weekends at the lake and had managed to amass a total of five carp in that time. They'd taken to calling the old lake fish 'the originals', but Sid had caught none of them, just a few of the smaller, pike lake fish, up to twenty-four pounds. Neil's forty-seven was a fish neither of them recognised, but they were unsure if it was a pike lake fish, or a thirty pounder from when they were fishing the Mere and had just whacked on the weight in the ensuing seven or eight years. Either scenario was possible, but it didn't detract from the fact that it was a stunning fish that had probably never been on the bank before.

Neither Buzz nor Rhodie had managed to get to the lake, mainly through work commitments, but a window of opportunity had opened when one of Buzz's contracts was put, temporarily, on hold. At the same time, Rhodie's wife decided to take the kids to see her mum for a few days and, out of the blue, they were all free to fish for three or four days towards the end of July. Sid and Stan managed to wangle a couple of days off, and so they all arranged to meet on a Thursday morning.

Since Neil's fish, another couple of large fish had been lost, as well as three thirties being landed. Chris had licked his opening night wounds and had taken a lovely thirty-three pound mirror, a week or so after Neil's success. The same fish was caught again at the beginning of July, from the same Poachers' Pads swim, and just prior to the arrival of the four of them, Bob had helped himself to a fine thirty-one pound common, from the point. A few other, smaller fish were also landed, but the real biggies were still conspicuous by their absence – unless you knew where to look.

'Look, just over there.' Sid's whispered command was heard by all of them, and they followed his pointed finger to the edge of the snags. He was atop one of the few trees that overlooked the snags, and could see perfectly the half dozen fish hanging motionless, just a foot below the surface. Three were relatively small, but the others looked to be in excess of thirty pounds.

Rhodie, as ever, was making the precarious journey out onto the snag tree, but the dry, dead branches were cracking and snapping as he made his way along the gnarled trunk. Stan and Buzz were more sensible, and were standing atop a couple of stumps, affording them a two-foot high advantage over normal standing height, and both could just make out the fish that Sid had spotted.

'Need to get a bit higher,' said Buzz, as he dropped carefully back to ground level and began to clamber halfway up the tree that Sid occupied.

'Oi, careful big fella. This is a one-bedroom flat, mate, not a three-bedroom house. Only room for a little 'un, not a great big lump like you,' declared Sid, then clung on for dear life as Buzz swayed back and forth on the trunk of the wispy willow.

'I'll huff and I'll puff,' he said, whilst Stan stood to the side, shaking his head and smiling.

'Yeah, and I'll drop and I'll bop,' replied Sid, still clutching the trunk with both arms. 'Now, don't make me come down there and sort you out, big fella. You know it'll only end in tears.'

Buzz stopped swaying and peered through the foliage out into the lake, and Sid preened himself and dusted himself down, claiming a minor victory, but knowing that recompense would be coming.

'Right, now that you've seen sense,' he said, 'just over there, to the right of Rhodie. See 'em?'

Buzz could see them, and could tell that they weren't what he was here for, so scanned around a little further. There was nobody at all fishing the old lake, and just two guys on the pike lake side, so there was little to disturb the fish. A whistle alerted them, and they looked across at Rhodie, who had managed to get three quarters of the way along the trunk, and so was about twelve feet out into the lake. He was peering down into the deep water under the tree, shading his eyes from the sun's glare to better aid his view. He looked up at his audience and pointed down, then spread his arms wide, careful to retain his balance on his precarious perch. He then held up three fingers before lowering his body onto the trunk and peering deep into the water. From above, a few small branches snapped off as Sid tried to get a better view, then a short, sharp expletive came from him. Stan expected to hear the cracking of branches, and then bone, but his mate was still in the treetop, jumping about like an agitated gibbon.

'Yeah, I see 'em,' he whisper-shouted. 'Three of 'em, about four, five feet down. Can't make 'em out exactly, but they look pretty big.'

Neither Stan nor Buzz were high enough to afford them a decent view, so both just relied on treetop telegraph and semaphore. Suddenly, Rhodie got very agitated, and began waving his arms about, and pointing down with both hands. At the same time, further expletives rained down with the branches, and seconds later Stan and Buzz, once again on their respective tree stumps, could see why.

One, two, then three fish rose slowly beneath the tree, the odd bubble pimpling the surface as they did so. They then moved ever so slowly from beneath the fallen tree and out into open water, just yards away from their open-mouthed admirers. The Common was in front, moving slowly, and all could see a fresh scar along her flank. Behind her came a smaller fish, a little over half her size, and it wasn't until that fish turned slightly that Stan saw the starburst of scales by its gill cover, then a slightly darker scale a few inches away. It was Taurus, the carp that Neil had caught, and it was eclipsed by The Common. Then, finally, another huge fish, a mirror, emerged from the cover of the tree and moved alongside Taurus, dwarfing it in both length and bulk. Undisturbed by Sid's wailing and Rhodie's waving, the trio of carp moved slowly along the margins, towards the Post Office, and Stan and

Buzz quickly followed. They kept pace with them for half a minute or so, then The Common moved off towards the island, followed by the other two, and pretty soon all were out of sight.

It seemed like they'd hardly been away. Buzz was in the Post Office, Stan in the South Westerly, and Chris and Sid in Island One and Two, respectively. Oh for a repeat of the last time they'd sat in these swims, in a different century. After their sighting of the carp, all three berated Stan for keeping their size such a secret, but he just hadn't realised.

'Honest, I probably see them half a dozen times a year, so I just haven't noticed how big they've become. I knew the Poached Mirror was getting bigger, especially when I had to put it back in the lake after we saved it from them poachers, but I'd had nothing to compare 'em against until now.'

The other three were still jibing him, but they knew exactly what he meant. How many times have we said, after not seeing a niece or nephew for a few years, 'Haven't you grown?' Well, the answer, from these carp was a resounding, 'Yes!'

'Neil's fish, Taurus, that's almost fifty pounds, and those two bloody dwarfed it,' Stan continued, 'How big does that make them? And Sid's Fish, that wasn't there, but I've seen it with the other two and they don't overshadow it like they do Taurus. That's gotta make that at least mid-fifties. Jesus!'

'Now, tell me Quill, my old mate,' began Sid, 'I believe you're a little torn whether to fish here or over at that other place, with the Leneys. Could I make a suggestion? Either fish here or get yourself bloody committed because you'd be out of your tiny, little mind if you decided to fish anywhere else.'

Rhodie took another swig of tea before joining in. 'Gotta make Sid right, there, which is obviously almost unheard of, but the strange little man in the cloth cap speaks the goddamn truth, Quill.' Sid doffed said cap and took a bow.

'Yep, they're right, mate,' agreed Buzz, 'this is the only place to be for the foreseeable. Look what happened last time, thought we'd found heaven then some bastard welded the pearly gates together. Who knows what these country folk'll do, mate? Them sailing boys were probably paying a lot more to sail than we do to fish, and you said yourself, you couldn't see 'em filling the syndicate with the same stamp of angler again. Next time it'll be guys like us, and then your troubles'll really start. Nope, gotta be here mate, every chance you get.'

'Yeah, how much better could it be,' said Sid. 'You bloody work here, so you can fill the place in with bait, if you want, or keep a little area primed, away from prying eyes, and telling only your good buddies about it. Gotta be good, ain't it?' Trust Sid to lighten the mood, thought Stan, thankfully.

'Okay, okay, I get the picture. Stop the bloody verbal assault. I know I was a bit torn, but that was before I saw what we saw today. No, I'll give old Jackson a call and see if I can get a refund; if not, tough shit really. It's only money, innit?'

That evening, Stan re-ran the home movie in his head. The Common, with a scar, obviously the fish that Chris had lost a few months back. Taurus, looking a similar size to when Neil had caught it. Then the Poached Mirror. When he had held it, last year, and lowered it into the lake he knew that it was a similar size to The Common, when they'd caught it years earlier. Now he was convinced of that fact. It had to have been ten pounds bigger than Taurus, possibly more, and The Common looked larger still. When they'd caught The Common, its weight had been breathtaking, unbelievable, beyond anything that had been caught in England at that time. Now, that weight had just recently been surpassed, but only by a pound or so, and how much weight could it have put on in the ensuing years? These thoughts, and derivatives of them, ran round and round in his head until the early hours of the morning, the odd splash from a distant, leaping carp only adding fuel to them.

'Stan! Stan!' Once again an early morning call from Neil had woken him, only this time he wasn't on the 'phone, he was in the mouth of the bivvy, his dark outline blocking the early morning light.

'Yep, what? Wassup, Neil? Bloody hell, I was well away there. What, you had one mate?'

'No, but your mate has.'

They arrived in Sid's swim within a minute or so, and his beaming smile lit up the early morning gloom.

'Oh, yes, Quill! Oh, yes!' Rhodie was already there, and Buzz was not far away, having also been awoken by Neil.

'What is it, mate?' he asked, obviously.

'A bloody great mirror carp, that's what it is Quill, An' I done 'im!' replied Sid, buzzing around the swim like a demented butterfly. 'Right, Rhodie, scales for you. Got yer camera, Stan?'

'Yep.'

'Cool. Ah, Buzz, me old mate, just in time to see what a carp looks like on the bank, fella. Here, grab this camera, you know how to work it, don't ya?' Buzz contemplated an acerbic response, but didn't feel up to a verbal duel at that moment. With the adrenaline running through him, Sid would make mincemeat of him, so he just quietly accepted the camera, and took up position.

Sid hoisted the sack from the margins, and they could all see the exertion on his face. This was gonna be a big fish.

'Wait until you see this, boys, it's gonna blow your minds,' he said, as he laid the sack down on the mat and began undoing the half dozen knots he'd tied in the cord. It was still a little murky, the sun still shielded behind the trees, but they wouldn't get much better light in this swim so the flashes would have to be employed.

As Sid revealed the fish, all they could see was scales, and they thought that it was a common. But, then, a piece of leathery skin was revealed before more scales, small and large. Eventually, it lay there before them and it was, indeed, mind-blowing. It was almost fully scaled, but not quite, and the colour of it was like beaten copper. All that the three of them could say was a joint, 'Bloody hell!'

It was a cliché, and was becoming more so for Stan, but a weight was immaterial, however, weigh it they did, of course, and then took copious photographs. In hindsight, such a stunning carp should have been seen in the full light of day, and although the subsequent shots did it no justice at all, Sid worried not. Forty-two pounds of virgin, fully scaled carp didn't come along every day, and he would remember the day for a long, long time, good photos or not.

A day or so later, Stan managed his first carp of the season, and his second, when he caught a couple of double-figure commons from a little spot in the edge. It just happened to be the same little spot that Buzz had taken the 48 from, and one that Stan had been trickling bait into for the previous few weeks. Apart from that, there were no more bites forthcoming to them – well, not from carp. Rhodie had decided to spod out about ten kilos of hemp and pellets on the second day, and for the next thirty-six hours landed a procession of progressively large bream. Stan had to almost order him to weigh one of them because it looked huge, and at sixteen pounds it bloody well was, but Rhodie was unimpressed. Stan, however, knew someone who would be, and later that day was on the phone to Bill to suggest a different method for him to try.

So that was that, a wholly enjoyable session with yet another, unknown whacker to add to the growing list. But the sight of those three carp would remain indelibly imprinted on four pairs of retinas for many months to come. The Common was obviously liable to slip up once or twice a season, as was the Poached Mirror. And what about Sid's Fish? Stan and Ted had seen it just prior to the start of the season, so who knew what its resistance to anglers' bait would be like?

This was getting more and more exciting, and Stan couldn't wait to get a call to say someone had caught one of them, although him doing the phoning would be much more acceptable. Maybe it would be a telegram – from the Post Office.

Part Six

IT WAS EARLY MORNING YESTERDAY

I WAS UP BEFORE THE DAWN

I REALLY HAVE ENJOYED MY STAY

BUT I MUST BE MOVING ON...

Chapter Thirty

Piper at the Gates of Dawn

Light snow was falling, gradually dusting the whole world in icing sugar, like a huge Christmas cake. Ted walked slowly towards the lake, afraid to even breathe in case he should shatter the silence. Just the light crunch of his steps in the thickening carpet of snow gave away his presence. But there was no one to hear, or so he hoped. He stopped by a large pine and eyed the landscape in front of him, looking for likely blind spots. He motioned forward, and the small group of men continued on their steady trek. Despite all of the necessary clothing, and the arduous exercise, the appendages still felt the cold, but he fought the urge to stamp his feet and moved ahead smoothly and quietly.

A shout alerted him and he looked to his left just as a huge stag careered across the glade, not ten yards from him, it's steamy breath wreathing its magnificent head in a cloud. Its antlers were tipped with snow, as were its back and flanks, and it slowed to a regal trot as soon as it realised that there was no danger, snorting derisively at the onlookers before trotting off into the thick pine forest.

'Piper at the Gates of Dawn,' muttered Ted, and the boss turned and smiled, nodding his head in agreement. Time to move back; Norway was lovely, and ideal for Artic manoeuvres, but now it was time for some hot broth and a game of poker.

Ted stood by the lake, a light dusting of snow glazing the landscape. He could see Neil and Quentin making their way along the south bank, towards him, so he moved from the cover of the trees and stood to survey the lake.

'Young Quentin, good to see you, lad. How's that there University treating you?' he asked.

'Really well, Ted, thanks. I'm really enjoying it,' replied Smiffy, clapping his gloved hands together to initiate a bit more blood flow.

'Where we off to then, Ted?' asked Posh, from beneath his scarf. 'Said you had something to show us.'

'I might, young Neil, just have to be real quiet. Real quiet.' With that he turned and headed east, back through Sutton Woods. They walked in silence for a few minutes, the whole world seemingly wrapped in cotton wool. Then, from a distance, they heard a familiar grunting, barking sound.

'Is that a stag?' asked Neil, pretty sure of the answer as he'd listened to them rutting for the month or so leading up to Christmas.

'More than a stag, lad. Quiet now, we're pretty close,' said Ted. The river was a short way ahead, through the trees, then on the far side was a clearing before the woodland encroached again. The trio of watchers crept to the river's edge and peered across at a glorious sight. Just on the far bank, no more than forty yards from them, was a magnificent red deer stag. Its antlers were huge, wide and many-tined and its neck was thick and muscular. The snowfall had increased a little out in the open, something they hadn't noticed in the shelter of the wood, and the deer had an almost albino look about it. Hot breath steamed from its nostrils and mouth, and it bellowed its authority across the woods.

'There, lads; The Piper at the Gates of Dawn,' said Ted.

Smiffy looked at Posh and shrugged his shoulders, but Posh smiled with the memory. 'Yeah, Wind in the Willows,' he said, excitedly. 'The Piper at the Gates of Dawn. He was, like, a god that piped in the sunrise every morning. He was a stag, or something like one. Ratty and Mole saw him, I think.'

Smiffy looked at his friend, slightly taken aback, but Ted chuckled and looked at Posh with a certain admiration. 'Just so, Neil, just so. And is this magnificent creature not worthy of that title?'

They turned back as the stag issued one more throaty declaration of power, before it turned and trotted, godlike, back into the cover of the woods. Within seconds all was still and quiet, and Smiffy looked at both Ted and Posh.

'Piper at the Gates of Dawn – brilliant! Wind in the Willows, eh? Sounds like I might have to be reading that pretty soon.'

Ted nodded. 'Right lads, time for a bit of Old Ted's rabbit stew, I reckon. Waddya think?' No answer was required as the pair of them had already turned and started moving swiftly towards Ted's cabin. A few months earlier, all had been vibrant and green, but it had still ended in rabbit stew.

With extra learning comes the added bonus of extra holidays, so Smiffy was back at the family home by the middle of July. A few weeks away with friends in Spain, and then he was back at the Mere, eager to wet a line in this place of their dreams. News of Posh's unbelievable fish, still the largest from the lake, had fuelled his every daydream since, and he had planned his summer assault with military precision. Unfortunately, not being at all militarily minded, his plans soon went out of the window when the sun shone, and the barbecues were lit. A cold cider or two helped to numb the senses a little, and dull the urgency, so it wasn't until early August that he and Posh made their first serious sortie together. Posh had spent quite a bit of time on the banks, mainly in his bailiff role, but had also managed half a dozen sessions in search of monsters. Apart from his one glowing success, however, the carp had been elusive, and he'd had to be satisfied with a couple of hefty tench and bream.

Their first couple of sessions coincided with high pressure and soaring temperatures, which weren't the least conducive to fishing of any sort, and were both curtailed prematurely in favour of a stroll to The Green Man. Then, guided by the weatherman, they planned an overnight trip towards the end of the month. Strangely, the weatherman had got it right, and a ridge of low pressure did, indeed, push in from the Atlantic, bringing strong southwesterlies, cloud and rain - ideal summer carping weather. Being strong, hardy lads they decided to sit it out in the teeth of the wind, knowing that the carp would also be braving the conditions, so Posh set up in the South Westerly and Smiffy in Island One. Well, the wind did blow, and the rain did pour, and by morning they were as wretched as two recently rescued rodents. On top of that, the carp were so conspicuous by their absence as to have been holidaying in warmer climes altogether.

After a trip to Smiffy's house to dry out and regroup, they wandered back to the lake, taking the long way round, but within a hundred yards knew that they need go no further. As they rounded the corner by the Poachers' Pads, right at the back of the wind, a carp slid out of the clear, calm waters and flopped back down, its wake rocking the lily leaves and shocking the gawping onlookers. As another followed suit a few seconds later, there was no one to see, because they were busy belting round the lake to retrieve their gear and 'reconsider their options'!

Within an hour they were both sitting very quietly at the back of the swim, five yards from the lake's edge. On their return they'd seen two more carp, both fairly small, rolling at the back of the pads. Rather than panicking and hurling leads about everywhere, Posh decreed patience, so they sat and watched as carp after carp rolled and bubbled in front of them. After fifteen minutes of this torture, Smiffy had put a garbled plan together and there was only one thing for certain in it – a peacock quill float. Posh had crept to the edge of the pads nearest the woods and had flicked out a light lead with a small pop-up on, a scattering of broken boilies and sweetcorn accompanying it. Smiffy, however, was determined to persevere with the float, so took the rod out and carefully slid the float into the rubber, attaching three swan shot just six inches from the hook. On the hook he impaled three bright yellow grains, then carefully flicked the float to the edge of the pads, five yards out.

Yeah, right!

Smiffy was a complete mess. His fingers were like bananas and with every roll of another carp, were getting fatter by the minute. He broke a rubber, then got the hook caught in his jumper. It took half a tin of sweetcorn before he actually managed to get three to stay on the hook, and all the while the carp were mocking him. Eventually, when he did cast, it went straight into the pads, and on the retrieval the grains all came off. He was on the verge of just chucking the whole lot in the bushes and going back to The Green Man, but then a moment of calm washed over him and, losing only four grains before getting three to stick, he watched as the float

plopped down next to the lilies. A twitch of the line and a turn of the reel handle, and all that was visible was a red tip – at last, he was bloody fishing! A few handfuls of corn were flicked out around the float and then he joined Posh at the back of the swim.

'That all seemed to go quite well,' said Posh, with barely a smirk. Smiffy looked at him, cap pulled low over his eyes, and declined to comment. At the back of the wind it was surprisingly warm, and they had soon stripped off their waterproof jackets in favour of the t-shirts underneath. Smiffy kept a steady eye on the float, but little was happening, and he gradually realised that the carp activity had slowed to almost nothing. Typical. He crept to the water's edge and looked out at the red tip, noticing a small bubble next to it that he hadn't seen just now. Then another joined it, and the float twitched a little. The third and fourth bubble were simultaneous, and the fifth coincided with the float lifting like a rocket, lying on its side and disappearing off into the big blue, all in the time it took the bubble to pop. The rod hooped, the angler winced as the carbon creaked and cracked, and the reel screamed a tortured scream. Whatever was on the other end obviously had an important appointment somewhere, and it was very late. Posh was now standing next to his mate, commenting on this and that, and Smiffy was totally oblivious to any of it. The carp had slowed to a mere crazed charge across the lake, and Smiffy felt in no control whatsoever. An eternity passed and was soon joined by another one. They chatted for a while, then went off in search of something more infinite, and as they left so Smiffy gained some line. Then more. Then he was reeling like crazy as the carp seemed to be intent on coming back and giving him a right good slap. It headed straight into the margins to his right, where a large reed bed had grown up over the summer, and Smiffy had to apply some severe side strain to avoid an inevitable disaster. This he did, just, then all was calm, and the carp seemed to realise that the last dash for freedom had sapped it of all its energy, allowing Smiffy to guide it gratefully into the net that Posh held.

Pandemonium and its pals had a party, there and then, and Smiffy and Posh happily joined in.

'What a bloody fight!' said Smiffy. 'I never thought I was gonna land the thing.' He massaged his shoulder and wheeled his arm round, then peered over his mate's shoulder to look at his prize. 'Bloody hell, Posh, that's a whacker, innit?'

Posh could see the length of the fish, but he'd seen it roll into the net and knew it had little depth, and was obviously shaped like a torpedo.

They lifted it onto the mat and gawped at the beauty of it. Long and lean, with a scattering of scales on its bronzed flanks, it may not have been as huge as Taurus, but it had fought like a bull and was definitely a personal best for Smiffy. At thirty-one pounds, it was his first thirty, but initially he was a little disappointed. Then he stroked its sides, and lifted it for the photos, feeling its muscles tensing, and realised that this was a fine way to break the thirty pound barrier. Posh could take years, decades, to break his PB, but **he** could do it tomorrow. Yes, this was a fine PB.

The rain had started to fall again and they had to rush to get the fish back so that they could cover all of their gear up. The brollies were still wrapped up, and the rest of the gear was strewn about the swim, so by the time they had everything under shelter they were soaked to the skin.

'Should try them brollies up before the rain, lads,' came Ted's dry remark. He'd emerged from the woods by the pads, in a long oilskin-type coat, and a large brimmed hat. The rain was dripping from the brim, but he was bone dry.

'I'm off for a spot of lunch; bit of rabbit stew warming on the stove. You're welcome to some if you fancy,' he said, continuing on his way. A quick look between them said all that was needed and within minutes they were trotting along after him, their coats over their heads.

'Good choice, lads,' said Ted. 'So, you caught anything, then?'

Chapter Thirty One

One of the Few

Just down there, to the right of the big, cracked branch.' Jim's arm was extended, pointing, as he watched from the top of the tree. Lee, below, followed the direction but could see little because of the sun's glare and the ripple on the water.

'Can't see, mate, sorry. I'll try to get a bit higher.' Unfortunately, Lee's bulk made tree climbing a precarious pastime, and he rarely got himself more than a few feet off the ground before the limb he was standing on began to creak and complain.

Above him, Jim took little notice of his companion's plight, and just continued to follow the half a dozen carp as they meandered slowly beneath the snags. They all looked quite sizeable, and one was considerably larger than the others, possibly in the upper forties. As he continued to peer into the depths, his thoughts drifted back to the rumours they'd heard, of huge, uncaught monsters that swam the depths of this lake. Initially, although he and Lee had heard of the tickets that had become available for this lake, via the Angling Times, they'd taken little notice. There were so many lakes that purported to offer 'peace and quiet, excellent fishing, specimen sized fish of all species, etc, etc.' that they barely got to the end of the advert before flicking to another page. But then rumours had filtered back about a couple of lads that Lee vaguely knew. They'd been caught poaching this big lake out Salisbury way and had actually caught a massive mirror before the police bagged them, and the fish was returned to the lake. The lake in the advert was a big lake, seventy-odd acres, and was out near Salisbury; could that be just a coincidence? At £600 it was a costly risk to take if it was just a coincidence, but then news came out early in the summer of a forty-seven pound carp from the lake, and previously uncaught as well – maybe they weren't just rumours.

Jim had called up the club secretary to see if there were any tickets left and, unsurprisingly, the offer of another £1200 for the coffers cemented their acquisition. They'd decided on a bit of caution, so had popped down one day in August just for a stroll round, to get a feel for the place. They'd chatted to a couple of the anglers that were almost lost on the huge lake, and it transpired that a different forty had been caught a few weeks earlier. Their stroll around showed little signs of carp, although a couple of large splashes towards a distant south bank had them

peering through their binoculars to investigate. On their way
home they talked excitedly about the
prospects for the next few months, and
decided to begin their campaign at the
beginning of September. It was a four-
hour round trip so they needed to be
sure that their time was going to be
well spent.

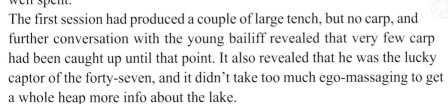

The first session had produced a couple of large tench, but no carp, and
further conversation with the young bailiff revealed that very few carp
had been caught up until that point. It also revealed that he was the lucky
captor of the forty-seven, and it didn't take too much ego-massaging to get
a whole heap more info about the lake.

So here they were, a week later, peering into the snags where Neil had told them
that the carp generally hung out. The snags were cut off from anglers by the
distances involved; the nearest swim being the Post Office, which was over one
hundred and fifty yards away, and had a few overhanging branches shielding it
from the snags. This, however, was where they were set up. Well, where Jim was
set up; Lee was around the corner in the South Westerly and feeling less than
confident about his chances.

The sight from the tree had spurred Jim on, and he sat with Lee and tea, trying to
devise a plan that could get his baits as close to the snags as possible. From his swim
he could barely see the far edge of the snags, due to the curve of the bank and the
overhanging trees, so even with one of his best casts he would be miles away. They
walked the bank to see where it would be viable to cast from, and it was only once
they were within about sixty or seventy yards that a cast from the bank became
possible. From the far side, the snags were hidden from view by a small point of
land, and even then it was out of bounds until you got to the left of the boathouse;
three huge oaks forming an impenetrable barrier between there and the small point
of land.

Frustration was getting the better of Jim, whilst Lee felt he would just like to get
his rods out as the snags were a far off land to him, and the island margins were
beginning to look more and more alluring. As the day moved inexorably towards
evening, Jim came to a decision.

'Right, I'm gonna wait until it's almost dark, then I'm gonna go down the bank and
cast as close to the snags as I can. Then, I'll get in the water and walk along the
margins until I can get the rod back out. There's a couple of trees we should be able
to pass the rod round, then it's big carp time!' He laughed at that and Lee smiled,
not sure whether to mention that they didn't actually know how deep the margins
were. Still, at least it meant he'd now be able to get his baits out by the island
before dark.

Jim's first cast fell yards short, the cramped bank space making it difficult to get a good swing of the rod. The second was much closer, but the hook and lead had hit an overhead branch and Jim was unsure whether the bait was still on. On retrieval it was, obviously, but if he'd left it then there would have been no bait – Sod's Law. The third cast, however, was absolutely spot-on, and he could envision the lead carrying on under the snags a further yard or so from its point of entry. Jim let out a little whoop of delight, mended the line, then gave the rod to Lee whilst he prepared to get into the lake. Another whoop left his lips a few seconds later, but it certainly wasn't delight, as the cool waters moved swiftly up his body to parts they really shouldn't reach. Steadying himself, and huffing loudly, he took the rod, and with his finger on the open spool, paid out line as he moved carefully back towards his swim. He calculated that he'd have to go about fifty yards before he could get out and start passing the rod around the tree trunks. Slowly, he made his way but then, with a sudden 'Whoa!' his footing went and he disappeared below the surface. Lee was unsure what had happened, and just looked round to see three quarters of the rod above the lake, held there like Excalibur. He had no time to panic before his friend came coughing and spluttering to the surface.

'Bloody hell! (cough, cough) Bloody hell! (cough, snort, splutter) Ooh, give us a hand Lee, grab the rod for a mo. Come on, I'm nearly ****ing drowning here, you twat!'

Lee grabbed the rod and remembered, just in time, to keep it down lest it caught in the grasping branches above.

'You all right, mate? What happened?' he asked, inanely.

'What happened? What the bloody hell 'd'you think happened? I nearly ****ing drowned, that's what happened. Jesus, it's bloody freezing. Mind that rod, mate, don't get it caught in the bloody trees. I ain't doing this more than once.'

He managed to find some firmer footing, then once again took the rod and moved, even more carefully, along the margins before, none too soon, coming to the spot they'd earmarked as the exit point. He passed the rod to Lee, dragged himself from the lake, then trotted back to his bivvy where he quickly stripped off, towelled himself down, and slung on dry clothes, shivering violently all the while. When he returned, five minutes later, night had fallen with a deep, dark thump, and the next part of the operation took much longer than they'd thought it would in the clear, easily visible, light of day.

Eventually, almost half an hour after that cast, Jim was standing in his swim with the rod tip underwater whilst slowly tightening up the line. He could feel it grating along the margin as the bank curved away from him, and he hoped that it wouldn't catch on any roots or mussel shells if a carp should pick it up. Once satisfied, he ran along the bank and threw about a dozen or so baits into the snags, before returning and putting on the kettle for a well-earned cup of tea.

Sometime in the night he thought he heard a buzzer, but fell straight back to sleep so was not on hand to land the nineteen-pound common for Lee. Nor to land the small, lightly scaled mirror for him an hour or so later. But he did hear his alarm, which bleeped twice in quick succession, the line pulling tight and the indicator holding close to the rod. He peered out at the red LED and knew it was the snag rod, but was loath to strike in case it was just a line bite, or a tench or something. That was his undoing. The carp were used to feeding confidently in the snags; they'd not been hooked in there for more than a decade, and Stan, Neil and a few others had regularly taken to flicking a few baits in there, just so that they could see them.

So the big, Poached Mirror just picked the hookbait up in its lips and moved slowly towards the next offering. The irritation in its lip was barely noticeable, and a usual occurrence when feeding in amongst the twigs, stones and general detritus below the trees. It moved deeper beneath the tree, in amongst its prehistoric jungle of branches, festooned with all manner of crustacea, the tugging at its mouth perturbing it just a little, so it began shaking its head to rid itself of the feeling.

Another bleep, another red LED. Jim got up and slid his feet into his trainers. He rummaged around below his bed until his fingers found his head torch, which he slipped onto his head and turned on. The beam picked out the rod and moved along it, highlighting the alarmingly curved tip, which was pulling round even more. It was just a matter of time when the line would ping from the clip and the buzzer would scream, but it would all be too late. He picked up the rod and struck fiercely, hoping to set the hook over one hundred and fifty yards, but that was unnecessary. He felt the rod buck in his hand as something on the other end moved slowly away. Leaning out as far as he dare, he pulled the rod back towards him, exerting the maximum pressure he could on the 3lb test curve, but to no avail. Moments later the rod was straight, the line slack, and any sensation of weight gone. He'd buggered it up, after all the planning and pain, he cocked the bloody thing up. The rod was thrown to the ground and he slumped back onto his bedchair, utterly dejected. There had to be a way, and he was bloody convinced that he would find it.

Gradually, the mirror became a little more agitated about its inability to free itself of the irritation, then a new sensation as it was temporarily halted in its course. Another shake of the head, then a flick of the huge tail and… freedom. The line slid along a branch and was sliced like cotton on the back of a razor sharp mussel shell. The fish moved swiftly through the branches, diving low, and out into the lake before slowing; the irritation still in its lip, but that would soon be gone.

Stan had watched the two guys packing away in the Post Office, one of whom had looked anything but happy. He'd assumed the guy must have lost a fish but was loath to ask. He didn't know what it was about these two, but he felt a certain unease in the air. Now, a few months later, he was watching them again, and the unease hadn't faded. There was nothing he could put his finger on; he'd spoken to them a couple of times since that first sighting, and they'd seemed okay, but there seemed to be an underlying air of menace. They'd done alright in their four or five sessions, both catching some of the commons, and the big guy having caught a twenty-eight-pound mirror at the end of October, but he'd have to keep an eye on them. That was for sure.

The lake was looking bare now; the last of the leaves having been blown from the trees a week or so previously by a typical autumn storm, and he didn't imagine that many of the members would persevere through the colder, winter months. The last few weeks had seen few anglers and even fewer fish; just a small common to the guy called Jim, and a twenty-pound mirror to Ben. He and Chris were going to give it a go up until Christmas, they'd said, but even without that they'd had a good season, taking nine fish between them, a couple of which were over thirty. Stan was sure that they would return next season and hoped that they were lucky enough to catch one of the real big'uns – they were certainly good enough, that was for sure, and really nice guys.

Then there was Bob – what a find he was! He'd plugged away through a pretty tough summer, but then had had the ultimate reward, and Stan and Sid had been there to witness it. Bob and Sid had met early in the summer, and their respective acerbic and cutting humour had been a joy to listen to as they verbally tore lumps out of each other. Many a day, Stan had sat there with tears running down his face as Sid goaded the dwarvish Bob, who'd growl and snarl and, with alarming speed, leap at Sid with fingers bent like claws. Invariably, Sid would avoid the clutches of his assailant, and would do that old Ali shuffle around the swim, but it eventually ended in tears, of one sort or another.

A big storm was brewing, typical of October, and Stan knew that he'd be wise to dispense with his stalking approach and settle down under a well pinned-down bivvy, just in case. His summer's fishing had been spent with just a rod and a bag of bits, stalking the mile or so of margins with float and hookbaits, and he'd been pretty successful, taking half a dozen carp and some lovely tench. The highlight had been a thirty-three-pound common from in front of the boathouse; a spot he'd been baiting for a few weeks whilst on his trips around the lake or into the woods, and the float had been in the water no more than a few minutes before it was being dragged all around the lake. He thought that more would come from the spot, but, apart from another, much smaller common, and a couple of nice tench, it had produced no more. He was certain that a longer, overnight session may have paid better dividends, and so it was that he'd kept trickling bait in for just the right occasion. And now seemed to be just that.

All three of them had managed to get the Friday off, so they would all arrive on Thursday afternoon. The reason for this wasn't so they could get an extra night's fishing in, but that England were, unbelievably, playing France in the semi-finals of the Rugby World Cup. Nobody had given them a chance, especially against the

Aussies in the previous week's quarterfinal, but they had been astounding and now, against the hosts in their home stadium, hopes were even higher.

'Ho ho, you don't hang about do ya, Quill? In like Flynn, there.' Stan had heard Sid's car pull up behind the boathouse so was fully prepared for the assault.

'Well, us old boys need a bit of a start on you young 'uns, don't we? And seeing as I seem to have done most of the work around here, I thought I might just take advantage, if that's okay with you.'

Sid flipped a hand dismissively before plonking down in Stan's lowchair. 'So, how big and how many?' he asked, as usual. Stan put the kettle on, which was given the thumbs up by his mate, then stood and looked at the lake.

'Well, I've only been here an hour or so, but I've seen a couple of things about sixty yards out. Difficult to tell what they were, because of the wind, but they weren't birds, that was for sure.' Sid then stood and walked to the edge of the lake. Stan was set up to the right, nearest to the West Woods, so Sid had quite a lot of water to choose from, and, knowing that Bob wouldn't be down until after dark, he took his time deciding where to go. The wind was picking up and pushing across them, from right to left, so the left hand side, out past the jetty, looked very inviting. He stood over there for ten minutes, hoping for leaping inspiration, but none was forthcoming, so he strolled back to Stan's bivvy and demanded more tea. They mulled over the possibilities, and Stan reminded him that the fish he'd caught, a month or so earlier, had been from no more than ten yards out. The lake here was quite deep, having been dug out to allow the keels of the deeper craft to safely moor along there, so there was a trench of about twelve feet in the close margin. Sid continued to ponder but then was shocked out of his revelry when a voice called from behind.

'You got room for a little un' in there, lads?' It was Bob, and he'd obviously done the classic 'I won't be down until…' double bluff.

Sid spun round and almost indignantly said, 'What you doing here? I thought you weren't gonna be here 'til after dark.'

Bob laughed throatily and smiled a huge smile. 'Ah hah, caught you out then, did I Siddie boy? Hurr, hurr, hurr. Well, you better be making your mind up real quick, boy, 'cos old Bob wants to go fishing – right now.' He winked at Stan, who just stood there smiling, then realised the wink was more a command, for tea. A true vocation, thought Stan.

'Come on lad, where d'you fancy, then? Nights are drawing in, soon be dark, let's be at it.'

Sid looked left and right, left and right, and felt suddenly under pressure; his normal cool demeanour warming ever so slightly. 'Errm, I dunno. I'm not sure, what about you Bob, where'd you fancy?'

Bob smiled again, raising his arms to signify that he wasn't bothered. This, in itself, could have been a double bluff so Sid furrowed his brow and put his chin in his hands. 'Only one answer – spoof for it,' said Stan. 'Winner chooses.'

The two protagonists looked at each other, then nodded and rummaged around in their pockets for three coins each. The first couple of rounds produced no winner, then Sid called spoof, to Bob's three. Sid revealed an empty hand, and stared straight into Bob's eyes. Bob's hand opened slowly, his face sullen, but then he thrust the three coins into Sid's face and danced a little jig, clicking his heels together and spinning in a circle. Sid's shoulders slumped slightly; he'd decided that he really fancied the left side of the swim, but was certain that was where Bob also fancied. Bob rubbed his chin dramatically and peered left and right.

'Come on, fer Chrissake, it don't take that long. Bloody moon'll be up soon,' moaned Sid.

Bob smiled, wickedly, then said, 'Here. I'll stay here, you can get yerself over there.'

Sid was slightly stunned, but in short order was striding back to his car, thoughts of monster carp in rolling waves occupying his mind.

The evening passed with laughter and banter, and Sid brought his usual left-field humour to the party.

'Did you know,' he said, apropos of nothing at all, 'that a camel sees things three times larger than they really are?'

'What?' said Stan, fuelled by a glass of wine too many. 'What are you talking about?

'Yeah, saw it on the telly. Three times the size. S'pose that's why they never die in the desert; they can always see an oasis, and it looks so close they never get worried about going thirsty.'

Bob was chuckling away to himself and said, 'So does that mean that llamas can see things one and half times as big, 'cos they're only half the size of a camel?'

'Could've done with a couple in the factory, when I used to work at the printers. They would have spotted any tiny hickies that the others used to miss,' said Stan, joining in the off-the-wall conversation.

'Yeah,' said Sid,' but you gotta watch out for yer llama, not good workers you know.'

'Really?' said Stan. 'What's up with 'em then? Obviously camels get the 'ump easily, but what about yer llama?'

'Feisty little buggers, easily annoyed, just like our stunted friend here,' said Sid, eyeing Bob warily. 'Thing is, if they play up, you know what you have to do?'

Stan could see the punchline looming, he just couldn't quite make it out. 'No, what?' he asked, resigned to the inevitable.

'Well,' said Sid, glowing, 'you have to fire a llama.'

It got no better after that, and soon they retired to their respective beds, in hope.

The morning was grey and windy, with a very light drizzle being blown hither and yon by the capricious breeze. Stan sat in the front of his bivvy, nursing a cup of tea and a small hangover. He'd seen a couple of bits and pieces, but nothing concrete, and was deciding when to reel his rods in for a stroll round the lake when, to his left and no more than five yards from the bank he heard a huge splash, and looked round just in time to see the flat spot in the deep margins, right in front of Bob's rods. Bob himself had appeared at the door of the bivvy, his head poking out like that of a dark green tortoise. He looked right, towards Stan, and said, 'Did you see that?'

Stan shook his head. 'No, but I bloody heard; it sounded like a whale!'

The lake was churned up and brown in front of them, and the deep margins in front of Bob must have looked mighty attractive to a feeding carp. Bob slowly walked down to Stan, rubbing his eyes and holding a cup, which Stan took without a word. 'I got one about five yards further out, just on the up-slope. Waddya reckon I should do – leave it there or recast it?' he asked.

'Where're the other two?' asked Stan.

''Err, one's about thirty, the other about fifty, I s'pose. Think I should move one?'

Stan cocked his head to one side and raised an eyebrow in that 'well, what do you think?' pose. Bob nodded and while Stan carried on with the brewing, Bob reeled in the furthest rod, rebaited, and just dropped it in the margins, a few yards to the left of where the fish had rolled. He flicked on the bite alarm, then crumbed up some boilies and threw them into the lake, half of them being blown back by the strengthening wind. Stan whistled and raised his cup, so Bob nodded and walked off towards him, but had taken no more than a dozen steps when the bite alarm absolutely screamed and line flew from the spool at an alarming rate. All was slow motion for a second. Bob stopped in his tracks, slowly turning his head. Stan held the mug of tea outstretched, not sure what was occurring, then watched as Bob spun round and ran back as if wading through treacle. The tea hit the floor as Stan joined in the race, and all the while line continued to pour from the spool.

Bob just held the rod and watched as the line on his spool grew less and less, and when Stan asked what it felt like, Bob had nothing to compare it with. Sid came shambling into the swim, and muttered something about tea, but none was forthcoming, so he bent down and picked up Bob's water bottle, gulping down huge draughts of water whilst the carp made a bid for freedom that Steve McQueen would have been proud of.

The light rain was getting heavier, but none of them noticed, and after ten minutes, with the carp almost half a lake away, they realised that this could be something very special indeed. Bob said very little for the next ten minutes, just concentrated on retrieving as much line as possible, and, realising that this was going to take a while, Sid put the kettle on and made them all a life-saving cup of tea.

After half an hour they saw a flat spot some thirty yards out, then the carp moved off rapidly to the left.

'Watch your lines, Sid,' growled Bob, and Sid strolled down towards his rods, knowing that they were nowhere close. But the carp still had some strength, and suddenly his right hand alarm was emitting the odd bleep.

'Quick, Sid, lift yer bloody rod, mate. I can feel the line rubbing,' Bob shouted, but Sid was already running. He picked up the rod and straightaway could feel a sensation coming back up the line. Oh, bugger, he thought, but lifted the rod high so that they could see what was happening. The carp slowed in its escape bid, and Bob regained some line, and Sid felt the line on his rod being pulled and rubbed. Fortunately, there were no trees between them, so he slowly walked back towards Bob, rod held high and bale arm off. Another flat spot appeared in the waves, ten yards out, then a great, grey flank rolled over.

'Shit!' muttered Stan, net in hand, and Bob just nodded. Sid was almost next to him, gradually retrieving what line he could, but Bob was quiet and in control. The fish rolled again, five yards out, and they could see the little bird's nest of line, perilously close to the carp's mouth.

'Easy now, mate' said Sid, but Bob just gave him a sideways glare and concentrated on the job at hand. Stan was kneeling down, net extended, and waiting to engulf the fish. It rolled again, so close, then again, but this time close enough and he carefully raised the mesh before feeling the weight of the fish safely inside.

Then all hell broke loose.

The carp thrashed the water to a foam, but to no avail. Bob screamed a deep, throaty scream and dropped his rod, before turning and giving Sid a lung busting bear hug. And Stan just knelt there and smiled.

'Bloody hell, Bob, you're not back in bleeding Mordor, y'know. I ain't a bloody Orc; I'm one of the good guys,' grunted Sid as Bob let him go. Bob was beyond care, the ache in his arm telling him that he had landed the fish of a lifetime.

Sid walked over to the net and joined Stan in peering down at the carp. 'Bloody hell, Quill, I recognise that, don't I?'

Stan nodded, 'You sure do mate, you were the last one to catch this, almost ten years ago.' Bob joined them and whooped at the sight of the huge fish.

'What is it then? Which one?' he asked.

'Sid's Fish, mate. It's Sid's. Last time out at fifty-two pounds, in the last century.

Might be a bit bigger now, though,' explained Stan. Bob was uncaring, and added a few more intricate steps to his earlier jig, incorporating a little arm-hooking spin with Sid.

At fifty-seven pounds it smashed his personal best into very small pieces, and you didn't need to have a camel's eyesight to see the grin on his face. After that, little else mattered, and the icing on a very large cake was England's defeat of France in the semi-final, which induced much merriment, singing, the odd little jig, and a fair amount of well deserved hangovers. All in all, one of the best weekends Stan could remember for a very long time.

Winter's grip was not far off, and pretty soon the lake was left to the carp, the few remaining waterfowl, and Old Ted. He'd watched carefully over the previous few months, and had taken note of a few individuals that he was a little unsure of. His sense of character had held him in good stead over the years, and he had no qualms about trusting it now. He would have to be vigilant in the coming season; there was still some danger here, and he wanted to be sure he was there to thwart it, if necessary.

Chapter Thirty Two
A Momentary Lapse of Reason

oxing Day at Peter and Wendy's was becoming a bit of an annual event, and a pretty good one too. The large sitting room was fairly crowded, as was the kitchen, obviously, and even Old Ted had accepted an invitation this year.

Stan and Jean mingled as usual, especially as they had the news to spread that they were to become grandparents for the second time. It had been their first granddaughter, Maisie, who had come barrelling through the door on Christmas Eve to break the news, but that was soon forgotten when she saw the huge Christmas tree, festooned with decorations and surrounded by hoards of presents. Her excitement was infectious, and pretty soon Stan had done the typical granddad thing and snuck a small present from beneath the tree for Maisie to open. Admonishment from wife and daughter meant little in the face of the glee on Maisie's face, and soon all was a blur of crayons and paper. Christmas Day was similar, but on a scale previously unsurpassed, and by early evening the house was almost quiet, apart from the odd snore from Stan. Ever was it thus.

The kids had to leave on Boxing Day, so Stan and Jean took the opportunity to recharge their batteries before the evenings festivities. Now, a dozen hours later, they were in full swing and all was well with the world.

'So, another grandchild, Stan. Bloody fine show,' said Peter, wobbling only slightly. 'Lovely to have 'em, I'd imagine. Difficult to know when young Quentin will grace us with one, few years yet, I'd imagine.'

'No rush, Pete. Give the boy a chance, he'll do you proud, don't you worry,' replied Stan, a hand on his hosts shoulder. Peter nodded and smiled drunkenly.

'To the children, and their offspring,' he declared, raising a glass. Stan raised his own and they clinked them together.

'And to the bloody fine parents, as well,' he added, to which Peter once again raised his glass, then clapped Stan on the shoulder and smiled.

'Stan, old man, got something to discuss,' he began, slightly seriously. 'Not sure if this is the time or place but, what the hell. Been having a chat with a few of the members. Bit of ill-feeling, bit disgruntled a few of 'em'

'Ill-feeling,' said Stan, 'about what?'

'Well, ill-feeling's probably the wrong word. Damn, I knew I should have left this 'til later. It's, well, a few of 'em didn't have the best of years, didn't bag many fish and, what with the price of the ticket, well, there's been talk of stocking the lake with a few more carp. You know, just to give everyone a bit of a chance.'

Suddenly, Stan felt remarkably sober, and a tad concerned. 'Peter, please, you can't be serious. How many times have I heard this? Bad anglers trying to hide their inadequacy behind the old 'there's no bloody fish in this lake' excuse. No, Peter, its bollocks, mate. You can't do it. Do you have any idea of the possible fall out from stocking the lake with new carp?' By now, Peter was realising that he really should have left this until another day, and was guiding Stan out of the sitting room and into the hall.

'Stan, I understand what you're saying, but..'

'No, I don't think you do, Peter. The possible diseases that a new strain of fish could be carrying could wipe out the existing stock. Wipe 'em clean out. Gone! I've seen it before, mate, and it's bloody devastating.'

'Stan, Stan, listen to me. I've been chatting to Stuart about this. He's just bought fifty good quality carp and put them in the Hatch. There's been no ill effects, so I'm going to have a word with the same chap. Apparently..'

Once again, Stan couldn't wait, 'Oh, you're joking, not in the Hatch. Why the bloody hell did he do that? He's got enough fish in there to satisfy everyone..'

'Yes, but nobody could…'

'Catch them,' finished Stan. 'Oh, Peter, it's such bloody vanity, it proves nothing. Please, do me a favour. Leave it for a few months, there's no rush. Wait until the spring to make sure that Stuart's fish are alright, then we can have a serious look at it then. Just leave it for now, yeah?'

Peter had also sobered a little, and could see and hear the intensity of Stan's feelings about the matter, and Stan's feelings were something he very much trusted. 'Okay, old boy, we'll leave it until the end of March, but then we need to give it some serious thought. But, for now, I think we need a top up.'

'Yeah, I reckon you're right. Thanks Pete,' said Stan. 'One other thing, though.'

'What's that?' asked Peter, a little worried.

'This music, it's gotta change. Frank and Bing and that are all right for a while, but we need to be getting people up, bit of boogying going on. What you got in that collection?' They walked across the sitting room to the CD player, and stacks of CD's, and began examining a few.

'What about a bit of Elvis?' asked Peter. Stan looked around and assessed the gathered throng.

'Nah, not a Blue Suede Shoes crowd, Pete. Something a bit more recent, I reckon.'

'I think we've got some Take That somewhere,' said Peter, to a look of derision by Stan, who then went back to squinting at the CD covers. Then he turned triumphantly, holding a disc in the air.

'Oh, yes! Here we go,' he said, and shoved the cover in Peter's face, who peered at it blearily, then beamed all over his face, raising a glass and drinking from it.

'It's Thriller diller night, Peter! Reckon we'll have Old Ted moon-walking across the floor before the night's out.' Peter guffawed and spat beer everywhere, whilst Stan slipped the disc into the player and turned the volume up to eleven.

It was close to midnight, and it was time to get **down**.

At the time it had seemed like such a good idea, but at three in the morning, with quite a few pints inside you, anything seems like a good idea. Now, though, Posh started to doubt the wisdom of the plan he'd hatched with Smiffy. Yes it was pike fishing. Yes, it was the first of January, but it was also bleeding freezing and his head hurt from the previous night's revelry. To be fair, the plan had been hatched at Smiffy's place on Boxing Day, or at least the early morning after Boxing Day, and they'd not had a New Year's Eve party planned, but then Jeff's mum and dad were off skiing, the place was empty, and a few of their old school mates decided, well, you know how it goes. And it went.. and went.. and went. Now here he was, standing by the lake, wrapped up like an Eskimo and waiting for Smiffy to arrive. Their planned nine o'clock rendezvous was many hours passed, and the early afternoon sun was trying to break through the watery clouds, but to little effect. Oh sod this, thought Posh, I might as well chuck a dead bait around whilst I'm bloody waiting. They'd decided to concentrate in front of the boathouse, mainly because it was closest and offered a little shelter from the chill, northeasterly that was blowing. But it also offered them some of the deepest water in the Mere, right in the margins, and their thinking had been that, sheltered from the wind and.. oh, what the hell! It seemed like a good idea at the time, so it might as well be tried out.

He impaled a slice of semi-frozen mackerel with the treble, and flicked it out ten yards to the drop off, feeling it flicker to the lake bed and come to a slow stop. He twitched it a little, to draw it down the slope, then put the rod on the rests and shoved his hands in his pockets; that wind was bloody chilly.

'Oh, I see, started without me, then,' said Smiffy as he strolled into the swim.

'Bloody hell, it lives!' replied Posh. 'Didn't think there was any chance you were gonna make it, not the state you were in when I last saw you.'

Smiffy laughed, then raised a flask and said, 'Yes, but look what I have – hot bloody soup! That's why I'm late, mate, been making us a bit of the old life saver.' He then unscrewed the lid and took out the two cups, filling them with a steaming brew that suddenly had Posh realising how hungry he was.

'Okay, I forgive you, but only this once. Now give that here, mate, and sling a dead fish into the lake. Let's at least pretend we're fishing.'

Smiffy slowly handed over the soup, then took a slow sip of his, the heat of it burning his top lip. 'Bastard!' he exclaimed, then laughed as Posh did the same. 'Yeah, maybe I'll get a bait out and let the bugger cool down a bit,' he decided.

Once they were both fishing, they moved back towards the cover of the boathouse in the knowledge that their alarms would alert them to any foolhardy pike in the area. As they stood there, slowly drinking the soup, they gradually came back to life and chatted about the previous evening, the previous season, Smiffy's University antics, and the prospect of the coming season. Smiffy was due to leave University in the summer, but was seriously considering staying on to take a further degree, which would stand him in very good stead for the course he wanted to go, that being into the National Trust.

'Yeah, one more year to finish my Ecology degree, then I reckon I'm pretty set. Spoken to a couple of people already and they seem to be crying out for new people at the mo, so it could be just the right time. Got some bloody good lakes as well, mate, and lots of 'em. Found out about a few round this neck of the woods, and the word is there may be a vacancy for the Forest pretty soon, so me and you could be doing some serious stuff in the future.'

'What, like this ain't serious enough,' said Posh, a little indignantly.

'No, I don't mean that, mate. This is the nuts, no doubt about that. But some of these Trust waters, they're untapped, nobody fishing 'em at all. Just something to think about when we've had 'em all from here, eh.' Smiffy smiled at that, and drained the cup of a selection of vegetables and pieces of chicken.

'Bloody hell!' exclaimed Posh, whilst dropping his cup and running to the rods. His alarm had been turned down low and all he'd heard was a faint buzzing, then he'd seen his indicator dancing beneath his rod. He lifted into a decent fish that took a few yards of line before kiting left towards the near margin. He walked down towards it, but then it made off back out into the lake, rising like a marlin before crashing back onto the surface.

'Hoo, hoo!' whooped Smiffy, seeing that it was at least a decent double, and grabbing the landing net in preparation. The fish kited back into the deep margin, but pretty soon the exercise began to take its toll and, with net outstretched, Smiffy scooped it up in the dark mesh.

'Happy New Year!' declared Smiffy, and shook his friend's outstretched hand. 'Waddya reckon, Smiffy?' he asked as his friend held it behind the gills and removed the hooks with the forceps.

'Ohh, I'll give you, errr, sixteen I reckon.' He then laid it down for Posh to examine, and pick up, to agree or disagree with his friend's assessment.

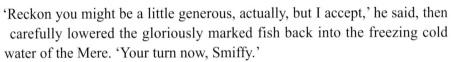

'Reckon you might be a little generous, actually, but I accept,' he said, then carefully lowered the gloriously marked fish back into the freezing cold water of the Mere. 'Your turn now, Smiffy.'

As the light began to fade, Smiffy managed to snaffle a small jack pike, but then the lack of soup and the creeping cold made up their minds for them, and they decided to pack up and head for the hills.

'Wonder how Old Ted is?' said Smiffy as they hoisted their rods and prepared to leave.

'Err, dunno. Saw him a couple of days ago, over by the point, not seen him since. What d'you reckon?' asked Posh.

'Well, might be nice to pop over and see him. And he's bound to have that good old rabbit stew on the range, ain't he?' said Smiffy, with a grin. With that, they rested their rods against the boathouse wall and made for Sutton Woods.

Once again, the winter was there to test them. The year had been full of new sensations and new dangers, especially for the occupants of the old pike lake, who had seen little like it before.

The Common and The Poached Mirror had both had cause to learn anew lessons they'd long forgotten, but those lessons were so easy to fade, so fleeting.

The winter claimed a few casualties, as it always did, it was like a sacrificial offering from the rest of the seasons. Amongst them, a common of decent proportions hadn't been able to overcome the trauma of capture towards the end of the year and died, lodged deep beneath the snags, never to be found.

But soon, the winter sun grew stronger, and spring's hands warmed it and spread it across the land. The fish moved from their semi-dormant state in readiness for the birth of spring, and the bounty it would bring. The coming seasons would see more dangers to face and overcome, or to succumb to and hence, battle to survive.

Chapter Thirty Three
Obscured by Clouds

ooking back, Stan couldn't believe how lucky they'd been. True to his word, Peter had left it until the end of the season, in mid-March, before broaching the subject of a new stocking of carp.

'Spoke to Stuart the other day,' he said to Stan, as they walked past the last house, and towards the West Woods. 'His fish seem to be fine, no ill effects from the introductions. In fact, a couple of the new fish were caught towards the end of the season, which cheered the locals no end.'

Stan was unsurprised by this, he knew that the new fish would be fine, it would be the originals that would suffer if there were any diseases transmitted. He forced a smile and asked, 'So, what's the plan then, Peter? I think we all need to sit down and discuss it, don't you? If we agree that there needs to be a top up of stock, we need to decide numbers, size, strains, when to introduce them. We can't just bung someone a few quid and drop a van load of fish into the lake, that would be suicidal.'

'Stan, Stan, I know. Believe me, I've given this a great deal of thought since Christmas and I value your input hugely, you know that, so I wouldn't dream of "bunging someone a few quid", trust me.'

Stan smiled a little, then carried on with his plan. 'Well, look, I'm up to my eyes for the rest of the week, and me and Jean are away at the weekend, so what about we sit down next week, the four of us, and decide on a workable plan.'

Peter nodded at the idea and they parted, with Peter arranging to talk to John and Simon in order to set up a committee meeting. He, however, didn't know what Stan knew, and that was that John was away on holiday from Saturday for a fortnight, not returning until the very beginning of April. That would allow just a little longer for any problems to reveal themselves at the Hatch. After that, however, it was going to be extremely difficult to stop the stocking, and Stan still had a very bad feeling about the whole thing.

'Stan, I think I owe you a huge apology,' Peter said. John, Simon and Stan were standing at the bar in The Green Man, awaiting Peter's arrival, and had just begun discussing John's holiday, when Peter came blustering in with his apology.

'What for, Peter? What are you talking about?' Stan had a horrible feeling that he knew exactly what Peter was talking about.

'You were right, Stan. About those fish, you were right,' began Peter. 'I've just got off the phone to a very distraught Stuart Goldsmith. His fish are dying, Stan. They found four of them today, washed up, bloated, dead for a week or so they think.' Whilst Peter took a huge swallow from his pint glass, Stan felt sick to his stomach. Those fantastic fish in the Hatch, how old must they have been? How many more would die? Oh, bloody hell, why don't people think!

'What, err, what sort of size, you know, the dead ones, what sort of size were they?' he asked, numbed. Apparently they'd been very bloated, beginning to decompose, but they'd estimated them to have been over twenty pounds each. That evening was not one of the best that they'd spent in The Green Man.

Within a fortnight the full extent of the tragedy had unfolded. More than a dozen of the original stock had been found, the last one seemingly having only just died – a beautifully scaled mirror of over thirty pounds. Stan didn't want to know anymore, he just thanked his lucky stars that Peter had seen sense at Christmas, otherwise, well, he didn't want to think what the repercussions might have been. And now the season was under way again. Less than half the members had rejoined, which had caused Peter quite some dismay, but it didn't take long for word to filter out, and mates of existing members soon filled the holes until there were almost fifty members again. Stan had interviewed most of them, and was pretty pleased with the mix. There were a few more serious carp anglers this time, but there were still a few that he knew would only fish two or three times a year. That was fine, as long as he and Neil kept an eye out he felt sure that it would be a good season – and it got off to a flyer.

Chris and Ben had joined again, as he knew they would, and they'd even popped over a couple of times in the close season to see if he needed any help, although he was sure it was for a good look round, really. But, hey, he would have done the same, and their offer was kind but unnecessary. Living near Portsmouth, they were less than an hour away, and he had a feeling that they would be very good, loyal members over the coming years, and hoped that they got their due reward. And within a fortnight of the start, they did.

As he'd expected, the start of the season hadn't been as hectic as the previous year, but there were still more than twenty anglers on the lake, and that situation didn't change for almost a week. By the second Sunday, however, the car parks were almost empty and Chris and Ben turned up at midday with a full three days in front of them. Up until then half a dozen carp had been landed, the largest being the thirty one that Stan had stalked the previous year, and a couple of good'uns had been lost as well. Chris and Ben decided, after a good look round the lake, to set up on the point of the old Mere, where Neil had caught Taurus from the previous season. A few fish had been seen in the area over the previous few days, and the departing angler had caught a small, double figure common during the night. Ben opted to fish the right hand side of the swim, looking out towards the pads, whilst Chris was behind him, fishing through a hole in the ever-burgeoning reed margin – a hole that Stan himself had fished a decade earlier with mixed success.

On his early morning stroll, on Monday, Stan stopped for a chat and was pleased to hear that Ben had landed a twenty five pound common from the pads, earlier that morning. Chris had seen a couple of fish at distance, out towards the boathouse, but had no plans to fish at that distance. He was certain that the fish patrolled the margins of the bay to his left, and the very point that he was on, so persevered with his close in tactics.

The next morning, Stan's mobile rang as he was in the bathroom. He picked it up, still with a mouthful of toothpaste.

'Yerrp?' he gargled. There was mayhem on the other end, shouting and whooping, and a voice that simply said 'YESS!'

He quickly spat out the toothpaste and readjusted the phone. 'Hello, who's that?' he asked.

'Stan? Stan, it's Chris, YESSS! I've 'ad a ****ing whacker, mate, a whacker! You coming down to witness it?'

'Chris? Bloody hell, mate, well done. Give me …. ten minutes. Sack it up and we'll do some good photos. You weighed it?'

'No mate,' Chris said, 'but I think it's that one that Bob had. Sid's Fish?'

Stan punched the air and just said, 'Excellent! I'll be there in ten. Put the kettle on.'

It was, indeed, Sid's Fish at a huge weight of fifty eight and a half pounds, and once again smashed it's captors personal best by many, many pounds. Stan couldn't have been happier for Chris, and he knew that Ben felt just the same. To them it was **their** capture, and it wouldn't be too long before Ben was holding another of their fish for the camera.

No further large fish graced the bank during May, nor June, although tales of lost leviathans were becoming more common. Stan suspected that a lot of the lost fish were either fabrications or else genuine losses but embellished a little, for whatever bizarre reason the captor felt necessary. Stan had managed a few short sessions and had carried on with his mobile approach with a little success, although he'd caught nothing that he felt warranted a wet weighsling. Neil, however, fared a little better.

He'd not managed to get many nights in during the first month or so of the season, and to be fair he was quite happy walking the banks, chatting to the anglers and generally getting to know everybody and everything. Not long after Chris's capture of Sid's Fish, however, he fancied a bit of a go. This was, in part, down to Ted. As usual, they'd spent a bit of time discussing nature and her ways, and Ted had waxed lyrical about the power of the moon and the sun; the new moon, and the last quarter being good for rabbiting, and trout fishing. Neil took this all in and then went onto the Internet to learn a little bit more about moon phases. It transpired that the moon was in its last quarter when Chris had his success, last week, so would now be new. Surely worth a little go, thought Neil.

He'd fancied the point, again, for obvious reasons, but there were other people who also did their homework, and a couple of old members had occupied the two swims on there. So, after a walk around for an hour, Neil opted to fish the Poachers' Pads. A couple of fish had been hooked there early on, but little else since, however Neil always fancied that the fish visited the area quite regularly and hoped that this would coincide with one of those visits. By early evening he had all three baits out, although the one he really fancied was on the spot that Smiffy had caught from the previous summer. He sprinkled a few boilies around each bait, but dispensed with the hemp and pellets as they had attracted quite a bit of bream and tench attention of late.

As the sun dropped to his left he heard someone behind him and turned to see Ted standing there.

'New moon tonight, young Becks. Good choice,' said Ted. 'Good spot, too. I sin a couple of carp leaping here first thing this morning, just on the back of the pads. Big as well.'

'As girt pigs?' asked Neil, wryly.

'Not quite that big, lad, but plenty big enough for a whipper-snapper like you, don't you worry,' Ted countered. They chatted for a further hour, whilst the sun sank and the bats came out to dance and spin, then Ted wandered away towards home, passing behind the point and stopping for a while, listening.

No sooner had Ted left than a fish rolled just as he had said, at the back of the pads, and Neil's confidence grew. An hour later, just after he'd nodded off, another crashed off to his right and he awoke with a start. No moon meant a pitch-black night, but as his eyes adjusted his mouth dropped at the scene above him. The sky was absolutely crammed with stars, more than he was sure he'd ever seen before, and it was almost impossible to identify any of the constellations because there were so many more stars masking them. He lay on his bedchair for ten minutes or so, marvelling at the sight, then spotted a shooting star to his right and wishing on it quickly. His eyes had barely closed when his wish came true and he was standing in the stygian blackness playing a carp of indeterminate size or whereabouts. The rod bucked and the reel hissed, but he had no idea what was really happening, feeling almost in a dream state, and it was with some surprise that he was soon peering down at a net full of dark, black carp.

His headtorch was like a laser beam and blinded him temporarily, but as he got his sight back, albeit with bright spots before his eyes, he gazed down on a long, leathery carp. Long, so long, but with very little depth to go with it. Nevertheless, he was sure that this was a big carp and so carefully slipped it into a weigh-sling and hoisted it onto the scales. The needle bounced around the forty pound mark, but then he realised that he hadn't zeroed the scales, so it was probably about thirty eight – hoo-bloody-ray! Once the fish was sacked and safely in the margins he sent a text message to Stan, knowing that he would be round early to take the photos.

As he gradually calmed down, he lay on his bed and stared skywards. What to call this one, he thought? As he scanned the star-filled sky, he made out Orion's Belt, then picked out the bright star above, at its armpit – Beetlejuice. He smiled to himself. Perfect, just perfect.

It was Jim and Lee's first session at the lake since last November. They'd spent the winter fishing a couple of ponds local to them, in Kent, and trying to devise a method to outwit the huge Mere carp that seemed to reside mainly in the snags. Then, by chance, Lee had picked up a copy of a carp magazine and read an article about a particularly snaggy lake in France, and the methods employed to extract the carp from there. Once he'd shown it to Jim they were both convinced that this would help them catch the fish, once and for all. The July session was just to get seen again; the plan they had couldn't be put into effect for another couple of months, when the nights drew in and the cover of darkness could be used to their advantage. Even so, it was nice for Lee to catch a fair sized common from the pads, the largest he'd had from the lake so far, but way below what they were both dreaming of. For now, though, that was fine. They'd pop down a couple more times over the next month or so before putting their plan into serious action, during September.

As Ted walked back to his cabin he mulled over what he had heard. He thought he'd recognised the pair fishing the point; a couple that had fished towards the end of last year. The big lad seemed harmless, but he wasn't sure about the other one – something about the eyes. They'd been talking about a lake in France, something about snags and braid. He couldn't hear it all, but he felt a little uneasy about it, it was almost conspiratorial. He'd have to keep an eye on this pair, just in case.

'Last chance I'll get before I'm off again, Quill,' said Buzz, on the other end of the line.

'No problem, mate, you can be my guest. It's not that busy at the moment. Haven't seen Sid much of late, what with his new baby and all that, he don't really have the time at the mo.' Stan was pleased to be hearing from his mate after a couple of months of radio silence, but he knew that was apt to happen if he was on a particularly sensitive job. 'When you coming down, then?'

A few days later they sat by the lake, in front of the boathouse, and mulled over the possibilities. August had been warm, with very little in the way of fish activity, but then there had been very little in the way of angling activity either, and the only guys Stan had seen regularly were Chris and Ben, Bob and a couple of bream anglers from Swindon. Invariably there would be at least half a dozen fishing at the weekend, but the weekdays were very quiet, so he and Buzz had opted for a few days in the middle of the week prior to the August Bank Holiday. The weather was still warm, but the forecast was for typical Bank Holiday weather – wind and rain – which would suit them perfectly. Choice of swim was difficult. It was so hard not to go into the Post Office and adjacent area, but Stan had been keeping an eye on the snags for a while and had seen nothing significant in there. Most of the decent captures, this season, had been from the south bank and as they sat looking across at the Poachers' Pads, they couldn't deny it looked a pretty good bet.

'Right, tell you what,' said Stan, 'you go over there. I quite fancy a dabble in the corner here. Not many people have fished it, really, and I just happen to have been dropping a bit of bait in there for a few weeks. 'Bout time I gave it a go, I reckon.' He'd indicated the reedy corner to the right of the boathouse, next to the West Woods bank, and Buzz looked at it for the first time.

'Hold on there, Quill. Are you holding out on me?' he growled. Stan laughed and put up his hands.

'Mate, it's up to you, you're my guest, you choose.'

This gave Buzz cause to furrow his brow and look askance at Stan. 'Hmm. Now he plays the old double bluff. It's worse than fishing with Sid. No, what am I saying? Nothing's worse than fishing with Sid.' Stan laughed and stretched.

'Well, come on, let's do some bloody fishing, for God's sake. Where d'you fancy mate? Clock's ticking,'

Buzz growled under his breath, then picked up the arms of his barrow. 'Best you're not scamming me, Quill, old boy.' Then he was off, round to the pads, leaving Stan grinning behind him.

At four in the morning, the sight and sound of something as big as a bear in the mouth of your bivvy is enough to make even the most hardened soul quake, and Stan certainly quaked for a few moments.

'Whaa! What the … bloody hell, Buzz, what the …'

'Ha! Hah! Old Buzz has just landed himself a monster. Come on, Quill, we gotta be weighing this old boy pretty quick. He fought like a lion and I'm not sure I wanna be sacking him up for too long, boy.'

Stan staggered along behind his large but extremely happy companion, following him back through the black woods to his devastated swim. It put him in mind of the first time he'd seen him, all those years ago, standing up to his waist in water, his sleeping bag still round his legs and his brolly and bedchair looking like they'd been mugged. How pleasing it was that, even after all this time, the effect of a run on a carp lake could still render his mate an uncontrollable wreck.

The sling was on the mat, but the net was nowhere to be seen. Headtorches on, they scanned the area for scales and camera, then Buzz went over to the lake and removed the bankstick he'd used to secure the net in the margin. He grunted with the exertion of lifting the huge fish from the lake, and a flash of torchlight on its flank gave Stan a hint as to its identity. Then, once laid on the mat, he was sure.

'It's Sid's Fish, mate. Bloody hell, it looks massive!'

'It is bloody massive!' exclaimed Buzz. 'Sid, hurr, hurrr, just can't get away from him, eh?'

Buzz grunted again as he lofted the scales and Stan shone the torch on the dial, reading it as the needle span to a halt.

'Fifty seven … fifty seven .. twelve. Yeah, fifty seven twelve. Bloody well done, Buzz, my old mate. Now what was that you were saying about scamming?'

Buzz laughed, then settled the fish down on the mat whilst Stan got the cameras ready.

'You sure you don't want to sack it up for a few hours, mate? Be light pretty soon.'

'Nah, come on, let's get the old girl back, she's had a hard night,' said Buzz, and after the photos that's exactly what they did.

Later that day, Stan was sitting with Neil and Ted at the back of his little swim, watching a couple of fish mooching about on the gravel shelf in front of the swim. The same gravel shelf that he'd lowered a bait onto a couple of hours earlier. The same bait that a very angry carp picked up a few minutes later and proceeded to take for a guided tour of that corner of the lake. Eventually, after twenty minutes of frantic battling, Neil netted a long, leathery carp for Stan, and recognised it straightaway.

'Beetlejuice!' he shouted, leaving Stan and Ted both slightly bemused because he had omitted to tell anyone of his naming of the fish. After the explanation, and the quizzical looks, they weighed the lovely beast at a little over thirty- nine pounds, and Stan smiled at Buzz as he realised that he probably had been scammed, just a little.

A fine session, for both of them, and one that probably wouldn't be repeated this side of Christmas.

All in all, the season was going along fine. Sid's Fish was becoming fairly popular, as were a couple of the others. It would be interesting to see where the others were hiding, but then it needed a few more people to be looking, really. For now, Stan was pretty pleased with the way things were going, he just hoped it stayed that way. Imagine if those fish had been stocked in the Mere.......

Chapter Thirty Four

Shine on You Crazy Diamond

Neil stood in the doorway of Ted's cabin, peering into the gloom. He'd waited by the boathouse for almost an hour, becoming more and more concerned. Ted was never late; never.

'Ted?' he called, tentatively. 'Ted, you in there?' From the next room came a retching sound and then a low groan, and immediately Neil knew something was not right. Walking slowly across the room, feeling as if he were trespassing, he called out again. 'Ted, it's Neil. You alright, mate?' Another moaning sound came from the direction of the small bathroom, so Neil walked over and carefully pushed the door open a few inches. Before him, Ted knelt on the floor, his head over the toilet bowl, and a low moaning came from him. Neil knelt down beside him and put a hand on his arm, at which point Ted slowly turned his head. His face was ashen, and wreathed in clammy sweat; a dribble of bile dangling from his lip.

'Bloody hell, Ted, what's happened?' Ted didn't have the will or the strength to answer, and just turned his head back to the bowl, a spasm of pain chasing across his face and causing him to double over. Neil realised he had to act quickly and was soon putting a plan into action.

He would have to move him, just to the door so that he could get him into the Land Rover, then he could drive him… somewhere. Stan! He had to call Stan, get some help. By the time Stan answered, Neil had pulled the Land Rover to the door and was making sure that Ted would be able to get in the passenger seat. A quick explanation got Stan up to speed, although he had little medical experience so couldn't think of anything better than Neil's idea. Into the Rover, through the woods and past the Mere to the main road where they'd meet up, then on to the hospital, ten miles away.

Moving Ted was traumatic, for both of them, and it took all of Neil's strength and Ted's willpower to get it done at all. Once in the car Ted slumped against the window, doubling over in pain every minute or so. Neil was beside himself. Ted was an old guy; it could be anything at his age, and Neil couldn't help but fear the worst.

Even at five miles an hour, the journey through the woods was a torture, and it was all that Ted could do to stop himself screaming with the pain. In what seemed like a hell's eternity, but was no more than ten minutes, they eventually reached the joyous tarmac of the main road where Stan was waiting, worried stupid. A quick look in the window told him all he needed to know, and he decided to go on ahead to alert the hospital of Ted's imminent arrival. Neil tried to balance haste with comfort, which was pretty difficult at the best of times, but in Ted's old Land Rover, almost impossible, but suddenly there was a 'Hospital' sign.

Stan's plan had worked and a small team of nurses were waiting with a gurney to receive Ted. His transfer was excruciating to watch, but then he was being whisked away down a corridor and through some plastic doors. Stan and Neil sat and waited for half an hour before Stan suggested that Neil go back to the Mere and let John and Daniel know what was happening. Although he was unhappy at leaving Ted without knowing what was wrong, he reluctantly agreed, and drove a whole heap faster leaving than he had arriving. Stan sat and fidgeted. Then he paced the small waiting room like an expectant father. The clock on the wall seemed to have hands made of lead, incapable of moving faster than a snail. After what seemed like hours, a nurse came into the room.

'Uh, are you Mr Wright's son?' she asked.

'No. No, just a friend. I don't think he has any family. How is he? Will he be okay?'

'He should be fine, hopefully you got him here just in time,' said the nurse. 'It's appendicitis, quite unusual for someone of Mr Wright's age, and pretty painful I would think. But it hadn't burst, which is a blessing, although it's very inflamed. We'll operate very shortly and, if all goes smoothly, he should be able to leave in the next couple of days.'

Stan's relief was palpable, and the nurse smiled at him in that practiced way. 'Oh, thank God. I didn't know, I mean, you know, with him being quite old, well, you think all sorts of things. So, a couple of days. Err, that might be a bit of a problem. He lives on his own, out in the woods. Got no one to help him, really. How long will it be before he's properly up and about?

'In the woods?' said the nurse, with a frown. 'Well, I would think that he'll be fully mobile within a week, but if you say he's on his own, in the woods, then I'll have to see how long we can keep him in here.' She was no longer smiling, and Stan began to wither under the gaze. At that moment, Neil rushed back into the room, and, seeing the nurse, immediately launched into a volley of questions. Before the nurse could reply, Stan took him by the arm and sat him down.

'It's alright, Neil, it's appendicitis, that's all. Should be out of here in a week,' said Stan, casting a sideways glance at the nurse. She looked back with a quizzical glare, then left.

'Bloody hell, is that all?' said Neil. 'I had mine out when I was about six, in hospital for about four days, that was all. Oh, mate, I tell you, I really thought it was, well, you know, something… big.'

Stan couldn't help but laugh. 'Well, Neil, I'm sure Ted will be most pleased to hear that the pain he was in was only something small!'

It was like drifting out of a dream. He could hear noises, see lights, but neither sound nor vision was in focus. To his left there came a groaning sound, and through the mists of anaesthesia he thought he could see Thommo in the next bed, his head bandaged but still seeping blood. Across the way someone cried out, once, twice, then fell silent. His memory faded in and out much the same as his senses; sound of cars, buses, a child shouting abuse at them as they marched along the road, Thommo sneering at a gang of youths, fags dangling from their own, sneering mouths. Then quiet, no kids, no shouts, just a car. Feet running, bodies swerving this way and that. Then blinding light before all-enveloping dark. Thommo groaned again, muttered about a fag, a nurse came and spoke quietly to him then faded in pastels and shimmering light, before the dark came again.

'Mr Wright?'

'Ted!'

'Mr Wright? Can you hear me?'

'Ted, you old bugger, you alright?'

'Mr Wright, how are you feeling?'

'Come on Ted, you old f......'

'Ah, there you are, how are you feeling?' Thommo faded like an early autumn mist and was replaced by the cherubic face of an angel. 'Everything went very well, Mr Wright. Caught it just in time, but no complications, so you should be right as rain in no time,' said the angel.

'Wha… Cough! Cough!' Ted's throat was as dry as the Sahara and as he ran his tongue across his lips he felt them, cracked and parched.

'Hold on, Mr Wright. Here you are, slowly now.' The angel gently lifted his head and held a beaker of cold water for him to sip. He wanted to take great draughts of it, but she let him have just enough to wet his lips before laying his head back down. 'Just rest for a while, now. I'll pop back in a little while and see if you're up for a little something to eat.' With that, the angel turned and left, leaving an angel-sized hole in Ted's memory. Sleep returned, and he dreamed of Thommo, and angels with flasks of cold, cold water. And a danger just out of sight, out of reach.

They'd planned it all to perfection. After reading the article that Lee had seen, he and Jim sat down and devised a plan to fish the snags with confidence, but most of it was of a dubious nature, to say the least. In the article, it had shown how to fish around corners and obstacles by the use of long banksticks, line clips and balloons as floats. The latter would be of no use, but they'd worked out a method of getting the line as far away from the bank as possible, utilising an extra long storm pole and rubberised rod rest. Next was the line, and it seemed that the only option, for both strength and indication properties, was going to be braided line, so Jim spooled up one of his big spools with a hundred quid's worth of line and prayed that it was going to be money well spent. The hooklink was a different matter, and Jim had decided he was taking no chances with the vicious mussels that clung to every underwater branch, so opted for the strongest material he could find – wire trace. If it could survive the ravages from a pike's teeth, then he was sure it would overcome the attentions of the razor sharp shells. So that was it; just one other thing – how to get it to where he wanted it? That was why they decided to leave it until later in the year, because the nights were drawing in, and under cover of the longer hours of darkness he could take out the bait in his small inflatable and drop it right into the snags.

It was all perfect, and after a couple of earlier sorties, the real work began in the middle of September. As Ted lay on an operating table, ten miles away, Jim and Lee turned up for the first of their three-day, midweek holidays. The fact that this also coincided with one of the most productive times of the year was no mistake, and when they saw that the swims were free, their confidence soared. That is to say, Jim's confidence soared. Ever the stooge, Lee just resigned himself to being the dumb henchman, when, in fact, it was he who was regularly catching carp on their trips. Jim dismissed this as necessity and concentrated on the task at hand.

By a little after nine o'clock, the sun had finally left the western skyline and Jim quickly inflated the small craft. The sound of the air entering the valve seemed so loud he was sure that all around could hear, but that was just natural paranoia. Within a minute or so the boat was afloat in the margin, and Jim was gingerly getting himself settled in it. He had a small headtorch with him, but he hoped not to have to use it, then, taking the baited hook and lead, and clamping it carefully between his teeth, he pushed away from the bank, leaving Lee holding the rod and paying out the line. He rowed away from the bank initially, so as to clear the right hand margin, then moved back towards the snags, the line tugging at the side of his mouth as he went. The wind was picking up a little so he had to be quite forceful with the oars and pretty soon he saw the outline of a branch in front of him. Suddenly panicked, he slowed himself and grabbed the lead, preparing to drop it over the side. The boat scraped alongside another branch and he realised he was losing control. Swearing quietly to himself he spun round and reached over the side, then let the lead drop from his hand. The boat had drifted a little further towards the bank when he realised that the line would, by now, have sunk and he would be unable to utilise the storm pole he had placed so carefully, earlier on. Oh well, too bloody late now, and he rowed back to the bank nearest the snags and dragged the boat out, hoisting it onto his head and walking back to his swim. By the time he had taken the slack out of the line, almost half an hour had passed since he'd set sail, and he pondered the random nature of his bait placement. But it was close enough, of that he was sure, and so he clipped on the indicator and flicked on the alarm.

He'd never used braid before, and by four in the morning he wondered whether he would ever use it again. The first twitchy take occurred within ten minutes of him setting the indicator and he struck the rod immediately, but to no avail. This time it only took twenty minutes to get everything settled, and although the bait placement was still a bit random, he'd managed to feed the line over the storm pole so was happier with that side of things. But not for long.

By midnight he'd been back out a further three times but was still fishless. What was happening? Line bites? Bream? Crayfish even? He knew not what it was; all he knew was that he was getting more frustrated by the second. Along from him, in the South Westerly, Lee was cursing quietly to himself. This plan was definitely not going anywhere, and he was getting the full brunt of Jim's frustration. Despite that, it was he who was playing the first carp of the session and was elated when he saw, in the torchlight, the unmistakable outline of a long, scaly mirror. He weighed it quickly, before sacking it, and at thirty-five pounds it was by far their best fish from the Mere thus far. Jim, strangely, didn't seem as pleased as Lee, and merely grunted when he trotted along to tell him, then turned over and tried to get some sleep.

'It's the braid, mate; it'll pick up everything. Bit of weed on the line, strong gust of wind, the lot. Suggest you try not to hit anything unless its pulled it out of the clip, or dropped right back.' This advice, from a mate of Jim's who regularly fished in France, wasn't exactly music to his ears, but at least it provided a few answers, and the following night, although another of little sleep, was spent more on the bank than in the boat. The wind meant that the alarm was constantly bleeping, until Jim had the idea of turning the sensitivity right down, then it wasn't until it was ripped from the line clip that Jim knew of any carp attention. The braid did its job, and although only a little over twenty pounds, Jim regarded the common as a huge success, and left the next morning knowing that this could well produce the result he was looking for. Before they left, Jim deposited a couple of kilos of bait amongst the snag in preparation for their return, the following Monday.

'Yeah, Ted. Poor Neil was beside himself, didn't know what to do at first, but he coped pretty well, I reckon.' Stan sat next to Ted's bed and munched on a couple more grapes. Ted was recovering fairly well, and desperately wanted to be out of there, but the doctor wanted to do 'a few more tests, just to make sure' so he was resigned to another couple of days in hospital before he could leave.

'Young Neil; he's alright, Stan. Copes well under pressure, that boy. How's it going over the Mere? Any problems?' He had concerns, but he couldn't put his finger on them so was loath to say anything to Stan, lest he thought it was just the ramblings of an old fool.

'Yeah, everything seems fine. Been a few fish out. Some guy had a thirty-five the other day. Lee, you know, the big guy who fishes with the other one?' said Stan. Ted's mind focussed a little – that was something to do with it, he was sure.

'Hmm, keep an eye on them, Stan. Not too sure about them two.' Stan nodded, having a similar feeling himself, then looked up at the clock.

'Blimey, gotta go, Ted. I'm actually going angling tonight, and I've gotta pick up Jean from Salisbury before that. You take it easy, mate. I'll give the ward a call tomorrow, see what's happening, then I'll come over and get you as soon as they say. Just rest up, mate, be plenty for you to do when you get back.' With that, Stan strode out of the ward and left Ted to his thoughts. Two more days. Bugger.

'Right, I reckon we've got it sussed now, Lee. Reckon we can get it all done in ten minutes, in and out.' Jim stood in the swim and looked along the bank, watching the sun glistened waves lapping the bank to his right. He was desperate to get a bait out by the snags and had been sorely tempted to try it in daylight, whilst no one was about, but then someone had set up on the Point, opposite, and although it was almost a quarter of a mile away, the guy would have to be blind to miss a bright yellow inflatable bobbing around in front of him. For now, he'd have to be patient, and just carry on feeding the fish. He'd spied three or four shapes in the deep, dark water beneath the snags, and was certain that at least one of them was on his list of desirables, so he went back and scattered a few more baits around the edge of the snags, in the hope of enticing them from beneath the tree. The evening seemed to drag on forever, but eight o'clock saw the last rays of the sun dance on the clouds and the sky turned blood red on the western horizon.

The plan worked perfectly now, and within fifteen minutes Jim was back in his swim, line adjusted, alarm on and ready to do battle. He felt so confident he thought he was going to burst, and barely acknowledged the fact that Lee had, yet again, caught a fine mirror from the island margins. A cursory glance of the thirty-pound carp, followed by some quick photos, was all the attention he gave it before taking up station in the chair next to his rods. He decided to sit by the rods for the first night, thermally wrapped and ready to pounce, and with a stack of Red Bull by his side. At eleven o'clock the indicator lifted an inch to the rod and the alarm gave a single bleep. Jim watched as the isotope slowly dropped back down, with no noise from the alarm. Nothing. A couple of minutes later the same thing was repeated and Jim put it down to the slight breeze that was blowing towards him. The indicator did not drop back this time, but Jim was so intent on watching the indicator that he couldn't see the rod tip bending and bending. As the pressure told and the line pulled from the clip, Jim was so surprised he almost tumbled backwards in his chair, kicking the rod in the process and watching it flip up in the air. He jumped up and grabbed the rod, heaving it round to the left and feeling a solid resistance. This was it! This was what he'd been waiting for. But he'd waited too long, too long.

Another mouthful of food and silt, and The Common's defences were gradually being lowered. It had spent much of the past few days grazing on the abundance of food beneath the snaggy branches, and was becoming less cautious and more greedy. The Big Mirror was less cavalier, having a vague memory of danger, but it still could not resist the bounty offered to it. Along with the four other fish, they grazed with carefree abandon beneath the night sky. Another mouthful and The Common sensed something not quite right. It blew the mouthful of food and silt back out, but something remained, and a distant memory was triggered once again. It shook its head once, twice, then tried to move off, but was halted in its tracks. This was bad, very bad. Using its huge paddle of a tail and its muscular frame it thrashed into the deep recesses of the snag tree, sharp shells grazing its sides and removing scales as it went. The pain was sharp, not usual, and the further it penetrated the refuge the more the pain increased. Its flesh was tearing inside its mouth, and along the side of its face something harsh rubbed back and forth. Panic had taken over but, for the first time in its long life, its power was useless. There was nowhere to go, and the more it tried to escape, the greater the pain, the tearing, the abuse. But it still had so much strength. It had fought not at all, not run a hundred yards across the lake, not thrashed its huge tail in anger and fear and torn away from its would-be captor. It had moved mere yards, and it still had one last chance. The pain was excruciating, like nothing it had felt before, but it had to try, and so, sensing an opening through the branches, used every muscle in its body and drove for freedom. Pain! So much pain. But then it was free and tore across the lake as fast as it could, its wary cohorts in hot pursuit. But the price for freedom had been so high, the hooklink slicing through the side of its face and ripping a huge lump of sinew and flesh from its mouth. As it slowed its headlong charge for freedom, shock began to take over and its senses slowed. It would need to hide, to rest, to try to allow its body to recover. But it was tired, so tired.

The rod bucked two or three times, but the braid was strong and Jim knew that he was in control. He held on for dear life, ignoring the screaming voice in his head that was telling him to loosen the clutch. Couldn't. Had to keep the pressure on. Once again the fish drove for freedom and the rod tip nearly hit the surface of the lake, but Jim held firm and began to see his name in lights. How big would this be? Would it beat the record? Imagine that. Suddenly, with a huge burst of power, the fish thrashed once more, and the rod sprung back, before going solid again. Bloody hell, thought I'd lost it, he thought. There was no more thrashing, just a steady too-ing and fro-ing. After ten minutes of this, Jim feared the worse, so put the rod in the rests and ran down to get Lee. When they got back nothing had moved and Jim sat down with his head in his hands.

'What about if I go out there, try to pick up the line?' suggested Lee. 'It might just be caught round a snag. That fish ain't coming off, not unless it leaves its head on your bloody hook.' The words filtered through, and after a few minutes Jim decided it was worth a go.

'You gonna be okay in that boat, Lee,' he asked, seriously. 'It ain't that big, mate. Be careful.' Lee just grunted and made off up the bank with the boat on his head. He'd also taken a headtorch, and as much as they'd tried not to use one, this time it might be a necessity. He entered the lake about sixty yards from the snags and slowly rowed out whilst Jim held the rod high. Within seconds Lee felt the line on his face, so took it in his hand and very slowly eased himself along it, and as he got closer to the snag he called for Jim to let a bit of line off, then watched as the line disappeared beneath the waves, going almost straight down. It was no good, he had to risk the torch, so shone it down through the water to see if he could spot the fish, but there was none. After a few moments of moving his head back and forth he caught sight of a glimmer and, concentrating, saw that it was the wire trace, attached to a branch six feet below. Oh bugger!

'It's gone, mate,' he called to Jim.

'What?' came the cry from out of the darkness.

'Gone. Hook's in a branch, I can see it. We'll need to cut the line.'

Stan had been woken by a small tench on one of the margin rods and after slipping it back into the margins and recasting that rod, had got back into bed. He thought he heard a shout, then another, and peering out could see a torch dancing on the far margin. But that wasn't the Post Office. The Post Office was off to the right, almost behind the island, that light was, well, it looked like it was coming from the snags.

'Keep an eye on them, Stan. Not sure about them two.'

Ted's words rang in his ears and he was suddenly very awake. More voices drifted back across the lake, but the wind was in the wrong direction so he couldn't make out their meaning. The light was still bobbing up and down, up and down. Are they in a bloody boat? He grabbed his car keys and made off towards his car, completely forgetting his rods. As he got to the car he knew the interior light would come on, but was pretty sure the island was definitely in the way this time. He left the headlights off and crawled along in second gear, driving by memory until he came to the end of the east bank. There he stopped and got out, walking quickly towards the Post Office swim. He could hear some more talk, so slowed a little to listen.

'Well I can't bloody bite it, can I? It's a hundred pound braid, Jim. I need a bloody knife, and a sharp one at that.' This voice seemed to be coming from the direction of the snags, and the bobbing light.

'Alright. ****ing hell, lost a ****ing great carp, now I've lost my ****ing rig.' The other guy came around the bivvy and walked swiftly towards the snags, not noticing Stan ten yards away. Oh well, thought Stan, bull by the horns, and strode along behind him. As he stopped by the snags, the guy in the boat was bobbing in the margins, awaiting the knife, so Stan moved towards them, turned on his headtorch, full beam, and said, 'Alright guys, got a problem?'

Rabbits in the headlights would be a perfect description of their reaction, and a gibbering, senseless response was all that they could manage before Stan put two and two together and made 'ban'.

'What d'yer mean? We ain't done nothing wrong,' said Jim, indignantly. Déjà vu, thought Stan, resignedly.

'Mate, I have no idea how many rules you've really broken, but have you any idea of the ramifications of using a boat on here without a bloody life jacket? Do you even know why you've been allowed to fish on here, what actually happened to leave this lake free for angling to take place again?' Stan was getting fired up now, real fired up, and although he knew that if things turned nasty he'd have little chance against these two, his feelings were getting the better of him and he felt no fear.

'Yeah, I know, mate. I'm really sorry. We're bang out of order, mate. Come on Jim, not worth arguing, we've been done, and that's it.' It was the big guy, Lee, and Stan almost felt sorry for him. The other guy kept on proclaiming his innocence until Lee finally flipped.

'For **** sake, Jim, shut up! Just shut up. It's all about you, mate, innit? Your swim, your plan, you to catch the biggie, you to be the hero. And me, I get to hold the rod, and hand you the bait, and hide the boat, and drive the car. Well I've had enough. I'm off, and if you're not ready when I've packed up you better think of another way of getting home.'

The silence was almost shattering after that, apart from the sound of Jim's chin hitting the floor.

'I'm really sorry, mate,' said Lee once more to Stan. 'This is a lovely place and we've buggered it up. Caught some nice fish though. Thanks. Might see you around.' He turned away and, dragging the boat behind him, made off towards his swim, followed by a very chagrined Jim.

When Stan picked up Ted the next day, he told him all about it, and how correct he'd been, but Ted felt no pleasure at that. What had they done that they'd blown their cover so completely? Something major must have happened, or something very bad.

So tired. The pain had subsided until just a dull ache was left, but the trauma could not be healed so easily. The great carp sought out the sanctuary of the island margins, beneath the weeping willow fronds, and moved very little for days. Its eyes gradually lost their lustre, and its great body the inability to fight. To fight the smallest of organisms. The wound was vicious, but there was no antibiotic to help

heal it, to help fight off infection. Slowly, so slowly the battle was being lost.
The final battle. After decades and decades of trauma and battles, of fighting
and surviving, finally the great carp had no more to give.
So tired, so very tired. So…

'Over there, Stan, beneath the willow. See it?' Stan and Neil were standing in Island Two, looking out towards the island, and Stan could see exactly what Neil had seen, an hour earlier, and he suddenly felt sick to his stomach. It was seventy yards away, beneath the trees, it could have been anything. Carp, pike, common, mirror. But Stan knew, he just knew.
'Yeah, I see it, Neil. Errr, better get a boat, get out and see what it is.' Neil trotted off to the boathouse to get the small rowing boat they had tied up there, whilst Stan stood and looked. Ted came up behind him in his usual silent manner, but said nothing at first. Stan sensed he was behind him, and said, 'Got a real bad feeling about this, Ted. Real bad.' Ted said nothing.
All three of them took to the boat and the closer they got, the sicker Stan felt. From ten yards away they could see that it was a common. From five that it was a big common. From next to it…

Stan could barely find the words. He sat on the bank, cradling the great carp in his arms, his eyes filling with tears. Bloody hell, he thought, it's only a bloody fish. But it wasn't; it never had been. Neil and Ted stood like pallbearers, heads bowed, looking on silently. The carp hadn't been dead long; there was no decomposition. In fact it looked in perfect condition, apart from an horrendous wound to its mouth and face. But it wasn't in perfect condition, it was dead. Gone. And Stan sat with it in his arms for five minutes, just marvelling at its beauty, its majesty, its vastness.
'What we gonna do, Stan, weigh it?' asked Neil.
'No!' growled Ted, almost the first word he'd spoken all afternoon. 'We bury her, proper. We don't need to know how big; we can see. We can see with our own eyes. Now we bury her.'
Stan looked up at Neil, then nodded. Right and proper, he thought.
They took her to the woods, dug a deep hole, wrapped her in a sack and lowered her down. Then she was gone.

A week later, Stan sat in his garden, drinking tea and reading Carp Talk. On the front was a picture of a common. '57lb' read the headline. It was a lovely fish. Beautiful. But only fifty-seven pounds. Stan stared into the middle distance. He'd held a carp so much larger than that, twice, and then he'd buried her. And nobody would know. His melancholy mood had hung over him like a cloud for the past week, but then a ray of sunshine burst through, and the clouds parted.
'Hello, Gandad!' came Maisie's lilting voice. He immediately perked up and looked

round as his granddaughter burst into the garden. 'Look, Gandad,' she demanded, and held up a jar of water suspended from a string. In it, Stan could see a couple of sticklebacks, and he beamed at Maisie.

'What have you got there, baby?' he asked.

Maisie peered closely at the jar and said 'Sticky backs, Gandad.' Stan laughed, Maisie smiled, then Laura walked in and presented him with his new granddaughter. Oh, well, life goes on, he thought. And if it goes on like this, then that would be just fine.

Smiffy and Posh walked away from the grave, although 'grave' was probably too grand a word for it; just a big oak tree, where a big carp had been buried. Saying very little they walked through the woods towards Ted's cabin. The leaves were turning autumn gold, and most of the creatures of the wood were busying themselves for the coming winter.

'He's been a bit quiet of late,' said Posh. 'I think the combination of the hospital and then The Common dying sort of knocked the stuffing out of him a bit.'

As they reached the cabin, Posh stopped and looked around. Something was missing, but he couldn't put his finger on it. He knocked at the door. No answer.

'Ted,' he called, 'you in there?' No answer. Oh no, not again. He pushed the door open, and walked in slowly, followed by Smiffy. There was no sound. The cabin was cool, which was unusual as the stove was on most of the time, but this time not.

'Ted,' he called, louder. Nothing.

'What's this?' said Smiffy, and Posh turned towards him. He was standing at the table, looking at something. Posh walked over to see what had caught his attention. A couple of books sat side by side, and on top of them was a maroon beret. He picked up the beret and quickly inspected it, then put it back on the table before looking at the books. 'Dune' sat next to 'Wind in the Willows' and his breath caught in his throat.

Smiffy picked up one of the books and noticed a scribbled note underneath so, putting down the book, he picked up the note and read it.

'He's gone, hasn't he?' said Smiffy. Posh looked at the books and picked up the well-thumbed copy of 'Dune'. That was what was missing; the Land Rover.

'No, he's not gone, mate; he'll always be here.' Posh looked around at the cabin, with a new sight, and thought, Yeah, this would be a real cool place to live. Then he went over to the stove and picked up a box of matches.

'Cup of tea, Smiffy?

I'm such a lucky man
I tried to be a stronger man
I've shed a tear or two, but that don't
make me a weaker man
It's made me a better man,
I've given all I can
To a world that sometimes thinks
I'm a lesser man
I remember all the things that
I've been through
Gave myself to all those people
I once knew
I'm such a lucky man

The Final Cut

The Final Cut

A particularly persistent ray of sunlight finally bursts through the thin, high cloud blanket and alights on the marginal waters of the lake, dancing along the rippling surface and revealing all beneath, to any who could see.

It alights upon the broad backs of two large carp, idly meandering close to the bank, and paints streaks of dark and light across their scaly shoulders.

From a nearby tree, two pairs of eyes feast on the sight, and two pairs of lungs fill with air, not to be exhaled for many seconds.

The carp slowly cruise closer: closer to a small selection of unnatural, yet irresistible morsels of food. Their senses are heightened by the aroma, and despite their natural caution, their equally natural curiosity pulls them ever nearer.

The watchers in the sky are yet to exhale as they watch the two fish move slowly towards their free offerings, and their baited hooks. The nearer they get, the larger they become, and it is soon obvious that these are the two largest fish in the lake, possibly in the land.

A huge mouth gulps at the lakebed, taking in silt and weed and a selection of the new food. Similarly, the whole mouthful is ejected. Then sucked back in. Then out. Then, having sifted the food from the surrounding detritus, it is swallowed. A barely discernible fin movement holds the great carp balanced in place whilst it feeds, then a mere flick of the tail moves it slowly forward, towards the next small feast.

Ten yards. Eight. Five. The carp move so slowly that they seem almost motionless, and the watchers think that their hearts might fail before the fish reach the turning point. Small motes of dust flick in and out of view as the rays of the sun intermittently escape from behind the shroud of cloud. A butterfly lands on an outstretched hand, unnoticed, then moves away skittishly. Beads of sweat sting staring eyes, but they daren't move lest they should alert the fish to their presence, ten feet below.

In. Out. Another mouthful is sifted then swallowed, another yard covered. The two fish are now content; there is no danger, just food. They have fed here for many years, without encountering any previous danger, surely? Ahead, a small pile of food, easy pickings. With one small exertion the huge carp is above it and, with one inhalation, everything is sucked in.

Pellet, corn, boilie.

Hook.

Another blow, but something is amiss. Suck, blow. There is pressure, tension, weight. Wrong! Something is wrong.

In times of danger there is only one response – flight.

'Shit! It's got it, hasn't it, Posh?'

They look carefully, the fish is over the hookbaits, its vast bulk impeding their view, but then all becomes clear. With a sudden twist of its body, the carp flees the scene, a monstrous bow wave in its wake. At the same time a scream of tortured gears heralds the spinning of the reel, lain on the grass. A second, no more, passes before the scream is accompanied by the cracking of branches as those previously aloft become suddenly earth bound.

A rod arcs, a reel continues to scream, and the biggest carp in the land flees for its life.

The players may change, but the song remains the same.

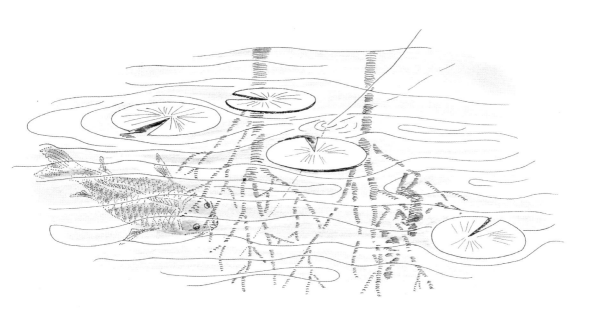